BUTTERFLY EFFECTS

Praise for the InCryptid Series

"The only thing more fun than an October Daye book is an InCryptid book. Swift narrative, charm, great world-building . . . all the McGuire trademarks."

—Charlaine Harris, #1 *New York Times* bestselling author

"Seanan McGuire's *Discount Armageddon* is an urban fantasy triple threat—smart and sexy and funny. The Aeslin mice alone are worth the price of the book, so consider a cast of truly original characters, a plot where weird never overwhelms logic, and some serious kick-ass world-building as a bonus."

—Tanya Huff, bestselling author of *The Wild Ways*

"McGuire's InCryptid series is one of the most reliably imaginative and well-told sci-fi series to be found, and she brings all her considerable talents to bear on [*Tricks for Free*]. . . . McGuire's heroine is a brave, resourceful, and sarcastic delight, and her intrepid comrades are just the kind of supportive and snarky sidekicks she needs."

—*RT Book Reviews* (top pick)

"While [*Spelunking Through Hell*] veers noticeably from the urban fantasy of earlier volumes, taking place primarily in strange realms with almost no humans in sight, it still bears all the hallmarks of the InCryptid series: a clever protagonist, snarky banter, unusual creatures, and an entertaining blend of action, romance, and horror (the secret behind Alice's enduring youth and vitality is especially unsettling). At heart a love story, this entry delivers both a satisfying payoff for fans of the series and an intriguing expansion of its universe."

—*Publishers Weekly*

"McGuire's characters are equal parts sass and sarcasm, set in an ever-expanding interdimensional world where Alice is on a journey highlighted by emotional chaos and roller-coaster pacing. Fans will be delighted by [*Spelunking Through Hell*]."

—*Library Journal*

"*Discount Armageddon* is a quick-witted, sharp-edged look at what makes a monster monstrous, and at how closely our urban fantasy protagonists walk—or dance—that line. The pacing never lets up, and when the end comes, you're left wanting more. I can't wait for the next book!"

—C. E. Murphy, author of *Raven Calls*

By the Same Author

Deadlands: Boneyard
Dusk or Dark or Dawn or Day
Dying with Her Cheer Pants On
Laughter at the Academy
Letters to the Pumpkin King
Overwatch: Declassified: An Official History of Overwatch
The Proper Thing and Other Stories
What If: Wanda Maximoff and Peter Parker Were Siblings?
Velveteen vs. The Early Adventures

The Alchemical Journeys Series

Middlegame
Seasonal Fears
Tidal Creatures

The Wayward Children Series

Every Heart a Doorway
Down Among the Sticks and Bones
Beneath the Sugar Sky
In an Absent Dream
Come Tumbling Down
Across the Green Grass Fields
Where the Drowned Girls Go
Lost in the Moment and Found
Mislaid in Parts Half-Known
Adrift in Currents Clean and Clear
Through Gates of Garnet and Gold
Seanan McGuire's Wayward Children, Volumes 1–3 (boxed set)
Be Sure: Wayward Children, Books 1–3

The October Daye Series

Rosemary and Rue
A Local Habitation
An Artificial Night
Late Eclipses
One Salt Sea
Ashes of Honor
Chimes at Midnight
The Winter Long
A Red-Rose Chain
Once Broken Faith
The Brightest Fell
Night and Silence
The Unkindest Tide
A Killing Frost
When Sorrows Come
Be the Serpent
Sleep No More
The Innocent Sleep
Silver and Lead

The InCryptid Series

Discount Armageddon
Midnight Blue-Light Special
Half-Off Ragnarok
Pocket Apocalypse
Chaos Choreography
Magic for Nothing
Tricks for Free
That Ain't Witchcraft
Imaginary Numbers
Calculated Risks
Spelunking Through Hell
Backpacking Through Bedlam
Aftermarket Afterlife
Installment Immortality
Butterfly Effects

The Indexing Series

Indexing
Indexing: Reflections

The Ghost Roads Series

Sparrow Hill Road
The Girl in the Green Silk Gown
Angel of the Overpass

AS A. DEBORAH BAKER

The Up-And-Under Series

Over the Woodward Wall
Along the Saltwise Sea
Into the Windwracked Wilds
Under the Smokestrewn Sky

AS MIRA GRANT

The Newsflesh Series

Feed
Deadline
Blackout
Feedback
Rise: The Complete Newsflesh Collection (short stories)
The Rising: The Newsflesh Trilogy

The Parasitology Series

Parasite
Symbiont
Chimera

Rolling in the Deep
Into the Drowning Deep

Overgrowth
Final Girls
Kingdom of Needle and Bone
In the Shadow of Spindrift House
Square^3
Unbreakable
Alien: Echo

BUTTERFLY EFFECTS

SEANAN McGUIRE

TOR PUBLISHING GROUP
New York

This is a work of fiction. All of the names, characters, organizations, places, and events portrayed in this work are either products of the author's imagination or used fictitiously.

BUTTERFLY EFFECTS

Chapter ornaments by Tara O'Shea

A Tor Book
Published by Tom Doherty Associates / Tor Publishing Group
120 Broadway
New York, NY 10271

www.torpublishinggroup.com

EU Representative: Macmillan Publishers Ireland Ltd, 1st Floor,
The Liffey Trust Centre, 117–126 Sheriff Street Upper, Dublin 1, D01 YC43

The Library of Congress Cataloging-in-Publication Data is available upon request.

ISBN 978-1-250-37513-1 (trade paperback)
ISBN 978-1-250-37514-8 (ebook)

First Edition: 2026

Printed in the United States of America

10 9 8 7 6 5 4 3 2 1

For Wing.
Ahem. Nerd.

Price Family Tree

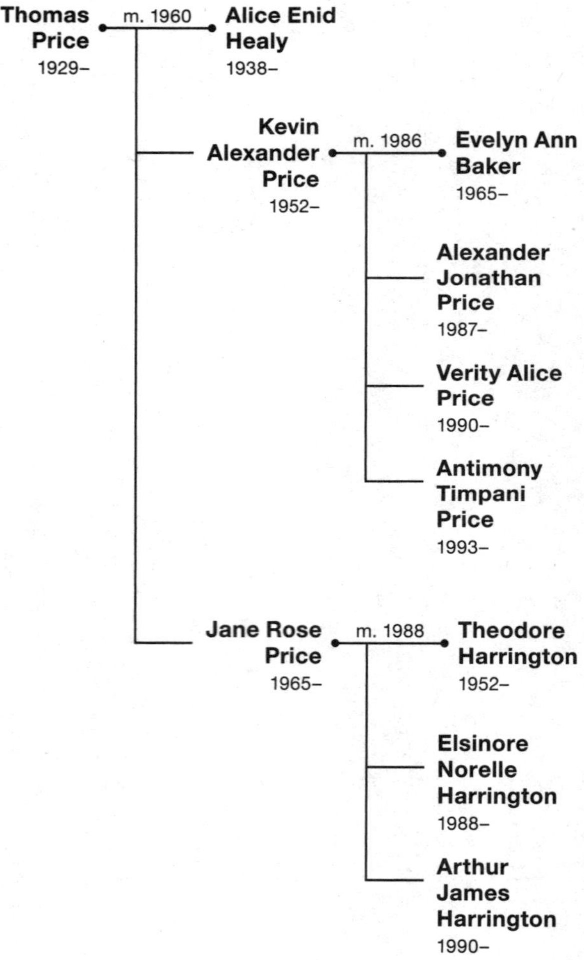

Baker Family Tree

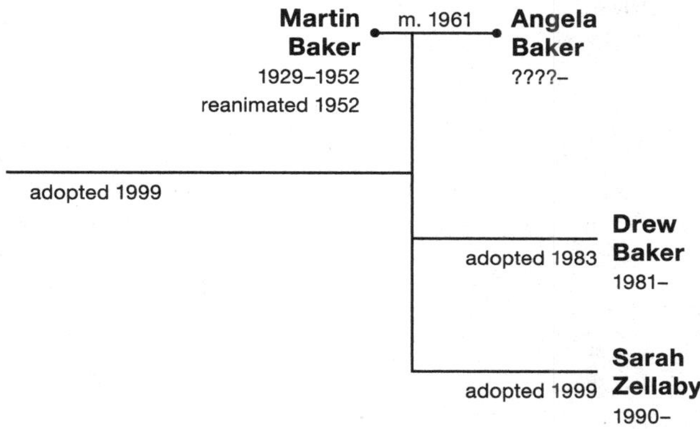

Chaos, noun:

1. The inherent unpredictability in the behavior of a complex natural system.

Chaos theory, noun:

1. A branch of mathematical and physical theory that deals with the nature and consequences of chaos and chaotic systems.
2. The study of unpredictable systems.
3. See also "impossible math."

BUTTERFLY EFFECTS

Prologue

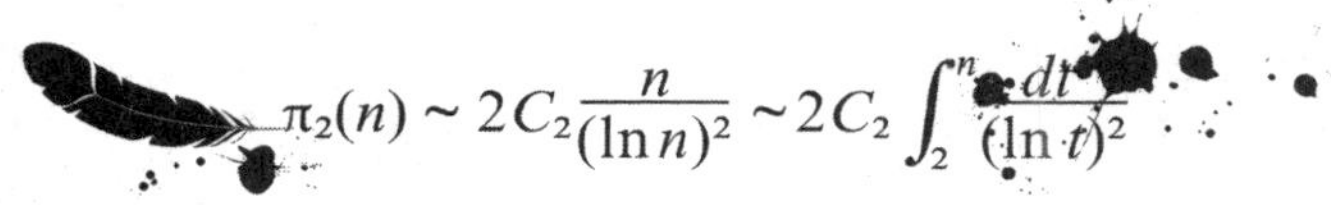

"Life is the gift we never asked for, can't return, and can't survive without. Treasure it, but never feel like you owe anything to anyone. You don't."

—**Jane Harrington-Price**

Columbus, Ohio
A little over twenty years ago

ANGELA WATCHED THE REARVIEW MIRROR anxiously as Martin pulled the RV onto the final street between them and home. All four children were asleep again, although they weren't in a single pile the way they'd been at the start of their trip. Instead, the siblings were on one side of the RV, collapsed onto the bed in a tangle of arms, legs, and foam-padded boffer swords, while their foundling slept curled alone on the couch, covered by one of the scratchy plaid blankets no one had any recollection of buying, but which seemed to respawn every time they cleaned out the RV, growing in the coat closet like a strange, invasive woolen mold. Angela didn't like the arrangement much. The girl was going to have enough difficulty without isolating herself.

The children were too young—all of them, even Alex, although he would have argued he was the eldest and that made him practically grown-up—to really understand what a cuckoo was, or what they could do. To them, "cuckoo" meant either the little bird that came out of the clock in cartoons or their beloved maternal grandmother, who made them cookies and put tomato powder on her cereal, and never forgot their birthdays. It didn't mean "predator from another dimension." It didn't mean danger, or destruction, or having your mind rewritten against your will.

They were going to learn. Angela was sure of that now. As soon as she called their parents, their education in the dangers of cuckoos was going to begin. She loved her in-laws. They were good, reasonable people who did their best to treat all intelligent creatures as equals. They were also humans. And humans could be small-minded and petty in a way that was really only accessible to members of the dominant species.

Evelyn was her daughter, had grown up in her house and only ever known her as a source of comfort and support. Evelyn had also been there when her new husband's mother had assaulted Angela for the crime of being a cuckoo, and while she'd intervened, it hadn't been immediate, and she hadn't stopped it from happening. Evelyn was human before she was anything else, and humans knew, on an instinctual level, that cuckoos were monsters.

This little girl wasn't a monster, not yet. She was seven years old, newly orphaned, and terrified. But none of that was going to matter when Kevin and Evie found out she'd been around their children. She was too young to have any real control over what she could do: her telepathic cries were loud and ceaseless when she was awake. She would insert herself into the memories of everyone around her without hesitation or finesse, and she wouldn't even realize she was doing it. It was a matter of survival.

Thanks to Kevin's family being profoundly weird in a way Angela still didn't fully understand, all of the kids were remarkably resistant to cuckoo influence, and had been able to reject Sarah's clumsy instinctive attempts to make them believe she was their sibling, but would their parents be comfortable with that? Would they be willing to let the children finish out their summer in Ohio, or would they be on the next plane out from Oregon, eager to defend their offspring?

There was so much to worry about, and none of it had been expected when they'd started their drive to Florida.

Martin pulled into the driveway, turning off the engine. "We're here," he said needlessly, voice soft to avoid waking the kids.

"Think we can unload the inanimate parts of the RV in the morning, just take care of the living right now?"

"I think that would be perfect."

One upstairs light was on—Drew's room. He'd never wanted to be defined by his species, and so while he shared the normal bogeyman aversion to bright or direct light, he'd chosen to give up his spot in the basement as soon as he was old enough to express an opinion, preferring thick curtains and a second-floor bedroom when he came back to Ohio during his school breaks. He liked to open them at night so he could air out the room. The family wasn't going to wake him by coming in. He was naturally nocturnal, and would be up until just before sunrise, when he'd close the curtains and sleep through the brightest part of the day.

Martin looked at it uneasily. "Think we should warn him about our new guest?"

"She's not a guest, Martin. Sarah will be staying with us for as long as she needs to be here. If she decides that's forever, we'll take care of her."

"Isn't that kidnapping?"

"It would be, if she were a human child. But she doesn't have any biological family that's going to claim her, and she's just going to adopt herself to anyone with a susceptible mind who comes near her for too long. She needs a home, Martin. We talked about this."

His expression of discomfort grew. "Yes, but—"

"Yes, but, what? She was a child when we had the conversation the first time, and she's still a child now. She needs a home." Angela glared at her husband, a silent challenge in her eyes. Sometimes it was easy for her to forget that he'd been human, once, had lived several human lives before he'd died and been put back together by a scientist with more jumper cables than good sense. Part of him would always be human, would always think like a member of the dominant species.

Part of him, even after the life they'd worked so hard to build together, would never really understand how cruel the world could be to people like her, or like Sarah.

"Still," he said, stubbornly, "should we warn Drew? I know bogeymen are as susceptible to cuckoo influence as humans are."

"She's asleep. Even the most powerful cuckoo in the world can't rewrite someone's mind while they're asleep. I'll tell him she's here, and we can give him the choice of whether he wants to meet her or not."

"Angie . . ."

"He's a grown man, Martin, and she's a little girl. She needs us. Are you going to be the one who lets a little girl down?"

He paused, then sighed, heavily. "Let's get the kids inside."

"Thank you."

✦ ✦ ✦

Morning broke, and Sarah McNally opened her eyes on an unfamiliar room. She froze, entire body going rigid. It hurt, having her muscles seize up like that, and she whimpered, just a little. Normally, that sound would have been enough to alert her mother that something was wrong. Patricia McNally would have come bustling into the room with hot tea and arnica cream, ready to ease her daughter into the day.

Sarah's eyes darted to the door, the rest of her still too stiff to move. It didn't open. Her mother wasn't going to come.

Because her mother was dead. The memory flooded back with the same suddenness it always did, laced with an acidic agony that burnt her thoughts when she let herself dwell on it for too long. Her parents were dead. They had gone for a car ride, and then they *died*, and she'd been at a sleepover at Amy's house, because she liked Amy and Amy's dad made the best waffles she'd ever had, so she hadn't been with them. She hadn't been able to say goodbye, and now they were gone forever, and everyone who saw her tried to take her home with them, like she was a lost puppy or something.

And now she'd been kidnapped.

Fighting the urge to curl under the blankets and cry, Sarah

forced her locked-up muscles to untense enough to let her sit up in the bed, clutching the covers around herself. She was wearing a nightgown she didn't recognize, white flannel with blue flowers, and it was warm and soft and she wanted to like it, but she thought you probably shouldn't like things kidnappers gave to you.

She slid out of the bed, toes sinking into the soft carpet, and padded soundlessly to the bedroom door. Testing the knob, she found that it was unlocked and slipped out into the hall, following the sound of voices. The children she'd met before were laugh-shrieking about something, and the heavy rumble of an adult voice rolled beneath them, tolerant and amused.

If there were children, it was probably safe for her to go there, and she didn't want to be alone in this scary new place, not when her parents were dead and she didn't know where her shoes were. She walked onward, taking note of the smudged wallpaper and the photographs on the walls. As always, the pictures confused her, a little. Why did people like to take pictures of other people so much? It wasn't like you could tell who you were looking at once there wasn't a mind behind the face to make it individual.

At least these people had a reasonable number of pictures centered on the places, not the individuals who were there. It was like a travelogue in pieces, spread out across the hallway walls.

Then she reached the kitchen doorway, and stopped dead.

The three kids she'd already met were at the table, along with the two adults from the front seat, and a new man, who was even harder to look at than the children, all of whom were a little fuzzy and hard to see properly. This man was blurry and smeared, like he was standing in a deep shadow that kept her eyes from focusing. It made her uncomfortable to look at him too directly. He turned his face toward her as she stood in the doorway, and the children stopped laughing, conversation dying out as everyone joined the new man in watching her.

The woman was the first one to react. She stood, pushing back her chair with a soft scrape against the linoleum, and moved toward the counter. "You're awake," she said, like Sarah might not have noticed. "Do you want something to eat? There's V8, and I can make you some sweet tomato waffles. They're my own recipe."

"They're *weird*," said the fairer-haired of the two girls among the children, leaning forward and speaking in a conspiratorial tone. "Grandma makes blueberry waffles too, and they're lots better. Tell her you want blueberry."

Sarah bit her lip. "I like tomatoes," she said, voice quavering.

"I know you do," said the woman. "It's the solanine—a chemical found in tomatoes. It's in other things, too, but tomatoes are the easiest way for you to get it. And my tomato waffles aren't weird, Verity, they're just not to your taste. I candy cherry tomatoes, chop them up, and mix them with the batter the same way I would blueberries. I didn't offer them to *you*."

"Sorry, Grandma," said Verity, shrinking down in her seat.

The new man moved then, rising from his chair and moving closer to Sarah, who flinched away. "She looks just like you, Mom," he said.

"We're a species with low personal variance," said the woman. "We never needed it."

"Can she see me? Sorry, that was rude—can you see me?" He shifted his attention to Sarah for his second question.

Sarah twitched but managed not to recoil. "I . . . Not very well? You're sort of blurry, and my eyes don't want to focus on you."

"That's because you don't look at people with your eyes," he said, and reached up, removing a chain from around his neck.

He suddenly snapped into perfect focus, becoming a normal man who looked a bit like the woman who was making her a waffle, and a bit like the man still sitting at the table with the kids. He felt like the basement back at home, cool and safe and stable, a place she could go to hide from storms, where she could be safe among the spiders.

"My name is Andrew," he said. "Most people call me 'Drew.' I'm a kind of person called a bogeyman, which means I don't like bright lights, and I'm wearing a special necklace that blocks telepathy from reaching me, which is why you can't see me very well."

"I can see you just fine now," said Sarah.

"I know," said Drew, with a complicated ripple of discomfort. "Mom, I think this one's yours."

"I wanted to wait," said the waffle lady.

"I know, but she was squinting at me like I was some invisible monster, and waiting isn't always better than honesty." He put the chain back on and went blurry again, the feeling of cellar-safety fading away.

At least now Sarah knew what he looked like, and while she couldn't see him properly anymore, she could track him as he moved back to his seat.

The woman popped a waffle out of her waffle maker, shaking her head, and carried it over to the table. "I have butter, syrup, and ketchup, Sarah," she said. "Come sit, and have breakfast. Did you want some V8?"

"Yes, please," said Sarah, suddenly shy. She moved to sit, waiting until she was settled, the waffle smelling amazing in front of her, to ask, "Are you my kidnappers?"

"No, sweetheart," said the woman. "We're your helpers. I'm so sorry about what happened to your parents."

"I'm sorry too."

"Do you have any grandparents we could call?"

"No."

That was typical of the kind of family cuckoos were generally attached to when it came time to hide their young. They didn't always have time to scout well enough to be sure—Angela herself had grown up with two sets of grandparents—but when they could, they left the babies with couples who had no strong familial ties outside each other. It helped with questions like "Why didn't you tell us you were pregnant" and "Why doesn't the baby look anything like you in the pictures." Still, it stung to know that was the case for Sarah. If she'd already had an existing family, they might have been able to help her reunite with them.

"I'm so sorry, Sarah. Did you want syrup? Or ketchup?"

Sarah hesitated. "Can I really have ketchup if I want it?" she asked.

"I always put ketchup on mine."

"She does," confirmed the man. "Has for as long as I've known her."

"Then ketchup, please," said Sarah, in a prim voice. "I like it better."

"Most of us do," said the woman, and reached for the ketchup. She exchanged a look with the man as she did. "There's something I need to discuss with you, once you're finished eating your breakfast, all right?"

"All right," said Sarah. She took the bottle, squirting thick red paste onto her waffle like it was frosting, pausing, and then adding another layer. She set the ketchup aside, picking up her fork. "Is it about me not being human? I heard you last night."

The woman flinched. "I'm sorry, Sarah. We thought you were asleep, but we still shouldn't have been talking about you."

"It's okay." Sarah shrugged. "But what's a cuckoo?"

Silence settled over the kitchen table, heavy and uncomfortable, and for a long moment, no one seemed to know what to say. Then the younger of the two girls piped up:

"A cuckoo is our grandmother, Angela Baker, and she makes the best spaghetti sauce in the whole world, and likes to do math so much she made it her whole job, and our mother says she's one of the best people ever to keep us from jumping off bridges during summer vacation, and so if you say anything mean about cuckoos, you're saying it about our gramma and I hate you."

Angela radiated amusement. "Thank you, Antimony, but no one is saying anything mean about cuckoos right now. Sarah was only asking what we are. And Sarah, we're just a different way of being people. We can be nice and kind or cruel and mean. We can be anything we want to be."

"Gramma wanted to be an accountant," said the boy, proudly.

"Yes, I did, Alex, and I'm a very good accountant, thank you. We don't see faces like humans do—we see minds. That's why Drew's wearing the charm that keeps you from looking at his mind too hard, because sometimes when we look at people's minds, we change them. It usually happens when we're scared, or when we're talking to strangers. We make them think they already know us, and then we change their memories so they remember knowing us. That's what happened to you when people started trying to take you home. You were scared, and that just made it worse."

Sarah's eyes were huge. "I don't want to change people's minds."

"That's good, because people can get hurt that way. A lot of cuckoos don't care about hurting people, but I do. I care a great deal."

"I don't want to hurt people," said Sarah. "How do I not do that?"

"I can help you," said Angela. "But you'll have to stay here if you want to learn."

"I don't live here anymore," said Drew. "I was just back to house-sit. So you won't be putting me in any danger of having my mind changed."

"You can't change my mind," said Martin.

"We're going home next week," said Alex.

"If I stay here, I can learn how to be a good cuckoo and no one's going to take me away?" asked Sarah hesitantly.

Angela nodded.

"Yes," she said.

Sarah looked around the room, then back to Angela, and nodded decisively.

"Then I'm staying here, and you're going to teach me," she said. "And I'm never going to hurt anybody."

One

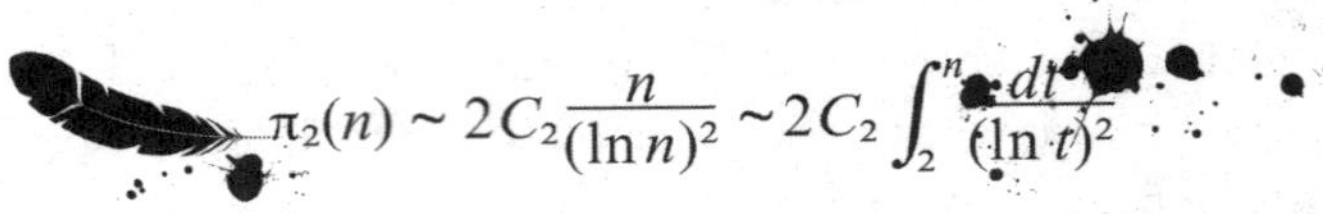

"Promises are always important. Promises to children are the foundations of who we are. Make them carefully, if you're going to make them at all."

—**Angela Baker**

An only moderately creepy suburban home in Columbus, Ohio

Now

WAKING UP IN OHIO MEANT waking up alone.

I was allowed to have Greg with me in Oregon and Michigan—both places had enough space for him in the nearby woods, and plenty of ways he could hide from anyone who happened to wander onto our property. Concealing a jumping spider the size of a draft horse is unsurprisingly difficult, although it's sometimes easier than I expected it to be: no one really wants to believe something like Greg could exist, which makes it easy for them to dismiss the evidence of their eyes. He's been mistaken for everything from a bear to a really good Halloween decoration. Greg doesn't care what people think he is. He cares that I'm safe and he's getting fed, and that's about it. Still, there isn't room for him in Ohio.

With the way they've been tearing down the local patches of woodland to build new housing developments, there's never *going* to be room for him. What wild space remains is home to a lot of species that have substantially more business being here than Greg does. Alex has made it very clear that if it came down to my spider or the local lindworms, he'd have to side with the lindworms. They live in Ohio, and Greg does not.

That's fine. I'm not *so* dependent on my emotional support spider that I can't be without him for a night or two—not yet, anyway. I may get there, with the way things have been going, and that will be a terrible thing, because so much of my family is located in places Greg can't go. Verity's still in New York, even though she keeps insisting she's going to move back to Oregon so she can raise the kids in the sort of wide-open spaces she enjoyed as a child, and my parents are in Ohio with my baby brother, Isaac.

In other words, flexibility is key if I want to keep in touch with my family.

I rolled onto my back, looking up at the ceiling. Every inch of it was familiar, from the cracks in the paint to the faint stains left behind by a baking-soda-volcano incident when I was nine. Mom's offered to paint in here a few times, but I've always asked her not to. I like having something in my world that stays stable. I haven't even rotated my posters since high school. The ghosts of old X-Men storylines and outdated *Magic: the Gathering* sets watched me from the walls as I rolled over again, this time out of the bed.

Everyone else in the house was awake. I could feel them starting to go about their days even through the anti-telepathy charms in my walls. Mom had no idea the charms weren't enough to keep me out of people's minds anymore, and as long as they could take the edge off sufficiently to let me sleep at night, I wasn't going to tell her. I couldn't read actual thoughts through them without making an effort, and that meant everyone had as much privacy as we had any real reason to expect in a house with multiple telepaths.

Speaking of telepaths . . . Isaac was awake and reaching for me, the way he did every morning. I could feel his frustration as the telepathy blockers prevented him from properly establishing contact. He'd come bursting through my bedroom door soon, when the agony of waiting got to be too much, and then he'd get another scolding from our mother. That wasn't fair to him. Lecturing eight-year-olds for not having developed patience has never been one of my favorite activities.

One nice thing about spending a reasonable chunk of my time in Ohio: I always have clothes in my room. I dug a pair of black leggings and a charcoal-gray sweater out of my drawers, pulling them on just as I felt Isaac's impatience reaching a fever pitch. Grabbing a brush off my dresser to run though my hair as I moved, I turned toward the door.

My name is Sarah Zellaby. I am a mathematician. I have what can charitably be referred to as an anxiety disorder, which I manage through a combination of mindfulness, meditation, and the presence of an emotional support animal—the aforementioned Greg, the giant spider. My biological mother was a monster. My first adoptive mother was very kind, even if she never knew I was adopted—I was foisted on her by the monster-mother, who'd dropped me on a doorstep knowing I'd be cared for whether or not the people inside had ever wanted children. After my first set of adoptive parents died, I was found and taken in by the Bakers, Angela and Martin. Angela and I at least share a species, and it's thanks to her that I'm not a monster like my first mother was.

I don't want to be a monster.

But no matter what I want, I am not and will never be human. I don't get to Pinocchio my way into someone else's species: I don't even get to try as hard as I used to think I could. I'm what's called a cuckoo, a telepathic ambush predator that exists to exploit. My species takes whatever we want, and doesn't care what gets broken in the process. Nice neighbors, right?

I mean, not really, obviously. Cuckoos are pretty much awful. Our actual species name is "Johrlac," which is too many consonants and not nearly enough vowels for my tastes, but we don't tend to use that for ourselves here on Earth. We're the descendants of the people the other Johrlac kicked out for sucking too much to stay in the neighborhood, and when they made our ancestors leave, they edited their memories just enough to remove a few basic details. Like how to do the math that would have returned us to our original dimension.

Because yeah, we're telepaths. We can read people's thoughts, manipulate their memories, that whole fun set of shitty behaviors. But we can also channel that energy into math that will literally rewrite realities, if we can just find the processing power we need.

I don't like to think about processing power.

Shaking my head to chase away the memory of the last time I'd needed processing power, I opened my bedroom door and the thoughts of the rest of the house poured through, like honey dripping from a comb. Shelby was trying to get her hair to behave before she left for work, frustrated by one curl's refusal to stay where she put it; Alex was getting breakfast in front of the kids. Mom was upstairs, doing quadratic equations in her head as she showered, and Dad was a dark smudge at the bottom of the pile of conflicting mental signals, all but unreadable.

My adoptive father, Martin Baker, is what we call a Revenant. It's a sort of depressing name for a really sweet guy, but given that the alternatives were "a Frankenstein" or "an abomination of science," I think it's okay. He used to be several human men, all of whom died in one way or another, only to get graverobbed and spliced together by a scientist with a dubious grasp on the concept of "ethics."

Something about the resurrection process makes Revenants all but impossible to read. If I hadn't lived with him for several decades, I wouldn't even have been able to tell he was in the house. That was obscurely comforting. I don't have a lot of limits anymore, and that makes the ones I do have all the more precious to me.

Because, see, about eight years ago, right before Isaac was born, my birth mother decided she had a right to come crashing back into my life and wreck everything I cared about. She and the other cuckoos on Earth had decided technology was reaching a point where it was too difficult for them to exist as telepathic predators. Even if humans can't tell us apart, cameras can, and our movements can be followed. Humanity was starting to catch on, and the cuckoos wanted out.

To achieve "out," they needed someone who could handle the massive equation they'd cobbled together, the mathematical function that would allow us to exit this dimension and head for a different one. That meant they needed what's called a Queen—a cuckoo who's gone through the rare fourth instar and unlocked a whole additional level of telepathic power.

And this is all getting a little confusing, especially when I'm trying to make it to breakfast at the same time. Let's step into an aside.

◆ ◆ ◆

All right: cuckoos, as I've mentioned, are both shitty neighbors and telepathic ambush predators. We're not originally from the dimension where Earth is located: our home dimension is called Johrlar, which makes the part where we're called Johrlac just a little egotistical, if you ask me. Which they didn't. The cuckoos have never asked me for anything in my life. They've just done it, and expected me to deal graciously with the consequences.

Which I have not done, but we'll get there.

Today's cuckoos are the descendants of Johrlar's exiles, who passed packets of ancestral memory from parent to child in order to make sure their kids would be born perfect little examples of a lousy, murderous species. Again, we'll get to that in a minute. The important thing here is "from another dimension." We didn't evolve on Earth, and our ancestors were clearly subject to different evolutionary pressures in the process of becoming what we are today: humanoid bipeds, pale-skinned, black-haired, and blue-eyed, with surprisingly little variance between individuals. Mom—Angela—and I are virtually identical, despite the fact that we're not directly related.

Part of this is because we're actually a form of insect. Surprise! We look like a species of goths, but we're closer to being giant, wingless wasps. The collagen in our skins is not human-identical, although it feels the same, and that keeps us from visibly aging in the same fashion after we reach our twenties. Angela could still go clubbing with college kids without it seeming creepy, if she'd had any interest in clubbing. Isaac and I would be able to do the same someday, once he was old enough to care about things other than Pokémon cards and chess. We don't get sick, and we don't get old, and we don't play nicely.

We have no hearts. Literally. Instead, our circulatory system is decentralized, and works via a series of muscular pulses. That would still be a problem, if we had blood in the human sense, but fortunately for us, we don't. Instead, we have a form of advanced hemolymph that keeps us oxygenated and moving. It has antibiotic properties, and we're rare enough that I don't know of anything Earth-based that's developed a resistance to it yet. So that part's neat at least.

Instars are insect life stages, the progression from nymph to imago, or full adult. Cuckoos have lost our exoskeletons, so we don't molt like normal insects, but we still change. The first instar is universal—the larval stage of our species, infants and children indistinguishable from the host species we're hiding among. The second is also universal. Isaac will reach it one day, and when he does, I'll be on hand to make sure he doesn't kill everyone in the house. (The second instar tends to cause temporary psychosis brought on by the sudden release of excessive quantities of ancestral memory, which tell the kid in question that humans are nothing more than meat to be farmed. Like I said, we suck.)

Most cuckoos stop there, mature enough to grow up and consider themselves adults, a little bit evil and a little bit nasty and a whole lot manipulative. Some, though, strain themselves hard enough that they go through a third instar, one that leaves them a little bit scrambled for several years, but results in their inherent power level going up. As to why a species of assholes doesn't pursue this greater power all the time, well. There's no way to avoid the scrambled period, because each instar is marked by physical changes. They're just internal ones, involving structures in the brain. We're literally out of our minds following the third instar, because our brains are reshaping themselves. Not a good thing for a species of ambush predators.

So why do it at all? Well, I did it because I didn't know it was a possibility. I'd been trying to save my cousin's life, and I'd accidentally slammed the buttons that began the process to give me an upgrade. I could have stopped there and been happy, truly.

But third-instar cuckoos aren't common, and those who try apparently have a nasty tendency not to survive the physical rearrangement of their minds when it happens with no one to take care of them. I'd been safe here in Ohio while my brain rebuilt itself, and when I'd felt well enough to leave, I'd returned to the world unaware of what had happened to me.

Only to get ambushed by my biological mother and her hive, who wanted to force me into my fourth instar in order to get themselves a fully adult cuckoo. Since we don't need to reach the imago stage to reproduce, we generally don't bother: we're all content to stop after the second instar, safe and secure and not rebuilding ourselves when we don't have to. But the equation that lets us rip holes in the barrier between dimensions is so large and needs so much power that only a queen can handle it.

Except even a queen can't really handle it. It's too big, and it's hungry. When I had that equation in my mind, I felt like I was wrestling a greased dinosaur that wanted to bite my head off more than it had ever wanted anything else in its life. The equation is a predator. The cuckoos usually kept it contained by breaking it into pieces and storing it around the world, but that didn't change the fact that it was a monstrous thing. An ender of worlds.

Completing the equation would have blown a chunk out of Earth big enough to destroy the planet. But what did the cuckoos care? We'd be somewhere else, and to them, that was what mattered. I was their groomed and chosen queen: I was going to set them free. And sure, I was going to melt my own brain in the process, but I got the feeling that for them, that was a side bonus. Get a new world to consume, and don't get stuck with a pesky queen in the process.

I've always tried to be a good person. I've always tried to behave more like a human than a giant wasp in a woman suit. And none of that had mattered while the equation was chewing on my brain, trying to force me to end everything so it could be free. I might have done it, except for one small thing that set me apart from all the other cuckoos, even when I hadn't been thinking about, even when I hadn't fully understood the ramifications:

I was in love. Deeply, helplessly in love, and had been since I was a little girl. His name was Artie, and he had the most soothing mind I'd ever touched. Something about his thoughts was *right*, like slipping into a hot bath on a cold night, or a bed with pre-warmed sheets. I'd loved him almost as soon as I'd known him, and miracle of miracles, he'd loved me the same way. *Really* loved me, not been manipulated into loving me by telepathic tricks. He was a Price, and Prices are part Kairos, another human-looking species that isn't, quite. Their Kairos heritage made them resistant if not immune to psychic manipulation, and while I could have forced my way into his mind, I couldn't have done it unintentionally.

Cuckoos don't do love, as a general rule. Hard to form those types of bonds when you're constantly measuring the world around you the way a lion measures an antelope. So no one realized Artie might be able to break me out of the mathematical fugue that was supposed to consume me and make it possible for the equation to direct my choices until the world ended in a glorious, concussive boom. He'd pulled me loose, and together we'd come up with a plan to use the minds around me as distributed processing power, letting me keep my self intact despite everything I was going through.

Unfortunately, I'd still been convinced I was going to die, so even as I turned the equation to my own ends, I'd been preparing for my demise. In an effort to keep my allies from hurting more than they had to, the last thing I'd done before the equation finished resolving and we were transported to a different dimension was wipe myself from their memories.

Meaning I landed in a whole new reality surrounded by people who had no idea who I was or why they shouldn't treat me like any other cuckoo. And one of them had been Artie, which hurt more than I ever imagined. To go from him loving me enough to pull me away from a mind-eating equation like it was no big deal to him looking at me like I was the enemy had been, well, bracing to say the least.

And then, when I was doing the math to get us the hell out of there and back to Earth, on the presumption that I'd done the math correctly the *first* time and not destroyed it on our way out the door, he'd touched me. Without his memories of growing up together, he hadn't realized how dangerous that could be. I'd erased his mind during the moment of contact, leaving him a literal shell of the man I loved, and what was gone was gone: I couldn't put it back. So I'd gathered all the memories I and his family had of him and used them to construct a new person in his place. A person who was almost him, but . . . not. People are made up of first-person experiences, not third-person memories.

And he—the new person, the one I'd constructed to occupy the empty shell of the man I loved—thought he loved me, because so many of the pieces I'd used to build him told him he did. I'd run away as fast as I could, unable to stand being anywhere near him. My father was a man who'd risen from the dead, but Artie was something new, and terrible, and entirely my fault.

One good thing had come from that whole situation: Isaac. My mother had been pregnant when she decided it was time for the cuckoos to get out of this dimension, and while she hadn't survived our time together, he had. He was brand-new and perfect when I'd hauled my friends and allies back to Earth, and Angela had been willing to take on the task of raising him. She was one of the only people in the world to have successfully raised a cuckoo who didn't start trying to murder everyone when she hit puberty—me—and we figured she had a decent shot at doing the same for him. All he needed was a suite of telepathic ethics and a little psychic surgery to remove that packet of ancestral memories before they could turn septic and explode all over his mind. No big deal, right?

Not for a family of telepathic wasps hiding in Columbus, Ohio, I guess.

◆ ◆ ◆

The kitchen hasn't really changed since the first time I'd seen it. Oh, they'd replaced the wallpaper right around the time I was finishing high school, and it was a new kitchen table, polished oak in place of the old walnut, but the fixtures and appliances were all the same. Dad's never been the world's biggest fan of avoidable change. He knows most of his kids are aging faster than he is, and he'll have to bury Evie and Drew someday, and probably his grandkids too, and he understands the world won't slow down to meet his sometimes-lumbering tempo, but he's never asked it to. He just asks Mom to buy two toasters when she has to replace one, so he can extend the period before something wholly new has to enter his space.

The only major change was the people. Alex was at the stove where I would normally have expected Mom to be, flipping pancakes with one hand and cracking eggs with the other. Dad was in his usual spot. Charlotte and Isaac were across from him, Lottie with a bowl of cereal and some pancakes, Isaac with pancakes and a plate of scrambled eggs covered in so much ketchup that it looked like a murder scene and a smaller cup of what looked like cocktail sauce, which he was carefully dipping each bite of pancake in before he ate it.

They brightened when they saw me, their thoughts taking on an effervescent, bubbling edge, like mental champagne.

"Sarah!" chirped Lottie. "You're still here!"

"Not f'long," said Isaac, more glumly. His thoughts were sparkling, but his tone was dour.

I sat down at the end of the table, close enough that I could lean over and put my arm around his shoulders. "Hey, you. You know I have to go. I'm sorry I can't be here all the time and always, but there are places I need to be, and people I've promised to visit. Do you want your auntie Verity to be all sad because I'm not coming to see her?"

"Auntie Verity's already sad enough," said Isaac. His eyes flashed briefly white as he raised them from his plate and looked at me. *She's always going to be sad, whether you're with her or not. And when you go to see her,* you *come back sad, because of your hospital friend. I'd rather you stayed here, where you can be happy, and didn't run away all the time.*

"You know I can't do that, Isaac," I said. "Greg can't be here with me, and I need Greg to be happy at all. If I stay here without him for too long, I'll start having nightmares again. And when I have nightmares, the whole neighborhood has nightmares."

It's not fair.

"Neither is talking only in our heads, because not everyone can do it," I said firmly. "Come on, buddy. Time for our outside voices, okay?"

He shot me a look, thoughts turning disgruntled. I shrugged, projecting neutrality in his direction.

Charlotte—Lottie to her family—was only a few months older than Isaac, and they'd grown up in each other's pockets. Because she was a Price by blood, she had the protection from mental manipulation provided by her father's Kairos ancestry. Even so, she could receive telepathic communication, and reply to them in kind. She and Isaac had both been slow to speak, not seeing the need for communicating with other people when they already had each other. Shelby had been briefly concerned she'd need to hold them back from starting formal schooling, since kids who sounded younger than their actual ages were likely to be the targets of bullying.

Alex hadn't initially agreed that the threat of bullying was a good-enough reason to keep them home, but Shelby had looked at him, shrugged, and asked calmly how many kindergarteners would need to have their minds melted by Isaac for the crime of being mean to Lottie before it would be a good-enough reason.

He'd agreed with her after that. Apparently, that agreement had been enough to make both children start catching up with their peers. They'd been talking more or less normally by the end of the month, and had been able to start school on the expected schedule. Because they refused to be separated and Isaac's official birthday was in November, they were both in second grade, and the only remaining trace of their delayed speech was in the way he would sometimes shorten words or create new contractions when he didn't feel like talking.

Well, that, and the way he slipped into telepathic speech if he thought he could get away with it. He and Lottie both carried anti-telepathy charms to school to keep him from accidentally answering the teacher without opening his mouth, but sometimes I was still concerned about being one bad playground argument away from a Stephen King novel.

I'd managed to survive elementary school in Ohio without going full Carrie White. I had confidence that my little brother could do the same. Probably.

"When are you leaving, Sarah?" asked Dad.

"I figured I'd wait until everyone had come downstairs for the day, so I could say my goodbyes," I said. "I'm planning to be gone for a few weeks this trip, just to make sure I can deal with everything in New York and then spend some real quality time with Greg in Michigan. I'll call when I head for Buckley, so you know where I am."

"I agree with Isaac: I wish you could stay longer," he said.

"And I wish I could have Greg here with me, but the Blue Fairy isn't granting requests right now," I said. "St. Giles's wants to have a serious talk with me about Mark's future, and that means I have to go. Everything else aside, we owe him."

Dad sighed. "I suppose we do."

Mark is a cuckoo. Like me, he's a pretty reasonable person who's not totally into the idea of psychically manipulating and abusing everyone around him. Unlike me, he didn't have anyone to hold his hand and help him get there. I never properly entered my second instar, thanks to Mom carefully removing every trace of my ancestral memories before they could rupture and wipe out my ability to see people as, well, people.

Mark didn't get those memories removed until much later, when I'd needed the processing space for the world-breaker equation and removed them with his permission. His instar proceeded normally, and the memories had spread through him like wine through cotton. He'd reacted the way cuckoos normally did, by having a brief mental break and trying to murder his younger sister, Cici. But Cici had been young enough to think he was playing a game with her. She'd evaded him for so long that his thoughts had time to calm down again, and he'd stopped seeing her as a target and remembered how much he loved her.

His love for his sister had been strong enough to drag him back over a line that should have been impossible to recross once he had crossed it. He'd been working with the cuckoos who took me purely because they told him that if he didn't, they'd kill his sister. The whole time, he'd been planning to kill me himself before I could end the world, assuming my family didn't arrive in time. But they had, and he'd been with us on our cross-dimensional bullshit adventure.

Like Artie, Mark had been seriously damaged by my attempt to solve, resolve, and destroy the equation. Unlike Artie, his mind hadn't been erased, just subjected to the kind of stress and trauma that could trigger his fourth instar. He was changing. But because he hadn't been primed for it by going through a third instar, he was trying to accomplish them both at once, and it had already taken eight years.

Eight years of catatonia while his brain physically broke down and rebuilt itself, and the staff at St. Giles's Hospital—a medical establishment catering almost completely to cryptids—got more and more nervous about what he was going to be if he woke up. Eight years of his human family having no idea what had happened to him. Cici had been twelve when he disappeared, and there was no good way of telling her he was alive, or how he'd been hurt, or anything. From her perspective, her big brother—the brother who'd loved her so much that he'd been able to defeat his own biology to stay with her—just walked away one day and never came back.

I spent time with him when I could, sitting by his bed and holding his hand and hoping that one day I'd pick up on even a flicker of sapient thought coming from him. I didn't know who or what he'd be if he ever managed to wake up. I just knew it was my fault he was in that bed, and I wanted him awake more than I wanted almost anything else that I could think of.

Without Mark, we would never have been able to make it back from the dimension I'd shunted us all into. Without all of them. And I owed them. I *would* owe them until the end of my days. I didn't get to rest and enjoy the love of my family until such time as I'd made sufficient amends for what I'd done.

If that was even possible.

I leaned over, pressing a kiss to Isaac's temple. His delight at the gesture washed over me, comforting and warm as a towel fresh out of the dryer. "I love you, little bee," I informed him.

He squirmed, embarrassed and pleased. "Don't be gross, stupid sister," he said.

"Sorry," I replied. "Can't help it."

Lottie giggled. I took a piece of pancake from Isaac's plate and dipped it into the cocktail sauce before popping it into my mouth. She made a face.

"That's weird," she informed me. "You can't put ketchup and stuff on everything you eat."

"Isaac does it," I said.

"It's still weird when he does it," she countered. "Yesterday he put ketchup in his fruit cup in the cafeteria. The lunch aide took it away 'cause she thought he was messing around and making messes."

Across the table, Dad's attention focused on Isaac. "Zach . . ." he rumbled, in a disappointed tone.

Isaac hunched his shoulders. "It tastes wrong when it's just sweet-sweet-sweet!" he said. "Tomatoes are only considered a vegetable for tax purposes anyway!"

I blinked, then looked over my shoulder as Mom stepped into the room, hair still damp and sticking to the sides of her face. "Was I like this when I was eight?"

"You were worse," she said sweetly. "You're the reason I learned how to make gummy candy at home. If I didn't send you to school with tomato gummies, you'd find ways to sneak tomatoes into everything, and it was scaring the other children. Not that you made it past seventh grade, whereas Zach is going all the way to high school, aren't you, buddy?"

"Yes, Mom," he said dutifully.

"With me," said Charlotte.

"Yes, with you." I knew she was smiling because she projected it to me and Isaac even as she folded her face in the appropriate ways. It's nice to spend time around people who telegraph their facial expressions. Makes it easier to react to them.

Sometimes I thought Charlotte was to Isaac as those therapy dogs were to the cheetahs in zoos. She gave him something to focus on and hang on to. Like me with Greg. Telepathy isn't an anxiety disorder, but being a telepath in a non-telepathic world can feel very similar. He'd been doing better than I did in public school from day one. Maybe if I'd been able to go to Portland and attend school with Artie, I could have made it to high school instead of having a nervous breakdown in the seventh grade and finishing out my education in this very kitchen.

Or maybe we'd just have ended up even more codependent than we already were, and I'd have fallen apart completely when I accidentally erased his mind, instead of just falling apart mostly. No way of knowing.

"Hi, Mom," I said. "You got the value of the variable wrong on your fourth equation. It should have been three, or the whole thing fails to resolve."

"I knew you'd catch that, sweetie," she said, crossing the kitchen to kiss my forehead before ruffling Isaac's hair with one hand. "You always were my little perfectionist. When do you leave?"

"As soon as Shelby comes downstairs." There was a clatter from the hall, telling me that she was doing precisely that.

"Aren't you going to eat first?" asked Alex.

"I'll grab something in New York," I said. "Promise."

Shelby stepped into the kitchen, nodding in my direction just as I stepped away from Mom and grabbed for the inherent mathematical structure of the world around me. I had to do the mental equivalent of squinting in order to see it, but once I did, I could see the chained functions that made up everything. Physics, matter, and distance, they were all equations, and equations could be modified.

I waved at Shelby, and I was gone.

There aren't really words for the way I can move around now that I've stabilized as a fully mature queen. "Spatial tunneling" is the closest we've really come. I basically just take the math that tells me my location and change it to something different. As soon as I release it in its changed state, it becomes an absolute truth, and reality is happier to change things about itself than it is to modify its underlying math. It does make an impact, leaving little errors in the math between the two points I've modified, and they need time to correct themselves before I can safely tunnel to the same location again. I try to think of it as drawing lines that are never allowed to overlap, a logic puzzle playing out in four dimensions at once. And even that is a simplification, because I don't know how to explain the beautiful crystalline network of numbers that is the equations that transport me. I reach out, I tweak, and I'm gone. Over and over again. It's that simple, and that complicated.

It's definitely not an ability that should have been extended to someone with my reasons for running away.

Two

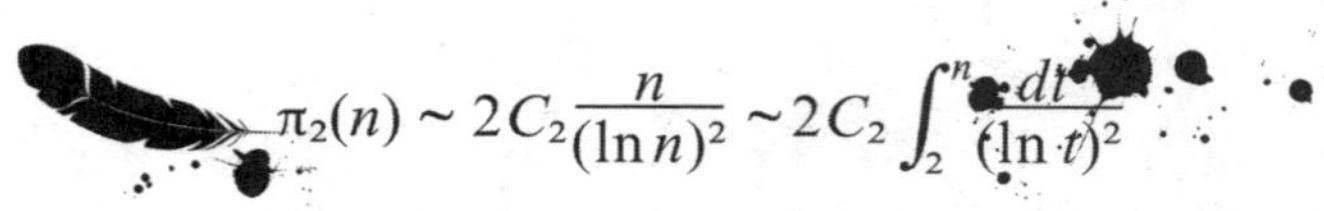

"People will always make assumptions about you based on who your family is. Whether you prove them wrong or right is up to you. Pick whichever suits you better."

—**Alice Healy**

The smaller bedroom in a rent-controlled Manhattan apartment

ONE MOMENT, I WAS IN the kitchen with my family, and the next moment, I was standing in the room I rented in New York. Unlike my childhood bedroom, it was barren, almost austere in its lack of decoration or clutter; there was a bed, for the times when I absolutely couldn't get out of sleeping here, and a dresser with a week's worth of clothing, but there wasn't much else.

It was, however, all spotlessly clean. I creaked open the door, and the sound of Latin pop drifted down the hall, accompanied by the smell of frying eggs and hot bacon grease. I could pick up Malena's thoughts from the kitchen, as bright and electric as her music. She was in a good mood. That was an excellent thing. An unhappy Malena can be dangerous.

Like me, Malena is a cryptid capable of passing for human. Unlike me, her species is actually native to this dimension. She's a chupacabra, a synapsid therianthrope whose biology would give most scientists the most confusing orgasm of their lives if they got an hour to study her. Is she a mammal? Is she a reptile? Is anyone going to figure it out any time soon?

Most of the time she's a Mexican-American woman who works as the handyman in the dragon-owned apartment building where my cousin Verity lives. Malena likes pop music, dirty fried eggs, and ballroom dance; while she no longer danced professionally, she had been teaching local classes, and had managed to acquire a loyal following of amorous retirees, aspiring competitors, and Broadway hopefuls.

She and Verity originally met on a reality dance competition show, *Dance or Die*, where they'd technically been up against each other, but had actually formed an alliance when the other contestants started showing up dead. They weren't the best of friends back then, but after Verity's husband died, Malena had shown up on her doorstep to drag her out of her depression. It hadn't worked well enough to make them roommates, but it had worked well enough to make Malena a semi-permanent fixture.

I was quietly glad of that. She only needed one bedroom, and was happy to sublet her spare to me for use when I was in the city. That kept me from needing to either rent a whole apartment on my own or—even worse—stay with Verity and her kids. Livvy and David are great kids, very sweet, very friendly, and very unaccustomed to spending extended periods of time around a telepath. It's the mental equivalent of going to the mall on Black Friday without earplugs.

Reaching out, I could tell Verity and the kids were in the building, and I'd be able to check in with them before heading to the hospital. I started walking quietly down the hall, following the sound of Malena's music.

I was almost there when she said, voice bright and friendly, "If you're not Sarah, you should know I don't have any of those silly human compunctions against killing people who invade my den, and maybe turn around and go the other way."

"Definitely Sarah," I said, stepping around the corner into the narrow, cream-colored kitchen.

Malena was standing in the center of the room. She folded her arms, eyeing me. "You ever hear of calling first? Texting? Maybe drawing up a nice schedule so I know when to expect the sudden appearance of my occasional roommate? I could have been in the middle of eating my breakfast."

"I don't care if you need to eat around me," I said. "It doesn't bother me."

She unfolded her arms in order to shake her spatula in my direction. "It will, once I put everything in the blender."

Chupacabra don't handle solids well. They're not strict sanguivores like Huldra, but they get horrific indigestion if they eat things that aren't pureed, or have less than about eighty percent animal protein. There was an industrial-strength blender next to the stove, already half full of what looked dauntingly like raspberry jelly.

Coagulated pig's blood is an acquired taste, and as a chupacabra who lived among humans, Malena had acquired it. Seeing me looking, she picked up her frying pan and began scraping bacon and eggs into the blender, a challenging buzz at the top of her thoughts.

Sometimes I like to imagine what it would be like if I could look at people's faces and know what they were thinking, rather than looking at their thoughts and guessing at what they actually wanted me to see. I guess the grass really is always greener on the other side of the fence.

"You want some?" she asked.

"No, thank you," I said. "There's a juice bar near the entrance to St. Giles's that does tomato-ginger smoothies, and I'm going to grab one before I go to see Dr. Morrow."

Some of the challenge faded, replaced by guilt. "This is a Mark visit, huh?"

Malena never met Mark—he showed up well after the producers of *Dance or Die* decided it was a good idea to summon a giant snake from another dimension on live television—but she knew his deal. He'd been at St. Giles's for long enough to have become a fixture, and Verity had visiting privileges, just in case he woke up while I wasn't available. As the only adult we knew of in the city with Kairos heritage, she stood the best chance of putting him down if he opened his eyes and started breaking things.

"Yeah," I confirmed.

"Is it a good Mark visit?"

"Not so much, no. I think Dr. Morrow needs the bed. That, or they've seen something on their scans that worries them enough for them to want to discuss it with me in person. Either way, I can't see that meaning anything great, can you?"

"No," she said, with a sigh. "I'm sorry, Sarah. And I didn't mean to snipe at you. Of course you can come home whenever you need to. It's your room. You're a better roommate than someone who'd want to actually be here all the time. It's just been a hard week."

"Problems in the building?"

"Just the usual. Rats got into the basement again."

"I thought free snacks were a part of your payment."

Even I could tell that the number of extremely sharp teeth in her grin was unusual. "Oh, and they are. I just have to catch them live and keep them for three days to be sure they haven't been poisoned with anything that might upset my stomach. No, rats got into the basement and half the tenants wanted to parlay that into a rent reduction."

I winced. A rent reduction is never an easy ask in Manhattan. A rent reduction in a dragon-owned building is sort of like asking the sun to turn blue for the weekend to fit the aesthetics of your outdoor wedding. "How many evictions?" I asked.

"None. But things were tense and shouty around here for days."

"Ick."

"Tell me about it." She put the lid on the blender and hit the puree button. The blender's contents mixed into an unpleasant shade of greasy brown, streaked with red from the pig's blood jelly. I watched impassively.

My diet isn't precisely human-normal, and it takes more than a blood smoothie to upset me. Malena turned off the blender and poured its contents into a glass, sticking a straw into the slurry and taking a long drink. She watched me as she did, and I could feel her confusion grow as I didn't recoil or look away.

"I don't know why you want to fight with me right now, but I'm tired and I'm worried about Mark and I only came through the apartment so I could check in with Verity, not because I needed some recreational arguing," I said. "I'm gonna go."

Malena lowered her glass with a sigh. "I'm sorry. I don't want to fight, I'm just—I'm in a rotten mood, and you surprised me."

"I hope you feel better," I said, and started for the door.

It always feels a little odd to get around normally right after I've opened a spatial tunnel between two points. Like being able to do it means I should do nothing else. But even birds walk, and they have wings. Sometimes the supposedly easy method isn't the best one available.

Malena didn't follow or call me back, just let me go. That was almost certainly for the best. She might be in the mood to fight, but I wasn't, and I didn't want to hurt Verity's most reliable babysitter. People tended to assume that because I wasn't a physical fighter, I would be a soft or easy target.

People can be so good at being wrong.

The hallway outside the apartment smelled of boiled cabbage and fried onions, which wasn't indicative of anything currently being cooked. Those halls were virtually designed to trap and retain smells, developing unique olfactory footprints over time. You could tell a lot about a building's demographics by the way the hallways smelled. I liked it. It was a very domesticated method of peeing on a fencepost, a way to mark territory without breaking any social norms. I passed closed door after closed door on my way to the elevator, then pressed the call button and stepped inside.

Verity had been managing this building for the dragons since the family drove the Covenant of St. George out of the city. It was part reward for the work she'd already done, part bribe to keep her from heading back to Portland to raise her kids. *See?* it said. *We couldn't save your husband, but we can provide you with affordable housing near a good school district.*

Verity preferred to live away from the bulk of the family, and property management seemed to suit her well. She liked her apartment, and I could feel her general contentment as I made my way toward the door. Well, contentment and deep frustration: David, still too young for solids, had dumped his entire bowl of soft cereal on the kitchen floor, and Livvy was laughing so hard that he was taking it as incentive to throw more of the contents of his tray. Ah, the life of a single mother.

I had a key, and from the level of chaos I was picking up on, Verity wouldn't thank me for taking the time to knock. I unlocked the door and let myself inside. "I'm just a burglar," I called.

Her laughter drifted from the tiny dining room. "You know if I believed you, this could get real messy, right?"

"I know you never believe me about that sort of thing," I countered, and followed her voice.

Livvy was sitting in a grown-up chair, as befit a five-nearly-six-year-old. Her booster seat brought her up level with the table, and she watched me gravely as I approached, eyes going enormous and laughter cutting off. David, on the other hand, kept making happy baby sounds and flinging things onto the floor. He had moved on to his napkin and sippy cup, and was going to be entirely out of throwables very soon.

"Because I can feel you coming," said Verity, crouched over and wiping cereal off the floor.

"Fair," I allowed.

The longer someone spends around a cuckoo, the more they'll become attuned to us. On the one hand, this makes it easier for us to modify their thoughts, as we seep through their defenses like water into the foundation of a house. On the other hand, it means they can tell when we're nearby. Our telepathy generates a sort of static, like a mistuned radio inside their heads, and they can use that to evade us before we're close enough to act intentionally.

Or . . . I guess I shouldn't include myself in that "us." As a queen, I could do a lot of damage without coming close enough for the static to start. But my family didn't know that, and they weren't *going* to know if I had anything to say about it. I can handle them being a little cautious when they know I'm around, and I can deal with Arthur hating me. I just don't think I could survive them being actively afraid of me.

Maybe it was cowardly of me, but I needed my family not to

be scared just because of things I hadn't done yet, and was never intending to do.

Verity straightened up, and I knew she was smiling because she thought the word *Smile* in sparkly cursive lettering, like it was a placard in an old black-and-white film. She did that sometimes, visualizing things to help me understand her facial expressions. I always appreciated it when she made the effort.

"The hospital called you, huh?" she asked.

I nodded. "Yeah. I'm supposed to come in and talk to them about Mark."

Verity nodded. "Dr. Morrow told me he was going to call. You want me to come with you? I can ask Malena to watch the kids."

"No, I'm fine on my own," I said. "I just wanted to stop in and say hello before I went over. Is it weird that I'm nervous?"

"No," she said. "It's natural. It means you care."

"I do care," I said. I wanted him to wake up. I wanted to get him back to his family, to his sister, to the people who really knew and loved him. And wanting those things came with a certain degree of caring about him. How could they not?

Verity reached over and put a hand briefly on my shoulder. "It's going to be okay, Sarah," she said.

"Is it?" I asked.

She didn't have an answer.

✦ ✦ ✦

New York is an embarrassment of riches. In addition to some of the best public transit in North America—I can't say *the* best, I haven't spent that much time in Canada—Manhattan itself is an incredibly walkable city. It may take a while, but you can get almost anywhere from almost any starting point. Right now, that was what I wanted. To walk through endless, teeming crowds and let myself sink into the chaotic music of a million minds, all of them consumed by their own needs and desires, all of them focused on getting through the morning.

It was only a little after eight in the morning; about half the people who passed me were on their way to work, hurrying to cram themselves behind desks and service counters for the next eight hours. Children ran by on their way to school, retired adults strolled with more leisure in their steps, and food-cart vendors thought longingly of selling me a breakfast burrito or a hot dog.

When I reached the juice bar near St. Giles's, I went in and ordered my smoothie, as promised. I needed to eat *something* before the day got too late, and there's nothing like a carrot juice, tomato, ginger, and honey smoothie to make me feel better. I can't say it does anything for my blood sugar, because we're not sure I *have* blood sugar in the classical sense—we've had so few opportunities to study cuckoos on a biological level that I have more questions than answers when it comes to my own body. Experimenting on myself has never been an option. Even if my parents would allow it, I don't like pain, and with as unpredictable as my abilities can be, I try not to push the issue.

The clerk didn't bat an eye or spare a thought for my order, which was far from the strangest thing he'd ever shoved into a blender, or even shoved into a blender since they'd opened that day. I accepted the cup with a smile, tucking a five-dollar bill into his tip jar, and left. No one noticed that I hadn't paid. Being a telepathic predator comes with its advantages.

The "no one notices Sarah" theme continued as I opened a metal grate in the sidewalk and descended the stairs on the other side, pulling the grate closed again behind me. This was one of the more-direct entrances to the hospital. Most people skipped it during the day, since it was difficult to use without being seen. I didn't have that issue.

The stairs ended in a wide, flat stretch of unused sewer tunnel. Humans weren't the only people involved in building the original city, and the cryptids who had a hand in things made sure the infrastructure for us to survive was present and solid enough to stand up for centuries. I followed the tunnel until I came to another door, opening it on the clean white hospital reception area.

It looked like every other hospital waiting room I'd ever seen: stark lighting, hard plastic chairs, and big potted plants that looked like they couldn't decide whether to die or put out another leaf that would somehow be half-browned even as it opened. There were no windows, and the walls were dotted with inspirational posters about health and safety. Many of them were illustrated with cheerful cartoon versions of common cryptid species—a dragon, a bogeyman, a lepidoular . . . a cuckoo. The picture of the cuckoo showed a girl who looked unnervingly like me staring directly at the viewer.

"LEARN THE SIGNS YOUR MIND HAS BEEN CHANGED FOR YOU," read the text. "YOU ARE NOT IMMUNE TO PSYCHIC MANIPULATION."

I looked at this reminder of what people thought of my entire species and shuddered before approaching the reception desk. A woman in a white jacket sat there, a horseshoe-shaped clip holding her hair back and a rabbit's foot dangling from one wrist. She looked up as I got closer, forcing a veneer of calm that almost managed to conceal her deep discomfort.

"Sarah, hello," she said. "Dr. Morrow has been waiting for you. Let me call and tell him you've arrived."

"Thank you, Michelle," I said.

She managed a weak smile, thinking about it as much as doing it, and picked up the phone, twisting her body so I couldn't see her mouth as she spoke. It didn't matter; her thoughts were clear. She'd been trying to trade shifts since she heard I'd be coming to the hospital, wanting to avoid running into me directly.

I'd never intentionally done anything to hurt the staff at St. Giles's. But when my Aunt Jane—Artie's mother—died, I'd blamed myself and come to Mark's bedside in a desperate attempt at self-soothing. I'd been too lost in my own distress to cloak my presence, and so I'd just stopped people from getting too close to me instead. When Michelle had approached me in her official capacity as one of the head nurses, I'd put her to sleep, and she'd stayed that way for hours, until my attention turned elsewhere and the telepathic whammy I'd put on her wore off. It was understandable that she didn't want to deal with me. I wouldn't have wanted to deal with me either.

She'd been pretty successful about avoiding me up until this point. This was the first time I'd seen her since the incident.

"Hey," I said, voice gentle. "I'm sorry about knocking you out that time. I was really upset, and I wasn't clamping down on myself properly. It won't happen again."

She leaned away from me, radiating distrust and disbelief. "I've spoken to Dr. Morrow. He says that if you touch a member of his staff again, you'll be banned from the premises." *Like you always should have been,* added her thoughts, so clear and loud that I couldn't help overhearing. *Cuckoos shouldn't be allowed inside the building.*

I kept my face as composed as I could. "I promise, it won't happen again."

"Good." She eyed me suspiciously as I turned to look at the posters on the walls, studying them like they were the most interesting things I'd ever seen.

There are a lot of reasons to hate being a telepath in a non-telepathic world. But one of the big ones is that since people assume their minds are private, unreachable things, they do the equivalent of going into their front yards in their underpants and screaming at the neighbors. I've spent years learning not to foreground every awful, hateful, prejudiced thing I want to think, but there's no reason for non-telepaths to do the same.

In human spaces, no one believed people like me could exist, and so they did nothing to guard their thoughts, but they didn't spend time thinking about how much they'd like to kill people like me. In cryptid spaces, everyone knew people like me existed, and could be anywhere, so when they knew one of us was nearby, they spent a lot of time and energy thinking about how great it would be if we were dead and hence not there anymore. Having no interest in becoming dead, I mostly avoided non-family cryptid spaces.

Cuckoos were always going to be the enemy. We were invasive

outsiders, predators who didn't care who we hurt in the process of getting what we wanted. No matter how much I tried to suppress my instincts, they were still there. I could pretend to be a nice person as much as I wanted, but when push came to shove, I would always put myself first. I would always be the monster.

I sank deeper and deeper into self-loathing, Michelle's unguarded thoughts echoing through my mind like poisonous vapors trapped in a windowless room, and didn't hear the doors at the back of the room opening, or the soft clack of taloned feet against the tile floor.

Dr. Morrow was a smart man who understood cuckoo physiology better than most. He stopped several feet away from me and half-spread his wings, shaking them so the feathers brushed against one another with a soft susurration. They rustled again as he snapped his wings closed, folding them nearly away behind his back. "Miss Zellaby," he said, voice formal.

"Making sure you weren't going to startle me, Doctor?" I asked, turning to face him.

He shrugged. "I put a great deal of faith in the anti-telepathy charms I've ordered for my staff, but there's having faith and then there's being foolish. I don't want to learn their limits firsthand. Thank you for coming."

"You don't ask me to show up very often," I said. "Have I fallen behind on Mark's bills?"

St. Giles's doesn't take any known form of insurance: they're probably one of the last hospitals in America that bills exactly as much as they need to in order to keep the lights on. But they do bill. They have to. Even if the staff donated their time, the supplies they use aren't free. Mark's care was magnitudes cheaper than it would have been anywhere else in the country: it was still several thousand dollars a month, which I was gladly sending to the administrative office. He needed to be looked after. I owed him.

"No," said Dr. Morrow. "But your friend's latest scans are . . . Walk with me."

Something about his tone made anxiety lance through me,

briefly coloring the world in gray. Dr. Morrow didn't say anything further, only gestured for me to follow as he turned, heading for the doors that would take him into the primary part of the hospital. There was no one here to listen in on us, but I still felt like we could use a little privacy. This was Mark's future we were talking about here, after all.

The hall on the other side of the double doors was even brighter than the waiting room, the air cool and scented with disinfectant. I followed Dr. Morrow to a small office with a backless chair in front of the desk and a more-standard armchair next to it. He sat down on the backless chair, allowing his wings to relax from their folded position to a half-mantled state, reaching for his computer mouse.

"Mr. Wilson has been in a catatonic state since you brought him to us," he said, without preamble. "During this time, we have observed morphological transformations in the brain, most specifically the frontal lobe and right parahippocampal gyrus. Sections of his brain have appeared to functionally liquify, triggering concerns about cellular necrosis, then reconstitute in a modified configuration. I know your species has visual differences from the mammalian bipeds I customarily work with. Are you able to look at diagnostic scans, or should I describe them to you?"

"I'll either need you to put down the anti-telepathy charm or explain them to me, but I can see them," I said. "I can *see* faces, I just can't interpret any useful information from them. It's like asking you to look into an ant's nest and tell the individual ants apart, or understand what they're feeling from the way they're carrying their antennae. It just doesn't work."

"Some entomologists develop that skill," he said.

"I'm sure some cuckoos learn it as well," I said. "I didn't. I tried, and it never worked. When I was a kid and upset about not being able to tell what people were sharing about their feelings, my cousin Artie used to draw me sheets of cartoon faces making these exaggerated expressions, and they helped, a little. I can tell when someone's smiling as opposed to frowning, and if their thoughts say they're happy and they're frowning, I can be careful about saying 'Wow, someone's in a good mood today' before I understand the situation. But the cartoon faces never really translated into understanding real faces. Too much nuance. A big frown and a small frown look pretty much the same to me."

"Fascinating," he said dryly. "I'm not putting down my charm."

He tapped his computer monitor and it came on, showing a scan of what I presumed was Mark's brain. He moved the mouse, and a second scan appeared next to the first. I frowned, squinting.

They were both brains, both images taken from the same direction and angle, but they looked nothing alike. Even my untrained eye could tell the structures I was seeing had very little in common. The second image even had some entirely new-looking areas, separated from the rest by deep ridges. Dr. Morrow indicated the first image.

"This is Mr. Wilson's brain the day you brought him to us."

"I didn't bring him," I protested. "My family did. I was unconscious at the time."

"You took them all to another dimension, you brought them here, even if it was by proxy," he said. He clicked his mouse again and the first image disappeared, replaced by one that was almost identical to the second.

Dr. Morrow indicated the second image. "This is Mr. Wilson's brain yesterday afternoon, when we took him for routine scans."

"All right," I said. "When was the other one taken?"

He turned to look at me, rather than the screen. "That's your brain, the day you came back from your transdimensional adventure. That's what his has been moving toward. Based on this and the recent changes to his vital signs, I would predict Mr. Wilson is on the verge of waking up. I wanted you to be here when he did, in case he lashes out at the nearest target available."

Three

$$\pi_2(n) \sim 2C_2\frac{n}{(\ln n)^2} \sim 2C_2\int_2^n \frac{dt}{(\ln t)^2}$$

"There is nothing in this world or any other that could make me stop loving you, no matter how much you test my patience."

—**Mary Dunlavy**

A patient room at St. Giles's Hospital, a private cryptid institution under New York City

I PULLED THE CHAIR UP NEXT to Mark's bed, reaching for his hand as I sat. As always, he lay motionless and unresponsive, eyes closed and face turned toward the ceiling. He looked enough like me to be my brother, and for all we knew, he was; cuckoo parents don't exactly give their children lists of siblings when they drop us off. I didn't think so, though. There had been a familiar hum to Ingrid's mind that told me she was my biological mother. I didn't get that from Mark.

Right now, I didn't get anything at all until I laced my fingers with his, holding him as tightly as I dared. Once our palms were touching and the skin contact amplified my powers, I tumbled into his mind like Alice tumbling down the rabbit hole—the fictional character, not my grandmother.

I once described the inside of Mark's mind as being like a damaged computer hard drive, all scrambled data and static-filled images. This time, as I tumbled, I didn't see anything like that. Instead, I passed flashes of memory and personality. None of it seemed conscious—the awareness that would have screamed "Mark" to me just wasn't present.

Still, this was more than I'd ever been able to find before. I focused on my descent. Diving into someone else's mind like this was sort of like being in a lucid dream, one of those ones that feel completely real as they're going on. That meant that even though I knew I was sitting in Mark's hospital room, I felt like I was falling. I imagined my body heavier, dropping like a stone, and the dream image of myself obliged, plummeting into the depths of Mark's mind.

It was a disorienting, vertigo-inducing sensation, and I had to clench my jaw to stop myself from taking the extra weight away. I fell past memory, past the flickering web of Mark's personality trying to reconstruct itself, and landed in a familiar white void.

For a moment, I just stopped, standing up straight and looking triumphantly around.

I'd been trying to reach this void for years. It was the bottom of the self. I'd been trapped in my own void by my mother, once, and rescued Artie from his when a cuckoo boobytrap left him stranded there. Because that was the thing about really deep mental work: it was a concept and an unreal space, but that didn't make it any less dangerous to the unprepared. There were traps in the deeps, and they could catch and keep a person who didn't know how to avoid them.

Mark's void had been blocked by the distortion in his mind, keeping me from getting deep enough to look for him. And now the distortion was cleared, and I could get to the base of his psyche.

This deep into his thoughts, it no longer felt like lucid dreaming. It felt like reality. I took a step deeper into the white endlessness and felt my weight shift onto my leading foot, felt the solidity of my body moving through the cool air at the bottom of his self. I kept walking, trying to adjust to the strange sensation of moving through someone who probably wouldn't have invited me in if he'd been awake to have a say. When I'd been in my own mind, I'd been at home, and when I'd been in Artie's mind, I'd been someone he trusted enough to welcome. Here, I was barely better than a stranger, and I was the one who'd broken him. I had to tread carefully.

I held that thought firmly as I moved deeper, the scenery—or lack thereof—around me not changing in the least. I was an intruder here. I might not be actively unwelcome, but I needed to assume he'd throw me out if he could.

And I would welcome it. Throwing me out would show an awareness of his own mind that Mark hadn't demonstrated before this point. It might hurt, but I'd accept the pain if it meant he was waking up.

I walked and walked, until I saw something breaking the line of the empty infinity around me. It was a chair, the fancy gaming kind that Artie had in his basement for years, designed for people who wanted to spend hours staring at a screen and battling their controllers. I angled myself toward it, and it got larger at an accelerated rate, every step I took carrying me an impossible distance forward.

As it grew, I saw the table and television in front of it, the bright polygons of some complicated video game flashing across the screen. There was no sound. That made more sense when I got close enough to see the figure in the chair: Mark, maybe fourteen years old, wearing a pair of headphones that swallowed his ears and made his head look small. He was watching the screen with a frighteningly focused intensity, tongue poking out of the corner of his mouth and eyes narrowed to bring the figures into sharper focus.

That's another thing about being in someone's mindscape: since everything I'm seeing is their thoughts, or sometimes memories, I can understand facial expressions when I'm on the inside. They're not images so much as the memory and intention of images, and Mark's face was perfectly clear. In here, I could see how much we looked alike, even if he was younger than I'd ever known him.

It made sense. Mark told Artie his ancestral memories had cracked when he was fifteen. I'd ripped those same memories out of his mind after they'd been given plenty of time to throw down roots and wind their way through his psyche, resulting in incredible damage when they were removed. This was a version of Mark that had existed before those memories, and might well be the oldest version of him that still existed.

I moved to stand next to the television, waiting for him to notice me. For what felt like an eternity, he kept focusing on his game. I could tell when he realized I was there: his eyes widened and his tongue pulled back into his mouth. He pressed a button at the center of his controller, then tossed it to the side, pulling the headphones down around his neck.

"What are *you* doing here?" he asked, voice sharp and aggressive.

"I've been trying to *find* you," I replied. "Mark, are you all right?"

"Asks the woman who took my brain apart," he said, almost sullenly. He turned his attention back to the screen, picking up the controller again, although he left the headphones around his neck. "Of course I'm not all right."

"I needed the space, and you gave me permission," I said. "I didn't have a choice. We'd all have died if I hadn't done that."

"Yeah, well, maybe I died anyway," he countered. "If I wake up, am I still me? Am I going to lose everything that makes me who I am?"

I winced. "I don't know," I said. "Artie . . . Artie didn't wake up at all."

His eyes widened again, this time with surprise rather than shock. "What do you mean?"

"While I was running the equation, he—he touched me. Bare skin on bare skin. And it jumped into him, and it ate him alive. He didn't wake up after that. I had to build him a new person to be before he could wake up. I didn't do that with you. You've been sleeping and healing for a long time now. I think you're getting better."

"How long?" he asked suspiciously.

"I don't think I should—"

"How. Long?"

"Eight years."

He surged out of his chair, dropping the controller again. Somewhere in the process of standing up, he went from fourteen to twenty, getting taller and broader across the chest and shoulders, face melting from boyish softness into something more severe. "You mean you left me in a coma for *eight years*? My sister—"

"Is fine."

He froze, sagging slightly, like I'd just knocked the wind out of him.

"I've been checking in with your family periodically. They don't know who I am, and they don't remember me between visits, but I know who they are, and I know they miss you very much. They have no idea what happened to you. They just want you to come home."

"Cici."

"Is twenty years old now. She graduated from high school in the middle of her class, but she didn't get expelled, and when one of the boys on the football team grabbed her ass, she broke his jaw. She's a little spitfire, just like you said she was. She's majoring in forensic science. She misses her big brother."

"She can't be twenty," he objected. A giggle sounded from off to the right, high and bright and playful. He glanced toward it. "She's not allowed."

"I'm sorry." That wasn't enough. That could never have been enough. "You remember how Ingrid said she was going to turn me into a queen?"

"Yeah."

"The last instar only triggers if you experience psychic trauma and have had your ancestral memories removed," I said. "I caused you psychic trauma in the process of removing those memories. I think you've been undergoing the third and fourth instars at the same time. That's why it's taken so long."

He stared at me. "That's not possible."

Cici ran into the space between us, a skinny urchin of no more than twelve in leggings and an oversized T-shirt that hung well past her mid-thigh. Her hair was gathered into two puffs on the sides of her head, banded with rainbow beads, and her skin was dark enough to make Mark look sickly as she grabbed his arm and yanked it down, pulling on him.

"Mark, come *on*," she said. "You promised I could have a turn. You promised, you promised."

"Cici, hey, chill for a second, okay?" He picked up the controller and handed it to her. "Go ahead and get your high score on, and I'll check in with you in a little bit."

She threw herself into his chair, already punching buttons with wild glee. Mark turned his attention back to me.

"You can't tell me she grew up while I wasn't there," he said.

"I'm sorry. But she's still young, and she has so much life ahead of her. She needs her big brother. She needs you to come home. Will you wake up, please? Will you at least *try*?"

Mark hesitated. "I don't know how," he admitted, after a long pause.

"Don't worry." I smiled brightly, offering him my hand. "I do."

"Just a second, okay?" He turned back to Cici, who was just a memory, but was still the little sister he knew, the girl who'd been enough to stop him from destroying his entire family the way every cuckoo before him had done. She mattered.

He knelt, reaching over to poke her in the middle of the forehead. She glanced at him, lower lip jutting out in an exaggerated, playful pout.

"Stop it, stupid brother," she said. "I'm playing."

"I know, but—I have to go with my friend Sarah now, and I don't know when I'll be back. Can you stay here and keep the game going until I see you again?"

Memory-Cici nodded enthusiastically, attention returning to the screen. Mark stood, sighing, and turned back to me.

"I know she's just my memory of her, but if I'm not going to see this Cici again, I needed to say goodbye."

"I understand." I did, too. I would have given anything to have had the chance to say a proper goodbye to Artie, and I was never going to get one.

This time when I offered him my hand, he took it, and he let me pull him along as I started walking back through the endless white void. The gaming setup dwindled in the distance, becoming a speck before vanishing altogether. We were once again lost in the nothingness.

"Where are we going?" asked Mark.

"Home," I said. "Back to the world where your family is, and your body is, and there's tomato juice and math and autumn afternoons and no zombie cuckoos trying to destroy the world."

"Wait—if you've been checking on my family for eight years, does that mean you did it? You finished the equation, and you didn't die in the process?"

"Yup," I said. "I am officially the first surviving cuckoo queen. Whee."

He eyed me, sidelong and suspicious. "What did it cost you?"

I glanced back at him. "What?"

"What did finishing the equation cost you?"

"I already told you Artie didn't wake up. My cousin Annie didn't get her memories back. My family doesn't trust me anymore, not the way they did before I went and forcibly reminded them that I was a monster."

He squeezed my hand. "You're not a monster. You didn't do any of those things on purpose."

"I still did them."

Mark didn't have an answer to that. We walked on.

✦ ✦ ✦

Bit by bit, awareness of Mark's hospital room returned to me. I opened my eyes and I was sitting next to his bed, his hand held in mine, machines beeping and buzzing around us. I looked toward him. His eyelids were fluttering, struggling to open. One of the machines began beeping more loudly.

"Dr. Morrow," I said, loudly.

Mark's eyelids continued to flutter. And then the screaming began. Loud, unending screaming, entirely mental, projected through the bond created by our skin contact. I jerked my hand away. The screaming got softer but didn't stop.

"Dr. Morrow!" I shouted, trying to be heard above the din. I clapped my hands over my ears, knowing the screams were entirely inside my head but unable to stop myself.

The door slammed open and the doctor was there, wings fully mantled and feathers atop his head standing erect, like he was trying to make himself look bigger to scare away a threat. He took in the room at a glance, then rushed forward, pulling something out of his pocket and shoving it down the front of Mark's hospital gown.

The screams in my head cut off abruptly as the anti-telepathy charm settled against Mark's skin. I lowered my hands from my ears, eyeing him as warily as a hiker eyes a rattlesnake. "Mark?" I asked. "You awake over there?"

His eyes stopped trying to open and he sagged back into the bed, motionless. Dr. Morrow closed his wings, and for several seconds it was just the two of us staring at Mark, waiting for something to occur.

"This is part of why I wanted to speak to you," said Dr. Morrow finally. "You were unconscious for a matter of hours, not days, and the sound of your awakening still reverberated through the hospital."

"I didn't know that."

"Does an infant know they cry upon being born? We do many things on instinct in this life, and we don't recognize them all. I was concerned that Mr. Wilson would do exactly what he's done, and while I took the steps available to me, your presence seemed the best way to blunt the impact."

I raised an eyebrow. "And did it?"

"I know this won't sound sincere to you, but yes, it did. To the best of my knowledge, no one is bleeding from the ears, and I credit that to you being here to take the brunt of the damage."

"What do you mean?"

"Your nose." He produced a handkerchief from inside his coat and offered it to me.

I took it gingerly, then pressed it to my upper lip. It came away glistening with thick, clear fluid. If I were human, that would probably have been mucus. But I'm not, and so I had to admit it was hemolymph, probably from a burst vessel somewhere in my sinuses.

People don't really realize how much of the human—or cryptid—skull is actually taken up by sinuses. The "telepath nosebleed" in movies and comics is a cliché, but it's a cliché with a basis in anatomy. When something puts too much pressure on my brain, those are the easiest physical tells.

I wiped my upper lip more vigorously, then tapped it with my fingertips, verifying it was dry. "Can I keep this?" I asked, holding up the hankie.

"Please," said Dr. Morrow. "Now that Mr. Wilson is awake, we'll have to discuss the further specifics of his . . . care . . ."

His voice trailed off as a strange humming sound filled the room, growing higher and higher, clear and crystalline as a finger being run along the rim of a perfectly cut wine glass. It hummed and sang and trilled, and I recognized it like a captive-raised bird might recognize the song its mother sang while it was in the egg.

I stood, only half-aware of the motion, turning my eyes toward the ceiling. The sound had no source and no direction, but it felt like an "up" in some indefinable way, and so that was where I looked for it.

Dr. Morrow mantled his wings again, lifting them defensively as he looked around the room. "Do you hear that?" he asked needlessly.

"It's beautiful," I said. "Is that Mark?"

"I don't think so."

Dr. Morrow moved to start checking the machines still connected to Mark's body, moving with a quick efficiency that I could only envy. The hum got louder.

"I really don't think it's him," said Dr. Morrow. "None of these readings—"

The hum got even louder, until I couldn't hear Dr. Morrow speaking anymore. It swelled and swelled, and then, just as it was becoming painful, popped like a bubble, filling the room with iridescent glitter that hung suspended in the air, twinkling and shimmering and turning everything prismatically distorted.

The glitter wasn't all that appeared. It was accompanied by five people in skintight bodysuits that gleamed like liquid metal as they moved. The suits were cut to look almost segmented, chest, abdomen and legs called out by subtle lines and joints. Two of the suits were a rich, jewel-toned blue, while the other three were red, black, and gold.

Their heads and faces were exposed, revealing straight black hair and eyes as blue as my own. I couldn't be certain, but I thought they all looked like me, identical interlopers from somewhere else entirely.

I stared. I didn't know what else to do. Dr. Morrow was less subdued. Feathers bristling like he was a cat facing down an intruder rather than a Caladrius in his own territory, he stepped toward them.

"What is the meaning of this?" he demanded.

The closest stranger cocked their head to the side, looking at him impassively. "Native life-form," they said. "Non-dominant species. Some sort of healer? Believes we are trespassing."

"Remove but do not revise," said one of the others. They raised a hand, turning it sharply in the air like they were opening a door. Their eyes blazed briefly white, and Dr. Morrow froze.

A third stranger stepped forward, eyes glowing white, if not as brightly, and Dr. Morrow's feathers smoothed themselves back into their normal, neutral position. Then he turned and walked out of the room, not saying a word.

"What did you *do*?" I gasped.

"The local creature would have interfered," said the first of them to have spoken. "Interference is not to be allowed."

"You are the cuckoo queen?" asked another.

"I— What?"

"She is," said a third. "She has reached the forbidden instar."

"Your crimes have been noted and documented, and will not be permitted to go unanswered," said the one who'd put the whammy on Dr. Morrow. "You will stand before the tribunal and answer for what you've done."

"I haven't done anything wrong," I protested. "I just wanted to help Mark wake up."

As I spoke, I realized none of them had looked at Mark since they'd appeared in the room. He was motionless in the bed, and with the charm blocking his mind, he might as well have been an inanimate object. My breath caught, and I promptly shoved all thoughts of him behind walls of simple math, hiding them from view.

They couldn't see him. Dr. Morrow had stuffed an industrial-strength anti-telepathy charm into his gown, and now he was invisible to these strange Johrlac. Because these *were* Johrlac, not cuckoos: the way they held themselves, the way they dressed, even the way they spoke, it all whispered of origins beyond this world. They were alien. To me, to Mark, to everything around them.

And they were surrounding me. Suddenly realizing the danger I was in, I whirled, ready to flee the room, and stopped as two of them grabbed my arms. They didn't bother avoiding my skin, seeming unconcerned about touching me directly, and as their fingers closed around me, I realized they were wearing gloves of some transparent, flexible material.

I struggled, trying to jerk away, and they held me tighter, pulling my arms straight. The one I was starting to think of as a spokesperson stepped forward.

"We have left you free for too long," they said. "That ends now."

The hum resumed, louder now, infinitely louder, until it was consuming everything and I finally understood the mathematics behind its rising and falling tones, the way it all fit together, the things it was trying to accomplish, and that didn't matter at all, that could never have mattered—

Because we were gone.

Four

ANTIMONY

> "Most people's parents take the grandkids to an amusement park and come back with too many stuffed toys. Mine come back with extra kids."
>
> —**Evelyn Baker**

Buckley Township, Michigan,
in a field on the edge of the Galway Woods

SAM WAS SOMEWHERE IN THE trees, having the absolute time of his life. Occasionally he emerged to show me something terrible that he'd found scuttling around in the underbrush, and after I had sufficiently admired it, with as much ooh-ing and ahh-ing as I could manage, he would swing away again, off to find some new living nightmare that had arisen in the paradise of horrors my paternal grandparents called their home.

Half the things he brought out, proud as a cat with a dead rat to present to its owner, were species I had believed extinct since before I was born. But they'd survived here, in Buckley Township, Michigan, where the town motto should really have been "If you see something, no you didn't. Shut your fucking mouth before someone hears you." Or possibly the simpler "Snitches get stitches."

After several hours of show-and-tell, Sam had brought me half the horrors the forest had to offer, and I had managed to burn a perfect circle in the grass approximately ten feet across, controlling the fire so completely that not a single piece of greenery outside my planned design had been so much as scorched. According to Grandpa Thomas, making fucked-up charcoal crop circles was an essential step in learning to properly control my fire. He'd be out in a little while to check my work, and until he came, I was supposed to keep reburning the ground I'd already burnt, reducing the cinders to ashes, reducing the ashes to finer and finer powder, until it looked like a volcano had erupted in an incredibly localized manner.

That was an interesting idea. If I reached deep down, beyond my own fire, would I be able to reach the magma slumbering beneath the surface of the world? How deep did the fire—and the magic—really go?

Grandpa might know. When it comes to sorcery, I tend to assume Grandpa knows basically everything there is to know. Like his wife, my Grandma Alice, he doesn't look that much older than my parents, but he's closer to his hundredth birthday than he is to his eightieth. Magic can do weird things to aging, on top of everything else it makes weirder than it really needs to be.

Grandpa is also the source of the sorcery in our family line. Unlike most forms of magic, sorcery seems to have a fairly strong genetic component, and our family didn't do sorcerers until he went and married in. Thanks, Grandpa. Or thanks, Grandma, I guess, since by all reports, she's the one who pursued him like a prize worth winning.

Sam popped out of the woods again, this time holding something that looked like a leech two feet long and equipped with a lamprey's mouth. It writhed in his hands, trying to latch on to his arm. "Annie! Look what I found!"

"That's a bloodworm, sweetheart," I called back. "Let me guess: it was sleeping in the mud and you decided it needed to go for a little field trip in order to understand why sleeping in the mud is the best thing in the whole world?"

"Something like that," he said, and beamed at me, lips firmly closed. Sam Taylor is a lot of things. Funny, loyal, protective, incredibly slow to warm to strangers, probably the love of my life, and oh, right, essentially a giant monkey. His father was a yōkai therianthrope from a species called fūri, and Sam inherited more from him than a great ass and a fondness for high places. Yeah. I'm engaged to a monkey.

He's more *Kingdom of the Apes* than *Curious George*, or we'd never have hooked up in the first place, but being with Sam means being cool with a guy who has a tail unless he's making a concerted effort to *not* have a tail—which is most of the time when we're not dealing with the wider human population—and who really, really doesn't like it when people show their teeth as they smile. It's all worth it, though. And it's not like my family has ever been all that hung up on "human" as a requirement for a partner. Sam loves me, and that's enough.

So anyway. I'm Annie Price—short for "Antimony," and no, my parents weren't hippies; they were working from one of the last predictions made by my missing Aunt Laura, who told them either I or my cousin Elsie would need to disappear under a name that was and wasn't our own. So we both got reversible names. I'm Antimony Timpani, and she's Elsinore Norelle. Not sure how that helped when I *did* have to go undercover, but hell, maybe the Covenant sorcerers know some tricks ours don't.

Sorcerers: right. Elemental magic-users who interact with the living pneuma of the world to do what they do, generally each attuned to a single element. I'm a pyromancer, which means I manipulate flame and heat and my magic tries to boil me alive if I piss it off. My adopted brother, James, is a cryomancer, manipulating ice and cold and yeah, you can say ice isn't an element if you want, but to that I say, take it up with the anima mundi. They get the final word on whether something counts as elemental or not, since they're the living soul of the world.

My grandfather, as I mentioned before, was the first sorcerer in our family, and the rest of us get it from him. But he was missing for a long time, meaning we were never properly trained. I was spending the summer in Michigan while he worked to fix that, at least sufficiently that we wouldn't have to worry about me losing my temper at my own wedding and burning the ceremony and guests to cinders.

While I was in Michigan, my grandparents' adopted daughter, Sally, was staying in my room in Oregon and spending time with James, who was her best friend before he was my brother. Never let it be said that my family has passed up an opportunity to be deeply confusing. We'd trade places at the end of the summer, with Sally and James coming back to Michigan while Sam and I went home. Grandpa would start training James the way he'd been training me, and we'd all get better at not hurting people by mistake.

And that assumed the world would keep leaving us alone for six months, which was probably optimistic verging on unrealistic of me. The world never leaves us alone for that long.

Still grinning, Sam bounced back into the woods with his horrible new friend, vanishing into the trees just as my phone began ringing. It had been long enough since my last attempt at burning the ashes down even further that my hands were relatively cool; I pulled my phone out of my back pocket and swiped up to answer.

"Hello?"

"Antimony?" The voice on the other end was male, harried, and only faintly familiar.

"Who is this?"

My phone number isn't a state secret or anything, but it's not something I share very often, either. If a stranger had it, I might have a serious problem.

"It's—" The speaker paused to cough. "It's Mark. Mark Wilson. Your awful family threatened to dissect me or something when we first met. We went to another dimension together, and we didn't get eaten by giant spiders while we were there, although I sort of feel like we should have been. I helped you murder most of the members of my species on this planet. I've been in a coma for—"

"Mark? You're awake?" It was my turn to pause. "How did you get this number?"

"Really? That's what you want to focus on? How I got your

phone number? Not why I'm calling you, or when did I wake up, or anything that *matters*? You people really are *terrible*."

"Sorry, sorry. I'm glad you're awake. I hope you're okay. Why are you calling me, and how did you get this number?"

"I got this number because Sarah thought it at some point, and it's a *number*. I can't not memorize numbers, even if I hadn't had good reason to want to be able to contact you if I needed to. Which I had and have. You're one of the only members of your asshole family worth talking to."

I couldn't fully blame Mark for his opinion on most of us. He'd sort of come crashing into the middle of a crisis, and hadn't seen us at our best. Unless by "best," you mean "acting most like characters from a really weird Addams Family knockoff."

"Right, okay," I said. "What's up? If you're awake, I'd expect you to be on the first plane to Cici by now."

"I will be, as soon as I'm cleared to leave the hospital. But I'm calling about Sarah."

I stiffened. "What about her?"

"She was here when I woke up. I was getting there on my own, and then she did some sort of deep-mind telepathic connection thing and helped me to the surface. It was a bit of a shock, waking up after eight years in a coma, and I screamed. A lot."

"I mean, I'd probably scream too."

Sam popped back out of the woods, shooting me a puzzled look as he saw that I was on the phone. I gestured for him to hold on a second, trying to focus on Mark.

"I don't mean vocally."

"Oh, you screamed in your head?" I hesitated. "Look, I don't know if this is a rude question or what, but the last time I checked in on you, there was something funky going on with your brain, and Dr. Morrow thought you might be going through another instar. Did you . . . ?"

"Oh my fucking God, have these assholes never heard of HIPAA? Did they just go around giving my private medical information to anyone who showed an interest in the freakshow?"

"No. Just those of us who were there for the initial injury, and might have something to contribute that could help with your recovery."

Mark huffed. "I guess I can allow it."

"Cool, thanks. Back to the instar . . . ?"

"Yes. Yes, I went through two additional instars, and am now on the same level of cuckoo maturity as Sarah. Happy?"

"Not particularly." The idea of a second cuckoo queen running around—or cuckoo king, or whatever—was honestly terrifying. Mark was more social than most cuckoos, and less inclined to kill people for fun, but he was still a cuckoo.

Honestly, I wasn't all that comfortable with having *one* cuckoo queen running around. My parents insisted Sarah and I had always been close, and I had the family photos, birthday cards, and D&D session notes to prove it. But all of that was gone. I didn't remember anything about her from before the moment I'd woken up under an orange, alien sky with a cuckoo collapsed on the floor in front of me. She'd deleted herself from my mind, and if she could do that to someone she claimed to care about, what could she do to everyone else around her?

"That's fine, I don't need you happy, just listening. When I woke up, I screamed mentally, and apparently it was *loud*. Loud enough that Dr. Morrow came rushing in and slapped an anti-telepathy charm on me. Just in time, too, because right after he did, a bunch of cuckoos, like, teleported into the room."

Goosebumps broke out all over my arms as I tensed. "What do you mean, a bunch of cuckoos teleported into the room?"

"I mean they weren't there and then they *were* there, and there were five of them, all wearing these weird sort of sci-fi jumpsuits, and they told Sarah they were going to hold her accountable for her crimes and grabbed her, and then they disappeared. I'm not her biggest fan and all, but like, her main crimes have been not blowing up the planet, self-defense, and being a self-destructive asshole. Not really a great reason to kidnap someone. Oh, and they said she'd reached 'the forbidden instar'? I guess they don't like cuckoo queens very much. I don't know. I've notified her family, meaning I called you and it's your problem now."

"What do you mean by that?"

There was a click as the line went dead. I lowered my phone, glaring at it for several seconds, then stuffed it back into my pocket. Cupping my hands around my mouth, I turned toward the forest and shouted:

"Sam! Come over here! We need to go inside!"

Sam, still standing at the edge of the woods, blinked and lifted his eyebrows, giving me a dubious look. "You don't have to yell, you know. I'm like ten feet away."

I lowered my hands. "Sorry, but this is an emergency, and I forgot you were there."

"Right. Time to move." He jumped, clearing the distance between us in one massive leap that would have been impossible for any less-simian biped, literally sweeping me off my feet as he started running for the house. He wrapped his tail around my waist, providing a sort of biological seatbelt. I sighed heavily.

"I can run, you know."

"I'm faster."

I couldn't argue with that and he knew it. I was more dangerous in the field, but he was terrifyingly fast when he wanted to be, moving with a speed that seemed impossible even after as many times as I'd seen it.

So he carried me and ran, and I breathed through my nose, fighting to keep the fire out of my hands until we could get to my grandparents and find out if this was as bad as I thought it was. Because I thought it was pretty damn bad.

◆ ◆ ◆

My family owns two houses in Buckley Township, which is a strange place to have most of our real estate holdings, but makes sense when you consider that Grandma grew up in one of them and Grandpa spent years magically confined to the other. The house from her side of the family is currently rented out to some really lovely people who have no idea the true owner of their home is back in town. The house from his side of the family is now the official residence of the Michigan Prices.

Which seems a little bit ridiculous to me, since if the crossroads had confined me to a single building for the better part of a decade, I would have burned the place to the ground before I voluntarily stepped through the doors again. But he liked his messed-up, possibly possessed house. Liked the porch swing with its infestation of tailypo, and liked the back steps where my grandmother used to sit when she came to visit him, and he had the right to make bad decisions for himself. Just as long as none of them led to another disappearance.

Sam bounded up the back steps and set me on my feet, letting go.

"Thanks, hon," I said, and kissed his cheek before opening the back door and stepping inside.

The kitchen, which hadn't been renovated since sometime in the nineteen-fifties, was a wonderland of linoleum, outdated appliances, wood-paneled cupboards, and peeling wallpaper that looked remarkably like rotting meat. Although that last may have had more to do with the house itself than any intentional decorating choices: the house, which had a name—the Old Parrish Place—had been the site of some fairly brutal murders before my grandfather took up residence there, and while our family's ghosts assure us the place isn't haunted, it sure as hell acts like it is.

"Grandma?" I called. "Grandpa? Are you around?"

There was no immediate reply, but as I stood there waiting for one, a mouse ran out of a hole in the wall behind the toaster, sitting at attention with its tail wrapped around its hind legs and staring at me with black oildrop eyes.

I turned to the mouse. "Do you know where my grandparents are?"

"The God of Inconvenient Timing is in his basement fastness, doing Great Works of repair and recovery," said the mouse, voice a little squeaky and high-pitched but perfectly comprehensible.

Aeslin mice can be accused of many things. Poor diction is not among them. "The Noisy Priestess fights a glorious battle against the laundry, but may soon be defeated, and has stated her Intention to summon you from the Pastures to come and assist with Pinning the Washing onto the Line, for lo, did not the Kindly Priestess once say, 'Many Hands Make Light Work, and Young Backs Lift Heavy Things'?"

It wasn't uncommon for the mice to answer simple questions with elaborate aphorisms, but like everyone else in my family, I'd been dealing with them since I was a baby, and knew how to translate mouse into English.

"Thanks!" I said, and hurried for the stairs, leaving Sam and the mouse behind.

Extremely short-form explanation, at risk of derailing the extreme importance of my search: Aeslin mice. Intelligent, talking cryptid mice who live their lives according to strict and evolving religious rules, usually centered around one or more idols. In the case of my family's colony, that means us. The family. We are their gods, and we take our duties to them very seriously. Almost as seriously as they take their duties to us.

The laundry room was, conveniently, in the basement, not far from Grandpa's workshop. I hurtled down the stairs, probably faster than I should have, hanging off the banister with one hand to keep myself from making an even *faster* descent that ended with a broken neck.

Reaching the basement, I trotted toward the wall that had been erected to block off the back third of the room and create a series of smaller functional spaces. The laundry-room door was open, sending light and steam into the rest of the basement. I stepped into the doorway.

"Grandma, we have a problem," I said.

She looked up from the basket of laundry she was sorting through, raising both eyebrows. "Is the problem your boyfriend's genuine inability to unroll his socks before throwing them into the hamper?"

"Sadly, no, and those aren't Sam's socks. Sam doesn't wear socks. His feet are too big when he's not pretending to be human, and he really doesn't like having things between him and the ground." He'd tried to explain it to me a few times, and the closest I'd come to understanding was "Imagine wearing oven mitts all the time for a full day, and how clumsy that would make you feel."

"So they're . . . ?"

"My socks, and you and Mom now have something else in common," I said, with a shrug. "I keep forgetting people are going to collect my laundry."

She looked at me and huffed, affectionately. "Of course you do. Little princess."

There was no anger in her words, only abiding fondness. Grandma was too busy looking for Grandpa to be there for most of my life, or most of her children's lives. Now that she was home to stay, she took far too much satisfaction in doing basic household tasks. It felt counter-feminist to me, like she was making herself smaller to give the rest of us the space to expand, but if it made her happy, she had the right to make the choice. Rolled-up socks and all.

"Anyway, Grandma, you got a minute? I think it's important. It feels important anyway, and I don't know what to do with it by myself."

"Sure, sweetie." She dropped the shirt she was holding back into the basket and walked around the sorting table, leaning against it with her arms crossed and her head tilted slightly to the side. "What's going on?"

This is my grandmother, the infamous Alice Price-Healy: short, blonde, bright-eyed, and perky in the way of the best children's librarians. Well on her way to ninety years old, which you'd never know by looking at her, since she appeared to be no more than thirty, and that only if you were willing to really stretch your estimation of her age. Tattoos covered the left side of her body, dense and colorful, and only serving to highlight the few stretches of unmarked skin. Those were where the tattoos she'd already activated and used up had been.

Throughout my childhood, her tattoos had always been changing, appearing and disappearing between visits like magic—which they were, technically, magical ink embedded in human skin to anchor acts of artificial sorcery powered by her own body rather than by the pneuma around her. Grandma was no more a sorcerer than Sam was. But, like Sam, she had her own talents, most of which revolved around horrible violence. According to the mice, she was a human wrecking ball even before she spent fifty years throwing herself into strange dimensions trying to find her husband. After, though . . . well. There's a reason her name sparks fear in all the wrong sorts of people.

I took a deep breath. "Mark just called me."

"Mark is?"

"Mark is the cuckoo who helped us rescue Sarah a few years before you got home. He's been in a coma at St. Giles's Hospital since then."

"All right, so he's awake, then. Why did he call you? And why do you look like this might not have been a good thing?"

"According to Mark, a bunch of strange cuckoos teleported into his hospital room while Sarah was there, seized her, and disappeared. He said they were wearing 'sci-fi jumpsuits' and called her current developmental stage 'the forbidden instar.' It all sounds sort of, you know, bad."

"Because it *is* bad," said a voice from behind me, male, with the kind of British accent that speaks of years of formal schooling geared at replacing childhood regionalisms with perfect BBC English. "Am I correct in assuming that 'sci-fi' is still a favored abbreviation of 'science fiction,' meaning your friend likely saw some sort of futuristic attire and simplified it to 'sci-fi jumpsuit'?"

"That sounds about right." I turned.

Having my grandfather around has been odd mostly because I was so used to not looking like any of the members of my family. The so-called "Healy look" has been dominant for generations: short, blonde, soft the way a bobcat kitten is soft, packed with claws and teeth and terrible ways to make you regret petting the kitty. I'm tall, brunette, and much more angular than the rest of my generation. Turns out, it's because I take after my grandfather.

Like Alice, he was covered in tattoos. Unlike Alice, his covered both sides of his body, and served as a clear warning to anyone who knew anything about sorcery, since each of them anchored some magical effect or other, and could be activated at will. The only clear patch of skin I could see below his neck was at the hollow of his throat, where he'd released the charm that had been keeping him from getting physically older before he could be reunited with his wife. They were both aging normally now, which was a nice change for our family.

He was wearing a plain white shirt, unbuttoned at the collar and sleeves rolled up to his elbows, and tan work pants. He could have been any man who liked to work with his hands, puttering away on his weekend.

"Then this is definitely bad," he said. "I don't think he saw cuckoos."

"But he—"

"I think he saw Johrlac. The kind that come from Johrlar."

"I don't understand why we act like they're not the same species just because of where they come from."

"Because in many ways, they aren't," he said. "The cuckoos are the exiles of Johrlar, the ones who've been expelled from their society and set to wander the universe forever. Instars are triggered by the appropriate level and degree of psychic exposure. A Johrlac who never goes beyond the second instar will not be the same creature as one who's gone all the way to the ending. They're related, but they're not the same."

"And these people snatched Sarah?"

"It certainly sounds like it. The few Johrlac I've met have been very focused on keeping their exiles from reaching full maturity—the forbidden instar, as you say. They don't want them to have access to the sort of power that comes with full maturation."

That didn't sound good. "Mark said the Johrlac said they were going to hold Sarah responsible for her crimes. Do you think they know about what happened when we went to giant spider world?"

"If they didn't know before they took her, they almost certainly know now," said Alice.

My phone rang.

I pulled it out of my back pocket, glaring at it. I was still dealing with the aftermath of my *last* unexpected phone call. I certainly wasn't ready for another one.

At least this time it was coming from a familiar number. I swiped my thumb up the screen, tapping the speaker icon.

"Elsie, hi," I said. "I'm here with Grandma and Grandpa. I've got you on speaker. What's up?"

"What's up is some asshole cuckoos dressed like they escaped from a production of *Starlight Express* just came in here and snatched Arthur!" she wailed. "We were in the living room, and then they were just *there*. They grabbed him, said something about gathering evidence, and disappeared. What the hell is going on?"

"Why do you think I would know what's going on?" I asked. "I don't know. But—"

"How many of them were there, Elsinore?" asked Grandpa, coming close enough to be heard without shouting.

"Er, three. Sir." Elsie still wasn't entirely comfortable with our grandfather being back from the dimension where he'd been lost for so long. It made sense. To her, he was a stranger who'd come swooping in and suddenly expected a familial relationship. He was technically the same thing to me, but I had the dual advantages of James's relationship with Sally and my own blazing need to learn sorcery from someone who actually understood the way it worked. It made accepting him easier.

"And what did they look like?"

"Like cuckoos! They all look alike!"

"If we were talking about members of literally any other species, I would feel the need to remind you that a refusal to see distinctions between individuals is a form of prejudice," said Grandpa. "As it stands, given that they're insects with very little morphological variance, I'll allow it. They were all cuckoos?"

"Yeah. Pale, black hair, blue eyes."

"And their, er, *Star Trek Express* outfits?"

Elsie snorted. "*Starlight Express.* It's a musical. About trains. Lots of glitter and spandex. They were wearing these weird bodysuits that were cut to look sort of like they were segmented. Like insect exoskeletons, only flexible."

"Yes, that was what I thought you were saying. What colors were the bodysuits? It's very important that you remember."

"Um. The one who seemed to be in charge was wearing red, black, and yellow."

"In that order?"

"Yes. Her chest was red, and her abdomen and hips were black, and then her legs were yellow."

"All right. The other two?"

"One was in all black with red stripes along his back. They wrapped around like they were supposed to look like wings. And the other one was a really deep blue on top, and this sort of two-tone orange and magenta on the bottom, that changed when she moved. It was all iridescent and very cool-looking, except for the part where they were in the process of abducting my brother."

"Thank you, Elsinore. You've been extremely helpful." He turned back to me, mouthing "Hang up," and making an exaggerated gesture with one hand, like he was hanging up an old-fashioned landline.

I blinked, then turned my attention back to the phone. "Thank you for letting us know, Elsie," I said. "I think Grandpa has some idea of how we're supposed to deal with it, so I'm going to go work on that with him now, okay?"

"I'm just getting used to this version of my brother," she wailed. "Bring him *back*."

"I'll do my best. Call again if you need anything." I hung up before she could say anything else. I felt a little bad about it, all things considered, but I didn't really see what else I could do.

When Elsie's brother Artie got pulled into another dimension with me, Mark, James, and Sarah during the whole "Cuckoos try to destroy the world" incident, he got his mind erased in the process of the rest of us getting out of there. I was there, I saw it happen, and I know it was an accident, but I can completely understand why Elsie blamed Sarah for the way things went down: most days, I blamed her too. Artie had touched her. That was all he did. He'd touched her, and she'd lost control of her powers, because cuckoos are too dangerous to be around normal people, and he was gone in less than the time it took to blink an eye. He left his body behind, because he didn't die: he was just deleted, like he'd never existed to begin with.

Sarah had built a new person to take his place, one who remembered a lot of Artie's life and shared some of his passions—but not enough to believably replace him. He'd started coming apart inside of six months, losing the memories that weren't properly anchored inside his head, forgetting things he should have known, and insisting we all call him "Arthur," because he knew he wasn't Artie.

Watching a stranger wearing my cousin's body like a borrowed suit had been hard on me. It had been a lot harder on Elsie. She was his sister, and she loved him—both versions of him—more than any of the rest of us. It had taken a cross-country road trip with Arthur and Mary before she'd started really spending time with Arthur on any sort of a voluntary basis. But somewhere between Oregon and Massachusetts, she figured out how to love him as he was, not mourn him for what he wasn't.

And now he was gone. Taken by the cuckoos, just like Artie had been, if a bit more physically. I slid the phone back into my pocket, looking between my grandparents. They both looked horrified in their own ways: Thomas's mouth was set in a hard, furious line, and Alice's hands were flexing like she wanted a knife, or a pistol, or something.

"Well?" I asked. "What do you know, and what are we going to do about this?"

Five

> "Breaking things is easy. A child can do it. Putting things back together, now, that's harder than most people can imagine."
>
> —**Frances Brown**

Buckley Township, Michigan,
the dining room of the Old Parrish Place

SAM AND I SAT ON one side of the dining room table, his tail looped around my left ankle like a tether keeping me from leaping up and throwing myself into danger. Both of us were tense, a state that wasn't aided by the fact that as soon as we'd gotten upstairs, Alice had gone for her revolvers and Thomas had gone to his study for some books. I tilted my head back, looking up at the ceiling.

"This is going to be bad, isn't it?"

I glanced at Sam. "What makes you say that?"

"I dunno. I've been hanging around with your family for a while now, and when people start looking for weapons and research materials, that means things are about to get messy and probably start sucking." Sam made a dour face. "I was enjoying our little summer vacation."

I bumped my shoulder against his. "You mean you were enjoying harassing every living thing in the Galway Woods."

"Hey, your grandmother said the forest liked me. I figure I should go on little play dates with it to make sure it keeps liking me."

"You are *so* weird."

He grinned. "Takes one to know one."

"I am *not* weird."

"You agreed to marry me. That's weird."

I rolled my eyes. "You do *not* get to play that card."

"Watch me."

We were bantering to distract ourselves from the elephant in the room: two of my cousins had apparently been abducted by cosplaying cuckoos, and they knew Sarah's teleportation trick. I didn't know whether we were looking at two separate groups or one coherent hive, but either way, things were likely to get very unpleasant before they settled down again. A little silliness now would spare us at least a little stress once things got started.

Alice came striding back into the room, an old-fashioned gun belt riding low on her hips and a knife strapped to her left bicep. She was pretty set in her ways, and if she looked more gunslinger than modern mercenary, well, she could still kick the asses of most of the mercenaries I'd met. Fifty years of practice will do that for a person.

"Sam, you're sort of optional here," she said, bluntly. "You can stay in Michigan and keep an eye on the house and Sarah's spider."

I groaned. "I forgot about Greg."

"How do you forget about a spider the size of a grizzly bear?" asked Sam. "He's roaming around in the woods. Half the horrible things I've brought to show you, I only found because he flushed them out. I saw him take down a peryton this morning. Just jumped up and snatched it right out of the air."

I whistled. "Wow. I wish I could have seen *that*."

Sam made a sour face. "No, you don't. Peryton are gross-looking enough without having pieces ripped off by a giant spider."

"Fair enough." Peryton are part of the vast class of cryptids that are best described as "not deer." Oh, they have hooves and antlers and the basic body plan of a deer, but all the not-deer are somehow *wrong*. Peryton, for example, don't have skin as such. They have a thick layer of gelatinous mucus that keeps their organs in place and helps to prevent their musculature from being covered in a layer of dust and grime, but it's not the same. They look like they've been flensed. Nasty pieces of work.

Sometimes I wonder what the hell evolution was thinking. And then I remember that evolution isn't known for thinking at all. It's not even selecting for the most successful forms, no matter what third-grade biology classes will try to tell you: it's selecting for "Can it make it to adulthood and live long enough to reproduce?" Everything after that is gravy in evolution's eyes.

"Well?" asked Alice.

Sam turned, blinking at her. "Well, what?"

"Well, will you stay here and keep an eye on the spider?"

He leaned back in his chair, eyeing her unhappily. "See, I sort of feel like you're trying to get me to agree to something by starting in the middle. Where is everybody going that I wouldn't be going? What is the plan here?"

Alice didn't answer immediately, looking over her shoulder instead, like she was hoping help was going to arrive. When help didn't seem to be forthcoming, she turned back to the two of us and sighed heavily.

"The clothing Elsie described, and that your friend Mark alluded to—"

"He's not my friend," I muttered.

"—matches descriptions of Johrlar cultural attire," she continued, ignoring my interjection. "It sounds like both Artie and Sarah were collected by representatives from the cuckoos's home dimension. Which would mean we're not dealing with cuckoos at all, except for Sarah herself. We're dealing with Johrlac, and that changes the situation considerably."

"How so?" I asked.

"Well, for one thing, much as it pains me to say this, we can't just go in guns blazing to get our people back. We don't want to offend an entire dimension, and depending on what's going on, they may not comprehend why we'd think they'd done anything wrong."

"Even if they have some stupid cuckoo law that lets them kidnap Sarah without feeling like the bad guys, that doesn't give them a right to put their hands on Arthur!"

"Actually, I think it does," said Thomas, walking into the room with a hefty cloth-bound book in his hands. He put it down on the table, already open to a diagram of a female cuckoo wearing a jumpsuit like the one Elsie described. She could have been a sketch of Sarah, except for an odd vacancy in the eyes: her face was entirely blank, no animation or emotion. Part of that was probably the fact that it was a black-and-white sketch, but it felt intentional, somehow.

He tapped the picture, very lightly. "Black, yellow, and red. The eusocial judiciary caste of Johrlar. For them to bring a judge to collect Arthur, they must have already determined to their satisfaction that he was not a person under their laws."

"The fuck you say?"

"The Johrlac don't consider telepathic constructs 'people,' even when they've been given ownership of an individual body. They're more on the level of 'horrifying perversions of the natural order.'"

"And what do the Johrlac do with these 'perversions'?" I asked.

Alice looked at me levelly. "They unmake them," she said. "Which is why the three of us are leaving for Johrlar as soon as possible. We need to get there before it's too late for us to bring him back."

"And Sarah?" I asked.

"None of our records mention cuckoos achieving the queen instar," said Thomas. "Now, we know that's because normally, when a cuckoo reaches queen, she destroys the world she's standing on in order to transport her people to the next dimension in the chain."

I eyed the book in his hands, hungrily. "You know, these records would have been useful when we were fighting the cuckoo hive that tried to kill us all in the process of forcing Sarah's final instar."

"Sadly, they weren't available until I returned home and wrote down what I'd learned during my exile, along with what Alice had learned in her travels," said Thomas. "I had bits and pieces. After encounters with multiple Johrlac and people who knew them, we've been able to put together an almost-coherent map of their society."

"The Johrlac took away the equations that can force the queen instar before they banished the cuckoos," said Alice. She turned, picking up a small leather bag from the buffet against the wall. "Sam, you asked where we're going. Now you know. Last chance: want to stay here and mind the house?"

"You mean, do I want to let you take my fiancée, who has disappeared on me *twice* now because she didn't think I needed to be there, to another dimension, filled with super-powerful, super-alien telepaths who are already planning to take her cousin apart, while I stay here and wait for you to bring her back in one piece? Lady, I know you've been out of touch for a while, but if you think I'm going to go along with that, you're absolutely out of your gun-loving, banana-shit mind."

"So that's a no, then," said Alice mildly. She shook out the bag over the table, and a handful of pendants on woven leather cords fell out. They were sturdier-looking than our usual anti-telepathy charms, their glass centers surrounded by a woven lattice of silver bars.

"These belonged to my grandfather," she said. "He designed and made them shortly after my parents encountered their first cuckoo. You could say the technology was in its infancy then; we didn't know how powerful the charms would need to be to offer us a measure of protection. This batch overshot the necessary by a country mile."

"The blood family of Frances Healy is naturally resistant to the mental influence of the cuckoos," said Thomas, picking up a charm and sliding it over his head. "I, unfortunately, am not the blood family of Frances Healy."

"Hey!" said Alice. "You were already cradle-robbing with me. No need to make it kissing cousins at the same time. Only reason I was okay with Sarah and Artie is because they're not actually related. They're not even members of the same species."

"Neither are we," said Sam. He took a charm, studying it carefully before he put it on.

"You're half-human, dear," said Alice. "That's close enough for this family."

"If you say so," he grumbled.

"Take a charm," said Alice, following her own advice even as she looked at me sternly. "I know we're resistant to cuckoo telepathy, but Johrlac are like cuckoos on steroids. They know what they can do, and they know how to do it. You need protection if you're coming with us, and we want you with us. These are your cousins. You should have a part in saving them."

"Got it." I leaned over and picked up a charm, slinging it around my neck. "All right. Is this where we leave an ominous note to explain where we went, to be found in a year when someone finally comes looking for us?"

"You really think your mom would wait that long?" asked Sam. "She'd be here in three days when you stopped sending her funny things you found on the internet."

"Hey, my meme game is strong!" I protested.

He rolled his eyes, tail tightening around my ankle. "Sure, sweetie."

"No," said Alice. "I have a better idea. Thomas, go call Cynthia to keep an eye on the house, while I let Mary know what's going on."

He nodded and ducked out of the room, heading for the kitchen. Alice took a step back from the table, clapping her hands together in front of her as she did. Only once: once was all she needed. "Mary, I need you," she said.

I scooted my chair closer to Sam's, leaning over to rest my head on his shoulder and watch the show.

Mary Dunlavy has been our family babysitter since my grandmother was born. Literally—she took care of Alice before she was out of diapers. You know how people sometimes ask children "Where did you get that mouth" when they smart off or talk back?

Well, no one in our family has ever needed to be asked. We got that mouth from our babysitter, who's managed to keep three full generations of us alive to adulthood, and is now hard at work on a fourth.

Most babysitters get to retire long before they hit the great-grandchildren of their original charges. Not Mary. Mary never gets to retire, because Mary's dead. Her retirement would involve a trip into the great beyond, and that's not the sort of thing she's particularly interested in doing.

With four children under ten currently in the family, Mary isn't always available when she's wanted. Alice waited several seconds, then sighed and tilted her face toward the ceiling. "Mary, come on. This isn't something frivolous. Tell the anima mundi this is a case of genuine need. The Johrlac have snatched Arthur and Sarah, and we need to go and get them back before something really awful happens."

"What the hell are you people *doing* over here?" asked Mary, from behind me. She sounded harried.

I twisted to look over my shoulder, offering her a sideways smile. "Hey, Mary."

"Hey, yourself," she replied, walking forward. Sam watched her with more wariness than I did, which made sense. He and Mary didn't meet under the best of circumstances, what with me being in hiding and her being his only source of information about what was going on. He liked her well enough now that she wasn't gate-keeping the details of my life from him.

When she reached the edge of the table, she kept going, walking straight through the wood. There had to be some advantages to being dead, or why would anybody with any common sense even bother?

Besides, sometimes Mary had to do the impressive ghost shit to remind us all that she was the adult in the room, no matter what it looked like. She died when she was sixteen, and so sixteen she's stayed, for decades now, and sixteen she'll keep staying until the day she decides she's done keeping us alive and moves on to her eventual reward. Whatever that looks like, I hope it's awesome. She's earned it.

She was wearing leggings and a thigh-length gray sweater, belted at the waist like some sort of a dress. It was perfectly reasonable attire for a modern babysitter, and we had almost certainly called her away from one of her younger charges. I felt a brief pang of jealousy at the thought. I'd been the youngest in the family for years, while the other members of my generation grew up enough to start considering kids. As a caretaker ghost, Mary naturally attached herself to the youngest person she felt any responsibility toward, which meant she'd been my near-constant companion for most of my life, always available if I needed someone to talk to or was having a bad day. And with the birth of the new generation, that had changed. I was expected to be a real grownup now, whether I wanted to or not.

I guess most people hit that transition a lot earlier in life, but I was still getting used to it, and I didn't like it much.

In addition to her babysitter-casual attire, Mary had long, bone-white hair, the only real physical indicator of her phantom state; her eyes used to look like a hundred miles of empty highway, which isn't actually a color, but again, ghost. She had a lot more leeway in the "What color are my eyes" category than most people get. Since she'd transferred her employment from the crossroads to the anima mundi, they had turned blue again, the way they'd been when she was alive. It hadn't unbleached her hair, but it made her look a lot less faded.

"Getting ready for a cross-dimensional retrieval mission," said Alice. "Hey, Mary. Can you let everyone else know that we're going to Johrlar for a little while? Or maybe a long while, I don't exactly know how long this is going to take. But assume we're out of calling range until I call and tell you otherwise."

"Slow down, Alice," said Mary. "Why are you going to the cuckoo's nest?"

"I just told you, they snatched Sarah and Arthur."

Mary froze. "What?" she asked, after a long, terrible pause.

"Johrlac, dressed in the standard uniforms they use on Johrlar, came here and stole two of my grandchildren," said Alice, with poisonous patience. "We think they want to delete Arthur because of the way he was created, and make Sarah stand trial for creating him. We need to get them back before anything permanent happens. So we don't have time to stand around here and make sure everything's filed and signed off on. We need to go."

"And you're taking Annie?"

"Chances that we could leave her without tranquilizing her are pretty slim, and having two pyrokinetics with us is never a bad thing. She wants to come, she's coming."

"And so is Sam," said Sam, resolutely. "I am not sitting out another field trip that could take my fiancée away for the better part of a year."

"No one's asking you to, dear," said Alice. "Mary, can you please let the rest of the family know? I could call them, but then I'd have to explain what's happening over and over again. At least four times, if I'm counting locations correctly."

"Any idea how long you'll be gone?"

"Time is always strange across dimensions," said Alice, apologetically. "We'll be back as soon as we can, but it may take a while."

Thomas came back into the room. "Cynthia is fine to check on the house until we get back, and has requested we not get trapped in any bottle dimensions or other inconveniences," he said. "She says she's just getting used to us being here full-time, and would rather not adjust herself again. She's also agreed to feed Greg until we return. She'll keep him supplied in sheep, and bill us when we get back. I got the distinct feeling that if we stay gone longer than she feels is appropriate, she'll start buying fancy sheep to run up the bill."

"Come back quick to avoid bankruptcy, got it," said Alice. "Mary?"

"Hello, Mary," said Thomas, moving to stand next to his wife.

"Hey, Tommy," said Mary, with a quick smile. They'd been

friends since he first came to Buckley, and they were always glad to see each other.

"Yes, Alice, I'll tell the rest of the family you've fucked off to another dimension again," she said, returning her attention to my grandmother. "At least this time you're doing it together, and I don't have to worry about you running off to find him. Don't get separated. Please. I don't think my nerves can take that again. You ever seen a ghost have a nervous breakdown? It's not pretty. None of us will enjoy it."

"We'll be back, Mary," I said solemnly. "I give you my word."

"I'll hold you to that," she said, and disappeared, throwing herself back into the ghost version of the world that existed outside the lands of the living. From there, she'd be able to quickly transport herself back to whichever of the children she was currently supposed to be taking care of.

If she could transport living people the way she moved herself around, we'd all be much happier. But alas, everyone has their limitations.

Thomas started for the door on the other side of the room, gesturing for the rest of us to follow. Sam untwined his tail from around my ankle and rose, offering me his hand. I took it and let him pull me after him, and Alice came after me, a small procession leaving the empty dining room behind as an almost-funereal silence fell over everything.

✦ ✦ ✦

Thomas led us all down to the basement, where he bent and rolled back the rug that had been covering most of the floor. Below it was a complicated circle, the exterior made up of crisp geometric symbols. They hurt my eyes if I looked at them too hard, and I could almost understand what they said. I had seen some of those sigils in my fire, dancing inside the structure of the flames.

"Everyone inside the circle," he said. "I'm driving this one." He looked to Alice. "I know you still have a few crossing charms tattooed on you, and I'm ordering you to use them if you have to. Just don't take any unnecessary risks."

Alice rolled her eyes. "Yes, dear. At least you didn't tell me to be careful."

"Believe me, I would, if I thought you would listen." He glanced to Sam, accurately identifying him as the one sympathetic person in this basement. "I swear those words cause her to become temporarily hard of hearing."

"Annie, too," said Sam.

Thomas sighed and opened the book he'd been carrying around since the dining room. He flipped past the page with the costume designs on it—convenient but not currently useful—and stopped, clearing his throat. Then he began to read aloud.

It began as a sequence of numbers, complex but not incomprehensible. Then it started getting strange. Letters and functions crept in, rapidly escalating to a point where he might as well have been speaking gibberish. Smooth, fast, fluent gibberish, made eldritch and fascinating by his British accent, but not a damn thing I could understand.

The symbols around the edges of the circle lit up one by one, glowing an unnerving blue-white shade that got brighter and brighter as he continued. Sam shifted closer to me inside the circle, wrapping his tail around my waist this time, and I leaned into him, grateful for the tether. At least if we were sucked through some incomprehensible portal into the abyss, we wouldn't be separated in the process.

Alice stepped up behind me, putting one hand on my shoulder and another hand on Thomas's shoulder, forming a line between the four of us.

And then, with a snapping sound, the entire circle lit up, bright as a supernova, so bright it made my eyes ache and water, and the basement was gone, and we were somewhere else.

Six

> "If you ever want to truly understand where you came from, you have to leave. Distance grants perspective. Distance, and a good sniper scope."
>
> —**Enid Healy**

Well, Toto, I don't think we're in Kansas anymore

THE LIGHT WAS DAZZLING ENOUGH to leave me temporarily blinded. I rubbed my eyes, trying to clear them, and listened to the sounds around me, none of which corresponded easily to standing in a basement. I could hear what sounded like enormous insects buzzing, a drone like small aircraft taking off, and the rustling of leaves in the breeze. I could feel the breeze, too, soft against my skin, warm as a spring afternoon in San Diego. It smelled like unfamiliar flowers, spicy and sweet and strangely compelling, and honey, and water somewhere in the near distance. There was a hint of salt to it as well, which coated the back of my throat and made me want to sneeze.

Sam's tail was still wrapped securely around my waist: wherever we were now, we hadn't been separated. I nodded to myself and tried to focus on what else I could pick up about my surroundings.

The Daredevil model of "lose one sense and your other senses are heightened" doesn't work exactly like that, but if you close your eyes and focus, you'll often find you can pick up on things you might otherwise have overlooked. As I focused, I could tell that the buzzing was divided into at least three registers, like I was hearing cicadas, bees, and some sort of cricket all at the same time. There was no electrical hum. Wherever we were, it wasn't near any power lines.

Little black spots were starting to appear in the burned-out white of my vision. I opened my eyes and blinked hard, and they got bigger, the world beginning to come clear in colorful blurs. I squinted my eyes shut again and rubbed at them as hard as I could, and when I opened them, I could finally see.

We were standing at the top of a low rise, surrounded by rolling hills like the English downs, but greener, as green as something out of a cartoon, and covered with patches of the most incredibly vibrant flowers I had ever seen. These were rainforest brilliant, hothouse bright, the kind of flowers that had no business growing in a climate as mild as the one around us, which felt more like Seattle or Vancouver than anything remotely tropical. Ahead of us, stretching out as far as I could see to either the left or right, was the bright flat disk of a lake, the waters so blue that they looked almost glacial. The far shore was visible, barely, a bristled line of trees against the distant mountains.

I couldn't see any towns or cities, or anything that looked remotely like civilization as I would recognize it. Except for my companions, there weren't even any people. I looked behind myself. There were trees in the distance, with twisting limbs and broad, waxy-looking leaves; they dripped with flowers and fruit, depending on the type of tree, and they looked entirely alluring.

"This is . . . a lot," said Sam, sounding faintly strangled. I turned to blink at him. He was gawking at our surroundings like a child at their very first carnival, and I abruptly remembered that he'd never been off-world before; this was his first non-Earth dimension. What a fun starting point.

"This is Johrlar," said Thomas, adjusting his glasses with one hand. He wasn't holding the book I'd seen before any longer; instead, he had a leather satchel slung over one shoulder. I couldn't tell whether he'd had that all along or it was something he had conjured somehow.

It didn't really matter, I supposed. Alice was crouching and rolling a bit of the dirt between her fingers, expression drawn into a look of profound seriousness. I turned to my grandfather, not wanting to interrupt her.

"Now what?" I asked him.

"Normally, the Johrlac would come looking for any strangers who snuck in through the back door the way we did," he said. "Thanks to the charms we're carrying, it should take them a little while to realize we're here, and by then, we'll have moved on from this point, which will make it more difficult for them to find us. Believe me when I say we'd prefer not to be found before we're ready."

"Is there a plan here?" asked Sam, shaking off his shock with admirable quickness. "Or are we going with the Price family 'Let's just run at it with our arms up and scream so it thinks we're too big to kill and goes away on its own' classic?"

"I thought we'd get at least a moment's awe out of you," said Alice, looking up from her examination of the ground. "Come on, we're in a whole new dimension. Isn't this *exciting*?"

"Oh, right, ooh, ahhh, new dimension, very cosmic, I'm so impressed," said Sam, deadpan. "Look, I'm a dude who's actually a monkey, because my dad was even more monkey than I am, and for all I know, fūri are originally from another dimension, so I'm less interested in being impressed than I am in getting home alive, preferably with a fiancée who remembers who I am and knows her own name. Can we have the plan?"

"Johrlac are telepathic, and don't tend to expect people who don't show up on their radar," said Thomas. "Some of them won't even acknowledge the existence of people who can't be read, which is, right now, us. We're basically inanimate objects unless we put our charms down. Much of the population is likely to ignore us unless we start trying to actively interact with them, which seems profoundly unlikely. We need to locate the city where Sarah and Arthur have been taken, and follow any members of the judiciary we can find back to their courthouse."

"How are we supposed to recognize members of the judiciary?" asked Sam.

"Some of the castes have actual reason to keep secrets from the others," said Thomas. "The judiciary, administrative, and intelligence castes all practice a certain measure of mental shielding to prevent contaminating the rest of the hive mind. They make up a large-enough percentage of the population that when you're in an urban environment, all hive members who leave their homes have to be visually recognizable. Hence the jumpsuits Elsie saw. We just find the Johrlac wearing red, yellow, and black jumpsuits, watch them for a while, and we'll know where we need to go."

"This is ridiculous," I muttered. "We're really going to just wander around until we find a city, and then hope we can stumble on someone who can show us where to go?"

"No," said Alice. She bounced to her feet, dropping the bit of dirt she'd been studying so intently. "Stay here."

She didn't wait to see if we would agree, only ran off into the foliage, vanishing into the thick sprays of flowers. Thomas watched her go, smiling indulgently.

"She just ran away," said Sam. "Did you see that? We were talking about plans, and she decided to just run away. Is this how you do this sort of thing normally? Just running away without saying anything?"

"Don't you know by now?" asked Thomas.

"No, because usually if I'm going outside to do stupid shit, I've got Annie with me, and we worked the trapeze together. She knows you can't just *do* things unless you want somebody to get dropped. So we don't do it like that. We make plans, we communicate them to each other, and then we follow them as much as we possibly can."

Thomas shot me a dubious look. I nodded.

"We try to communicate as much as we can," I said. "I don't like being dropped on my head."

"Fascinating," he replied. "A Price that plans. You really do have more of my family in you than I would have thought possible. I've never been here before, but your grandmother has, and she assured me that if my transit spell deposited us in the countryside, she'd be able to find us easy passage to the nearest city. I assume she's gone off to secure that passage, whatever form it may take."

Sam continued to look unconvinced. I nodded again.

"So she's what, off hotwiring us a car?"

"The local equivalent," said Thomas. "The Johrlac were able to subjugate most of the occupants of their world and put them to work. As a consequence, they never spent much energy on the invention of machines that could do those same jobs for them."

"Are you saying they mind-controlled the horses, and so they never made cars?" asked Sam.

"Essentially," said Thomas. "Your grandmother grew up with her own mother's horses, and while she's not the rider Fran was—no one is the rider Fran was—she's a fairly decent horse thief. She'll be back soon, I'm sure."

"*Did* horses evolve here?" I asked.

"Not as such," said Thomas. "Johrlar never did much in the way of true mammals. This is an insect-based world, and large herbivores are unheard-of here. The only mammals I know of to have a large population on Johrlar are—"

"Kairos," said a new voice.

I turned, Sam turning with me, and watched as a small group of people—six in total, so while they were small, they still had us well outnumbered—pushed their way through the nearest patch of tall, bell-shaped flowers. They were holding long polearms that resembled jagged bidents more than anything else, with shafts made of wood that gleamed like it had been dipped in crude oil and heads of polished steel.

And they looked human, as human as Thomas and I did, and substantially more human than Sam, who was still in his mostly monkey form. A few of them could have been related, but they didn't have the eerie similarities of the Johrlac; their skin and hair colors varied from dark to light, and their faces were entirely different.

The man at the front of the group, who had dark skin and short-cropped black hair, aimed his bident at us and smiled unpleasantly, showing far too many teeth. Sam stiffened beside me, tail tightening around my waist.

"Did you really think you could come to the territory of the fortunate and not find yourself confronted with the children of fortune?" he asked, words accented but understandable. He kept smiling as he shifted his position slightly, swinging the bident from Thomas to me. "This is our place, and we brook no intrusions."

"I'm sorry," said Thomas. "These were the coordinates I had. We intended no trespass or disrespect against your people."

"Intent isn't the same as action," said the man. "You intended no trespass, but you have trespassed all the same. We have little enough territory remaining to us. Why should we tolerate your coming here and treading upon what is ours?"

"I'm a distant relative, if that helps," I said. My great-grandmother, Frances Brown, was half-Kairos. It's where my side of the family gets our natural resistance to cuckoo mind tricks, and why we so often find ourselves dealing with ludicrous coincidences. Sam liked to say that my family's only plan was "Just wing it," and he wasn't far wrong, because being part-Kairos meant "just winging it" worked more often than not.

The man looked at me, eyes narrowing. "It doesn't help," he said. "What dreadful bower must have borne you, to stand so before us?"

"Uh, excuse me?" I scowled at him. "Don't talk about my mother like that."

To my surprise, he laughed. The other five Kairos began moving forward, their bidents held at menacing angles, clearly keeping an eye on us.

"This will be a delightful conversation," he said. "The three of you will come with us now."

"My wife—" began Thomas.

"Is already lost if she's gone into the green," said the man. "You will come."

Jabbing their bidents at us to illustrate their point, the Kairos surrounding us urged us to start moving. I looked to Thomas, waiting to see how he would react.

To my surprise, he sighed and began to go in the direction they were urging us. "Alice will be fine," he said, in a low voice. "Much of our time together since we were reunited has been focused on her learning that she's not alone any longer, and me learning that she spent fifty years relying on luck and skill and didn't die. So I trust her to come and find us, and I'd really rather not start our time in this dimension by getting into a throw-down with a bunch of the locals."

"I don't like this," I grumbled.

"Neither do I," he said. "But this is so far from the worst thing I've had to deal with that it barely rates a complaint. All right?"

"All right," I agreed, and we kept walking, into the flowers, into the trees, away from the flat silver waters of the distant lake.

✦ ✦ ✦

The Kairos led us through the brush for what felt like hours, finally emerging at the edge of a small village that wouldn't have looked out of place in the American Southwest. The houses, which stood independently, ranged in height from one to three stories tall, and looked like they'd been built entirely from adobe bricks and fistfuls of some sort of thick, rubbery mud. There was no glass in the windows, which had been set to line up with one another, allowing any breezes that blew by to penetrate all the homes at the same time. The rooftops were flat.

"Verity would love it here," I murmured, soft enough that only Sam could hear me. He snorted, mildly amused but still wary.

Ladders made of what looked like thick bamboo lashed together with ropes made from braided leaves leaned against the front of the houses, allowing people to access the higher floors without going through the interior, and many of the windows had braided baskets hanging from them, some heavy with unidentified objects, others clearly empty.

And there were people. Maybe that shouldn't have been a surprise, this being their village and all, but it looked enough like a sound stage from some low-budget science fiction show that I almost expected the place to be deserted, or occupied by a few extras from central casting. Instead, hunters with more of those strange bidents carried the carcasses of what looked like massive isopods and centipedes to hang them from hooks; groups of children sat cross-legged on the ground with adults leading them in counting games or story circles; unarmed adults hung laundry on lines or cracked the exoskeletons on the slaughtered insects, extracting the meat within. All told, I counted more than eighty individuals, and I wasn't taking care to count every single one of them.

Like the six who'd come to intercept us, they all looked human: drop any of these people on the street in Portland, give them a knit beanie and a paper coffee cup, and they'd fit right in. Their range of skin tones included a few more extremes than I was used to: people so pale I could see their veins, or so dark that their skins seemed to swallow the light as it touched them, and a pair of women with gorgeous dark brown hair and skin yellow enough to verge on gold, but they were all within the spectrum possible for people on Earth. They wore loose, layered clothing in greens and browns, clearly designed to make it easier for them to vanish into the foliage: some, like the initial six, had pieces of exoskeleton stitched or strapped to their attire, providing bright splashes of color that would, paradoxically, also make blending in easier. Hard to hide among the flowers when you were the only thing in sight without petals. Red seemed to be the dominant color—almost everyone I saw had at least one piece of shockingly red cloth integrated into their outfits, worn proudly as their primary adornment.

This wasn't any community or culture I'd ever seen before, but they still looked so mundane that it was almost shocking when

I heard a few of them speaking in low voices and realized they weren't speaking English.

Weren't . . . Wait. I looked back to our original six, who had ranged out to surround us in a loose circle. I frowned, then turned to Thomas. "Why do these ones speak English and those ones don't?"

"An excellent question, Antimony. Why do you think that is?"

I scowled. He did that a lot—set little tests for me rather than answering my questions. He said it was part of his duty if he was going to be teaching me sorcery. "Kairos aren't telepathic," I said. "If anything, they're the opposite, since they're resistant to most forms of telepathy. But this isn't magical. I'd be able to feel it if this were magical."

"Are you so sure?"

"Yeah, and I'm pretty sure that 'being held hostage by strange aliens' is not the best moment for a pop quiz, okay?"

Thomas almost looked amused as he nodded. "Fair enough. Kairos are resistant to telepathy, yes, but not immune, and Johrlar is a telepathic world. Focus on what you hear."

I blinked then, frowning, and tried to pay attention to the ongoing drone around us. It hadn't gotten any quieter as we moved, although it was steady enough that I'd started to almost tune it out, letting it fall into the background. As before, it was divided into three registers, deep, deeper, and high and shrill. But as I focused on them, I realized there was a fourth register, almost inaudible against the greater wall of sound. I held up three fingers, making solid eye contact with my grandfather, and then, deliberately, raised a fourth.

His smile was the smile of every teacher I'd ever had, in school settings and otherwise, when I finally got the answer to some tricky problem or landed some complicated trick. It was approval and satisfaction and a certain amount of smugness, like my cleverness was somehow down to him. In this context, I didn't mind.

He nodded. "Johrlar is a telepathic world," he repeated. "That means most of the species that have managed to thrive here are sensitive, on some level or other. They hunt, evade, mate, and protect their young without visual or verbal signals. It's only natural that some of the vegetation would pick up the same abilities."

"That's ridiculous," said Sam. "Plants don't have brains. They can't be telepathic."

"Don't they?" asked Thomas. "Even on Earth, we have clonal colonies, large groups of genetically identical plants that communicate within themselves, passing information as well as nutrients through their roots. Their brains aren't like ours, being more decentralized and deconstructed, but I'd argue that they're thinking all the same. Now, Annie. What do you see?"

I looked around the village, noting the presence of a flowering vine that had seemed almost inconsequential before, the local equivalent of morning glories. The flowers themselves looked more like some sort of weird rainbow orchid, presumably optimized to attract bees and beetles I had never even dreamt of.

"I saw those vines where we landed, too," I said. "Are they one of those clonal colonies?"

"I can't be sure, but I'd wager yes," said Thomas.

One of the original six nudged me to walk a little faster, and said, "The mind-mind flowers grow in discrete groves, and we build our settlements near their roots. They translate for us, and on the occasions when we find travelers like yourselves, they smooth the edges between our tongues. It isn't without its drawbacks—none of us have actually learned to speak our mother tongue in generations, and I have little doubt that without the presence of the flowers, we'll find that it's been lost. But we understand each other, no matter where we wander, and we understand those who come from worlds beyond the sky, and we understand the heartless ones."

I blinked. Sam spoke first.

"You call them mind-mind flowers?" he asked, incredulously. "Isn't that a little, well, ridiculous?"

"No, we call them mind-mind flowers," said the man. He paused, frowning. "Or, I suppose, we call them whatever it is you're hearing in translation. We call them what they are, and that word translates itself for others."

"Does it apply to names as well, I wonder?" asked Thomas. "If I say my name is Thomas Price, will they hear those words, or 'twin cost'?"

"Both," said the man. "Delightful, isn't it? You can communicate with any of us, down to the littlest babe."

The idea of babies being able to make their wishes known in words was at once positive and unsettling. It would definitely lead to some social changes, and explained why the various groups of children seemed to be entirely mixed, containing everything from toddlers to tweens.

"Wait," I said. "If you haven't *learned* to talk, does that mean you used to live someplace that didn't have these mind-mind flowers?"

"Of course," said the man. "We are Kairos. This is not our world."

"Meaning what . . . ?"

"Meaning you are strangers here, and while you seem to intend but little harm, appearances can deceive. Still your tongues and stay your questions. We're going to the Eldest Living."

He waved the group onward, and we walked deeper into the village, Thomas looking unnervingly serene for a man who'd been held captive in another dimension for decades and had now been effectively taken prisoner again, Sam mostly just looking annoyed. He kept his tail looped around me, limiting how far we could be separated, and I kept a hand on it, making it clear that right now, the anchor was more than appreciated. I didn't know this place or these people, even if they were distant relatives of mine. I definitely didn't want to deal with them alone.

Thomas's serenity was odd, considering that we still hadn't seen a sign of Alice. He kept walking, looking around himself with interest, and didn't seem like he was getting ready to bolt into the brush. That probably meant he had a plan. I just wished he had a way of sharing it with me.

He glanced over at me and winked, broadly. Oh, he definitely had a plan. I'd just need to wait to find out what it was.

Holding to hope with one hand and Sam's tail with the other, I took a deep breath and followed my grandfather into the unknown.

Seven

"When all else fails, do your research. When your research fails, restock your first aid kit."

—**Jane Harrington-Price**

In Johrlar, going deeper into an inexplicable village

THE VILLAGE WAS LARGER THAN it looked when we first arrived, extending into the trees in several directions and at irregular angles, as if they'd been trying to emulate the shape of something dropped from a great height. Sam eyed the ladders and staggered rooftops as we walked, and I knew he was assessing how useful they would be if we needed to make a swift escape. He didn't say anything. None of us were talking anymore.

Some of the houses were hidden by bamboo, or by impossibly large broad-leafed plants that hung over them, providing shade and camouflage at the same time. And the trailing vines of the mind-mind flower were everywhere, making it clear that the communication network extended throughout the village.

We were approaching a massive tree that appeared to have grown from multiple trunks that were now all fused together, forming a hollow almost as deep as the tree was big around. Its branches were thick and twisted, creating a wonderland of bars and connections. Any children's play place in the world would have done well to erect a model of that tree. Its leaves were amethyst purple and glittered in the light, while its flowers were multi-petaled confections, almost like exploding carnations, black as onyx and almost as dazzling as the leaves.

Beetles the size of my fists scuttled across the bark, their carapaces flicking open to display the diaphanous lines of their wings. They didn't flee as we approached the tree, only moved almost languidly out of easy reach.

Sam twitched.

I gave him a curious look.

"I don't get a lot of annoying monkey urges," he said. "Mostly they have to do with covering my teeth and not wearing shoes. But I'll be damned if those beetles don't look like some sort of ultra-fancy snack food."

I wrinkled my nose. "Okay, one, ew, and two, 'Hey babe, I wanna eat bugs' was not the confession I was expecting from you today."

"None of this is what I was expecting!" complained Sam. He shot a glare at the man who had brought us here, who hadn't said a word since announcing that he was taking us to the Eldest Living, whoever that was. Then again, it might well be the tree. It's dangerous to make assumptions about species and cultures you don't belong to.

I patted Sam's tail with one hand. "Sorry we wound up in another dimension instead of spending the evening watching videos on YouTube and getting lost in the forest."

He sniffed. "You better mean that."

The man who'd been leading us thus far turned to face the entire group—me, Thomas, and Sam, and the other five Kairos who'd come to intercept us at our landing spot. He raised his bident.

All the other Kairos stopped walking. Not wanting to get stabbed with a bident, we did the same.

"You will be polite," said the man. "You will be deferent. You will be courteous as befits your position—guests in our home, with no cause to expect anything beyond the most basic of hospitality. Do you understand?"

"Sure, I guess," I said. His word choices were strange, and I knew they weren't actually his own; they were supplied by the mind-mind flowers, providing the easiest translation they could find.

I didn't trust it. It was like having a conversation with a generative text engine, only I didn't know what data sets it had been trained on, or whether he had any way to control what he said to us. Maybe he was explaining the manner in which we were going to be executed, and all we could do was stand by and politely agree, since we had no way of knowing what we didn't get to hear.

Sam's tail tightened, pulling me a few inches closer to him, and I knew he was having similar thoughts. Thomas, however, looked utterly relaxed, which didn't match up with my grandmother's tales of what a paranoid and cautious man he was. Either she'd been exaggerating to make the rest of us like him when he wasn't around to correct her, or he had a plan.

Oh, I hoped he had a plan.

The man eyed me. "There will be no trouble. There will be no violence. The Eldest Living will answer for you what may be answered, and will tell us what is to be done. Do you understand?"

"We do," said Thomas. He sounded almost bored. "May we continue?"

"No weapons may be brought into the presence of the Eldest Living," said the man.

He looked utterly nonplussed when all three of us started laughing. Sam actually uncoiled his tail from around my wrist so he could wrap it around himself as he bent double. It wasn't *that* funny, but we were all wound-up and out of our normal environment, and that added an edge of hysteria to the laughter that would have been entirely over the top in any other circumstance.

The man, looking puzzled, stepped closer to us and prodded at Thomas with his bident. And Sam moved.

It's difficult to describe or overstate just how fast a fūri is when not trying to seem unthreatening. One second Sam was next to me, laughing uproariously, and the next he was in front of Thomas, one hand on the shaft of the stranger's bident, holding the weapon up so that its tines pointed at the sky. It was like he'd clipped across the distance between them, only touching down on one frame out of every four.

His lips were drawn back, displaying large, square teeth. They weren't pointed or even particularly sharp, but they looked strong, and it would take a braver person than me to look at that display and think it was a good idea to keep doing whatever had caused him to make that face.

"No," he said, with absolute calm. He shoved the bident toward the man as he released it, and the man staggered back several feet, unable to keep his balance in the face of Sam's force.

"Why are you laughing?" demanded the man, not advancing again. He held his bident in front of himself like he wasn't sure what he was meant to do with it, clearly uneasy and off-balance.

"Even if we wanted to spend the next hour debating what you do and don't consider a weapon, all three of us *are* weapons according to any reasonable definition," said Thomas. He held up one hand, fingers flat and facing upward, and briefly lowered his eyebrows. A ball of flickering red flame burst into being above his palm. He moved his hand and the fire moved with it, making his control clear. "My descendant and I are elementalists, and as you can see, her partner is fūri. He can have a careless person's arms off their body in seconds. Asking us to put our weapons aside is the same as saying that we can freely go. May we go?"

The man looked increasingly flustered. He turned to his companions, saying sharply, "Keep them here," before he turned and ducked into the hollow trunk of the massive tree.

Sam scoffed as he moved back to my side. "Coward," he grumbled.

"Most people are when faced with giant angry monkeys," I said, bumping my shoulder against his. "Look at those branches. You think we'll be here long enough to play trapeze up there?"

"It's not trapeze if we don't have swings. It's just Olympic-level jungle gym." He paused, sounding much calmer as he added, "I sure hope so. Lots of good geometry up there."

"Of course they have good geometry. This is the Johrlac world.

They're all mathematicians." I looked over at Thomas. "Is that speciesist? If I say they're all mathematicians?"

"Normally any statement that begins with 'they're all' is going to be a little bit prejudiced, but in this case, no," he said. "A fondness for mathematics is as natural and inborn as everything else about them. Johrlac can no more help their love of numbers than they can decide to trade hemolymph for hemoglobin and become true mammals."

"Good to know," I said. "Should we have heard from Alice by now?" I didn't want to worry him. At the same time, I wanted someone to reassure *me.*

He glanced up at the sky, apparently trying to calculate how long it had actually been. If he could manage that, he was a better navigator than I was: normally when I was trying to measure time by the motion of the sun, there was only one of them, and I was on a planet whose orbital axis was familiar to me. Here, there were either three suns or two suns and a very large moon that was reflecting enough light to seem lambent in its own right, and I had no idea how long the days or nights were supposed to be.

"She's fine," he said finally, looking back down at me. "Alice is . . . Alice is extremely Alice when she needs to be. I don't know a better way of putting it. She's either following us or she's still getting transport under control, and either way, she'll show up when the time is right. And she'll be all the happier and easier to deal with because she's been punching giant ladybugs or something."

"Why did we need another world full of giant insects?" asked Sam plaintively. "Greg's okay, but one's enough. I'd like to go to a dimension full of things that don't go above four legs apiece if that's cool."

"There are plenty of non-insect dimensions," said Thomas. "Some of them are even pleasant places to visit. Ithaca, for example. But the Johrlac evolved from insects, and it makes sense that their world would be more of the same. I'm so sorry Sarah got abducted to a place that doesn't suit your sensibilities."

"Yeah, well, someone should be," grumbled Sam.

The man from before stepped back out of the tree, looking cautious and relieved at the same time, like he didn't particularly want to be in our presence, but was glad to know what he was coming back to do.

"The Eldest Living will see you now, weapons and all," he said, making a sweeping gesture with his bident.

The three of us moved to stand closer together. "Thank you," said Thomas, and we walked past the man, into the shadows of the tree. The scouts, all six of them, remained behind.

✦ ✦ ✦

Inside the trunk it was surprisingly bright, thanks to the many small openings formed by the interweaving of the trunks; they allowed shafts of sunlight to shine through, which then hit any one of a number of shining reflective disks hung from the high walls of the tree, bouncing the light back and forth between them. The end result was an odd mosaic of light and shadows, dazzling and dark at once.

The center of the space was occupied by a ring of chairs clearly designed for human-shaped bipeds, surrounding a pile of pillows and soft fabrics. Settled at the top of the pile was a woman. True to what I assumed was her title, she was quite possibly the physically oldest person I had ever seen. Her hair was white and wispy; her skin was deeply seamed with wrinkles and looked softer than the cloth below her. Her fingers were straight, but her knuckles were huge, like knobs on the length of a stick. She turned toward us as we entered, and smiled.

"Our travelers," she said, and her voice was sweet and clear. "How fortuitous. Right time, right place, my friends. Please come and have a seat."

"These are your people?" asked Thomas. He approached the chairs without hesitation. Sam and I did the same, following his lead.

"The village? Yes. I've been guiding them for a long, long while now. I'll be done guiding them soon enough: the correct time for my departure approaches."

"I am Thomas Price," said Thomas. "This is my granddaughter, Antimony, and her betrothed, Samuel. We're here because two more of my grandchildren have been abducted from their homes by the Johrlac, and we need to get them back. Your scouting party stumbled across us shortly after our arrival."

"Right time, right place," she said. "If they found you, you can be sure a detachment of the heartless ones was not far behind. You must have triggered something when you came through the dimensional wall."

"You know about dimensional travel?"

"We do." She looked up, toward one of the beams of light. "We were a domestication project for the heartless ones, many generations ago. They were looking for people who could take the place of the underclass they had sent into exile, who could do the tasks they had no interest in performing for themselves without losing their minds, and they found the Kairos. They found Caerus, the world of our beginning, and they came for us in such numbers that the only thing the timing could do was send us into the arms of potentially kinder masters, leaving the cruelest to hunt in vain. They brought us here, believing they could tame us, believing our resistance to their minds would make us sturdier over the long tail of time. And they set us to work. But we never forgot where we had come from, and we told our children, and we remembered that we were Kairos. We remembered that we didn't belong here. We remember still."

Well. This was interesting. We'd only known about the Kairos for a few years; before that, our family's occasionally improbable luck had been chalked up to chance and turned into a running joke. It wasn't until Mark that we'd learned we owed our sometimes-tumultuous relationship with coincidence to a streak of non-human heritage. Given the presence of jinks and mara on Earth, I had never really considered that the Kairos might have an extra-dimensional origin.

"If you were brought here as a slave population, what changed?" asked Thomas. His tone was polite, but I could hear the hunger for knowledge under the civility of it all: like the rest of us, he wanted to understand more than almost everything else.

"The heartless ones could read our intentions, even through the dampening effect of the timing, and that made organization difficult, but with, well, time, they paid less attention, and the timing was forever working in our favor. When we reached the right coincidences, we broke free, all but the barest few of us, and we made for the wild places of their world. Once we were here, the timing hid us better than they could seek, and we vanished into the green. We've been here ever since. Some of us have escaped to other worlds through the crossings. That would be how you"—she nodded toward me, eyes sharp within their nests of wrinkles—"could come to be. We are no more of Caerus. We wouldn't know how to be. This is not our world, but it is our home, and this is where we die."

"Why did your hunters bring us here?" asked Sam.

She switched her attention over to him. "You, I don't recognize," she said, after a moment. "The girl is of the Kairos, if not entirely, and the man is of whatever sister species birthed her. You, though . . . I don't know you."

"Human," said Thomas politely. "We're from a place called 'Earth.' It's not far from here, as the dimensional axes are measured. Someone who was traveling one step at a time could get there in no more than five hops."

"And they have evolved there a sister species?"

"Three, we think," I said. "Humans, jinks, and mara. We're all considered primates, evolved from the simians that also live there."

"Fascinating," said the woman. "What is special about these 'humans'?"

"To be honest, I don't know for sure," I said. "They're cross-fertile with several other species, including Kairos, and they're capable of sorcery, sometimes—interaction with the pneuma. It's not universal."

"It was more common once, but we spent centuries with an extradimensional predator feeding on our world and destroying anyone it found who could manipulate the pneuma," added Thomas.

The woman looked impressed. "Still, to have any hope of manipulation of the pneuma without death is a rare attribute. It serves you well. Now. Why are you here?"

I hesitated, looking to Thomas to see if he was going to supply any answer. He shook his head, saying nothing, which meant that it was down to me. I looked back to the Eldest Living. "My grandfather already told you. Two of my cousins have been abducted by the Johrlac, and we're here to get them back."

"Why?"

"Why were they abducted, or why do we want them back?"

"Yes."

"They were abducted because my cousin Sarah is a member of the species you call the 'heartless ones.' A descendant of their exiles. My family adopted her as a child." I didn't know how the mind-mind flowers would translate the concept of "cuckoos." Not knowing which of my words were actually being transmitted to the people around me was surprisingly frustrating. This was an aspect of the universal translator that *Star Trek* never bothered to address. "She managed to complete the full cycle of instars to become a queen by their standards, and I guess that attracted their attention. She's not theirs, and we want her back. They also took another of my cousins, Arthur. He's . . ." How was I supposed to explain Arthur? "He's like me. Part-human, part-Kairos. He's also part-Lilu." More Lilu than anything else, since his father was fully Lilu, while his mother was a mixture of Kairos and human. I was starting to feel like my family tree needed a pie chart.

"I don't know why the heartless ones took him," I concluded, choosing a simple white lie over the complicated truth. "They just appeared, grabbed him, and vanished again. His sister's incredibly upset about it, and the rest of us want him back."

"So you crossed dimensions to retrieve them?"

I shrugged. "We had the capability, and it seemed like the least we could do. Are we prisoners here?"

She blinked. "No. The Kairos do not keep prisoners. You're free to go whenever the timing allows."

"Meaning . . . ?"

"Meaning you might try to walk away and find yourselves lost in the green, or pursued back here by the flesh-stripper beetles, or forced to flee from a detachment of the heartless ones. They would reclaim us if they were allowed. They patrol this area often, looking for signs of our encampments."

"So we're in more danger because we're with you?"

"We would never have found you if you weren't in danger without us."

I turned to Thomas, ready to throw my hands up and demand to know what we were supposed to do with these people. I don't like being talked in circles.

Catching my frustration, he turned toward the Eldest Living. "We need to get our people back, and then we'll go," he said. "Is there anything you can do to help us?"

"We maintain what peace we have by never interfering in the matters of the heartless ones," said the Eldest Living. "We remain below their notice, and they leave us to our own devices."

Sam frowned. "But you just said . . ."

I grabbed his hand. "No, Sam, it's fine. Let's let the Eldest Living get her rest, and we'll just go on our way. I'm sure Alice is looking for us by now."

"Why are you calling her 'Alice' and not 'Grandma'?" asked Sam.

"In the field, names are easier," I said. I turned toward the door, hoping he and Thomas would follow, hoping Thomas had managed to catch the same contradiction I had.

The Eldest Living didn't call us back, only sat in her nest of soft fabrics and watched as we walked away.

The scouting party was still outside, bidents at the ready. They straightened as we emerged, attention fixing on the three of us. I offered their leader an easy smile.

"Hey, sport," I said. "The Eldest says we're free to go. Hope that's cool by you."

He frowned, looking momentarily confused. "Honor to the Eldest," he said, after a moment's consideration. "You have offered us no offense. We merely wanted to be sure you presented no danger to our people as a whole. May the timing guide you."

"Right back at you," I said genially, and kept on walking, Thomas and Sam close behind. No one moved to stop us.

"Keep moving," I said, voice much lower, and angled for the trees.

We almost made it before someone shouted behind us.

"Run," I suggested.

We ran.

Eight

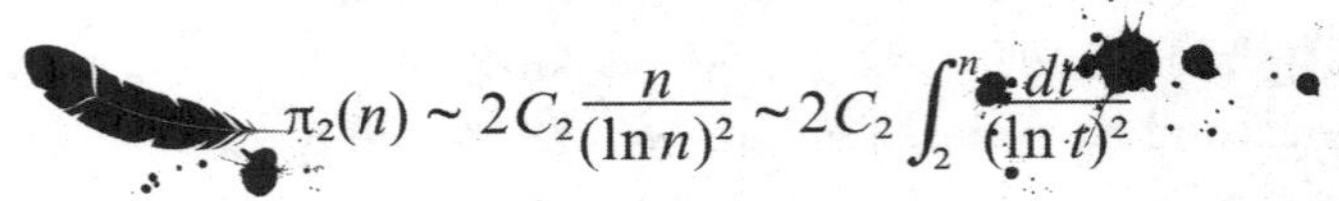

SARAH

"Biology makes a lot of choices for us. That's inevitable. You were always going to be a biped, you were always going to have your mother's thumbs and your father's funny eyebrows. But everything else is up to you. Figure it out."

—Angela Baker

Location? To be honest, I have no idea, but I have my suspicions

THE TRANSITION WAS SEAMLESS, PAINLESS, and swift. One moment we were in Mark's hospital room, and then I was wrapped in diaphanous veils of mathematics, the numbers sliding rapidly by, so smooth and fluid that I could barely follow them. If I focused on a single line, I could watch it evolve and branch, but I would be lost as soon as it encountered another function and combined with a series of numbers I hadn't been watching. This was math taken to the point of poetry, so advanced it became its own language, and like all languages, it told me stories about the culture that had defined it.

Math is a constant. To go back to the absolute basics, two plus two is going to be four whether you're a human, a cuckoo, or a silica-based organism that has just figured out how to think as an individual being. But the way we write it down can vary from person to person, and will absolutely be impacted by the assumptions of the mathematician. This was math starting from a lot of assumptions I didn't know or understand, and it was holding me so tightly that it was something of a wonder I could think, much less move.

We weren't in the hospital anymore. We weren't anywhere. The world was a sheet of brilliant, eye-searing blue in front of me, and deep, textured darkness behind, crackling red around the edges. Even as the thought formed, part of me understood that the words "blue" and "red" had no meaning here: I was looking at the Doppler shift, seeing the expansion and contraction of the universe in real time.

Flashes of gray-violet and white-pink began to gather around the edges of my vision, ultraviolet signals of the transition ahead. I caught my breath, abstractly relieved that I still could—I had breath to catch, which meant I had lungs, and a body, and the ability to make decisions about both those things—and braced against the transition I knew was about to hit.

I needn't have bothered. We slid through the phase shift without hesitation, the numbers continuing to dance and twine around me, and this was infinity, this was forever. I was going to spend the rest of my existence in a silken cocoon of mathematics, and I wasn't certain time could find me here: it seemed possible that this would just continue until the Doppler shift resolved itself and reality settled into a calm, motionless infinity, no longer conflicted, no longer expanding or contracting or anything at all. I didn't like the idea, but none of this had been my decision.

Then, like the bubble dropping Glinda in front of Dorothy and the others, the cocoon popped and disappeared, leaving me standing on a perfectly normal tile floor, head spinning and aching from the absence of the sheltering numbers. The five people who'd surrounded me in Mark's hospital room were standing around me, none more than an arm's length away, unruffled by the transition. They weren't saying anything or moving much, and so I decided to take a moment to focus on my surroundings.

We were in a small room, barely large enough for the six of us to stand without touching each other. The floor was made of pearlescent gray tile, while the walls looked like they'd been made from rough bleached paper, off-white and almost exactly the color of human bones that had been baking in the sun. There were no windows, and no doors. There was also no furniture. I put a hand against my temple, trying to steady myself.

Wherever we were, there wasn't a human inside my range for receptive telepathy. Given how enormously expanded my range had been since I completed the queen instar, that almost certainly meant we weren't anywhere near Earth.

Cuckoos—Johrlac—can't see the color red. We don't have the right receptors in our eyes. I can see red when I'm around humans, because I've borrowed the concept from their minds, and their eyes guide me to what's red and what isn't. Well, the Johrlac who had taken me were no longer wearing red and black. Instead, they were wearing black and gray, and the gray part of their jumpsuits was patterned in fractal arcs, ultraviolet detailing a human captive would have missed.

Well, bully for me.

"Do not move," snapped one of the Johrlac in black and gray. "You have been arrested, and will not attempt to evade custody."

"My head is spinning," I said. "I'd ask if I could sit down, but since there aren't any chairs, I'm just going to stand here and try to keep myself from falling over. Assuming that's all right with you?"

I couldn't see their minds at all, couldn't read the shape of their thoughts or what they might be thinking. But I could tell when two of them exchanged a look, moving somewhat closer to each another. Their eyes glazed over white for a moment, and I strained mentally, trying to pick up the thread of their conversation. I didn't want to listen in. I just wanted to feel less like I'd been cut off from the world.

"Fine," snapped one of them. "We'll send the request for seating. Your time among the mammals has made you weak, aberration. You were always going to be a disappointment to your hive. We did not expect you to shame your species."

The words were clearly intended to hurt, but they missed their mark, mostly because I didn't care what these people thought of me. They were strangers who happened to share some essential biology with my own; I'd erased my own biological mother's mind and left her to be ripped apart by giant spiders. Blood has never been the yardstick I measure by.

"Who are you people, and where are we?" I asked, lowering my hand. "I think you owe me at least a few answers, considering what you just did."

"What we just did?" asked one of the blue ones. "We removed an invasive species from a fragile ecosystem."

Those words sounded so much like the ones I'd heard from my own family whenever they needed to justify themselves that I paused for a moment, blinking, before I asked, "Have you been reading my mind?"

"You are a criminal. You have no right to expect privacy of the mind," said the other blue one.

"I haven't broken any laws," I protested.

"Your existence says otherwise," said one of the gray ones. "For a cuckoo to achieve maturity, others must die. The dimension in which you were raised remains intact, and we found no other cuckoo minds in your vicinity: you are guilty of the extermination of your species on your world of birth."

It all sounded so reasonable when it was laid out like that, like a logic problem that had a right answer and a wrong answer, and had to be resolved.

"I didn't do that on purpose," I objected. "I only acted to save my world. It was self-defense."

"Was it self-defense when you erased the self of the human you believed you loved? Or was it the cuckoo need for control lashing out under the pretense of preserving some intangible greater good?" The gray one cocked their head to the side. "I can see you were afraid, and that you were so deep into wrangling the equation you were trying to complete that you had the convenient excuse of your distraction, but you should have noticed his intrusion into the mathematics. And instead of acknowledging it, you pulled him deeper in and made use of him like he was merely a tool for your employment, like his existence was inferior to your own. You acted as a cuckoo. Your crimes are greater than your excuses, and you will pay for them."

A ripping sound from across the room caught my attention. Honestly, I was grateful to have something to distract me from the horrible things the stranger was saying. I needed them to introduce themselves, or at the very least to drop their mental shielding long enough for me to get their pronouns. I wasn't used to being this devoid of context.

A knife protruded through the paper wall, and as I watched, it slid downward, cutting a clear channel. Two people in black-and-yellow jumpsuits stepped through the opening, both holding knives, and each gripping one side of what looked like a simple kitchen chair. They put it down in the center of the room, looking to one of the people in blue, and I realized with some relief that I could feel their minds. They were both female, bright and eager to do their jobs.

I withdrew my thoughts as soon as I knew how to address them. They'd give me their names if they wanted to share, and until then, the relief of having the correct pronouns was going to be enough to keep me going. Sometimes it's the little things.

"We have brought the chair, Inspector," said the first of the pair. "Have we fulfilled your request?"

"Yes," said one of the people in blue. "Fix the wall as you leave."

"Yes, Inspector," chorused the two, and they turned in unison to make their way back to the opening they'd created. I watched them go, all but despondent. Having a moment where I'd been able to claim context on my situation had been wonderful: losing it was terrible.

But at least now I could say with certainty that I was on Johrlar. I'd never seen the dimension my species originated from, but nothing else explained being surrounded by this many Johrlac.

"Well, sit," said one of the Johrlac in gray and yellow. "You asked for the chair, and it was brought before you. We're not here to serve your comfort, prisoner."

The slit in the wall was already disappearing, seemingly mending itself from the bottom up. The minds of the two Johrlac who had brought the chair were already gone, making me suspect the paper had some sort of anti-telepathic quality, blunting the thoughts of everyone on the other side.

"Do you have any weapons?" asked one of the blue ones.

I turned to blink at them, startled by the question. "What?"

It would have been a foolish thing to ask any other member of my family, even Elsie; Isaac and Charlotte didn't carry weapons to school as far as I knew, but every one of my relatives over the age of fourteen was armed at all times, ranging from a few knives in Verity's case to a veritable walking armory in Alice's. I, on the other hand, generally counted on my telepathy and giant spider to get me through, since both of those things were more useful on a general basis than a handgun small enough to hide in my clothing.

"Weapons," repeated the blue one, impatiently. "Are you carrying any weapons right now?"

"No. You snatched me from a *hospital*."

"Good. You will remain here, inside this room, and not make any attempts to escape our custody. If you do, it will go poorly for you, and will be considered during your sentencing. Do you understand?"

"Sentencing? What? You're not going to be sentencing me. I don't acknowledge your authority over me."

"Criminals never do," said the blue one. Their eyes flashed white, and all the strangers blurred for a moment, becoming intangible before they disappeared, and I was left alone in a prison cell with paper walls.

Exhausted, I sat down in the chair and dropped my head into my hands. What the hell was supposed to happen now?

✦ ✦ ✦

After taking an unknown amount of time to feel sorry for myself—as if the last several years of my life hadn't been shitty enough without adding in an entire dimension of self-righteous assholes who happened to be related to me—I sat up, took a deep breath, and began trying to figure out my next move.

Technically, I could cross dimensions the same way they did, if I just had the equation I needed to get myself back to Earth. Issue there: I didn't have the equation, and while I might be able to work it out if they left me alone for long enough, the only method I knew for building world-jumping equations was based on cuckoo math. It was brute force and brutality, not the elegant Doppler shift of the Johrlac method. The cuckoos had presumably understood their methods, once, but that knowledge had been excised from their minds before they were exiled. Everything they knew, they'd rebuilt painfully from basic principles: those first cuckoos had known they were from another dimension, one where math could open doors and smooth passages, and they'd pushed and pushed and pushed against the possible until it finally agreed to yield to them.

Cuckoo math was like using a nuclear weapon to do the job of a housekey. It left devastation in its wake, and if that wasn't bad enough, it was massive. They used enormous, sprawling functions to achieve simple means. Writing their math down took reams of paper; I could probably have reached the same conclusion in Johrlac math on a Post-it. And when you're talking about arithmancy, you're not using paper.

You're using minds.

The Johrlac had almost certainly sent a team of six just so they'd have the processing power necessary to run even their streamlined version of the universal math without straining or endangering any of their arithmancers. I didn't have those extra minds. I just had me. If I put together the equation that would let me leave without having anyone to help me hoist it up, I would destroy a large portion of this planet, and melt my own mind in the process. Not optimal.

I slumped in my chair, rubbing my temples with my forefingers. The Johrlac had come as soon as they heard Mark's mental shriek, but they hadn't realized Mark and I were different people. That made a certain sense—he hadn't really been packing a lot of personally identifying information into his screaming—but it was also sloppy. They should have realized they were hearing the screams of a male cuckoo while they were busy arresting a female one.

Paper walls might be good for quick repairs and even quick construction, but they didn't have a lot going for them in the sturdiness department. I stood, turning to take a look at the chair itself. It was made of what looked like hard-pressed paper mâché, the same stuff as the walls, and had no metal or wood, nothing harder than stiff cardboard. Interesting. I turned back to the walls.

It wasn't a large room; a few long steps took me to the wall that had been cut before. I touched it experimentally. It was warm and rough under my fingers, slightly yielding, but still solid. I pressed harder, and quickly discovered there was a limit to the amount of give it would offer me.

Right. Only one thing to try. I pushed the sleeve of my sweater up, pulled back my fist, and punched the wall as hard as I could.

The impact reverberated along my arm all the way to the shoulder and I yelped, jumping around and trying to shake the sudden ache out of my hand. It felt like, well. Like I'd just punched a wall. There wasn't even a dent to show where I'd hit. If I was getting out of here, it wasn't going to be that easy.

I waited until the pain had dulled down to a roar, then prodded the wall more gently with my fingertips. Paper, yes, but hard paper, almost like a form of drywall. I took a disgusted step back, then paused, reviewing the contents of my pockets.

They'd been oddly concerned about weapons for people who'd already taken me captive and allowed themselves to remain within arm's length for an extended period of time. So maybe they weren't worried about themselves. Maybe they'd been worried about the walls. And in a place without metal, maybe the definition of "weapon" was a little bit broader than I usually considered it.

I stuck a hand into my skirt pocket, rummaging around. I had a pack of tomato-flavored novelty chewing gum—from Japan, naturally—some loose change, a Metro card, and my house keys. I pulled them out, considering their sharp, irregular edges, then turned back to the wall.

Gripping one key firmly between my fingers, I pressed it against the wall and leaned on it like I thought it could support me. To my deep relief and delight, it punched through almost as soon as I shifted my weight onto it, and I began to pull downward, sawing as I pulled.

I was rewarded with a rough gash in the papery substance, opening slowly but inexorably in the path of the key. I didn't hear anyone on the other side, which might mean I wasn't in any immediate risk of being caught. Emboldened by the thought, I pulled harder, until I had opened a wide-enough gash to shove my hands through and start pulling to the sides, rather than straight up and down.

I stuck my head out, finding myself looking at a long, perfectly straight hallway made from the same tile-and-paper combination as the room. The two workers I'd seen earlier were standing across from the wall I'd been busily cutting through, leaning against the opposite wall and watching me with the patient interest of schoolteachers watching a child perform a trick. I froze. They kept watching me, silent and unmoving.

Several seconds ticked by. When they didn't move or sound up any alarms, I started sawing downward with my key again, opening the gash in the wall wider and wider, until I was able to grip the sides and pull them far enough apart to let me step out into the hall.

Something about the room where I'd been left was clearly responsible for the telepathic dampening, because as soon as I was in the hall, it was like the world acquired another dimension that had been quietly suppressed before. I could see the two people in front of me properly, and identify them as individuals who looked nothing alike. They were both female Johrlac, close friends if not lovers, and members of the same creche group, whatever that meant. Their names were—

They didn't have any names. I stopped, blinking at them in bemusement. The one on the left took pity on me.

"Names are meant to be shared aloud," she said. "Not like castes or gender or anything else innate. We know you're not from here, so we're not going to take offense, but if you want to know our names, you need to ask us."

Oh. That made sense. "I'm Sarah," I said. "Who are you?"

They flashed amusement at each other, eyes still on me. "My name is Fetch," said one.

"My name is Carry," said the other.

"We're assistants," they said in unison.

I blinked again, more slowly this time, trying to put my thoughts into some semblance of a coherent order. Finally, I said, "Those are your . . . names?"

"And our tasks," said Fetch. "I'm most frequently sent to retrieve things that have been put in other places."

"And once she finds them, I carry them back to where they're intended. I'm one of the best we have at my job," said Carry, proudly.

"That sounds very . . . I'm sorry, did you change names when you got these jobs?"

They radiated bewilderment at me. "What do you mean?" asked Carry. "We were born to these positions, and we'll hold them until we're too old to continue any longer. Once that happens, we'll be renamed and released from service."

"I . . . What?"

"You're a cuckoo, aren't you?" asked Fetch. Unlike the others, she didn't sneer when she said the word "cuckoo": it was just a question on her lips, an innocent inquiry that needed to be answered.

I nodded.

"That explains everything," she said sagely. "You can't possibly be expected to understand."

"Now," said Carry. "We waited as long as we could to see if you'd figure out a way out of the room. It's a primitive solution, but it makes sense and you're loose now. Let's go."

"Go where?"

"Not here," said Fetch. "We can't stay here. The authorities will be back soon. We can explain everything once we're someplace safe."

I hesitated. I didn't know these people, and they were trying to get me to go someplace unfamiliar with them. Normally, that would have been a big-enough red flag that I would have declined the offer and gone looking for my own way out. Normally, I wouldn't have just been abducted by members of my species who didn't want to talk to me or answer any of my questions. If Fetch and Carry were willing to explain things elsewhere, then I was willing to let them.

"All right," I said. "Let's go."

✦ ✦ ✦

The first place we went was a large closet of some sort, filled with shelves of cleaning products that were unfamiliar and utterly comprehensible at the same time. Instead of plastic jugs, they had large gourds and hollowed-out sections of some kind of bamboo that just happened to be bright purple and as wide around as a dinner plate. The air smelled of citrus and herbs, sharper and subtly spicier than the bleach and Lysol I was accustomed to at home.

Fetch grabbed a woven bag from one of the shelves, tossing it at me. It hit me squarely in the chest, and I grabbed hold of it without thinking. "Remove what you're wearing and put that on," she said.

I blinked at her in dismay. Carry looked over her shoulder.

"Don't worry about it," she said. "We've all got the same configuration—quite literally. I'd guess that your ancestors came from the same hive structure as ours. You have nothing to show that we haven't seen."

Johrlac don't process visual stimuli in the same exact way as humans, but we can see. My cheeks heated with embarrassment, although my clear blood meant I wouldn't have to deal with the secondary mortification of visibly flushing. I turned my back on the pair of them, opening the bag and taking a look inside.

Inside the bag was a black-and-yellow jumpsuit like the ones the two of them were wearing. I took it out, giving it a good shake to remove the wrinkles, then pulled my sweater off over my head.

The jumpsuit was ribbed and looked tight enough that I wasn't sure I could get it on over my bra. I glanced over my shoulder. "What do I do about—?" I asked, gesturing vaguely at my breasts.

"Remove the chest cover," said Fetch. "The suit will lift your breasts sufficient for modesty and comfort, and it isn't made to accommodate such a garment."

"Oh," I said. "Okay." It wasn't, really, but since I wasn't here to get into an argument with the cultural fashions of Johrlar, this was the best I was going to get.

At least the jumpsuit allowed me to keep my underpants on.

The years I'd spent helping Verity get ready for dance recitals came in unexpectedly handy as I hopped and wiggled the jumpsuit over my hips and then pulled it up to cover the rest of me, sliding my arms into their holes and pulling the fabric tight before zipping the whole thing up the front. It was as tight as I had assumed it would be, and fit me perfectly for all of that; the species-wide lack of variation apparently lent itself well to universal tailoring. I brushed my hair back with a sweep of my hand, looking down at myself, and had to admit two things:

First, that if I could take this jumpsuit home with me when we were finished here, it would do *numbers* at the next comic convention Annie decided to drag me to. All I'd need was some dramatic eyeshadow and maybe black lipstick and I'd look like the best evil hive queen network television had never produced. Second, that even outside of a comic convention, I looked pretty damn good in this thing. It fit, it was flattering in its construction, and the color suited me. I could do worse.

I stuffed my original clothing into the bag the jumpsuit had come out of, then turned to face Fetch and Carry, slightly spreading my arms to give them a better look. "Well?"

They looked me up and down, satisfaction radiating from the pair of them. "Very good," said Carry. "You look much better this way. More appropriate."

"Appropriate for what?"

Fetch shook her head. "I told you, we'll explain everything once we're somewhere safe. You're a queen; it should be easy enough for you to partition your thoughts. For now, if anyone asks or reaches, your name is Gather. You're an assistant from the precinct on the other side of the city, here to assist with the volume of work expected to accompany the trial. You've just arrived, and have had time to meet no one apart from your fellow assistants. You don't know anyone else."

"That's the truth," I said.

"Then this should be easy. Do you know what a reach feels like?"

"I'm not even sure what a reach *is*."

Fetch frowned, the expression echoing through her thoughts. "Right, right. You know what you can do, but not what it's called or how it works. I've seen this before, in other cuckoos, but never in a queen."

"That's because cuckoos don't survive long enough to go queen," said Carry.

"This one clearly did," said Fetch. "A reach is where you extend a mental hand to check someone's identity. Name, caste, purpose, pronouns. The foundations. You did it to us as soon as you were out of the dampening field."

"I'm sorry, I don't understand what you mean by 'caste.'"

"All right. Just focus on your partition: your name is Gather. Your caste is service. Your purpose is civic assistant."

"I thought names were meant to be shared aloud."

"They are, most of the time. Not when it's someone of a higher caste asking in the course of performing their duties. Ignore the contradiction: they like to feel important sometimes." She shrugged. "Your pronouns are whatever you like."

"Female." I looked around the room. "Where are we?"

"Janitorial closet. The janitor on this floor, Sterilize, is a cousin of mine and has agreed to let us use this space. He and I played together as children, and no one will question him having been seen doing me casual favors."

"Does everyone have names that match their jobs?"

"Until we're beyond jobs," said Carry. She glanced to Fetch. "Is this really going to work? She could be feral."

"She hasn't attacked us yet," said Fetch amiably. "And apart from a slight untidiness of thought, she seems perfectly tame. She'll be easier to understand once we're safely away from here and can explain. Now, Gather." She turned on me, switching smoothly to telepathy as she said, *I need you to do everything I've said, and come so, so quietly. We're getting you out of here. Do you understand?*

I nodded. *Yes.*

Excellent. Let's go.

She opened the door and the three of us proceeded out into the hall, all walking silently and virtually in unison as we moved into the uncertain future.

Nine

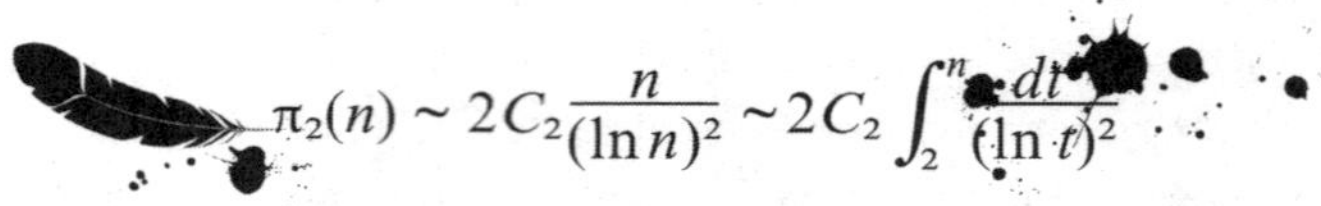

"It's not for us to judge the way that other people decide they want to live their lives. Even if those people are bog-stupid sometimes, it's not our job to judge them."

—**Alice Healy**

Moving through an extra-dimensional civic service building in the company of two near-strangers who need to explain more

HOLDING THE PARTITION FETCH HAD suggested at the front of my mind was difficult at first, because it was so unfamiliar: my name was Gather, I was a civic assistant, and I was here to help. It was tempting to embroider the identity I'd been functionally assigned, to start adding frills and caveats, but in the end, I stuck with the simple skeleton my new maybe-allies had provided.

We moved through the building in a rough wedge formation, with Fetch at the front and me following in synch with Carry behind her. As we walked, we began passing other Johrlac, wearing more of those strange jumpsuits. Which, I suppose, weren't so strange here; if everyone was wearing them, then I was the strange one for finding them odd.

They seemed to divide the people based on their jobs, or maybe by castes—I still wasn't clear what distinguished the concepts. Johrlac in gray and brown seemed to be janitorial: we passed them emptying wastebaskets and scrubbing floors. Both janitors and civic assistants repaired walls, placing pieces of fibrous brown material in their mouths and chewing until it broke down into a thick gray-brown paste, which they then smeared on any cracks or breaks in the paper walls around us. The first time I saw that happen, I managed, barely, to control my urge to gag.

Wasps built nests. Why shouldn't we?

And no one gave us a second look. I had a jumpsuit and a public partition which I pushed forward every time we saw anyone who wasn't a part of our trio, and that seemed to be enough. We passed through a large room filled with desks, each occupied by a Johrlac in a brightly colored jumpsuit, their eyes flashing white as they did whatever job they had been assigned. There was no metal, no plastic. Some things, like the desks, were made of wood, but I didn't see anything I would have considered a computer, or even a typewriter.

There was paper, flat white sheets of it, and people dressed like Fetch and Carry sitting at desks around the edges of the room with pens in their hands, apparently transcribing something. I couldn't see or even conceive of what. As we crossed the room, one of the workers, a man in gray and black, turned to look at us.

"Assistants," he said, the first word I'd heard spoken outside the service closet. Fetch smoothly shifted her trajectory to move toward him, and Carry and I followed. He looked all three of us up and down, his thoughts showing nothing more than a flicker of curiosity. "I require a research packet."

"Yes, assessor," said Fetch.

"I was told there had been two of you assigned to our division," he said, with what might have been a flicker of suspicion.

"There were, assessor," said Fetch. "I am Fetch. It is my responsibility to collect and categorize information and provide it freely to my secondary function, Carry. The two of us were unsuited to the demands of the trial. We needed a third function to smoothly provide all that you required. It is complex, when a matter involves the rights of three species across four dimensions. This is Gather. She serves the function of collating the information that it might be delivered to you more swiftly."

"Are you saying you are unsuited to your purpose?"

"No, assessor. I am saying my purpose involves the swift and accurate location of information, and that purpose is better fulfilled with a collator present."

"Hmm." He looked at me, eyes glazing white, and I felt his probe against the surface of my mind. I froze, suddenly glad I hadn't elaborated upon the simple partition I'd been assigned.

He brushed his mind over mine, and I thought nothing that would betray me, allowed myself no relaxation of thought, only pushed forward what I had been told was safe: my name was Gather, I was a female civic assistant of the service caste, and nothing else mattered in this moment.

He withdrew with a small sound of distaste. "You locate large pieces of information and this one breaks them down into digestible pieces, to be transmitted by your third?"

"Yes, assessor."

"Very efficient. I've been saying for transits that we needed to increase the number of assistants assigned to this division. It sounds like your labor is being fairly distributed. Are you on your way to the archives now?"

"Yes, assessor," said Fetch. I realized she was projecting, when she hadn't been before, radiating helpful willingness to serve like her life depended on it.

Which, for all I knew, it might. I had no idea how this society would react to someone being unable to perform their job—or function, I supposed. If my new friends could be executed for helping me, they were taking an even-greater risk than I'd originally assumed.

"What are you carrying?" He turned his attention abruptly to me. "Your function requires no physical efforts."

I managed, barely, not to jump at the sudden weight of his regard. I had almost forgotten the woven bag that held my clothing. As I stared at him, reaching for something he might believe, I realized what was strangest about this whole encounter: all four of us were members of a telepathic species, and judging by the eyes of the people around me, they weren't shy about using their telepathy here on Johrlar. And despite this, we were speaking aloud, and all speaking the same language somehow. It didn't make sense. Why wouldn't they communicate telepathically? Charlotte and Isaac certainly did, and when I was a child, that had been my primary method of talking to my cousins. Telepathy was easier and more pleasant than speech.

But telepathy also made it difficult to lie. Maybe that was the key: these people wanted to be able to keep their secrets just as much as human bureaucrats did, and fully opening their minds would have rendered that impossible. I centered my partition a bit more solidly, wanting to give him no reason or excuse for pushing past it, and said, in a level tone, "No, assessor. It doesn't."

"Then why . . . ?" From his current position, he could see our eyes. He'd know at once if we started communicating in silence. I needed to come up with a feasible lie based only on the things I already knew.

"I am sometimes called upon to collate and reconcile such large amounts of information that I become distracted. I was in a distracted state while moving from my original assignment to this one, and I dirtied my original uniform. I am taking it to be cleaned."

"We are shortly to embark on our afternoon leisure time, assessor," said Carry politely. "We will deposit Gather's soiled belongings at the sanitary point before acquiring our middle meal, and will return in plenty of time for the remainder of our shift."

"Ah," said the assessor, seeming to lose interest in the mystery of my bag. "Very well, then. Continue."

He turned away from us, back to staring into the distance. As I watched, his eyes frosted white, but I didn't feel his mind brushing against mine. Fetch gestured for me to follow as she resumed walking for the other side of the room. I fell into step behind her, feeling at once more and less secure about our escape. My partition had been enough to hold against a quick inspection from a bored researcher, but would it hold up against anything more intensive? And what the hell were these people doing, anyway?

We continued onward, leaving the room for some sort of wide, open atrium. The ceiling was high and delicately domed, thin glass panels held into a filigree that looked almost like the veining on a wasp's wings. I looked up at it, trying not to gape at the sight of three suns traveling across a blue and yellow sky. I had no idea what the filigree might be made of; I'd seen no metal since arriving here, apart from what I'd carried with me.

More Johrlac moved through the atrium, some talking quietly, others with whited-out eyes. Fetch steered us around the white-eyed ones, creating a clear space between us and the people who were actively using their telepathy. I began to think we might actually get out of here.

Then we approached the doors. They were made of sliding paper panels, at least four of them, so that people passed through one set and into a sort of airlock, then waited for the first set of doors to close before the second could be opened.

They were flanked by Johrlac in blue jumpsuits, like the ones who'd taken me from Mark's hospital room. They might even have been the same Johrlac; without mental contact, I had no way of telling them apart. There were two of them to either side of the first doors, and two more inside the airlock, flanking the second doors.

Fetch glanced over her shoulder, feeling the tension rolling off of me, and reached back to touch my wrist with one hand. *We're almost there,* she thought. *Remain calm and focused, and we'll be out before you have time to hear a cicada's cry.*

I took a deep breath, beginning to loop through the familiar, comforting chain of the Fibonacci sequence, one and one adding up to two, two and one adding up to three, and onward to eternity. We moved closer to the doors, slowly enough that I had plenty of time to see how the process worked. The people would approach, speaking briefly to the Johrlac in blue, who would then look forward, eyes flashing white, before the first doors opened. Meanwhile, the same process—or something similar—was occurring outside, people entering even as others made their exit.

Then we were approaching the doors.

"Business?" asked one of the guards. That felt like the right word. I didn't have a better one under the circumstances.

"Afternoon leisure, officer," said Fetch.

"All at once?"

"We are assigned to the same task within the research division. It is most efficient if we act as a unit even when outside our duties."

"Case?"

The mental static rolling off of Fetch drew tighter, turning somber. "The unauthorized instar detected in the dimensional cluster designated," and then she was off, reciting an algebraic equation long and complicated enough to make my head spin, even as my fingers itched to pin it on a piece of paper and begin ripping it apart.

I recognized part of it from the equation I'd used to get us all back to Earth after our first, unintentional visit to Greg's dimension. She was talking about Earth. She was talking about me.

That wasn't really much of a shock, given the situation, but it was still unsettling to know for sure. I kept my face composed and my posture loose, mirroring Carry as best I could, while the Fibonacci continued to roll, familiar and friendly, through the surface of my thoughts.

"Yes," said the guard, and nodded, eyes flashing white.

Barely able to believe our luck, I watched the first set of doors slide open. The three of us stepped through into the airlock, the guards stationed there watching us impassively. The doors closed behind us. The doors opened in front of us. Fetch started smoothly forward and we followed, exiting the building.

Once we were outside, we paused again, waiting for the doors to close behind us before beginning down the steps. Fetch remained calm, back straight and chin up, and I emulated her, not gawking as I wanted to.

We were on an alien world. We were on the world where my species had evolved. I had never been overly eager to see it for myself—had never even considered that it might be possible—but now that I was here, I wanted to see everything. I wanted to spin in circles and stare at the buildings and streets surrounding me.

I kept walking calmly forward, eyes fixed on the back of Fetch's head.

The building where I'd been held resembled nothing so much as a giant paper wasp nest, the outside soft and irregular, made of gray-brown paper. There were windows, not only in the great atrium, but scattered around the exterior of the building.

It was a common architectural style: about two-thirds of the buildings I could see shared it. None were labeled in any way. The other buildings were roughly split between muddy domes that looked like termite mounds and complicated wooden structures with open sides, allowing the air to pass cleanly through.

And everywhere I looked, there were Johrlac. The streets were stones pressed snugly into the earth; no concrete, no drivable surfaces. I didn't see any vehicles. There were wheels: a few of the people I saw were using wheeled chairs to move, either self-propelled or drawn like little carriages by bright-shelled beetles the size of goats.

You're staring, said Fetch, sounding amused. *Try not to. We need to get you to our hive. Once we're there, you can stare all you like.*

I nodded, not replying in case it somehow stood out. She sent a wave of satisfaction in my direction, and we walked on.

We were almost out of sight of the municipal building when an alarm started to sound, high and droning, like the descent of a thousand wasps. Fetch didn't look back, and so neither did I. All three of us just kept walking on.

✦ ✦ ✦

The air on Johrlar was hot and moist, like the air in Florida. I was used to it from summers at Lowryland, but that didn't mean it was something I dealt with on a daily basis. By the time we turned down a narrow byway lined with tall, broad-leafed trees like banyans, their trunks made up of dozens if not hundreds of accessory roots, I was overly warm and felt faintly nauseous, my morning smoothie consigned to the deep past.

Things I initially assumed were birds flitted through the branches. One of them froze as we passed nearby, and I realized they were heavy-bodied moths with ragged-looking wings, large enough to disturb the leaves the same way songbirds would have.

Neither Fetch nor Carry paid them any mind, and so I struggled to ignore them, dismissing them as commonplace and unremarkable. Gather would have known what they were, would have grown up with them flying outside her window, would no longer take any more notice of them than I did of the pigeons in New York, or the squirrels in Oregon, or the tailypo in Michigan. I just had to keep walking.

We continued for what felt like half a block, then turned and walked deeper into the trees, until a mottled gray-brown structure came into view. It was made of the same papery substance as the larger buildings, resembling nothing so much as a house-sized wasp's nest; it had been constructed around several large bamboo poles and the entirety of one of the multi-trunked trees, with windows winking at us from irregular points around the structure. The color was oddly soothing, and I realized after a moment's thought that it was the same mottled, lightly decaying flesh shade as the house in Michigan.

It looked like home.

Fetch led the way up the path, and as Carry was still maintaining her perfect calm, I followed without asking any questions or betraying any specific interest in the location. The door was once again made of sliding paper panels, but there were no guards here: instead there was a lever, which Fetch pulled. The doors slid open, allowing us into the airlock.

That was the only lock involved: there were no keys or latches I could see. The three of us piled into the airlock space, and Fetch hit a button on the wall, which caused a warm, dry wind to blow briskly through the room. Several small beetles I hadn't noticed before blew off of our clothes and hair, smacking against the far wall. There were sticky-looking flowers planted at the four corners of the room, high up where the walls met the ceiling; one of them extended a quick tendril, snatching a beetle out of the air before it could find a safer place to land.

I blinked. Fetch smiled. "I suppose you wouldn't have cleaner plants where you're from," she said. "They're harmless to anything as big as we are. They keep the bugs out of the house." She held a hand out toward the nearest of the plants, which reached down with a tendril and caressed her fingers before withdrawing, apparently realizing that it couldn't eat her.

Carry pulled another lever, and the interior doors slid open, revealing the house. Fetch motioned for us to follow, heading inside.

The first room of the house, which I assumed was cognate to a living room or parlor back on Earth, was large and high-ceilinged, with several windows scattered around the edges, and some surprisingly soft-looking furniture set in the middle, what looked like a couch and several easy chairs, all well padded and welcoming. There were no decorative pillows or anything like that, just plush fabric in a surprisingly delicate shade of yellow fading into orange. I blinked, and realized it was so delicate because it wasn't fabric at all; it was soft cellulose, pressed into a massive flower petal. The furniture was actually furled flowers.

Looking at the room from that perspective, I could see how all the furnishings had grown up out of the floor or from the walls; the shelves were some sort of hard fungus, the chairs were closed flowers, the table was probably some kind of toadstool. There wasn't much in the way of what I would have called ornamentation: no pictures on the walls or books on the shelves.

"You can put your bag down," said Fetch magnanimously.

I dropped the bag on the nearest couch. "Explanation time now."

"You did very well back there," said Carry. "If I hadn't known better, I would have sworn you were domesticated."

"I would like to know what's happening, please," I said. "I don't think I'm being unreasonable by asking."

"We did say we'd explain," said Fetch, with a heavy sigh. "First off, you should know we've been hoping for something like this to happen for quite some time, and you can speak freely here. We've been encouraging the growth of a sort of fungus in our walls. It puts out hyphae and forms a mycelial mat that surrounds the hive and makes it difficult for anyone to casually read the people inside."

"Best of all, it's normally occurring in this region," said Carry. "People are constantly having to call in the mycologists to have their property treated, but the treatment is expensive and we're young people just starting our careers in earnest; no one's going to question us allowing it to fester for a little while longer. We've encouraged the growth three times and had it removed twice, but it just keeps coming back, and people have started to suspect this whole grove may be infected. It keeps them from building nearby, and it allows us to maintain our privacy."

"You'll be as safe here as you can be anywhere," concluded Fetch.

"Where is here?" I asked. "I mean, I'm assuming Johrlar, based on everything I've seen so far, but I can't be certain, because no one's been telling me anything."

"This is Johrlar," said Fetch. "More specifically, this is the territory of Neyvar, and the capital city of Ka'krin. I could give you our address, but I doubt it would mean anything."

I didn't say anything, just blinked at her. I had never considered that Johrlar would be more than just a single undefined location, but it made sense. Earth was huge. It had continents and countries and cities. It wasn't just one place, undistinguished and unvaried.

"Was there something you specifically wanted to know about Johrlar?" asked Fetch. "Because we could show you, or at least tell you. We were both born and went through creche here in Ka'krin, so we don't have firsthand accounts of other cities, but I'm sure we could find them if you wanted more information—"

"The only information I want is why I'm in Johrlar to begin with," I exclaimed. "I didn't come here voluntarily."

"Well no, you wouldn't have," said Carry, sounding baffled. "No cuckoo ever does."

"Let's start there: you know what a cuckoo is. You called me a queen. The people who took me said I had reached 'the forbidden instar.' What does that mean? How can an instar be forbidden? The way it was explained to me, instars are a natural part of our life cycle. We don't have a lot of control over them, or how they progress. They just sort of happen, and we go along for the ride."

Fetch and Carry exchanged a look. "You ask for information beyond our caste," said Fetch politely, turning back to me. "Would you be willing to speak to another to know what you require?"

"I'm not going off to see the Wizard or anything here, but if you have someone who can tell me what the hell is going on, I'd be more than happy to hear it," I said sourly.

Fetch and Carry exchanged another look, this one more complicated, their eyes flashing white as they "spoke" to one another. Carry broke off, heading for the sliding doors to the outside, and pulled the lever, leaving me alone with Fetch.

"She will return," said Fetch. "We anticipated your questions might be foundational in nature, and so we have a third who has agreed to speak with you on the matter. Carry is notifying Annalist, who will hopefully be able to join us shortly. If you're willing to restrict yourself to questions of smaller scope, I can do what I can to answer them, but if you would prefer to go in order, I can also provide you with something to eat and a place to rest until such time as aid is available."

"Okay—why did you break me out of there? And why did you have to? What were those people going to do to me?"

"We broke you out because we need your assistance, and as to why we had to, you would never have been allowed to leave of your own volition. A cuckoo queen is too dangerous to be allowed among the general population, and your comfort wouldn't justify the risk. They were going to make you stand trial for your many crimes, and after you had inevitably been found guilty, they were going to punish and neutralize you."

"Why do I have the feeling I wouldn't enjoy this neutralization process?"

"Because it would be extremely painful? There is no reversing an instar. Once complete, they are forever. Your neutralization could not be achieved through a simple resetting of the self. You would have to be removed entirely."

"So they were going to kill me because of crimes they decided I'd committed?"

"Yes. In mind, if not in flesh."

"If they care so much about cuckoo crimes, why aren't they spending more time arresting cuckoos for murder and genocide and all the other bullshit they get up to? The worst thing I ever did was skip out on the check for my morning coffee!"

Fetch radiated polite bemusement. "I don't know what a check or a morning coffee are, but I assume they must be small infractions, like tardiness or carelessness with an assigned job. I am sorry you believe yourself to be law-abiding. This must be so much more painful when you've made an effort to live an unblemished life."

"Question stands. If the people here on Johrlar think they get to hold us to their legal standards after they exiled our ancestors, why are they not popping in and grabbing cuckoos every single day? Cuckoos killed my adoptive parents in order to kick off my development the way they wanted it to proceed. That's murder."

"Ah," said Fetch. "A simple question: the judiciary does not interfere with cuckoo affairs when they do not break our laws."

I looked at her flatly. "Meaning what? Murder is okay here?"

"Murder is only wrong when it involves killing actual people."

I couldn't think of a single thing to say to that, and so I just stared at her, radiating shock and disappointment in her direction. She shrugged.

"I cannot change the entire cultural development of our species, Sarah, or I would have long since done so for other reasons. The individuals you live among may mimic intelligence, may present themselves as if they were worthy of your attention, but they are little better than the beasts of the field and forest. They are not truly sapient, nor can be without full connection. When cuckoos kill them, it is like children smashing companion creatures out of malicious curiosity. It would be better if they didn't, but the crime that has been committed is destruction of property at most, not *murder*. 'Murder' is the word used when Johrlac kill Johrlac, or when cuckoos kill cuckoos. Murder outside of judiciary limits is forbidden, and will be punished accordingly."

I took a deep breath. "All right. So these people, these Johrlac authorities, came to take me because I had committed crimes in their eyes—crimes bad enough to be worth punishing. Would it have done me any good to fight against them?"

"Only if you wished to enable the destruction of more of these almost-people you seem attached to."

I frowned at Fetch. She looked politely back, not seeming to understand why she'd said anything wrong. I'd never realized how much I'd picked up the habit of emoting from the people I lived with; I'd been told dozens of times that if someone was wearing a telepathy blocker, I could come off as robotic, so flat of voice and affect that I seemed disengaged. Now that I was facing a Johrlac raised among and by her own species, I could not only understand but see how incredibly over-animated I was in comparison. She pushed emotions at me, but her face rarely moved to match them, never transmitted "smile" to match the feelings she was so fiercely having.

It was strange, and unsettling in the extreme.

"So I couldn't fight back without making things worse," I concluded. "Are they really planning to kill me? Isn't that murder?"

"Murder is allowable for the judiciary when acting for the good of the collective," said Fetch. "They will be killing you and thus removing a threat. A cuckoo queen is one of the great monsters of our kind, too feared and abhorred to be allowed to stand."

"Why?"

"Because the cuckoos have been cast outside the collective, and they act for themselves, not for us." Fetch pushed earnestness and sincerity at me. "They are individual. To be individual is to be uncontrolled, and the uncontrolled is dangerous."

"So shouldn't all cuckoos be considered a threat?"

"No." She seemed genuinely surprised by the question—so surprised that I was momentarily taken aback, sure that I must have missed something. "A cuckoo is a small thing, easily swept aside. We encounter them rarely. They can't travel on their own, can't reset the self, can't do anything of meaning. They are inconsequential. And they were made to be incapable of queening."

"Excuse me?"

"The process of reaching a fully mature instar requires community support and the aid of the collective. Cuckoos have neither of these things. They should be unable to achieve a queen instar."

For a moment, I couldn't speak. I could only stare, overcome by how much even the people responsible for the cuckoos didn't know about them. Finally, I caught my breath, and said, "I don't know who told you that, but that's not correct. Cuckoos are fully capable of reaching the queen stage. It's how they move between dimensions."

"What do you mean?"

"When they've exhausted a world—when they've eaten, spoiled, and destroyed as much of it as they possibly can, and yearn for new challenges—they force a queen to mature. And then they pump her head so full of math that she loses track of who she is. She falls into a white void of swirling infinity, so packed with arithmantic equations that she's coming apart around the edges, that she'll do *anything* to make the maelstrom stop. While they have her there, pinned like a butterfly under glass, they tell her it's easy. They tell her the math can be resolved, and all she has to do is finish the equation. But what they don't tell her is that if she does, she'll blow a hole in the side of the dimension she's currently in, a hole so big that it blows all the cuckoos right through and into a whole new world they can eat for breakfast."

"But . . . no one could survive that. It would harm the queen," said Fetch, sounding horrified. Oh, good. They could show animation.

"The queen's not supposed to survive it." I looked at her levelly. "Finishing the equation will make the storm stop, absolutely. It just wipes away the queen as it's dying. She's not supposed to survive. The cuckoos prime their queens like bombs and use them as escape hatches."

"That's terrible! They shouldn't have been able to do that!"

I would have been so much happier if they couldn't. If I'd just been allowed to go on as I had been, living and limited and so in love with Artie that sometimes I couldn't see straight. Not perfect, not by a long shot, but . . . happy. I'd been happy, and I hadn't been happy like that since they'd forced me through my final instar. The closest I could come was going to the middle of nowhere with Greg and letting the simplicity of his thoughts soothe me. And that couldn't last. That could never last.

"They did it anyway."

"They can't . . ." said Fetch, sounding increasingly frantic. "They can't have knowingly acted to *harm* a *queen*. It's against everything we are! I could *never*."

From the way she said it, she meant that literally. She sounded like even trying to harm a queen would destroy her.

She shook her head, hard, like she was trying to shake away something sticky and foul. "It's not possible, they can't— You're here." She sounded momentarily triumphant. "If the process of maturing destroyed the queen's mind, you wouldn't be able to be here."

"I was able to create a distributed processing system to absorb the brunt of the equation before it could consume me. It still took pieces of my memory, but not as many as it could have without the extra processing power. It wiped out the minds of the people I used to process the numbers, but I lived. What does it say about your judiciary system that my crime wasn't being forced into an instar I never wanted, but surviving the process?"

Fetch sagged. "It says the cuckoos are monsters, if they can harm a queen so. But more, it says we were wrong. I knew this already—how can a natural stage of existence be incorrect?—but I thought there might be some nuance to the situation that I was missing. I'm only an assistant, after all. I lack the intelligence to fully understand the law."

"Okay, hang on," I said. "How does getting a job work here?"

"There is always a list of positions which will need to be filled in sixteen to nineteen seasonal cycles," said Fetch. "The administration maintains it, and sends the breeding assignments to the nurseries. Members of the appropriate professions are offered the opportunity to reproduce, and upon the production of healthy young, those offspring are given jobs and names appropriate to their purpose. Then we just have to wait for the memories to mature. Is that not how work is assigned in your culture, Sarah? What does a Sarah do, anyway? I do not recognize the title."

Oh, for the love of . . . "Sarah isn't a title or a position, it's my name," I said. "It was given to me by the humans I was originally left with." I didn't remember much about the McNallys—youth and trauma will have that effect on the mind—but I remembered that they'd loved me very much, and they'd died never knowing I wasn't really their daughter.

"I don't understand."

"I don't have a job right now. When you ask 'What does a Sarah do?' the answer is something like 'Math, and spending time with my family—I have a little brother, his name is Isaac, and he needs cuckoo role models to look up to so he doesn't grow up to be a total asshole like most members of our species—and taking walks with my pet spider.' I'm not required to do any one thing just because someone thought we were going to need the position filled before I was born."

"That sounds . . . scary," said Fetch. "I've never tried to live without knowing exactly what was going to happen next. But it also sounds kind of wonderful and very exciting."

The doors opened, and Carry stepped through, followed by an older male Johrlac in a blue-and-gray jumpsuit. I frowned. The jumpsuits meant something, that much was obvious, but this was the fourth design I'd seen incorporating the shade of gray that had corresponded to red when I'd been able to view it through human senses, and that seemed irrational. Johrlac can't see red. They had no reason to be designing around it.

"What do the jumpsuits mean?" I blurted.

The man paused, radiating confusion. Clarity broke through, and he straightened. "You mean our uniforms."

"Er, yes."

"They have developed a fascinating means of saying hello in your hive," he said. "It is considered impolite in most professional capacities to look beyond the partition of the people with whom you interact, and many do not have a range of more than two body-lengths. The uniforms allow us to distinguish one another during working hours, that we address others properly and according to our need."

I blinked, very slowly, before turning back to Fetch. "I'm sorry. I know I'm at a cultural disadvantage here, and I think I must be misunderstanding. Did he just say that you all wear uniforms so you can *tell each other apart*?"

"One civic assistant is exactly the same as any other," said Fetch, reaching almost frantically for Carry. "Why does it matter if they address me, or Carry, or Collate?"

"I— Because— I—I don't even know how to begin answering that sentence," I said. "Do you ever *not* wear uniforms?"

"When we are outside of working hours, we may dress as we prefer," said the man. "I assume you are the cuckoo queen?"

"You must be pretty sure of that assumption, since I'm starting to think the people who run this place will kill you dead if they find out you've been talking to me," I replied. "My name is Sarah."

Carry had reached Fetch. The two tumbled into one another, Fetch clinging like she was afraid the sky might fall, Carry stroking her hair to soothe her. There was nothing sexual about it. They were like puppies, seeking comfort in the familiar. My talk of harming queens had unsettled Fetch more than I'd realized.

"Sarah," said the man, rolling the syllables of my name in his mouth like they were the most fascinating thing he'd ever heard. "I am Annalist."

"Analyst?" I asked.

"Annalist," he said, stressing the word slightly to make it clear that we were not saying the same thing. "I gather and remember history. It is what I was made for."

"All history?" I asked, feeling suddenly, strangely fragile. I was on a world I should have known as well as I knew the family compound in Portland. I should have known the bird-sized moths and the cleaner plants, the uniforms and the social structure, and I didn't know any of it. It had all been taken from me by the people who'd decided to exile my ancestors, and while I couldn't say I was sorry to have grown up the way I had—I loved my family, my friends, my life, and my world—I still resented the fact that the choice had never been mine to make.

"I approached Fetch and Carry after my records were accessed," he said. "The judiciary came to me to request information regarding cuckoos. How you can be intercepted, how you can be restrained. If you have ever produced a queen."

"What did you tell them?"

"Everything."

Ten

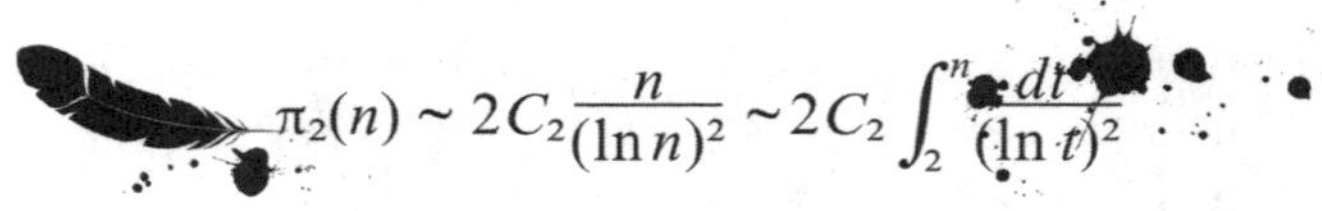

"History wasn't always history. Once upon a time it was just people making mistakes, the same as they are today. Don't give it too much power over you."

—**Mary Dunlavy**

In the home of Fetch and Carry, talking to a historian

I stared at Annalist. He turned his face away.

"It is my great shame that my lineage was involved with the original exile of the cuckoos. As their descendant, I am among those tasked with remembering the great betrayal, and what we did to our own people—for the cuckoos were our people in those days. We were all one hive, and my lineage was part of its destruction."

This is why we listened when he approached us, said Fetch, and I realized with a start that she was speaking inside my head. I'd grown so accustomed to this world of telepaths communicating out loud that I'd almost forgotten she could do that. I flashed her a sidelong glance. She had positioned herself behind him; he couldn't see her white-out eyes. *He knew what he spoke of. He knew what would be done to you, because he knew what* had *been done to your people. And he knew what you could do for us.*

I tried to focus on Annalist. He was radiating guilt and regret so loudly, it was a ringing in my ears, in the deep space that has nothing to do with actual sound.

"It's nice to meet you, Annalist," I said. "What can you tell me about cuckoos?"

"Nothing, unless I first explain the collective. Carry, how much time do you have remaining on your afternoon leisure?"

"Not long, Annalist," she replied. "Fetch and I will be required to return to our duties shortly. Sarah will remain here. It isn't safe for her to return with us, and we cannot risk the safety of a queen."

Fetch flinched at the very thought, looking momentarily sick to her stomach.

I wanted to object to the idea of being left behind, alone in an unfamiliar world, but I couldn't find a good reason. She was right that I'd be safer here, behind closed doors and walls laced with anti-telepathy fungus. I was still trying to adjust to the idea that I'd been arrested because of things I'd done in self-defense or without truly understanding the possible consequences of my actions. It didn't seem right.

Annalist nodded. "Very well." He returned his attention to me. "Do you know what you are?"

"Um. Sarah? A cuckoo? Biologically speaking, a giant telepathic wasp that's decided to masquerade as a mammal for reasons I presume are connected to the evolutionary pressures of Johrlar? Increasingly annoyed with this whole situation?" I was channeling my cousin Annie a bit by the end, my frustration beginning to overwhelm my customary calm.

"That is a sufficient starting place," said Annalist. "We are the Johrlac, however much we may seek to divide ourselves internally. We were born to the lush green places of this world, and we grew there, peaceful, for a time. In the beginning, all were of one hive, until our cousins, the Apraxis, realized they had no need to find or gather their own histories: they could plant their larvae in the bodies of our workers and wait. When the larvae matured, the Apraxis would know all that the worker had known, and would be enriched, while we were lessened."

"Wait," I said. "Are you saying *Apraxis wasps* come from Johrlar too?"

"Yes," said Annalist, with a flicker of annoyance at the interruption. "You know of them?"

"They're a problem on Earth. We kill them when we find them, but it only takes one to start a new hive, and they don't have any natural predators."

"Ah," said Annalist. "I suppose that is to be expected."

"Excuse me?"

"The Apraxis stalked and preyed upon us, year on year, until we could no longer tolerate the pressure. Our hives began to change in response to the danger. Our advantage over the Apraxis was our unity, which could protect even the farthest-ranging scouts. Unity was born from the strength of our minds, which grew beyond theirs, and so we bred for smarter children, greater unity, larger minds. Our forms began to change."

I nodded slowly. Evolution in response to predatory pressures wasn't unheard-of, even on Earth. I still didn't understand how we'd ended up looking so damn mammalian, but there might not *be* an explanation for that, depending on when in our history it had happened; sometimes evolution just does what seems funny at the time, and the survivors get to cope with the consequences.

"We grew larger. Our wings were lost, and we became as the crawling creatures of the forest, but it mattered not, for we found that the eldest among us could move things with a thought. Those that had completed the process of maturation were able to reorder the world from inside the hives, and it became clear that power should be seated in their mandibles. We began to take shelter in the colony homes of the wood-chewing ants which dwell below the loam. Their colony minds were large and slow and decentralized, and they were willing to tolerate us for our contributions. We grew fleshy as our exoskeletons sank below the surface of our bodies, increasing our flexibility and our ability to be of use to our hosts."

"So . . . we started as wasps, and then became naked ant mimics so we could practice being better telepaths?"

Annalist nodded. "The first true collective formed below the ground, as we were given time to bring more and more of our number through the full cycle of instars to maturity. The first great queens compiled the unwritten equation, and on a single night of brilliance and beauty we rose from the earth and opened a rift between worlds, pushing the hated Apraxis into the void. Upon rising, we found we could no longer bear the confinement of the soil, and we returned to our trees, building nests and forming hives, still cradled within the collective."

"Ah." So this was a creation myth draped in the trappings of history: what he was describing would have taken centuries at the absolute least, generation after generation of proto-Johrlac dying in the dark underground as they fought to force their own evolution. It wouldn't have happened in a single generation just because they had sufficient queens. But that was the flaw in what seemed to be a purely oral tradition of information-keeping: not enough space for all the details.

No one knew better than I did how limited the space really was inside a mind. Even if you went ahead and deleted all the unnecessary memories and personality traits of the person providing the storage, you'd run out of room before you could encompass an entire history. So why not simplify, leave out the bits that didn't change anything, and ignore the fact that simplification will always omit something that someone believes mattered, once upon a time? I didn't say any of that, only thought of collapsing functions and mathematical shortcuts and nodded, pushing understanding toward Annalist.

"The first collective endured long enough to begin the building of our civilization," said Annalist. "We found other hives of Apraxis; we exiled them as we had the first, cleansing them colony after colony from the world as we wished it should be. We found other groups of Johrlac, and we absorbed them, as we were further along in our collective than they were. One of them, dominating the continent to the east, had almost as large and advanced a collective as our own. They fought back, but our collective was the stronger, and they were absorbed. We did not, at the time, understand what it would mean to allow a second collective to fester within the first, and so we did not break it down as we should have."

"What is a 'collective'?" I asked. I was already fairly sure I knew, but I wanted to be certain, and I wanted him to say it.

"A collective is the unity formed by the joining of mature minds that guides a community's progress and progression," he said, with no trace of distress. "A collective encompasses all its parts, and guides them as necessary."

"A hive mind. You're describing a hive mind. But you're all individuals. You seem to have personalities beyond what the hive would assign to you. How is that possible?"

"Individual workers are partitioned to preserve a measure of autonomy, since without it, we become less efficient," said Annalist. "The queens cannot conduct the sweeping of every floor and the collection of every scrap of information. It would be too much. It must be decentralized in order to remain efficient. If the collective wishes, it can shut down that autonomy and reclaim it at once. That is why we must work swiftly and in secret, because if the collective realizes we plot against its wholeness, it will remove our ability to act. We will become of the one, and will no longer desire as we currently desire."

"All right, let me see if I'm following this correctly: the collective is a hive mind, and you all belong to the hive mind, but it lets you have your own lives so that it doesn't have to do all the work. Only if it figures out that you're using those lives to do things it won't like, it might smash you flat?"

"In the most primitive of terms, yes. The collective could know everything we know, if it only cared to look into us and learn. We must remain beyond suspicion."

"You said you let a second collective fester. What does that mean?"

"It means we killed all their known queens, which should have dissolved their collective, but they had managed to hide a few of their younger queens within the masses of their population, and so their collective endured. It was weak and fragile, and still it connected them. It kept them from accepting our collective as their own, from assimilating as they were intended to into the greater good of the Johrlac. Their incubators dreamt unapproved dreams. They filled their young with ambition and ideals that were not our own. Those young grew to disrupt systems, to demand independent thought, to attempt to change their stations after they had been born to them. They were . . . inappropriate. They were dangerous. And they were like an infection in the hives that sheltered them, tainting everything they touched."

Annalist paused, looking at me. "I hope you can be like your ancestors," he said, inexplicably. "Again and again, we routed their queens, and each time we did, they would simply prepare the next, for some of them had retained the memory of the process, and continued passing it along the generations. Hives collapsed. Innocents died. And still their collective endured, until all the historians and annalists were called together to give our advice. My ancestor was among that number. His suggestion was deemed the best."

"He said you should banish them."

"Yes, but not only that. He said when we had battled the Apraxis, they had been ejected from this world as a danger to the Johrlac, but it had worked only because they had been unable to return. So he suggested we excise each member of the second collective and open their minds for analysis. Once this had been done, the queens would examine them for the knowledge of how to cause a queen, the equations that allowed for manipulation of dimensional barriers, and the instinct toward collective, and they would remove those things where they were found. After the members of the second collective had been successfully edited to eliminate the danger they might present, they could be pushed through the rifts we had opened for the Apraxis, and we need never concern ourselves with them again."

"Our afternoon leisure is concluded," said Carry abruptly. "Annalist, will you remain here with our guest?"

"I have concluded my labors for this period," said Annalist. "I must finish my accounting, and will then discuss what is to be done from here with the Sarah. Please, return to work."

"There is food in the kitchen," said Fetch. "We will return when our shift is ended."

I wanted to ask them if they would get questioned about my absence—or rather, Gather's absence, since they'd claimed to need "her" in order to complete their current assignment. But they understood this system and I didn't, and I needed what Annalist was currently willing to tell me.

Inwardly, I was seething. Cuckoos were almost defined by their sociopathic lack of concern in the well-being of anyone else, even other cuckoos. The only thing that seemed to overwhelm that disconnection was parenthood, and that for only as much time as it took to get the baby to a suitable host parent. They just didn't care about anyone but themselves. Since cuckoo children were loving and compassionate and as empathic as any other intelligent child I'd ever met, we'd all been assuming they inherited their misanthropy from the ancestral memories they received during gestation. I'd always wondered how an entire intelligent species could evolve like that, and what advantage it could possibly have conferred back on Johrlar.

Now I knew. It hadn't evolved at all. Their ancestors had been psychically edited to resist the call to community, and then they'd passed that revision along to their own children. Punishment as pathogen, turning political prisoners into monsters.

Fetch and Carry turned, heading for the doors. They didn't look back or say goodbye. They apparently didn't feel the need.

Annalist was back to watching me, earnestly pushing hope in my direction. "Do you understand?" he asked.

"I understand that you took political prisoners, edited their minds to make it impossible for them to settle peacefully somewhere else, and threw them through the wall of the world into a place you'd been filling with killer wasps since the moment you'd figured out the math that would allow it to happen," I said. "Anyone would have turned a little sour after that."

"We had no idea they had been left with sufficient fragments of information to rebuild the transit equations until they had already done it, and were loosed upon the universes," said Annalist, voice turning subdued. "We believed that, without the urge to collective, they would be unable to raise their own children; they would have no creche keepers or workers suited to childcare. We didn't anticipate the number of realities which contained intelligences close enough to our own to nurture the young up until their first instar."

Well, that explained why everything I'd discussed with Alice said that cuckoos were mostly an issue for dimensions with a reasonable mammal population: they needed people who could understand the care needs of their babies well enough to keep them alive. That realization was small in the face of the new layer of horror Annalist had just added to what he'd already lain down:

"You were *hoping* their babies would all die?"

He radiated discomfort. "Less hoping, more . . . certain. There was no way to remove the urge for collective without also truncating the parental urge that would have allowed them to nurture their young."

"Well, I guess your little editing project didn't work as well as you hoped it was going to," I snapped.

"I feel you are angry with me," said Annalist.

"Because I *am*," I said. "I know you personally didn't have anything to do with this, even if you want to keep talking like you did—it happened centuries ago, probably millennia at this point, and the math doesn't work if I try to assign you blame directly—but you keep using the first person like one of your ancestors being involved means that you're directly culpable."

"Because I am," he said, earnestly. "I hold the memories of my ancestors and my collective, and they made this decision on their own, freely and with all the information they had available at the time. There is nothing they did that I would have done differently had I been put into their position."

All right. This wasn't going to get us anywhere. I took a deep breath. "You said you hoped I could be like my ancestors," I said. "What did you mean by that?"

"Before they were edited into cuckoos, your ancestors destabilized the collective by their presence. They caused ordinary people to question whether they could hope for something more than the position they had been born to fill. They made people *want*. You are a cuckoo queen who has survived the barrier that was meant to prevent your kind from ever arising again. If we can keep you alive long enough for the collective to be forced to face your existence, you may cause unrest, and that could be enough to set us free."

I blinked, very slowly. "Oh," I said. "So that's why you went to Fetch and Carry. Because you thought I might be useful."

"Because I am a proper Johrlac, who serves the queens, and I wanted to *save* you," he said, earnestly. "My ancestors condemned yours. I am ready to atone for what they've done, and to welcome you home to what should always have been your own."

My stomach clenched uncomfortably. I rubbed it with one hand. "Speaking of welcoming me home, Fetch mentioned food?"

"Yes," he said, with some relief. "We will eat."

✦ ✦ ✦

The kitchen was the first thing I'd seen that really made me believe these people had any form of advanced technology rather than depending on plants and fungus to provide all of their creature comforts. The room looked almost familiar. There was a sink, complete with running water, and a cold box that was clearly plugged into the wall. When I opened it, a light came on. It contained several bamboo tubes full of various liquids, and plates of cooked meats under a light film that looked like a thinner version of the substance that made up the walls.

"What do you like?" asked Annalist, opening the box and poking at its contents.

"I have no idea," I said. "I've never eaten anything from this dimension, and I doubt you'll have anything I'd recognize from Earth. Hit me with whatever's easy."

"Very well," he said, and began pulling things out of the cold box, piling them on the counter. "I appreciate how reasonable you're being about this entire situation."

"Come again?"

"You *are* a cuckoo. I had expected substantially more resistance when you were told that we wanted you to help us."

"Fetch and Carry got me out of custody. I can't imagine the people who snatched me from my home were planning anything good for me."

He began mixing things into a bowl, making a sort of salad. "You were to be held in the dampening chamber until they had finished gathering the evidence against you. Our law requires you be given a trial. It doesn't require that you be allowed any defense, or that you be permitted to open your mind to display memories which might prejudice the viewing gallery against the judiciary."

"So a show trial, in other words."

"Yes. The punishment for the crime of being a cuckoo queen is death. It has never arisen before, but it was set many generations ago, to be prepared for precisely this situation. By setting the punishment long before the commission of the crime, we can avoid the appearance of bias."

"I thought you couldn't harm a queen."

"I can't. Fetch and Carry can't. If we were to try, our minds would turn against our bodies, and the resulting conflict could be fatal. The other queens are not so limited."

I opened my mouth, then paused, huffing out the air through pursed lips. "So you can't kill me, but the people who should understand where I'm coming from can?"

"Yes," he replied, calmly. "You are a threat to their power. No queen can be uncontrolled. They needed to retain the power to destroy what threatens the collective. No one is saying *you* are a particularly terrible queen, only that all cuckoo queens are forbidden. The punishment for murder, which you are also charged with, on a scale which is frankly impressive, is revision. Either punishment could be applied to you."

"What is revision, exactly?"

He poured one of the liquids onto the bowl of greens, chunked vegetation, and meat he had been preparing, then carried it over and set it on the counter in front of me, along with a small three-tined fork made of polished wood. "You should be aware, as you have performed the process."

I blinked. "I have done no such thing."

"But you have. Our researchers have been traveling along your path. They found evidence of your having removed foundation memories from your allies on Pteracercus, of revising the reality experienced by a native of the same world, and of fully erasing and rebuilding the individual you refer to as 'Arthur Price.'"

I bristled, food forgotten as I glared at him. "Don't say Artie's name. This doesn't involve him."

"Oh, but it does. He is evidence of what you've done—perhaps the best evidence we could ask for. He will be a key part in your trial."

"What?"

"If you cannot be found before the trial arrives, I believe they may try him in your stead."

"They can't—they can't *do* that! He's not even here!"

Annalist looked at me, radiating bemusement. "Oh, but he is. He was collected shortly after you were. He'll stand trial, one way or another."

Eleven

ANTIMONY

"Oh, Kevin, look at her. She's beautiful. And I can already tell she's going to be so much wonderful trouble."

—**Evelyn Baker**

Crashing through the forest on a dimension populated by asshole telepaths and weird luck-benders. So, you know, business as usual.

We ran through the jungle, and the jungle did not do a damn thing to make this easier. It wasn't like fleeing in a fantasy novel, where the trees will conveniently get out of your way and the only puddles will be plot-relevant. The ground was a mixture of slippery leaf litter and unexpected, sucking mud; insects moved through both, some of them large enough to be truly unnerving.

"Have these people never even heard of the square-cube law?" demanded Sam, wrapping his tail around my waist and jerking me out of the path of an eight-foot centipede with razored mandibles that snapped shut on the spot where I'd been running only seconds before.

"I think they rescinded it," I snapped, sweeping dangling vines aside with hard swipes of my hands, which were superheated to the point where even *I* could feel the convection. It baked off my skin, turning the air wavery, and when I touched the vines, they charred and blackened. So did the hanging bristle worms that had been hiding among them. Big difference: the worms were large enough to scream as they died, thin, whistling shrieks that sounded like teakettles, if teakettles could feel pain.

Thomas was five or so feet ahead of Sam and me, throwing literal fistfuls of fire at anything that moved. Neither of us was being particularly careful about the risk of burning the forest down. Honestly, while ecological destruction is never a good thing, I was less concerned about starting an inferno than I was about being caught by the people we could hear pursuing us into the green.

Then one of them screamed, high and agonized, and the yelling changed qualities, going from the loud, boastful shouts of people who were certain they were going to win to the terrified shrieks of people who had just been reminded that some things were larger than they were. I looked down at the muddy ground as I ran, reminded of how many things that live in mud and hunt when disturbed can be slow to rouse. We were setting off every trap this forest had to offer, and as long as we didn't slow down, we might be able to stay ahead of them.

Then something started crashing through the trees ahead of us, and I realized maybe speed alone wasn't going to be enough to save us.

Thomas seemed to have realized the same. When he hit the next patch of fully solid ground he stopped, hands raised and wreathed in flame. Sam and I pulled up next to him, Sam unwinding his tail and leaping into the nearest tree, where he crouched and prepared to leap for whatever came to attack us. I balled my own hands into fists and lit them, my flames forming a smaller corona but burning much hotter, almost white compared to Thomas's red. I wanted to hurt fast and hard and end this, whatever it was.

Something flashed through the greenery ahead of us, scything off trees and branches as smoothly as a swung axe, and with far less resistance. A creature that looked like a mantis shrimp, if mantis shrimp came in size super ultra mega large, flowed through the gap this had created, antennae waving.

That wasn't the only thing waving. Alice, straddling the thing's carapace just behind its raptorial appendages, was beaming and waving vigorously. She had a firm grip on one of its antennae, and looked remarkably uninjured for a woman who was riding a giant predator.

"Hey, everybody," she called. "You ready to go?"

✦ ✦ ✦

Looking affectionately resigned, Thomas shook his hands, extinguishing the flames around them. "What took you so long, dear?" he called.

"I had to find a domesticated troupe, and then convince the dominant male that I didn't represent a threat. Good thing stromopods are a pretty common draft animal in this dimensional cluster. I know how to talk to them. I was only able to convince three to come away with me, though, so somebody's gonna have to double up."

I lowered my own hands, flames going out. "Yes. Riding double is absolutely the issue, and not the part where we're being asked to ride giant mantis shrimp."

"Stromopods, please," said Alice. "Mantis shrimp are smaller, and found in Earth's oceans. These nice fellows are closer to lungfish in a lot of ways; they have gills *and* functional lungs, so they do just fine both above and below water. They don't need to submerge more than once every few days. They can still punch like a cannonball, if you're worried about predators."

"I was worried less about predators than I was about the giant-ass stromopods, but good to know," I said. The creature she was sitting atop was definitely fascinating, with an exoskeleton that clearly said it was close to if not at the head of the local food system. Nothing with plentiful predators could go around with a shell that looked that much like clown vomit. The stromopod was streaked in at least a dozen shades of brilliant neon, all of them blending into one another like it thought it was establishing camouflage.

"Annie please let me ride the giant murder shrimp with you," said Sam, words quick and staccato. I turned to blink at him. He was staring at the stromopod, the fur on his head and cheeks puffed out in the start of a threat display.

"Afraid I'm going to get eaten?" I asked.

"Nope," he said. "Afraid *I* am."

Thomas chuckled, walking toward Alice and her mount. She tugged on the stromopod's antennae, turning it slightly to the side so he wasn't walking directly toward those striking claws. She smiled as she did it, making it clear that she wasn't worried.

"I miss anything?" she asked.

"We found some distant relations of yours, who were apparently imported by the Johrlac at some point to serve in a domestic capacity," said Thomas.

"And how did that work out for them?"

"You mean how did abducting a group of people who can actively manipulate coincidence to turn events to a desired outcome work out? Well, the Kairos we met are living in the deep woods, and seem to have established a fairly permanent settlement there, although it's unclear how much contact they have with the local Johrlac. The representative we spoke to indicated that their presence might explain the Kairos on Earth, and why they'd have such a small population and such a scant presence in the official records."

"Extradimensional imports don't usually have a lot of breeding stock," Alice agreed. She tugged on her stromopod again, turning it fully away from us. "Come on. We need to get on following Sarah, assuming she's someplace near here."

"What do you mean, 'assuming'?" asked Sam. "She's on Johrlar, we're on Johrlar. She has to be near here."

Alice looked over her shoulder at him, an expression on her face that I could only really describe as "oh isn't that adorable." "Sam, how big do you think this world is?"

"I don't know. The size of a League of Legends map, I guess? I never really thought much about how big other dimensions would be. I've never been able to visit one before."

"The key is in the name," said Thomas. "'Dimension.' Our dimension isn't called 'Earth,' Earth is just the world we're from. A world that's in a dimension, one that contains lots of other things, like our entire solar system."

Sam's face fell. "Are you saying we might not even be on the right *planet* right now?"

"No, the transit keys we have are for Johrlar-the-planet, and they'll have brought us to the right world. But Sarah could be hundreds of miles from here. Annie? You're the most attuned to her. Do you hear the static?"

"I'm wearing an anti-telepathy charm," I reminded him. "I can't hear the static right now."

"Maybe we need you to," said Thomas. He paused, looking thoughtful. "We're all protected from telepathy right now. Why did the mind-mind flowers work on us?"

"The what?" asked Alice.

"The universal-translator foliage the Kairos were using," said Thomas. "Given that they claimed the flowers rendered infants capable of speech, I'm not sure they know any actual language any longer. They're just relying on translation of intent, rather than intentional vocalizations."

"Huh," she said. "Fascinating. I've seen similar in the Johrlac cities, but the Johrlac *do* have a language, which they speak readily. I suppose they keep the flowers around for visitors. And I have absolutely no idea why they work. That's a question for the family scholars. I am not among them."

"You're smarter than you act," said Thomas, and she laughed.

"Visitors?" I asked. "Who would *want* to visit this place?"

Alice shrugged. Her stromopod was moving faster than we could, and she kept having to pull it to a stop so we could catch up. "Johrlar produces the best mathematicians in the known multiverse, and they're always generous with their calculations and their time. They want to help everyone else understand math as well as they do."

"Well, maybe not *as* well," said Thomas. "I'm not sure they'd like it if everyone else could start bending space and time by doing algebra."

"Please don't introduce time travel to this situation," said Sam. "I really could not deal with that right now."

"No time travel, just personal tesseracts," said Alice. "They have fine universities here, and living libraries made up of people who are happy to discuss scholastics with anyone who asks. I visited several times to consult with their cartographers. I'm hoping we've landed reasonably near to Ka'krin. That's their capital city. The climate is correct for Ka'krin, and my location tags were originally designed there, which would imply a close arrival."

"If these folks are all that friendly, why are we skulking around and stealing livestock, instead of heading straight for the nearest train station and just getting ourselves to town?" I asked, sourly. "This is starting to feel like a big waste of time."

"They're friendly, but they're . . . insular," said Alice. "The Johrlac believe they have the best way of doing everything, via their collective. You don't establish a world-spanning hive mind without developing at least a slight superiority complex."

"And given that they just abducted two members of our family, we can't assume they'd be happy to see us at the moment," said Thomas.

"We think they'll be happier to see us after we steal a bunch of their stuff?"

"They respect problem-solving, especially when performed by members of what they perceive as limited species," said Alice. "As long as we don't harm their animals, they'll understand we were only doing what was necessary to achieve our goals. And they're not likely to be happy in the least after we free Arthur and Sarah from their custody. Johrlac don't put a lot of weight on family."

"Who needs family when you have a hive mind?" asked Sam sourly. He looked surprised as Alice nodded agreement.

"Oh, I'm so pleased that you understand," she said. "That makes this all so much easier."

We had left the jungle behind, and were now following her massive stromopod across open field. Not far in the distance, two more of the creatures were peacefully picking through the grass, using their claws to pull it out of their way as they dredged squirming things out of the soil below. They didn't appear overly picky about whether they wound up eating clods of dirt and plants at the same time, but kept on grazing without pause regardless of what they shoved into their mouths. Alice pulled hers to a halt and slid down its carapace. "Sam, you're with me," she said, and trotted toward the others.

Sam shot me a helpless look before following her, looking about as enthused about the idea as I felt. Alice waited patiently for him to catch up, then led him on to the waiting stromopods, reaching out to touch their sides while waving for him to do the same.

Thomas watched fondly. I shook my head.

"I don't mean to speak ill of my elders, but I think Grandma's off her rocker," I said.

He glanced at me, smiling. "Isn't it wonderful?"

I blinked. "How is my grandmother having the survival instincts of a puppy wonderful?"

"She's not like us, Annie. She can't call down fire or burn away what frightens her. She has no connection to the pneuma. She's not even like your beau—Samuel may not be a sorcerer, but he can protect himself easily when the need arises. Alice is just a normal human woman with a broad streak of good luck and excellent aim with a pistol. And she spent *decades* roaming dimension to dimension, refusing to let go of the idea that I was somewhere out there to find. She never lost hope. She still believes things can be better."

"I'm not sure that's always the best thing to believe," I said.

"Maybe. Maybe not. But at the end of the day, I'd rather have someone who remembers how to hope at my back than someone who's completely given up on the idea of things getting better."

As I watched, Alice boosted Sam up to sit astride the stromopod's back. He didn't need the assist, but was clearly trying not to startle the creature, and accepted it willingly. She waved her hands, apparently instructing him to grasp the antennae, and I saw him gasp and smile as the creature turned to trundle back in our direction. Alice trotted alongside, keeping pace easily.

When Sam reached us, he pulled on the antennae, and the stromopod stopped. I pulled myself up the side of the creature, sliding into position in front of him and leaning back against his chest.

"You want the reins?" he asked.

"Nah. This way, if anything comes to bother us, I can set it on fire while you handle the driving. Besides, you know I don't like the idea of operating a large motor vehicle."

"This is more like a horse than a car."

"Same deal."

Alice was leading Thomas to the third stromopod. Thomas was better at following her instructions than Sam was; that, or this one was more prepared to be mounted, after seeing both of its friends get ridden off, because they were on their way back in no time.

Alice climbed back up the side of her own stromopod, and waved for the rest of us to follow her as she turned it and began riding off, moving parallel to the edge of the forest. "Does she know where she's going?" asked Sam.

"Hope so," I said, shrugging, and we followed her.

After we'd gone what felt like about a mile, Alice looked back. "Most of the life forms on this planet are insects or crustaceans," she said. "Not as many spiders as you'd expect, a lot of annelids, no true mammals or even reptiles. The invertebrates got real ambitious in the skeleton department at some point, and most of them are chordates now, which helps with getting larger than we necessarily want them to be, but that's neither here nor there. What matters is that life on this planet evolved along different lines."

"Okay," I said, dubiously. "What does that have to do with the price of coffee?"

"A surprising amount, really," she said. "Life seeks out the places it's most suited to when it comes time to start building permanent settlements. Fūri build in jungles, humans build on plains—there are always exceptions, but we'll preferentially move toward wide, flat spaces where we can see dangers coming. And Johrlac build on estuaries. They like the mud and the presence of brackish water. If we're lucky and we've been dropped near Ka'krin, moving toward the coast will basically guarantee we find it. It's large enough that it swallowed the whole river estuary a long time ago, and extended fairly deep into the surrounding jungles."

"You're enjoying this way more than I'm comfortable with," I said. "I would like an adult."

"I think we'd all like an adult, sweetheart," she said. "And I guess I am enjoying this. After finding Thomas, the people who helped me recover made me promise to stay home for a while. I'm not supposed to go dimension-hopping without a really good reason. It's nice to be home. It's *so* nice to have a little stability back in my day-to-day life. But I got used to things being a lot more exciting than they usually are in Michigan. You don't spend years building a relationship as one of the best pan-dimensional bounty hunters out there and then go cold turkey overnight."

"I guess that makes sense," I allowed, glancing over at Thomas to see how he was taking this. He was riding his own stromopod serenely, looking untroubled by the things his wife was saying. "And I guess you have good reasons to stay home for now."

"I do," said Alice.

"We've been working on the idea that she has backup now, and needs to stay where her backup can find her," said Thomas. "As long as she lets me come with her, I don't care if she needs to run into danger from time to time in order to stay happy and healthy."

"How is running into danger *healthy*?" asked Sam.

"Mental health counts too," said Alice.

He groaned, leaning his forehead against my shoulder. "Every time I start to think maybe your family isn't completely deranged, I'm reminded of how wrong I am," he complained. "Every single time."

"I am what I was made to be," I said, twisting to kiss him on the temple. "But I love you, and I do not share my grandmother's unreasonable desire to go roaming through hostile dimensions for fun."

"Thank fuck for that," said Sam fervently.

"And thank fuck for *that*," said Alice up ahead of us, pointing to something in the distance. She had managed to guide her stromopod to the top of a small rise; we hurried to catch up with her, Thomas and Sam each urging their own steed to move faster.

In a matter of seconds, all of us were lined up along the top of the rise, looking down into what must have been a fertile bowl once, fed on the sediment deposited by the large river we could see running toward the sea. The estuary was gone, swallowed by city.

The capital city of Ka'krin was large, sprawling to virtually fill the bowl; there was no farmland left that I could see, unless they were farming trees. Patches of the city had been all but swallowed whole by trees, their branches rising high and green into the sky.

The buildings were mostly irregular and brownish-gray, like a series of wasp's nests driven onto spikes. The rest were boxy and solid, and glass panels winked up at us from all the structures, and from the depths of the forested places. I didn't see any roads running either in or out of the city, although there was a bridge across the river, and a tall structure like a monorail running off into the distance. No trains moved there; it was just a long flat path, elevated from the ground and approaching the city. Ships dotted the bay, but I couldn't make out anything resembling a harbor.

"How are they . . . ?"

Alice looked at me. "Don't assume the things you see have the same functionality as they would in a human settlement. Try looking at them in context."

Looking in context, the monorail would work as a path for trading caravans and people riding beasts like our own. I squinted. Some of what I'd taken for supports were actually winding ramps, slope shallow enough that pedestrians could make their way to the top. And the glinting windows weren't as irregularly placed as they'd originally seemed; they were angled to catch light from all the suns above us, and would provide the foundation for an excellent solar network, if that was the ambition.

There was a large stone structure at what I assumed was the center of the city, a squared-off replica of the lumpy nests around it, rising like an irregular fruit into the air, ringed with balconies and dotted with more of those windows-slash-solar panels. It was next to a bumpy organic structure that was almost as tall but less visibly constructed. It seemed to "fit" better, for lack of a different word.

I peered down at the green rim around the city just in time to see a massive beetle coming in for a landing, having launched itself from somewhere in the cliffs off to the side. It tucked its wings away and trundled into the city proper, its rider a tiny speck in the distance.

"They don't use motor vehicles because they don't need them," I said slowly. "Do they use electricity?"

"Yes. Thanks to the cycle of the suns, night lasts only a few hours here, but while it's happening, the city lights up like anything. It attracts enormous moths, which the hunters will bring down before the suns rise again. That's about half of how they supply meat to the city. Moth is surprisingly filling."

"That is . . . actually really clever," I said. "Turning the whole city into a moth trap? Not the worst plan I've ever heard someone come up with."

"They also have water purification, advanced medical technology, and everything else they need to be a stable, thriving society. It helps that the hive mind keeps them from wanting much more than the necessities: you'll never meet a Johrlac who's focused on accumulation of personal wealth. It isn't needed, since no one would imagine letting someone else go hungry or cold or uncared-for."

"That sounds . . . pretty okay, really," said Sam carefully.

"It is, as long as you don't mind being born into whatever position you'll be expected to hold as an adult, with no opportunity for self-determination or upward mobility; if you're cool with reproduction happening only when assigned, since the gestating parent will determine the base telepathic encoding of the child; and if you don't object to the elderly being used as bait for the larger aquatic isopods," said Alice, tone remaining calm and unwavering. "I know we're not supposed to judge the way other cultures decide to organize themselves, but I kind of hate these people. They've never made a choice based on anything other than the benefit of the community as a whole, and that sort of very specific big-picture altruism leads to a *lot* of personal cruelties."

"And they have Sarah?"

"Maybe not here in Ka'krin, but somewhere," said Alice. "Come on."

She pulled on her stromopod's antennae, guiding it down the rise and onto the side of the bowl, where its many sharp legs found easy purchase as it began to wind its way toward the city. Sam and Thomas guided their mounts to do the same, and together, the four of us made our descent.

✦ ✦ ✦

It didn't take us long to reach the city. Pedestrians wandered the streets, all dressed in those brightly colored jumpsuits, otherwise identical. It wasn't just their faces: there were only two haircuts I could see, both long enough to be tied back, although one was shoulder-length and the other stopped at the chin. The two haircuts didn't seem to be connected to genders; males wore their hair long and females wore theirs short, and vice-versa. Some of them were accompanied by dog-sized beetles, or rode in carts pulled by equally unreasonably sized insects.

I could have gone my entire life without seeing a four-foot-long cockroach trundling down the sidewalk on a leash.

There were no motorized vehicles that I could see, but there was still a distinction between sidewalk and street. The sidewalks were narrower, and sometimes transitioned into what I would normally call boardwalks, raised on stilts and leaving the street below. The street, in contrast, was wider and used by various carts and draft animals, which moved smoothly and fluidly. There were no traffic lights, and yet people still took turns, waiting at corners for the opportunity to move. It was all dauntingly polite, and very, very silent.

Compared to a car, a giant riding beetle doesn't make any noise at all. The draft centipedes and stromopods clicked on the ceramic tile of the street, but it was a soft sound, like the tapping of fingers on slate, nothing like the roaring of an engine. Alice led the way, turning her mount toward the central building we'd spotted from above.

It was massive, far larger than it had looked from the rise: at least five stories as I measured building height, with multiple entrances and exits. It was shorter than most high-rise towers, but it was also apparently made of some lumpy organic material rather than steel or concrete, which made its height all the more impressive. There was a nearby stone building, even taller, but nowhere near as busy.

As we drew closer to the central building, it became obvious that some of the open-fronted buildings around it were a sort of hybrid between stables and parking garages; there was one right outside our destination. Alice turned her stromopod toward the garage, stopping it in front of a man in a red-and-brown jumpsuit. He jumped, startled, before reaching out to put his hand on the stromopod's front claw.

"Where did you come from, big fellow?" he asked—the first speech I'd heard since we reached the city. Like the Kairos, he sounded like he was speaking English, although his speech didn't match the motion of his mouth. I understood every word. I glanced around, finally finding a cluster of mind-mind flowers growing under the eaves of the roof.

He didn't acknowledge Alice as she slid off the other side of her mount, moving to help us ease our stromopods up into position. She pressed a finger to her lips, signaling us to stay quiet as we slid down the sides of our own animals.

The garage attendant looked increasingly confused as he collected the three animals and guided them inside. He didn't seem afraid of their claws, and I felt an odd pang of regret as I watched them walk away. They hadn't been affectionate or even particularly friendly, but they'd been with us, and I was sorry to see them go.

Still silent, Alice walked back to the corner and waved us all over to join her. She looked around, making sure that no one was in close range, then said, in a harsh whisper, "Some of these people know me. I've been here before. They won't think it's strange if I've come to consult the cartographers again."

"Alice . . ." said Thomas, warningly.

"I'm not asking you to let me go inside alone. I'm just saying it works better if I'm the one who takes off my telepathy blocker. They're used to me, and I'm part-Kairos. They can't dig deep enough to find out why I'm actually here if I just keep thinking hard about why I want them to believe I'm here."

Thomas took a deep breath. I could almost see the moment where he decided she was making sense and worth trusting. I managed not to nudge Sam and point it out to him. It wouldn't have done any good. Thomas had been working on his "The woman I love is going to do ridiculous bullshit and I just need to put up with it" responses for longer than Sam had been alive.

"All right," he said. "But please remember how much it would upset me to see you taken apart by hostile telepaths."

"Yes, dear," she said, and leaned in to kiss his cheek before she removed the anti-telepathy charm from around her neck and turned to stride toward the nearest set of doors into the massive central building.

The rest of us followed, unwilling to let her get too much distance from the party. She walked straight up to the guard next to the door, flashing him an enthusiastic smile. "Hi," she said, bright and bubbly as anything. "I'm Alice? Price? I have an appointment with the cartography department? Can you let me on in?"

He turned slowly to look at her, eyes glacial blue for a moment before they flashed firefly white. He nodded, expression never wavering. "We remember you, Alice Price. We had heard rumor that your long quest was finally ended. That the matter of Lemure had been resolved."

"There were some developments, and they've left me with new leads to follow, but everyone who's traveled through this sector knows that your maps are unrivaled, and I need help." Alice kept smiling, but a manic gleam was creeping into her eyes. "I can find him if I just keep going, I know it. Are you willing to help me keep going?"

Something about the way she said that made me feel like she wasn't speaking solely to the guard in front of her. The fact that his eyes had yet to stop glowing reinforced that impression.

"Your quest is an admirable one, Alice Price," said the guard. "We are proud to have offered you aid in the past, and have sincerely hoped that one day, your long road would lead you to victory. If we are able to in some way facilitate that goal, we would be glad to do so. Do you remember the way?"

"I do," said Alice. She tilted her head slightly to the side. "May I enter?"

"You may," said the guard. The white light in his eyes flickered out, and they were once more blue and serene as he pulled a small lever next to the doors.

They slid open smoothly, and Alice stepped through, moving with the sort of casual slowness employed by a woman with no need to hurry—or who was trying to keep the door open long enough for her less-visible companions to slip through.

On the other side was a sort of makeshift airlock, with strange flowers clustered in the corners and vents at the very top of the walls.

"Oh, I remember this part," said Alice lightly, for all the world like she was talking to herself. "Never liked it much. The decontamination jets always mess with my hair, and I don't care to have my hair messed with."

Thomas bit his lip in obvious amusement. Apparently, she was telling the truth.

His acceptance of her statement gave me the beat I needed to brace myself. The door closed behind us, and gusts of compressed air blew out of the vents, pushing my hair to the side. Multiple small beetles and flying insects were blown off of us and into the plants in the corners, which began to devour them with disconcerting speed and enthusiasm. I knew about Venus flytraps and the like, of course, but this was more Audrey II than anything outside of a horror movie had any right to be.

Sam's tail tightened around my waist again, and I glanced up at him. He was grimacing, unsettled by the air hitting his face. I put a hand on his tail, giving it a gentle tug, and, when he looked at me in surprise, offered him a smile. He was putting up with all of this for my family, because Sarah and Arthur needed him to be willing to try. That was more than worth a little clinging.

The air stopped, leaving everyone's hair in disarray. Alice reached up to smooth hers back into place as the interior set of doors slid open, revealing a large atrium that extended upward for several stories, terminating at a domed ceiling of glass panels, like the segments on a wasp's wing. That comparison caused everything else around it to click into sudden focus. The gray-brown material used for most of the buildings we'd seen? That was "paper," the same kind wasps back on Earth used to make their nests. These were just massive wasp's nests, even down to the mud. All the other building materials were just filling in the gaps they couldn't cover with what came naturally.

The floor wasn't "paper." It was polished ceramic tile, like the street outside, which made it another form of mud. They had textured it such that it was lightly rough beneath our feet, providing the traction and grip that would otherwise have been absent. A single rainy day could have turned this entire place into a slip-and-slide without that texturing.

Alice walked through the open doors, stopping about six feet deeper into the atrium and gesturing for us to join her. We clustered close around her, and I watched as people walked by our group without pause or sidestepping, even when it meant they nearly bumped into one of us. Only Alice appeared to register with them on any meaningful level.

She looked around herself, eyes sharp, expression serene. I tried to follow her example, peering at the people as they passed.

They were all Johrlac, naturally enough, and watching them I began to truly understand why their species had never bothered to evolve facial recognition. Every single one of them was functionally identical, tiny differences of gender aside. And they *were* tiny: they all had the same face, the same delicate bone structure and pale skin. They all looked roughly the same age, too. If not for their jumpsuits and hairstyles, I wouldn't have been able to follow any single one of them across the atrium.

Very few of them were carrying anything. A few had sections of bamboo larger around than the average industrial thermos, and others had scrolls that could have been made from the same material as the walls, but the vast majority were empty-handed. It was strange, especially in comparison to what I would have seen in a busy human building around this time of day.

The doors opened behind us, admitting two more Johrlac in black-and-yellow jumpsuits. They ignored us as they walked across the atrium, heading for a doorway on the other side.

"Alice Price," said a voice, brighter and more enthusiastic than the other Johrlac we'd spoken to thus far. I turned. An older woman in a blue-and-red jumpsuit was walking toward us, eyes glowing white and hands outstretched in greeting. She looked more like my grandmother than she did like Sarah, old enough to have faint seams around her eyes and at the corners of her mouth, but still oddly young compared to the demographic I would have expected in this sort of building on Earth.

Alice turned toward her, beaming. "Verix!" she exclaimed. "I didn't think you'd still be working here at this point—haven't you reached retirement age yet?"

"They'll pry me from my map room when my legs give out on me," said the woman, still sounding jovial. "I did my duty by the collective, and now the collective does its duty by me." She paused, and for a moment, I thought she was looking at the rest of us. Then the moment passed and she took Alice's hands, squeezing her fingers for a beat before letting them go. "You need reference? Come, come."

She turned and walked briskly toward another doorway—not the one she'd arrived through. Alice laughed and followed her, Thomas by her side. Sam and I trooped dutifully along after them. We were in too deep to back out now.

Besides, the architecture was really working at reminding me that what we called "cuckoos" were just extremely well-adapted wasps. And even with the anti-telepathy charms, getting caught could have dire consequences if they decided to treat me as an invader in their hive. Arthur was reminder enough of that.

We had all adapted to the idea of Arthur. We'd had years to do it, and as time had passed, he'd become more and more clearly his own person. First the grafted-on memories had fallen away, and then he'd replaced them with memories of his own, experiences he'd had that Artie hadn't, opinions Artie had never held. While there were still similarities, and probably always would be, no one could really look at him now and take him for the same person.

No one had expected Artie to be the first member of our generation to die. It wasn't a race he'd ever been interested in joining in on, while Verity and I had been vying for first place since we were children. Arthur was proof that he was gone.

And if I offended these people, I could join him.

Alice and the older cuckoo—Verix—weren't slowing down. They moved through the doorway and into a long, smooth-walled hallway. There were fewer people on this side of the atrium, but more of them were carrying scrolls. All were in the blue-and-red jumpsuits, reducing what little variation I'd been able to track before.

At the end of the hall, Verix pushed open another paper door, revealing a room like the inside of a honeycomb. Hexagonal cubbies covered the walls, each one containing at least one rolled scroll, while several large tables dominated the center of the floor.

A few people worked at smaller tables around the edge, their aims unclear from where I stood. They straightened and stood as Verix entered, pulling brushes and styluses aside.

"What do you need, Alice Price?" she asked, with a wave of her hand. "Whatever you require of our archives will be offered up to you!"

"You're doing an excellent Verix impression, Collective, but she never sounded that enthusiastic about being asked to do her job," said Alice, with audible boredom. "Please either let her surface or leave me to my research. I know where things are kept in here."

Verix's face fell, joviality replaced by annoyance. "We offer you the courtesy of the familiar," she said. "You do us no courtesy by rejecting it so bluntly."

"Forgive me," said Alice. "Among my people, wearing someone else's body like a puppet isn't viewed as a courtesy. We call that 'body-snatching.'"

"If you have need of assistance, please call," said apparently-not-Verix, and turned to walk out of the room, followed by the researchers from the smaller tables.

Alice watched them go, waiting until the last of them had made their exit before turning to the rest of us. "All right," she said, voice gone low and tight. "We're in."

"Uh, can you maybe explain what's going on right now?" asked Sam.

"They know me," she said. "I've done some jobs for them in the past. So when I show up asking to see maps, they're pretty well inclined to let me see them. It helps their reputation in the region if they're assisting me with bringing criminals to justice."

"And how does that explain why they're ignoring us?" he pressed.

"Oh, that."

"Yeah, that."

"Right now, the three of you represent a telepathic dead zone. When they try to 'look' at you, there's nothing there. So they either dismiss you as non-sentients, some sort of mechanical assistants, or they don't notice you to begin with."

"That doesn't make any sense at all," I protested. "If they can see us, wouldn't they realize they're just not picking up on our thoughts for some reason?"

"How much media have you seen where someone has an invisibility cloak or a magic ring or something, and because of that they could sneak around anywhere and no one would notice them?" asked Alice. "They still made noise. They still had a smell. They just couldn't be seen. But people dismissed them as not really there, if anyone noticed them at all. Most people don't jump first to 'Someone invisible is lurking around in the corners.'"

"I guess that makes sense," said Sam, slowly.

"Who is your friend?" asked Thomas.

"Verix used to be a cartographer for the Ka'krin municipal government. Meaning she traveled off-dimension charting things for them, which is why she had to take a name distinct from her profession. We met in a bar on Fraith. I was following a guy who'd skipped bail in six different dimensions, she was trying to find someone who'd guide her through a nasty bit of local geography, and we figured out that we could help each other. She was a nice lady. Reminded me of you, a bit." She looked over at Thomas, the ghost of a smile tugging at her lips. "The whole 'I come from an insular community that told me what was right and what was wrong and went out of their way to make sure I knew there were no other ways of doing things worth consideration, and then I got out into the world and started to see more and more evidence that sometimes other ways were better, or kinder, or whatever' thing. It was nice, spending time with someone I thought might actually get it."

"What happened?" he asked, more gently.

"What always happens to the Johrlac who leave home for whatever reason; she stayed gone long enough that she stopped dreaming the collective's dreams in the way she'd been told was ideologically pure, and she went home before they could label her a cuckoo. Now she's back on Johrlar, and she's never going to be allowed to leave again. They let her keep the name she used when she was off-world, but the person I knew is gone. She's been subsumed and diluted. Every cartographer in this building has a homeopathic amount of Verix in them."

"That's horrible," I said, staring at her. "How is that not . . ."

"Murder?" Alice shrugged. "They do things differently here. If we want their hospitality, we just have to deal with it." She crossed to the hex wall, sifting through the scrolls until she found something that suited her. Pulling the scroll free, she walked it back to the table and unrolled it, revealing an elaborate map of some forested area.

"Where is this, dear?" asked Thomas.

"Mul," said Alice. "It borders on Ithaca. The Johrlac have done a substantial amount of mapping there over the years; they have some fascinating coastal weather phenomena."

"I see." He moved to join her in studying the map.

I stared at them. "What are you doing?"

"They'll be back to check on me soon enough," said Alice. "I'm buying myself a little time. If I play this right, I can get access for several days by saying the bounties I'm on are complicated enough to require it. Mul is a good starting point, because it changes often enough that I would believably want a map even if I'd just been there."

The door slid open with a soft whispering sound, and another Johrlac in red and blue stepped inside, several scrolls in her arms. She stopped at the threshold, staring at Alice. "You," she said.

Alice lifted her head. "I'm sorry. I'm Alice Price. I have the permission of the collective to be here," she said.

"You," repeated the Johrlac. Her eyes flashed white, and she stiffened, like she'd been jabbed by an electric prod. When she spoke again, her voice was firmer, more level: "Alice Price, we are informed of something very interesting by our cartographer, whom you may remember. You knew her by the name Lybee."

"Lybee," said Alice, sounding horrified.

"We have been given a fascinating story by Lybee," said the collective, tone remaining level. "She informs us that her service to the Professor of Interdimensional Studies at the University of K'Larth was brought to an early end by the death of her employer, who had been controlling your assignments across known space. Further, she states that you vanished in the wake of his death, and have not been known to be working since that time. What are you doing here, Alice Price, who is clearly not on any bounty?"

Alice opened her mouth, then froze, head snapping back and eyes going wide. She made a pained sound. Thomas lunged, looking like he was about to grab her, but pulled himself up at the last possible second, looking almost like he was about to be sick.

"Such fascinating thoughts in your mind, Alice Price," said the collective, idly. "Who do you think you would become if we removed a few of them? How many of these memories do you truly need to be content? Only tell us why you're really here, and we won't need to threaten you so. Oh, rage, rage, little mammal. Yes, we know you view this as an assault and an offense, and we do apologize for the transgression. But you are a threat to the hive, and threats to the hive cannot be allowed to stand unchallenged."

Alice's mouth worked, but no sound came out.

"Oh, you've learned of the Kairos, have you? Little coincidence-benders. We thought they could be domesticated, thought they could be tamed, but they refused the gifts we offered them, refused the greatness that could have been theirs in favor of living in the jungle like roaches, scurrying and scuttling and hiding under leaves to evade our eyes. We always suspected you were of their messy kind, that it might explain your strange resistance to our desires. Lybee, though . . . you let her in. You allowed her passage beyond your barriers. She knows the pathways of your mind. Relax, Alice Price. Allow us to understand you."

Thomas tensed, hands beginning to crackle with heat, and I knew he was only a moment away from grabbing her. I tensed in turn, ready to tackle both my grandparents to the floor.

The door slid open and a trio of Johrlac in red, black, and gold jumpsuits came storming through. "The cuckoo queen is gone," reported one of them, in a loud voice.

Alice sagged for a moment, then collapsed to the ground in a puddle of limbs and harsh, heaving breaths. Thomas dropped to his knees beside her, gathering her into his arms as Lybee turned on the new arrivals.

"What?" she asked.

"The cuckoo," repeated the Johrlac that had spoken before. "She is not located in the holding cells any longer. We can find no sign of her within the building. The cuckoo is gone."

Lybee moved closer to the trio, her eyes blazing white. In response, they lifted their chins, their own eyes mirroring hers. The four of them were silent for a long time—more than thirty seconds, maybe more than a minute. Then they broke apart, Lybee turning back to Alice, who was sitting up and panting. A thin trickle of blood had run from her nostril to her upper lip, and the look she was giving the Johrlac was pure hatred.

"You are no longer of high concern," said Lybee, dismissively. "You may go about your business. Once you leave this room, the right of research is rescinded, and you will not be allowed reentry. Leave this dimension. You are no longer welcome here, Alice Price."

The four of them turned then, storming out of the room without looking back.

Twelve

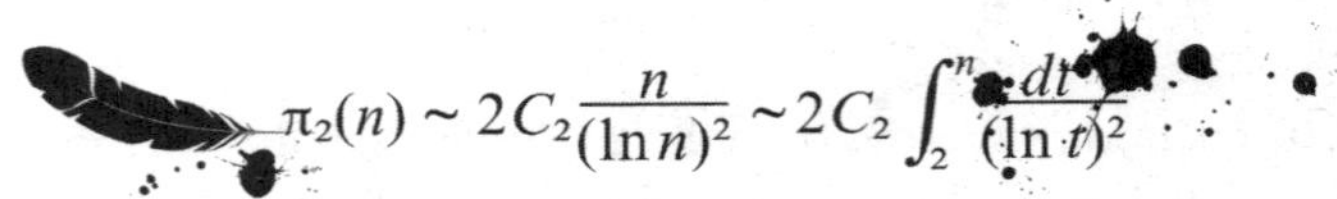

SARAH

> "I don't have much. But what's mine is mine, and if you try to do it harm, well. You'll learn why I've never needed much, either. A lady can do a lot of damage when she's looking after everything that matters."
>
> —**Frances Brown**

In the home of Fetch and Carry, preparing to absolutely lose my shit

WHAT."

I was almost proud of myself for how calm I sounded. My mouth was dust and ashes, my eyes were burning coals, but my words? Oh, my words were calm as anything. If there had been a Miss Johrlar competition, I could have won the Congeniality Award.

Right before I shoved it up somebody's ass. Okay, maybe I wasn't that congenial.

Annalist didn't appear to recognize the danger he was in.

"As the physical proof of your transgressions, this Arthur is entirely able to stand trial in your place," he said. "He can be brought before a jury, who will consider him in his totality before passing their judgement against you. Of course, in your absence, they will be unable to take your motivations into consideration; he will be judged in isolation, which may or may not be to his benefit."

"And what happens if they try him and find me guilty?"

"He will be destroyed, of course. The criminal may not benefit from the crime."

The thought that the courts of Johrlar would consider Arthur to be me attempting to benefit in some way from what happened, rather than the living, breathing punishment for my actions, was almost hilarious. But Annalist wasn't laughing, and it was clear from the grave way he was watching me that none of this was intended as a joke.

"No," I said, pushing my salad aside untasted. "I won't let that happen."

He blinked, bewildered. "But your freedom is more important than his survival."

"Oh? And why the hell is that?"

"You are a queen. He is not even Johrlac."

"Species is not superiority."

"But . . ." He stopped, clearly frustrated. "I believe this is a place where our upbringing differs sufficiently that there is no point in arguing. Please, however, listen as I tell you that some among us have been waiting for a queen capable of challenging the collective for a very long time. Longer than either you or I have been alive. If we are able to bring you into direct contact with the collective, on their own ground, you will be able to challenge them for supremacy, and if you win . . ." He paused for a moment, apparently lost in the sweet dreams of what would happen if I defeated the collective. "If you win, freedom for all who they control. Freedom for our continent. Perhaps, in time, freedom for our world."

I stared at him, resisting the urge to snarl. It wouldn't do any good, I knew; it was a reflex I had learned from Istas, and Sam, and the other therianthropes I had been spending time around. Their instincts told them that snarling at danger would drive it away, and I had picked up on that, and Annalist wouldn't even be able to read the expression if I tried, and so I just swallowed it, one more hot coal to burn in the banked fire that was my gut.

"I'm not responsible for your freedom," I said, keeping my voice as tight and level as I could. "I'm not responsible for anything to do with this damned dimension. You threw my ancestors out because they didn't meld properly with your collective, and as far as I'm concerned, that's the sort of thing that absolves me of needing to give a damn what you want me to do. I want Arthur back, and I want to go home."

"If you go home before your name is cleared, they'll simply come to collect you again, and we might not be able to release you a second time," said Annalist. "It was only a combination of luck and timing that allowed us to remove you from custody; expecting the same sequence of events to occur again would be either arrogant or foolish, depending on how we wanted to address the matter."

"I don't care," I said, coldly. "These people have no authority over me. I didn't fight this time because they took me by surprise. They won't take me by surprise again." I stood, leaving my salad behind. "I am not interested in solving all your world's issues. I am not interested in saving your people. I want *my* people, and I want to go home."

"If you want to save your people and return to your home, you will need to face the collective and you will need to win, or you will never know peace again."

Annalist looked at me levelly. "I am offering you a way out of this. I am offering you an escape. If you have any wisdom left in you after your upbringing, you will take what I am offering, and you will utilize it to win."

I stared at him until he turned his face away.

"Eat your salad," he said. "If you're worried for your friend, eat to protect him. You will need calories to keep your mind operating correctly, and you will need every ounce of strength that you can muster to have a prayer against them."

"Them who?"

"The collective."

"What *is* the collective?"

Annalist sighed heavily. "Queens are rare. Too few survive the final instar. It seems less make it through the transition with every year that passes. At the current time, the collective is five queens, no more. It has not been this weak in centuries. You can overcome it with a well-placed strike. You can become the collective, and then you can abandon Johrlar, and our region will have no collective. If a new collective must arise, it will rise according to the old ways, naturally, without a predetermined queen to guide it, and we will be able to determine how we want our lives to be lived, not how we are to be ordered to live them."

I paused, trying to order this in my mind. Finally, I said, "So you want me to go up against the central hive mind that controls your culture, destroy them, and leave you without anyone at the top of the food chain? Is that correct?"

"Yes," said Annalist. "That is what we are asking of you."

I stared at him for a moment, then finally reached for the salad. I didn't want to sit and eat. I wanted to rush off and rescue Arthur so we could go back to Earth and resume never looking at or speaking to each other. It was a painful penance. It was the one I'd earned.

But at the same time. Annalist was right: I needed to keep my strength up if I was about to get into a psychic battle with a five-person hive mind. There was only one of me. That meant victory was going to be a narrow thing if it was possible at all, and I really did need to be ready for a fight.

I didn't like the idea of traveling to another dimension to destabilize their government, but the Johrlac had shown that they could reach me on Earth without difficulty, and the collective had shown they were willing to do it. Worse, they'd touched Arthur. He wasn't Artie, was never going to *be* Artie, but he was all I had left of Artie, and for that, I loved him. For that, I owed him all the protection and comfort I could possibly offer.

When Dr. Frankenstein's creation woke up, he ran away and abandoned it to whatever existence it could manage without him. When my creation woke up, I didn't do too much better. I ran, as fast as I could, from the stranger with my Artie's memories. It was harder on Elsie and the others: for them, Arthur was a stranger with Artie's face. I couldn't see that part. For me, they looked totally different and always had. The mind was its own thing. But I understood one thing Dr. Frankenstein never did: I understood that running away didn't absolve me of my responsibility. Arthur wouldn't be in this situation if it weren't for me. Arthur wouldn't even exist if it weren't for me.

I had to fix this, no matter how much I disliked what that involved. And if these people wanted to arrest me for crimes I couldn't possibly have known I was committing, they started it. Whatever happened next was well and truly on their shoulders.

Annalist winced, putting a hand to his temples. Fortunately for me, that gave me the chance to set my salad—still untouched—aside before the wave he was reacting to could reach me.

I had been hit by Johrlac telepathy before. It had broken upon and overwhelmed me, leaving me stranded in the caverns of my own mind. This was something different. It slammed down, and I understood why they were all so afraid of the collective, why they were willing to gamble everything on a stranger from another dimension when it meant that there was a chance this overwhelming force would be removed.

It was the mental equivalent of having a weighted wool blanket dropped on my head while it was being carried to the dryer: hot, wet, and absolutely smothering. I gasped, struggling to breathe through the bulk of it. If I tried to stand up, I would fall; I was certain of that much. All I could do was sit frozen, the presence pressing down harder and harder, heavier and heavier, until I thought I would be crushed under its weight.

Be aware, boomed a voice, and I had just enough presence of mind remaining to wonder how overwhelming it would have been if I hadn't been in a house with dampening fungus in the walls. Fetch and Carry weren't here. What was this going to do to them?

Be aware, the voice repeated. *A prisoner has escaped from our custody, a cuckoo who claims to have achieved the forbidden instar and ascended into queendom. She lies. She will lead your mind astray, denying you the ability to properly serve your hive. Her corruption, if it taints you, will make ascension impossible: your own chances to achieve collective will be unmade if you assist her. She is disorganized and untidy of thought. She does not know the proper addresses offered by a person of manners. She does not know how to speak without disrupting. You will know her by her incivility of thought, and by her strange dress. She does not know our systems. If she is able to acquire a proper uniform, it will be incorrect for the position she is trying to embody: you will easily uncover her for the pretender she is. Do not attempt to apprehend. Do not make direct contact. She will be apprehended, she will be tried for her crimes, and she will be destroyed.*

As quickly as it had come, the presence receded. I sat up straighter, reaching for my salad with shaking, unsteady hands. Annalist looked like he was on the verge of passing out completely.

"Well," I said, with forced lightness. "I guess physical descriptions don't make a lot of sense when you're talking about a world where everyone looks basically the same. Does the collective realize they've just declared open season on their own people? Once you say 'Oh she might be wearing the appropriate uniform, but she won't be who you think she is,' everyone becomes a potential target."

"The collective is aware that we find ways of maintaining our individuality in the face of their authority," said Annalist. "They were us once, before their apotheosis. They were happy as us, but they resented them. Now that they are them, they will make any effort they can to keep us from becoming them."

I blinked. "I'm sorry. I didn't . . . What?"

"To become the collective, you must reach the queen's instar. To reach the queen's instar, you must— Wait, I'm sorry. You are a cuckoo. Do you know the path to queendom?"

"I know how it was explained to me, but it was explained to me by another cuckoo," I said. "Can you explain it as you understand it, and I'll tell you if my understanding matches your own?"

I finally picked up the odd wooden fork, stirring it through the salad bowl before taking a bite.

This wasn't the first time I'd eaten food from another dimension, and as with before, I found I didn't have any way to describe the flavors filling my mouth. How do you describe an apple to someone who's never tasted one? The greens were spicy and sweet at the same time, the chunked-up vegetables rich and savory, and the meat more like the fleshy parts of a lobster's claw than anything else. It was like I was being given food for the first time after a lifetime of being asked to eat those hard little pellets that pet owners feed to their captive animals, and in addition to being delicious, it made me so angry I could barely focus my eyes.

This wasn't my world, but it should have been. Whatever my ancestors did or didn't do, I'd had no part in it, and no opportunity to decide where I ended up. Earth was my home now, always would be: it was where I kept my stuff, where I knew what types of tomato I liked best, and where I had my family. But my choices should have been different, and this salad, which spoke to my hunger as nothing else had ever done, should have been commonplace.

Annalist was watching me, waiting for me to swallow and come back to the conversation. I finished chewing, unwilling to rush even for the sake of what he had to offer me, and turned my attention back to him.

"You like it?" he asked, almost slyly.

"I need you to tell me how someone can become a queen."

"Very well." He inclined his head. "The first instar, the universal zero, comes for us all. We are born to it, innocent nymphs, and from there will proceed to one of two paths. Most will mature, crack the egg of their buried memories, and become productive members of society. In some, that egg will be absent or malformed, refusing to hatch. They will continue on as nymphs until something triggers them to enter their second instar, and then they will mature stronger than they might have been otherwise. Zero is all, first is most, second is those who are challenged to it. Those are the easy changes, the worker stages. Most can survive them."

I made a noncommittal noise and took another bite of salad, watching him carefully.

"The third instar must be triggered from the outside, when another mature Johrlac puts pressure upon the mind of the one who seeks maturity. It leaves the individual stronger and more able to access their natural gifts. Some will begin to show flickers of potential at three that indicate what type of queen they would be. In the earliest days, only the queens were allowed to populate the hive."

That might have worked when we'd been more like wasps, but as modern Johrlac were bipeds built for live birth, rather than egg-laying, I couldn't imagine being responsible for the population of an entire hive would be a lot of fun. The very idea made my hips hurt.

"Once a third-instar individual has settled and stabilized, they can be pushed over the edge into the fourth instar. Queens are creatures of community: like the third instar, their transformation must begin from the outside. The exact mechanism is not communicated, because it must be restricted for the health of the hive. Queens will vary in power and potential, depending on the strength of the push which cracked their shells. The greater the danger, the stronger the queen."

"And that's why you're assuming I can stand up against a collective of five, since I was in a lot of danger when I changed," I said. "Why is it 'queen,' and not 'regent' or something else gender-neutral?"

Annalist looked baffled. "Why would we choose an untrue title for our rulers?"

"Because men can reach the fourth instar?"

"But they can't. It would take too long, and even if they survived, they would be dangerous. There are no male queens."

"I'm already dangerous," I protested. "I can bend space, and no one's around to teach me how to do it safely, which means I could seriously hurt people, or even collapse chunks of space and time if I'm not careful. And my telepathy is too strong—I erased the mind of the man I loved, and I didn't even realize I was doing it. I have no idea how strong I really am or am not, based on the scales you're using, but all queens are dangerous."

"Yes, which returns us to where we began: the collective will do whatever is necessary to prevent unauthorized queens from rising out of the population."

"Uh-huh." Given that the more advanced instars were all externally triggered, it would actually be possible for the collective to prevent other queens from rising. I just wasn't sure why they'd bother. "And why is that?"

"Each mind added to the collective dilutes its purity of purpose," said Annalist. "When a single mind controls the collective, there is no dissent or disagreement."

"And there's also no collective. One person isn't a collective; it's an individual."

"Be that as it may, there have been collectives controlled by one or two minds, and those were harmonious times."

Meaning a single queen would rise and seize control of the minds of the entire population? The thought was horrifying. I swallowed, staring at Annalist. "The current collective is five people."

"Yes."

"You said that was a small number."

"We try to maintain a collective of eight or more, for the sake of flexibility."

"How did they rise?"

"The first two were chosen by the previous collective to ascend and take their positions. The third was injured at a game with her brothers, and their efforts to call her back from her injuries were invasive enough to trigger her third instar. From there, she was able to convince her parents to press against her mind, and the pressure brought on her fourth instar. It was a shock to everyone when she broadcast her wishes over the city, and the existing queens took her into their number rather than executing her because they saw the potential in her range and strength. The fourth survived the collapse of a collective on the other side of the continent, and the fifth is the first to have been chosen by the new queens. Her name was Collate before her recategorization. She lived in this house with the others, once."

"Are Fetch and Carry helping me because they're angry at their friend for becoming a queen without them?"

"Nothing so simple as that. None of them wanted to join the collective. Fetch and her friends are what we call 'individualists,' people who believe individuals have the right to live their own lives, guided by their preferences and personalities, not at risk of revision because they displease a queen, not assigned to a profession from birth. We are eusocial insects at our core, but a hive may function without forcing forms of behavior upon its members. Collate was the strongest in her belief that self-determination was a right worth exercising. Her apotheosis was a punishment. She was revised, then triggered into ascension, and now she controls the city with the rest of the collective, and what little remains of their friend is worn away day upon day. They would burn this city to the ground if I allowed it—or if their own minds did. None of us can directly harm a queen. They fought back when Collate was taken, and now, even the thought of bringing harm to a queen harms *them*. They could never start the fire."

"If you allowed it . . . ignoring their conditioning, how do you have the authority to stop them?"

"I am of a higher professional position, but more importantly, I am a keeper of the histories. I know and understand the ways in which collectives have collapsed. Attacking the people they control rarely destroys them. It is more likely to strengthen their position, as it causes all those who have not been incapacitated to flock to the feet of those they consider strong protectors."

"This *really* doesn't sound like it has anything to do with me."

"Every queen is the living seed of a potential collective. They look upon your existence as a threat. They know not the exact shape of your strength, only that you were able to navigate a crossing between dimensions with multiple people and a large piece of your innate territory. That whispers to them of great and terrible power. You could overthrow them."

"Is this why people don't use their telepathy even as much as I do back on Earth?" I asked. "I used to dream of being a telepath in a telepathic society, where everyone would be sharing thoughts and there wouldn't be secrets or hidden meanings or misunderstandings. But here, it's like everyone's afraid to do more than brush up against somebody else's mind—how does that work?"

"The collective—"

"The collective changes. You just told me that. And if there's more than one collective, that means they aren't some unquestionable authority. So you must always be this reluctant to lower the barriers between you and everyone around you. How does that even work?"

"In the days before the cuckoos, we were better at unity," said Annalist. "We had never considered that anything else might occur. We left our barriers down. But then, out of the disharmony, came conflict. Came discomfort, which grew and grew and left little room for lowering of barriers. We became insular once we realized we *could* have conflict with our own, and in the rise of the collectives, we discovered that only through self-protection could any trace of singularity be preserved."

I shook my head, looking down into my half-empty salad bowl. How had I eaten that much of it—and when? "It seems silly, to be able to be so close and to spend so much time trying to be far apart."

"The collectives must be obeyed," he said. "How did you learn the way to apotheosis? It seems impossible for someone as isolated as you to have found the path."

I frowned, trying to formulate an answer. It seemed suddenly hilarious that half my salad was gone. What was I, some sort of grazing animal? Laughter bubbled in my gut, and I swallowed it, blinking slowly as I refocused on Annalist's face.

How long had his eyes been glowing? It wasn't bright, but it was present, a pale, lambent light behind his irises, brightening his sclera until they were so white they were almost bleached. He was doing something. Telepathically. I recognized the glow, even if I didn't know the purpose or intent.

"What are you doing?" I asked. "What did you do to me?" Then, and most importantly: "Who are you?"

"Any Johrlac born and raised to Johrlar would recognize the taste of marikana pollen, but we assumed you would have no such frame of reference, and indeed, you didn't. You knew nothing. You know nothing. You offer no true challenge, whatever you may think you do."

I stabbed my fork at him, vaguely aware that we were too far apart for me to do anything other than posture uselessly. Still, at least I was trying. That seemed like the only thing left that I could really do at this point. "Put something in my food?" My voice was starting to slur. Oh, I didn't like that.

"Yes, little cuckoo, we put something in your food," said Annalist. He rose, taking the fork from my hand and placing it carefully on the counter. "The collective is essential to the survival of our species. You are outside the collective. You will always be outside the collective. There is no world in which you overcome our unified voices and make yourself their equal, much less their superior."

I had never wanted any of that. I had never even wanted to *be* here. Johrlar was the land of my nightmares, the place that birthed cuckoos and stole freedom away. Stole family and peace and comfort. As a child, I'd prayed for the Blue Fairy to grant Pinocchio's wish and then come to do the same for me, to make me a real girl with red blood and a heart seated firmly in my chest to drive that blood along, to close my mind and let me sleep in singular peace. I'd never wished to go back to Johrlar. All this talk of overcoming and equality, it was so much noise, empty and meaningless. He threatened me over something I wasn't trying to achieve.

"We had hoped to find out how you claimed your current instar before the pollen took hold, but it doesn't matter that much. According to the scouts who visited the backwater dimension you consider 'home,' your apotheosis destroyed all the other adult cuckoos in your world. It will be decades before any of what you've left behind could rise to challenge us, and by then, we'll be prepared.

We'll destroy your Earth for the crime of threatening us, and take its residents to serve us." He chuckled, dark and cold and nothing like the polite academic who'd been speaking to me before—because he wasn't, was he? Annalist wasn't here anymore. I was speaking to the collective. "And if you still wonder why no one wants to touch your mind, this is the reason: your thoughts are inferior, and we don't want to be tainted by them."

He circled the table where I was seated, and I tried to track him. The effort made me dizzy, and my eyes slipped closed without my willing them to do so. I was still awake enough to feel my head hit the table, but nothing more than that, and when my body hit the floor, I was solidly unconscious.

✦ ✦ ✦

The white void around me was infinite and featureless. I pushed myself to my feet, taking a few steps into the nothingness, noting that my feet remained stable on the same plane: there was a floor, even if I couldn't see it. There were no distinctions between up and down, the floor, ceiling, and walls, but I existed here, and as long as I existed here, I could figure something out.

"Hello?" I called.

My voice echoed into the distance, bouncing off surfaces I couldn't see before finally bouncing back to me, distorted, yet still clear enough for me to understand. I scowled. Fun.

"All right," I said. "So you brought me here, set up some little test or trap or whatever, and then knocked me out so you could . . . what, exactly? What is the goal supposed to be? Am I supposed to start crying and wailing and begging for your mercy? Or open my mind all the way so you can get inside and go rooting around the shelves for whatever it is you think you need?"

"We wanted to meet you, Sarah McNally-Baker-Price-Zellaby," said a voice from behind me. It was sweet, female, calm, and sounded exactly like my own did when played back over a recording. It was my voice, stripped of bone conduction and transformed into a stranger's. She had no accent, which was interesting. None of the people I'd met on Johrlar had had what I would think of as a recognizable accent.

This wasn't just another country; it was another *planet*, in another dimension. I wasn't sure the people were actually speaking English—it would have been strange if they were, and on a planet of telepaths, it wasn't too far out of the realm of reason to assume that they might be using some sort of universal translator. I should really have asked when I had the chance.

Oh, wait. "What language are you speaking?" I asked.

Non sequiturs have a power all their own sometimes. There was a pause before the stranger said, sounding bewildered, "The tongue of the collective. We have never bothered to name it. All queens speak the same language. Why would we seek another?"

"Language evolves to suit its surroundings," I said, and turned to face her.

Unsurprisingly, she looked exactly like me. More, even, than Fetch and Carry had; this was an idealized space, and we both appeared as the ideal Johrlac. Any scars or bruises had been wiped away by the transition from reality to the nebulous solidity of the mindscape. She was wearing a jumpsuit like all the others: unlike the others, hers was a solid, almost iridescent black, gleaming and shifting with the light every time she moved. It made her hair seem less glossy than it actually was, pulling blue highlights out of the black, and making her skin even whiter than it would normally have been.

"You would be a *massive* hit in the goth clubs back home," I blurted.

She blinked. "I understand all the words there are," she said. "I have no idea what you just said."

"Goths are a subculture of people who like to wear black and listen to gloomy music and put on too much eyeliner—although I guess that's a judgmental way to describe it, since they wouldn't put on that much eyeliner if they didn't feel like it was just the right amount. So I guess they're people who like to wear black and listen to gloomy music and put on a perfectly reasonable amount of eyeliner that some people will consider excessive, because some people don't really have a sense of whimsy after they turn nineteen."

She blinked again. "I still have no idea what you just said, only that you said a lot of it," she said. "Please do not attempt to explain further."

"Why not? I thought you wanted to meet me. And all those names aren't mine. Just Sarah Zellaby."

"You've used all those names at one point or another, and they all belonged to you when you used them." She tilted her head. "Unless you intend to abandon all names and enter into our collective, they belong to you still."

"If that's the case, you're missing one. I don't know what my birth mother called me." And I never would, either, since Ingrid had been one of the adult cuckoos whose minds I wiped clean in order to protect my family. Whatever name she might have called me by was gone forever, erased from her memory before she met her inevitable end at the fangs of the giant spiders who hunted where I'd left her to shamble and fade away.

Maybe I was a monster after all. Who but a monster could do that to her own mother without a moment of hesitation or regret? And sure, she'd tried to kill me first, but that didn't make it normal for me to be able to do that to her so easily.

"Mm. Very few people do," said the collective. "Names are given by the hiring authority, not by the gestating parent. Allowing parents to involve themselves in naming would introduce too much sentiment into the process, and might result in familial bonds forming where they do not provide any social benefit."

"What do you do with children after they're born, if they aren't allowed to stay with their parents long enough to form familial bonds?"

"Children are raised in creches," said the collective. "We group them according to age. Many will form sibling bonds during this time—we have found no way to stop the process, and attempts to interfere have only accelerated it past the point of tolerability. The current levels of sibling entanglement are acceptable to us. How were you raised?"

"By humans for the first years, and by a cuckoo and her Revenant husband for the rest. Surrounded by cousins and siblings and people who taught me how to be a person one day at a time."

"And how did those lessons serve you when you turned on your own people?"

"About that." I smiled, the sort of smile I'd had to learn by riding along inside my cousin Verity's skull when she went to her dance competitions. She wore her smiles like they were weapons when she went to face her peers, honing and sharpening them until they were as terrifying as they were attractive. The woman with my face recoiled. We were inside the mind here, and she didn't need to understand faces to understand what my expression really meant.

"You sit here, all comfortable and safe and sure of yourself in an environment you're actually evolved to suit, and you judge me for not knowing your rules when I had to grow up in another dimension, with only the knowledge of your culture that you allowed my ancestors to retain? I don't think you have the right. I don't see what in this world or any other justifies you thinking that you have the moral high ground here. You have no right to judge me. You have no right to judge my cousin, either, who didn't do anything wrong. You're going to give him back to me, and then you're going to let us go home."

She smiled, less fiercely than I had, but still. The fact that she was able to smile at all proved she was paying attention, and learning more from me than I was learning from her. The math was tilted too far in her favor. She was supported by the power of five people while I was supported by only one, myself, and that wasn't fair. Not that she cared. Not that any of these people cared about what they were doing to us.

"Ahh, but you see, that's where you're incorrect," she said. "Your cousin, as you call it, is not a person, therefore we cannot let it go anywhere. It can be removed from our keeping, if you're brave enough to try, but we doubt you will be. We have the measure of you now, Sarah Zellaby, and you're no threat to us. Come peacefully. Stand trial as we intended you to do. Give up this idea that you can face us. We refuse it."

I raised an eyebrow, reaching out mentally as I tried to follow this projection back to its origins. I hadn't gone far before I encountered a junction, and realized this wasn't a member of the collective, as I had been assuming: this was the entire collective, five queens braided together and presenting themselves to me through one impeccably designed persona, like the Wizard of Oz in a black jumpsuit with no Emerald City in sight.

"If you hurt him in any way, I will make you pay for it on a scale you have never even imagined," I said, and mentally snipped one of the five ribbons of thought feeding into the braid that was "her." The effect was immediate and electric. She jerked like I'd jabbed her physically with a pin, eyes widening. At the same time, her hair became a little less smooth, her jumpsuit a little less flawless. Her projected perfection was a group project, and I had interfered with the group.

Oopsie.

"What are you doing?" she demanded. "Stop that right now."

"Stop what?" I asked innocently, and broke the second thread. "I thought it was just the two of us in here, sizing each other up. Was I wrong about that?"

"We are not singular," she said. "We are never singular. Even a . . . a *cuckoo* like yourself should understand that. We are the collective. We control this city and this territory, we are the voice of these people. Our desires are their desires, our dreams are their dreams. We speak with the voice of Johrlar."

"Oops," I said, snapping the third thread. This time, she staggered, looking almost like she was going to vomit. "Does that hurt? Why don't you stop me?"

"We will," she said, eyes wide with fear. She began backing up, opening space between us. It wasn't real—distance was just a concept here, not a real thing that could extend between people—but when I reached out for her, she was farther away. I couldn't quite grasp the remainder of the braid. It was too far removed from me.

"We *will* stop you," she said, terror in her voice. "You think you can come here, to our place, our *territory*, and threaten us so? We will stop you. We will end you. And once we have destroyed everything you are, we will rewrite you, so that even in death, you answer only to a name you didn't choose. You are a threat too great to be endured, and we will not stand for it."

She vanished then, winking out like a computer program being disconnected. The white went with her. I stared for a moment at the space where she'd been, then spun and looked behind me. There was nothing there but true void, black and empty and endless. I turned back to where the collective had been, and the blackness was there as well, consuming everything.

Frustrated, I sat down to wait for myself to wake up.

Thirteen

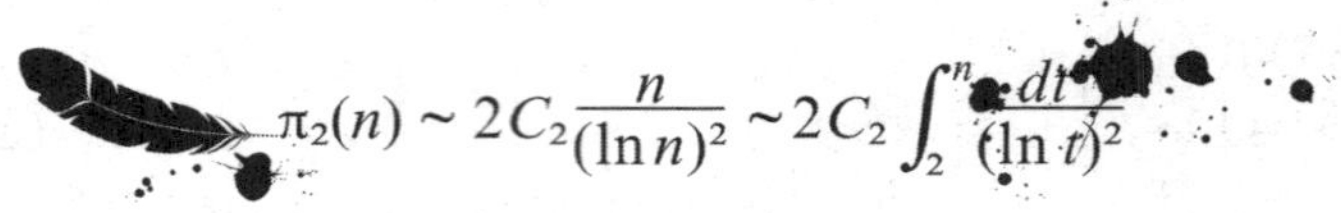

"Any man who'd drug a lady's drink deserves to meet the sharp end of the shovel, preferably face-first. Self-defense is never a crime."

—**Enid Healy**

In the home of Fetch and Carry, waking up on the kitchen floor

I HAD TIME TO COUNT WELL past three hundred thousand before I felt the blackness around me starting to erode, falling away like a riverbank in the rain. It was replaced by more darkness as it dissolved, but I could feel the change; I was ascending through the layers of my own mind, moving back toward consciousness. I didn't fight it. I didn't try to help it, either. Depending on what had been used to put me under, "helping" might result in the void trying to yank me back under.

By going limp, I could just allow myself to drift higher and higher, not resisting or encouraging the transition from deep unconsciousness to waking up. When the air around me started to lighten out of dark and toward dusky dawn, I closed the inner idea of my eyes, shutting out the world and allowing the transition to proceed without me doing anything to force it.

Bit by bit, something hard appeared below me, and the air around me became warm and humid, sticky in a way that dreams could never really be. I heard the soft woosh of my own breathing, and the hissing of the wind around the windows, and decided that I had waited long enough: I opened my eyes and I was back in the kitchen, the remains of my salad spilled on the floor all around me, alien lettuce in my hair.

It was still reasonably crisp. Given the temperature and humidity, and again drawing on my summers at Lowryland, where we'd often left sandwich fixings spread out across the counters in our tourist rentals, I guessed I'd been unconscious for maybe twenty minutes. Still longer than I liked when the collective might be looking for me. They had to know where Annalist was when they took him over.

I sat up and plucked the lettuce out of my hair with the same motion, wrinkling my nose at the scrap of greenery even as I tossed it aside. I would normally have felt bad about making a mess in someone else's home, but these people had set me up to be drugged and thrown to their collective, whether they'd known they were doing it or not. They could deal with a little dressing on their tile.

My head was spinning as I pushed myself up into a crouching position and straightened, moving slowly so as not to make the dizziness even worse. It helped that the room was dim, quiet, and—except for me—empty. I blinked, realizing what was different.

Annalist was gone.

I turned to the doorway, walking back into the front room. My head was still spinning, and my vision was blurry around the edges, the last of the drugs working their way through my system. I massaged my temple with one hand, trying to chase away the first stirrings of a headache. I couldn't allow myself to collapse here. Not when I didn't know where Annalist was. Not when the collective might be coming.

He wasn't in the front room, which was probably for the best. I preferred the idea that he'd knocked me out while the collective had him under their control and run for the hills as soon as they released him to the thought of the collective sticking around in his skin to gloat over my body. I kept walking, storming toward the closed front door.

Had he been working with the collective since the beginning? Were Fetch and Carry in danger? Or had he spoken of revolution, expecting it to come to nothing, and attracted the collective's attention in the process? It was impossible to know whose side Fetch and Carry were really on without asking them, and I couldn't trust telepathic communication when I didn't know whether the collective had taken them too.

Regardless, they didn't deserve to come back to a damaged house, and so I hit the switch to open the doors rather than telekinetically forcing them. If they were innocent, they were about to learn that they'd been betrayed by someone they trusted. No point in adding property damage to the shock.

The doors repeated their alternating airlock behavior before they let me outside, neither pair willing to open until the other was closed. After what felt like far too long, I was stepping into the humid air and strangely conflicting sunlight, the trees around me filtering it into dappled shadows. The same insects I'd seen before were still flitting and crawling in the branches, painfully visible.

Visible, and undisturbed. No one had passed this way in at least a few minutes. I paused to watch the insects buzzing around, making note of their colors. Most of them had gray patches that I could only assume would turn red if I had a human around to borrow color vision from; it would explain why the Johrlac had so much red in their uniforms if they were just replicating things they'd seen in nature.

I wanted to drop all my shields and broadcast a challenge to the collective. I also wanted to find Arthur without them finding *me*. So I pulled back as hard as I could, pushing forward the partition Fetch had instructed me to create: I was Gather, a civic assistant, and if using an identity she'd helped me to cobble together was a risk, it was a smaller risk than trying to come up with something on my own. The uniform I was wearing seemed like it would do half the work for me, anyway: most of the people I was likely to encounter would just assume they knew me based on what I was wearing, and if I could avoid answering any direct questions, that would be more than good enough.

I made my way carefully down the meandering lane connecting Fetch and Carry's home to the main thoroughfare, not seeing a single other person until I reached the walkway and looked down the street. If the collective was sending people to collect me, they weren't in any hurry to get it done. Johrlac moved in the distance, heading to and fro on their unknowable errands, and none of them spared me so much as a second glance.

A woman walked by, pulled by a spider the size of a cocker spaniel. The sight made my guts clench. How long had I been gone? Had anyone thought to try explaining to Greg that I wasn't going to be back any time soon? Not that most of my family could reach him on a level he'd be able to understand. Alex and Shelby would have to agree to take Isaac to Michigan before that could happen.

The woman noticed me watching her and paused, shooting me a curious look. I knew it was curious: I could feel the confusion washing off her like heat off a summer highway. I turned hastily away, clamping down on my own thoughts and emotions as tightly as I could manage. She didn't need to know that I was scared, lost, and hopelessly missing my own giant spider, who was very far away but safe, which put him one up on the cousin I owed the world to. After what I'd done to him, Arthur was my responsibility, now and forever.

At some point I'd begun heading back toward the building where I'd been held. I paused, trying to decide whether I needed to turn around and go looking for someplace else to start, then shrugged and continued onward. The collective could find me wherever I was. If I'd been held in the administration building, they might have Arthur there now. I could bust him out and . . .

And what? What was I going to do once I had him? I still couldn't stand to be around him, and it wasn't like I could manage a dimensional crossing unsupported. I might have psychic powers beyond what should be trusted to an individual, like, ever, but that didn't make me omnipotent. Trying to do the math with no one around but Arthur would risk either erasing my own mind or swallowing his for a second time. Could I even build a new person on a brain that had been wiped clean more than once?

I had no idea, and finding Arthur was a priority no matter how I wanted to look at things. Worst case, I could bust him out and run for the hills with him, find someplace isolated where we could hole up and get on with our lives. Best case, I could seize control of the collective as Annalist had been encouraging me to do—although I was no longer sure whether or not that had been some sort of a trap—and maybe that would give me the processing power I needed to get home.

Problem with being a Price: the majority of my relatives have the kind of luck where every lottery ticket is a winner and every missed flight is the start of a *Final Destination* film, their ludicrous connection to coincidence kicking in to keep them from meeting an untimely death. It means they've never really developed much of a skill for planning, since they genuinely haven't needed it. And that means they've never taught me how to plan.

Stop. Breathe. I stepped into the shadow cast by one of the buildings, leaning against the wall and trying to focus past the adrenaline the collective's visit had caused to flood my system. I needed to think like a Baker, not react like a Price. Not that I had ever really been either: I had been a McNally, and then, after my family had died, I had transformed myself into a Zellaby, taking my name from a cautionary tale that felt like it could have been written about my species, whether or not the author had ever known us.

John Wyndham could have been a cuckoo like me or Angela, divorced from the ancestral memories that were supposed to dictate his life and trying to find a way to navigate existence in a world that was disinterested in his success. It was an oddly appealing thought, the idea that some of the people I'd grown up trusting were the same sort of creature I was.

I wouldn't have needed to guess if I'd been allowed to grow up on Johrlar. I would have known. Every role model I had would have bled clear and spoken without opening their mouths, and I would have been surrounded by a society of my peers.

And based on what I'd seen so far, that wouldn't have done much to make me a better person.

I breathed slowly in and out, focusing on what was going to happen next. The collective knew I was here. Of course the collective knew I was here: they were the ones who'd chosen to bring me. But they knew I was loose, and that was new information. Had Annalist been under their control the whole time? Now that I'd had a moment to think, I was pretty sure he must have been, since he'd drugged my salad before their message about my escape came through. Were they also controlling Fetch and Carry? If that was the case, the collective had *wanted* me to escape, and that was a distressing thought. How much of what had happened since my arrival had they been manipulating?

Did it matter? Even if everything had been scripted on their end, I'd been reacting naturally, and I was going to have to deal with the outcome of my actions. The collective was only as in control as I allowed them to be.

So: plan. Get back into the administrative building, locate Arthur, break Arthur out. Once we were free, I could attract the collective's attention on purpose and find out how to get us home. They'd been five strong when they came to study me, and they hadn't been able to stop me from blocking their entanglement. I didn't think I was necessarily their equal, but I was definitely something they hadn't been expecting, and I could exploit that.

Taking another deep breath, I pushed away from the wall, turned, and stepped back onto the sidewalk, rejoining the general flow of traffic. None of the people I could see seemed to be upset, or to be hurrying for any reason beyond efficiency, which clearly motivated much of what happened here on Johrlar. I still didn't know what their society was based on, or what most of these people could possibly be doing for work. Did they have accountants? Dentists? I supposed they must have a medical career track, although even that felt a little odd, given the level of technology I'd seen so far.

I tugged on the cuff of my jumpsuit as I walked, then paused. The fabric felt like heavy silk of some kind, mixed with a slick textile that was definitely synthetic. They might have more-advanced technology that they were simply not choosing to share with prisoners and tourists. That would make more sense than them being a completely green-tech pastoral society, given everything I knew about the Johrlac from records and, yes, sometimes prejudicial stories told by people who'd survived them long enough to write their experiences down.

A whole life spent thinking my people were monsters hadn't exactly left me prepared to judge them fairly, but fair or not, I really didn't see how they could have built all of this with nothing more than bamboo and natural fibers.

I rubbed the hem of my sleeve again, trying to decide what it felt like. Silk and . . . rayon, maybe? Something slick and sturdy and stain-resistant. I wasn't the seamstress in our family, and Elsie wasn't here. Not that she was speaking to me at the moment anyway.

Arthur still thought he loved me. Intentionally or not, I'd programmed him that way, and he couldn't just shrug it off because he was tired of it. Elsie, though . . . Elsie *knew* she hated me, and nothing I could say or do was going to change her mind about that.

And it shouldn't. However sorry I was now, I killed her brother. I was the reason he was no longer walking in the world. Mistake or not, I did that. Only me. She deserved to hate me for the rest of her life, if that was what she needed. I was pretty sure that was what she was intending to do.

On the sidewalk ahead of me, a man stopped walking and turned around, looking in my direction. His eyes flashed momentarily white. I met his gaze without flinching or looking away, allowing him to reach out and touch the partition I had so carefully constructed. I felt him pushing against it, checking it for weak spots, and pushed back, shoving him out of my mind. His eyes flashed again, brighter this time.

My apologies for the intrusion, said a voice in my mind, mild, male, and polite. *We have been informed of an intruder in our midst, and your presentation matched the information I had been provided. Please tender your forgiveness.*

How would a civic assistant reply to that, I wondered? With no idea what message his jumpsuit conveyed, I could only guess, and decided erring on the side of politeness was unlikely to get me into any real trouble. *I am on my way back from afternoon leisure,* I replied. *I apologize for wasting your time with unnecessary suspicions.*

There: show humility and take responsibility for his mistakes. Not that they'd been mistakes, but I wasn't telling him that, and if he believed me, he might never know.

Apologies accepted, he said. *Please continue. I would not want you to be late on my account.*

He turned and began walking briskly away, not sparing me another glance. I rolled my eyes and turned back toward the administrative building, pausing to watch the people going in and out.

They all seemed to be moving with the same level of urgency, not rushing as I would have expected if they'd been responding to news of a dangerous criminal's escape. I approached the doors as calmly as I could, sure with every step that the guards were going to realize I wasn't meant to be there.

As I drew closer, I could hear the people entering giving their explanations for their presence. I waited to hear an assistant explain his presence, then stepped forward and did the same for my own, changing only the name.

There was a pause as the guards considered my story, and I tensed. If they decided I was lying to them—

"Case?" asked one of the officers on the door.

Ah. This, I knew. "The unauthorized instar detected in the dimensional cluster designated," and then the long algebraic equation. I was suddenly, fiercely grateful that the Johrlac used math in their naming system. I could no more have recited a phrase that long than I could have sprouted wings and flown away. But an equation? That was child's play.

The guard's eyes glazed over for a moment. "Your co-workers

have already returned to work," he said. "You departed at the same time."

"I was delayed by the collective's announcement," I said. "I am not customarily assigned to this location. Several people have stopped me to ask whether I had seen anything that might lead us to the missing prisoner."

The guard gave me a hard look, glaze blooming into earnest white. I pushed my partition toward him, holding it high and steady. I felt him pushing against its edges, checking their solidity, looking for holes in my defenses. When he didn't find any, he pulled back, the light in his eyes shutting off.

"The prisoner is unlikely to be found anywhere near here," he said. I nodded, taking this as an informational statement. That was apparently the correct response; he pulled the lever and the doors slid open, allowing me to step inside.

In a way, this was the real test. Outside, it had been me, the guard, and all the room in the world to turn and run if he hadn't believed my story. In the airlock, it was me and the two guards stationed there, their faces masks of impassive neutrality. They barely even looked at me.

Before when I'd been in the airlock, I'd been leaving. This was an arrival, and that came with the same wind-based decontamination as my arrival at Fetch and Carry's home. The air hit me and the bugs went flying, impacting with the far wall and sticking there as the plants in the corners unwound their tendrils and pulled them to their deaths. I wanted to study the various insects that had been blown off of me, to see what I could learn about this dimension from the shape of their wings and the shine of their bodies.

But a civic assistant who had lived here all her life would have no such curiosity. She would already understand. So I buried my questions beneath another layer of partition and continued staring straight ahead, waiting for the doors to open. When they did, I proceeded forward, into the vast atrium on the other side.

Johrlac of every caste strolled in all directions, distinguished only by the visual cues of their jumpsuits, walking with the calm, unified purpose of people who had never been required to make decisions for themselves. I loosened my partition slightly, letting myself hear the ambient hum of the minds around me.

They formed a single unbroken note, and I skimmed along the surface, looking for the threads of the collective. To my surprise, I didn't find many. These people knew what they were supposed to be doing, understood the rules they lived by, and were happily performing their duties without being forced into compliance. This was how you could organize a hive mind without omnipotence: the collective didn't need to be everywhere or know everything. They just needed to wind things up and get them started, then watch for deviation. Yes, that meant they couldn't stop it before it happened, but in some ways, that was better. Letting things go wrong allowed them to make corrections, which was constantly reinforcing the idea that they were in control.

Two Johrlac in brown-and-red jumpsuits hurried across the floor to one of the doorways there, dragging mops and buckets with them. The people whose paths they cut across stepped smoothly out of the way, letting them pass without breaking stride in any measurable way. It was like they all had access to an unseen grid, telling them what was going to happen next.

It was nice, in a terrible way. No collisions, no one cutting anyone else off, no conflicts over space. I spent enough time in libraries and academic settings to know the controlled chaos that would normally have defined a scene like this one, and it was nothing like the smooth, regimented ease in front of me. It was like the whole room had been choreographed. It was—

Wait. Brown and *red*?

I looked at the two Johrlac beginning to mop the floor. Yes: brown-and-red jumpsuits, the red bright as a firetruck, blaring and undampened. It would have been a bold fashion choice . . . if anyone in this room had been capable of perceiving the color red. They weren't, and so I shouldn't have been either.

I took another look around the room, moving with perhaps

more urgency than was safe if I wanted to fit into the throng surrounding me. All I saw were Johrlac, ignoring me as they went about their business. Johrlac in a dozen different jumpsuits, yes, but still members of my own species.

Then I blinked, and like a hidden object in a mobile game, I saw the figure pressed against the far wall. They were short and lithe, visibly younger than the workers surrounding them, wearing a solid-red jumpsuit that looked like it had been made by stitching pieces of other suits together, effectively creating a camouflage suit. Their hair was scruffy and brown, pulled into a high ponytail that fell shaggy along the sides of their head, breaking up their outline and allowing them to blend better with the ridges of the paper walls around them.

I started toward them, watching the crowd carefully. It was easy to move among them as long as I paid attention: they generally wouldn't deviate from the paths that they were on, preferring to proceed in straight lines whenever it was possible to do so. There were a few near misses as people stepped in front of me and didn't stop, forcing me to weave around them, and I was sure I would have looked odd if anyone had been paying attention, being the only person here without a clear map of the space. But no one seemed to care.

The person against the wall didn't appear to realize I was approaching them until I was only about ten feet away. Their head snapped up, eyes widening—brown eyes, which just confirmed that this person wasn't Johrlac. Hair dye exists, but I didn't see this particular world dedicating a lot of resources to developing cosmetic contacts.

I sped up slightly, wanting to reach them before they could run. I wasn't quite quick enough. They bolted, less concerned about being spotted than I was, and ran for the nearest open doorway. I scowled and followed, walking as fast as I dared, weaving between the people with focused dedication. They ignored me, I pursued the stranger, and for a moment, life was simple.

Then I came around a corner, entering an empty stretch of hall.

No: not empty. The stranger was there, pancaked up against the wall like the color of the jumpsuit they wore was going to protect them. There was nowhere left to run: the hall ended here, becoming wall and closed doors rather than any sort of exit route. I slowed down, still not trying to frighten my quarry more than absolutely necessary.

I dropped my partition as far as I dared, trying to listen on a mental level. Audibly, they weren't making any sounds. That wasn't surprising. Mentally, they weren't making any sounds at all. If I pushed harder than felt wholly safe, I struck what felt like a glossy dome, something solid and slick. It was like my probes slid right off the surface. Yet I knew they weren't wearing any sort of anti-telepathy charm; I could pick up on the concept of red from them, which meant *something* was escaping.

Maybe that was the answer: they had taken the time to lock everything they considered important away, blocking me from their thoughts, memories, and identity, but hadn't thought to start blocking basic concepts, like the color red.

I stopped about three feet away from where they were "hiding," dropping my voice to avoid attracting any more unwanted attention, and said, "I can see you."

"No you can't," they replied hotly, in a high, barely pubescent voice. "You can't see me at all."

"An interesting theory, but I followed you here, which sort of implies that I *can* see you," I said. "If I couldn't see you, I wouldn't be following you."

The stranger was quiet for several seconds, clearly thinking about this and not liking the fact that it was patently true. "I— well— You *shouldn't* be able to see me."

"No, probably not," I agreed. "Did you make that jumpsuit yourself? Is it supposed to hide you?"

They finally peeled their face away from the wall, turning to look at me. Their eyes were very wide. I couldn't pick up on what they were actually feeling, but here on Johrlar, being able to tell anything from a person's expression was barely shy of a superpower.

I gentled my voice still further, talking to the stranger like they were a wild animal I was afraid of spooking. "Hey," I said. "You don't have to be afraid of me. My name's Sarah. What's yours?"

"Name?" They paused, considering their options. "You're a cuckoo," they said finally. "That's what you are. You could be someone who's just been called home by the collective of queens to be reabsorbed and set to what they call honest work, but if you were, you wouldn't be able to see me, and so you're a cuckoo, and that's why you can see red, even though you oughtn't to be able to, not a bit of it. I couldn't have been expected to know a cuckoo was lurking around in the halls. That's a no-one-knows thing. So I didn't do anything wrong."

"No, you didn't," I affirmed. "You didn't do anything wrong. Who are you? Why are you here?" The question I really wanted to ask—*What* are you?—would have been rude beyond belief, and so I had to leave it floating between us, silent but still visible, at least to me.

"Ikko," said the stranger, after a long, contemplative pause. "Here to watch what happens. The collective's been all in a tizzy for days now. They're supposed to be arresting somebody for doing what they're calling awful, awful things on a whole different world, and I'm supposed to be watching for that person to come through so's we can try to intercept them. Only trouble is, all you wasps look just the same to me."

"Want to hear a secret?" I asked, and leaned closer before I said, in a conspiratorial tone, "We all look the same to each other, too. That's why we have to wear the jumpsuits. It's so we can tell each other apart."

Startled, Ikko giggled. That moment of surprise caused her shields to drop enough that I could get a glimpse of her mind's surface, coming away with two salient facts: first, that she was a girl, and second, that she wasn't supposed to be here. Oh, the mission she'd described was real, but it wasn't intended to be hers. She was still a child by the standards of her people, the local equivalent of twelve at best, and they didn't want to risk her.

"Well, Ikko," I said. "It's very brave of you to be here. This is a dangerous place for someone to be on their own."

"You're on your own. Is it all dangerous for you, too?"

She looked at me with wide brown eyes, waiting for my answer, and I realized I didn't have one. I hesitated. Was it dangerous for me? Yes, absolutely. The whole collective wanted me, and my "hide directly under their noses" tactic would only distract them for so long. I didn't understand how anything here worked. I didn't know how long it would take for them to notice the blank space I created in their perfect pattern. And when they did, they would destroy me.

I could handle them in the mindscape, where they were devoting a portion of their strength to holding me down in the void, into making a pleasant face to come and talk to me. Could I really deal with all five of them when they had full access to their resources and were standing on home ground? I'd been so angry about Annalise's actions that I hadn't really stopped to think my own through the way I should have.

"It's very dangerous for me here," I said honestly. "But I don't have anyplace else that I can go."

"You can come back to my village with me," said Ikko. "The Eldest Living would be happy to hide you if you haven't been re-assumed into the collective. You see me. That means you're using *your* eyes, and not theirs. It's how we know a safe wasp from a stinging one."

"I would be happy to come back to your village," I said. That was overstating things a bit, but it would get a child out of a dangerous situation that she wasn't supposed to be in, and that made it true enough for me. "If you can promise I'll be allowed to leave after I've been there, I think it would be safer for the both of us."

"Safe is as safe does," said Ikko philosophically. She pushed fully away from the wall. "You know how to exit?"

"I don't, actually," I admitted. "Last time I went out, I claimed afternoon leisure, which I'm guessing is sort of like a lunch break. But that isn't going to work twice in a row. You have any ideas?"

"You can work the doors. That makes it easier. You look like an adult wasp—you're an adult?"

I nodded.

"Great. Tell them you've been called for a reproductive assessment. They'll let you leave. Nothing suspicious about a reproductive assessment."

"All right," I said. "Lead the way."

She did, walking back down the hall and waiting at the door for me to follow. The atrium was exactly as it had been before, busy and bustling and as flawlessly choreographed as a Broadway musical. I forgot to slam my shields back up before we stepped into the open, and for just a moment, I could see the tracks telling them where they should step, the guidelines set down by the collective to order their movements. I could also see the allure. It hadn't been clear before, but as soon as I understood what it was like, the simple brilliance of it all slammed down.

I forced my partition back into place, shutting out that terrifying appeal before it could convince me that I needed to surrender myself to the collective. I looked at Ikko, who was watching me, eyes wide again. I was sure if I'd been able to brush against her emotions, I would have found concern and even a little fear lingering there. I was supposed to be one of the nice wasps. What would happen to her if I gave in to the urge for community and fell into the collective when she was right beside me and I knew where she was well enough to grab her?

My partition came up, and the trails were gone, the call of the collective going silent. I approached the doors, Ikko by my side, and waited for the guards to acknowledge me. They turned their attention to me, minds brushing against my partition, and I detected neither surprise nor true recognition from that touch.

"Business?" asked one of the guards.

"I have been summoned for a reproductive assessment," I said, keeping my voice level and faintly disinterested, like this was something that happened every day.

The guard's mind brushed against mine again, harder this time, with an insistence behind it that made me feel like dropping the partition would be the correct choice. I summoned the memory of Verity's first pregnancy, and the emotions that had been rolling off of her as we made our way to St. Giles's for her prenatal appointments. She'd been excited and scared, in awe of the tiny life she was building inside her own body, and terrified of the idea that she'd have to set that life loose to crash through the world on its own terms. I pressed those emotions flat and gray, trying to reduce them to something that would suit this place, these people.

Pushing them forward, I lowered my partition enough to let the guard reach through and touch that emotional response. He studied it for a moment, eyes gleaming white, then pulled back with a nod.

"Acceptable reason to depart during working hours," he said, and his eyes flashed a brighter white, obscuring pupils and irises entirely.

The door slid open behind him. Ikko and I stepped into the airlock, and the guard didn't comment on my silent companion, or ask Ikko where she was going. Between her jumpsuit and the slick surface of her mind, she genuinely wasn't there for him.

Once we were outside, she giggled and seized my hand. The skin-to-skin contact was enough to plunge me beneath the shell of her mental defenses. I saw the village she was taking me to, the ancient woman she referred to as the Eldest Living, her parents and siblings. And more, I heard a word I hadn't been expecting to encounter here, however far away we were from Earth.

We were on the public street, surrounded by Johrlac on all sides, and so I couldn't ask aloud, only hold on to Ikko's hand as we walked, and wonder what in the world a runaway preteen on Johrlar could possibly know about the Kairos.

Fourteen

ANTIMONY

"Never underestimate the power of gossip."

—**Jane Harrington-Price**

The map room, in the aftermath of a terrible proclamation

THE DOOR CLOSED BEHIND THE four Johrlac, and Alice sagged in Thomas's arms, sobbing into his chest. He held her tightly, watching the room like he thought it was going to attack us at any moment. It was . . . bracing, seeing the two of them like that. They were supposed to be untouchable, my powerful, terrifying elders, but here they were, brought low by a single group of Johrlac operating at a lower instar than Sarah. If they could do this to Alice, what could the queens who controlled this society do to the rest of us?

Sam apparently had the same thought. He stepped closer to me, large hands resting on my shoulders. "I know they took two of your cousins, and that's a bummer, babe, it really is, but you have a *lot* of cousins, and I only have one of you. Do you think we could make with being someplace that isn't *here*? Like, I don't know, some other dimension entirely? I never got to see the one with all the giant spiders. That sounds better than staying here."

I looked up at him, sighing. "You know I can't do that."

"I do," he said, with what sounded like genuine regret. "But *you* know I had to try, right? I love Sarah and Arthur, I really do.

with an insistence behind it that made me feel like dropping the partition would be the correct choice. I summoned the memory of Verity's first pregnancy, and the emotions that had been rolling off of her as we made our way to St. Giles's for her prenatal appointments. She'd been excited and scared, in awe of the tiny life she was building inside her own body, and terrified of the idea that she'd have to set that life loose to crash through the world on its own terms. I pressed those emotions flat and gray, trying to reduce them to something that would suit this place, these people.

Pushing them forward, I lowered my partition enough to let the guard reach through and touch that emotional response. He studied it for a moment, eyes gleaming white, then pulled back with a nod.

"Acceptable reason to depart during working hours," he said, and his eyes flashed a brighter white, obscuring pupils and irises entirely.

The door slid open behind him. Ikko and I stepped into the airlock, and the guard didn't comment on my silent companion, or ask Ikko where she was going. Between her jumpsuit and the slick surface of her mind, she genuinely wasn't there for him.

Once we were outside, she giggled and seized my hand. The skin-to-skin contact was enough to plunge me beneath the shell of her mental defenses. I saw the village she was taking me to, the ancient woman she referred to as the Eldest Living, her parents and siblings. And more, I heard a word I hadn't been expecting to encounter here, however far away we were from Earth.

We were on the public street, surrounded by Johrlac on all sides, and so I couldn't ask aloud, only hold on to Ikko's hand as we walked, and wonder what in the world a runaway preteen on Johrlar could possibly know about the Kairos.

Fourteen

ANTIMONY

"Never underestimate the power of gossip."

—**Jane Harrington-Price**

The map room, in the aftermath of a terrible proclamation

THE DOOR CLOSED BEHIND THE four Johrlac, and Alice sagged in Thomas's arms, sobbing into his chest. He held her tightly, watching the room like he thought it was going to attack us at any moment. It was . . . bracing, seeing the two of them like that. They were supposed to be untouchable, my powerful, terrifying elders, but here they were, brought low by a single group of Johrlac operating at a lower instar than Sarah. If they could do this to Alice, what could the queens who controlled this society do to the rest of us?

Sam apparently had the same thought. He stepped closer to me, large hands resting on my shoulders. "I know they took two of your cousins, and that's a bummer, babe, it really is, but you have a *lot* of cousins, and I only have one of you. Do you think we could make with being someplace that isn't *here*? Like, I don't know, some other dimension entirely? I never got to see the one with all the giant spiders. That sounds better than staying here."

I looked up at him, sighing. "You know I can't do that."

"I do," he said, with what sounded like genuine regret. "But *you* know I had to try, right? I love Sarah and Arthur, I really do.

They're my favorite fucked-up weirdos in your family. I just love you a hell of a lot more."

"I would certainly hope so, since you're supposed to be marrying me." I looked back to Alice and Thomas. She had stopped crying and was wiping her eyes, while he dabbed at her upper lip with a handkerchief he'd produced from a pocket. He looked over at us, expression hard.

"Being part-Kairos isn't enough to protect against the full focus of a hunting Johrlac," he said. "Never has been. We grew careless in assuming it would be sufficient. We won't make that mistake a second time."

"No, we won't," said Alice. She pushed herself away from him, then staggered slowly to her feet, swaying in place as she worked to get her balance back. "I should never have taken off my anti-telepathy charm." She pulled it out of her pocket and slipped it back over her head, adjusting it until it hung under her shirt, directly between her breasts. She paused when she was done, pressing the heel of her hand to her forehead.

"Shouldn't have stopped drinking the cooking sherry, either," she muttered. "My head is ringing like a damn gong. How long do we think this is going to last?"

"You have more experience with the Johrlac than I do, dear," said Thomas.

"Yeah, but you have more academic research," she countered. "Anything in there about them giving people chronic migraine as a form of punishment?"

"I'm not sure they've ever thought of it," he said. "Let's not make the suggestion."

"I want to suggest a few things," she said, tone leaving no question of whether or not those things would be bloody and violent. She looked around at the rest of us. "I heard you just now, Sam. If you really want to bail, we can't stop you. I wouldn't even blame you—this isn't your family yet, not quite, and this may be your one opportunity to hit the bricks. But you'll still be stuck in this dimension, because we don't have the resources to get you home."

He huffed, then slumped where he stood. "That, and you'll probably hate me forever, which is totally fair, because I'd hate me forever too. These people are—they're not great people. I've always been a little weirded out by the way you'll all accept that cuckoos are universally evil unless they're related to you, because that's not the kind of racist or speciesist you try to be. But now that I've met more of them, I'm wondering how you ever got close enough to learn that some of them *aren't* complete and total assholes."

"Well, our son married a cuckoo's daughter, and that sort of opened the door, although not until after I'd decked the mother of the bride at Kevin's wedding," said Alice. She was looking better by the moment, her color improving and her balance getting more stable. She had started to prowl around the edges of the room, peering at the cubbies full of rolled scrolls.

"How many major family decisions have you made via fist-fight?" asked Sam.

"Most of them," answered Alice and I, in unison. I shot her a look. She shot one back, clearly amused, but didn't comment, only continued peering at the various scrolls.

"What are you looking for, dear?" asked Thomas.

"I'm not sure, but I'll know it when I see it," said Alice. She paused at one of the cubbies, beginning to poke around inside it with more focus. "If you need something else to be pissed about, Lybee being here means they knew what Naga was having her do to me, and they allowed it. His other Johrlac helpers—the ones who came before her—may be here, too."

"The thought had already occurred to me," said Thomas, voice going dark and somewhat dangerous. When he sounded like that, he wasn't a man I'd want on the other side of a fight I couldn't get out of. "But if I go around setting everyone who hurt you while I was detained on fire, I'm going to get the sort of reputation that brings unwanted guests back to the house. I can let her live, for now. Unless you'd prefer I didn't . . ."

"I'm not that kind of malicious," said Alice. "Sometimes I wish

I were, but I haven't been since I outgrew putting my hair in pigtails."

"I miss your pigtails," said Thomas.

"You're the only one," she replied, pulling out a map scroll and moving to open it on the table. "Look at these directional arrows. Caerus borders on Johrlar, but it doesn't border on Earth."

"You know, if you gave the dimensions names that didn't correspond to specific planets, it might be easier for other people to tell the difference between them," said Sam.

"Might be," Alice agreed amiably. "Alas, we do not live within that happy filing system, which was established long before anyone in this room was even considered, much less conceived. Whoever started it was thinking from the perspective of 'Well, this is obviously the part of the dimension that *matters*.'"

"Arrogant," said Sam.

"Yup." Alice tapped the map, gesturing for Thomas to come closer. "Based on these pathways, the Kairos on Earth definitely arrived by way of Johrlar."

"It makes sense," I said. "They were here, and Johrlac are good at moving between dimensions. At least a few Kairos must have stumbled into the right place at the right time to make their escape through the transit paths."

"Yes," agreed Alice. "You can't really keep people who treat coincidence like a trusted friend confined for very long. We're keeping this." She rolled the map back up, shoving it into her pack. "If nothing else, we can return it to that village you saw. Show them how they're supposed to get out of here, assuming they even want to. This is their home after this long spent living here. They may not feel like Caerus has anything to offer them."

"Where do fūri come from?" asked Sam abruptly.

Alice blinked at him. "You know, I'm not entirely sure? I always assumed Earth. More of our local cryptids evolved there than came from some other dimension. Why?"

"Because if we're from another dimension and somebody

showed up with a map offering me a way back to a place I'd never been or seen and didn't know anything about, I don't think I'd want to go. I like it where I am."

Alice nodded. "Same here. I'm not packing my bags and heading for Caerus any time soon. But these Kairos were brought here to serve, and they've been hiding in the woods since they got away from the people who wanted to own them. Maybe they'll feel differently than we do. The polite thing is to give them the choice."

"And the clever thing is not to get ourselves caught here by standing around arguing about it," said Thomas. "What do you think the chances are the charm will keep them from catching you again, when they already know you're here?"

"They know I can move between dimensions—or think they know, anyway, even if I can't do it anymore. And I know, from past experience, that the way the tattooed crossings work doesn't disturb the math the Johrlac need to keep track of things. Meaning they won't think it's that strange for me to have just disappeared from a locked room."

"Alice . . ." said Thomas, a warning note in his tone. "Did you know they were going to catch on that quickly?"

"I don't want another argument about being careful, so no, I didn't," she said. "I knew there was a chance, but I had no way of knowing they'd already have recalled Lybee, or that she'd walk in on us like that. I wish I *had* known, because then I could have been braced to give her a more knuckle-forward hello. She knew I wasn't consenting back when she was messing with my memory. She was inside my head—she knew I didn't understand what she was doing, and she did it anyway. If I'd been trying to engineer an encounter with her, I would have made sure I was in a *much* better tactical position. Believe me, if I see her again, it's going to go very differently."

That wasn't the most soothing declaration of innocence I'd ever heard, but I could tell it mollified him; he relaxed as she spoke, and by the end, he was nodding.

"All right," he said. "So is there anything else we can do here?"

"I don't think so," said Alice. "They don't keep municipal blueprints, because that's not how building works here. As far as I'm aware, they don't write everything down for long-term storage. I always wondered why they wrote *anything* down, since they store it all in their mental filing systems. I suppose the Kairos answer that question."

"Why did they need the Kairos anyway?" I asked.

"Only the queens have access to any form of telekinesis," said Alice.

"Like how Emma Frost unlocked a whole bunch of new powers when she was possessed by the Phoenix Force?" I asked.

"I have no idea what that meant, but you sounded quite confident, so I'm going to nod and say that yes, that is probably a reasonable comparison," said Thomas.

"It's an X-Man thing," I said.

He didn't look enlightened, but he didn't ask any follow-up questions, so I presumed the topic was closed. I turned to look around the map room. There were two entrances: the one we'd come through, and the one Lybee had entered through. The only windows were more like skylights, set high above the shelves themselves. I nodded toward them and Sam grinned.

In the twinkling of an eye he was halfway up the wall of hex-shaped cubicles, moving almost faster than the eye could see. When he ran out of hexes, he launched himself across the room to snag on a shelf, dangling for a moment by his fingertips before flipping backward onto the narrow top, balancing on the balls of his feet. Stable, he moved closer to the windows.

"Annie, what is Samuel doing?" asked Thomas.

"Checking for other exits," I said. "Give him a second and he'll be back on the floor for you to look at disapprovingly."

"It's not that I don't approve. It's more that he seems to have a rather . . . negotiable relationship with gravity."

"You still haven't spent much time around Verity, have you?"

Thomas grimaced. "I make her somewhat uncomfortable, given the background I share with her late husband."

"Yeah," I said uncomfortably, turning my attention back to Sam.

Verity—my older sister—had always been a big fan of firsts. She'd been the first, and so far only, member of our generation to get married, the first to move out, the first to know what she wanted to do with her life. The first to find herself widowed and raising her children as a single mother. Her husband, Dominic, had been ex-Covenant, just like Thomas. Sometimes they even sounded the same. It wasn't really a surprise that she wouldn't want to be around our grandfather, given the similarities. It was still a tragedy that she wasn't building a relationship with him—or improving her relationship with me. Verity and I had never been the closest siblings, but she was still my sister, and I worried about her all alone out there in New York. And then I catch myself thinking things like that and realize I'm in danger of turning into my mother, just like I always said I wasn't going to let myself do.

Families are complicated.

Sam met my eyes and nodded, tail curled high behind his back. I nodded back, moving into position beneath the central skylight. He was bigger and heavier than I was, so I wouldn't be able to do much beyond breaking his fall, but that might be better than nothing, depending on how this went.

Sam leapt.

He impacted the central skylight with all four limbs at the same time, landing with hands and feet both pressed to the frame. He hung there for a long moment, suspended by his fingers and toes. The frame began to detach from the wall, jerking downward what felt like a quarter-inch at a time. Sam leapt free of the skylight, sticking to the wall above the shelves and looking delighted as his impact allowed him to punch twenty delicate holes into the grayish material, clinging on.

The skylight frame continued to detach, finally falling to clatter to the floor with a remarkably anticlimactic thudding noise. The lack of metal in their construction was definitely showing. Alice moved to pick it up, turning it over in her hands before passing it over to Thomas for further examination.

"Fascinating," he said. "The panels are extremely thin glass—I would expect it to be impossible without some sort of machining, but the substance that holds them in place is organic, and feels related to the glue some insects produce to build their nests. The material holding everything together is bamboo. They must heat it and bend it into position. It's beautiful, and would do a reasonable job of keeping the place climate-controlled."

"And we can get out now," said Sam, dropping down from the top of the shelves and moving to stand next to me again, his tail snaking around my ankle. "If they're expecting us to be moving around in here, it might be better for us to move around the outside of the building."

"As long as they still can't see us, that may be the most sensible way to do this," I agreed, looking toward my grandparents, who exchanged a speculative look before nodding their agreement.

"Sounds like a plan," said Alice. "Then they can really wonder where we went."

"Samuel?" said Thomas. "If you would be so kind?"

Sam smiled, then unwound his tail from my ankle, grabbed me, and jumped.

It only took him a few minutes to ferry all three of us up to the opening. I pulled myself through the hole and then helped my grandparents out onto the flat surface of the nearby roof, which crunched and flexed uncomfortably under our feet, but showed no signs of caving in. Sam came up at the very end, carrying the skylight with him. He pulled it back into the opening it had fallen out of, tugging until it seated itself with an audible *pop*.

"Seemed like it would fit back where it had come from," he said, shooting me a pleased look. "Now they won't have an immediate pointer to where we went, unless they go checking the outside wall. People don't normally think to do that."

"Well done, Samuel," said Thomas.

"Thank you." He preened.

I smacked him on the shoulder. "You broke it and then you fixed it. Don't be too smug."

He smiled at me. "You know you love me."

"Yeah, I do," I agreed, and kissed him on the cheek before taking a frank look at our surroundings.

The walls around us were never fully smooth, but rounded and ridged, like the outside of a wasp's nest. The top layers of the papery building material crunched underfoot, and there was no predicting where the next window would appear. Neighboring trees overhung the structure at some points, and I watched as a butterfly with wings like dinner plates went gliding silently by, flying with long, smooth wingbeats that were nothing like the rapid fluttering of the butterflies I knew from home.

Sam leapt and landed on a tree branch, looking instantly more comfortable than he had while we were all inside. He looked around, then leaned back down toward us and said, "There's a lot of activity down on the street, but no one's pointing at me."

"They're not going to register you as anything worth pointing at if the anti-telepathy charms continue to hold," said Alice. She looked around, then gestured farther up the slope of the building. "We should head this way. If I remember the layout correctly, that will take us toward the holding cells, and we might be able to find our people and get out of here before something else goes wrong."

"Alice . . ." Thomas hesitated, expression twisting. "I hate to ask this, but is there any chance the collective was actually able to modify your memory while they were inside your head before? I don't know if we should be letting you take the lead."

"My memory's been manipulated before, and while I can't swear I would know, I still remember why we came here," said Alice. "We're getting my grandchildren back. I'm not feeling any urge to lead us straight to the collective, or to betray my allies. I think I can be trusted for right now, and if it starts to look like I can't be, I won't fight back."

"All right," he said, and turned toward me. "Annie? What do you think?"

"I think I've trusted Grandma Alice for my whole life, and I can trust her now," I said. "I'm happy to let her lead the way until she gives me a good reason to feel otherwise."

"All right. Alice? Show us where we need to go."

Alice smiled brilliantly, then turned and began hiking up the slope of the building, not looking back as she moved toward the next slope in the sequence. We followed after her, although Sam stayed on the tree limb as long as he could, only dropping down onto the side of the building when he clearly had no other choice remaining. The four of us hiked grimly and silently from there, occasionally swatting away palm-sized flying beetles.

"I hate to say this in case it jinxes us or something, but at least there aren't any mosquitoes," said Sam.

I flinched. If the mosquitoes were to scale with everything else we were seeing around here, they would be a genuine threat. "Died to extradimensional mosquitoes" was not how I wanted future generations to remember me.

"Nope," said Alice, with what sounded like genuine cheer. "There aren't mosquitoes on this world. Why would sanguivores evolve when nothing bothered to develop blood? You'll find various parasites that feed on hemolymph or ichor, but nothing that wants blood."

"That's a relief."

"Sweat, now . . . sweat can get you into trouble."

"How does that work?" I asked. "I thought sweat was effectively filtered blood."

"It is. It's also an excellent source of salt and other minerals that the swarming flies adore, no matter what dimension you're in. They'll come after us if we hold still for too long. Call it good motivation to keep moving!" She flashed me a nearly manic smile and kept climbing the side of the building.

Sam stepped closer to me, voice low as he said, "She really

scares me sometimes, you know that? Like, she is genuinely terrifying when she's trying to be."

"Oh, no," said Thomas. "This isn't her trying to be terrifying."

"What is it, then?"

"This is her forgetting what terrifies the rest of us, and being honest for a change." He smiled a bit at our expressions, shaking his head. "She spent a long time alone, and leaning in to being the monster everyone around her was afraid of kept her alive. She's been getting better, I promise."

He turned and hurried after her, climbing the slight slope of the building without hesitating or looking back at the pair of us. I blinked, feeling obscurely like I'd just been scolded. Sam's tail wrapped around my waist and tugged me forward as he continued onward, and after a brief stumble, I let myself be pulled, hurrying to catch up to him.

Still no one at the street level seemed to realize we were there. They went about their business, ignoring the figures climbing the side of their central building. We really were invisible. It was kind of amazing how much dependance they placed on a single sense. It made me wonder how their society dealt with cuckoos like Angela, the ones who couldn't receive telepathic messages. Would one of them be able to see us, forced to use their eyes instead of their minds?

And on we climbed, higher and higher, away from what little we knew, into the silent heights of the structure.

✦ ✦ ✦

We reached a point where the building began to climb directly upward, rather than following the soft curves and slopes of a wasp's nest. Alice cocked her head, looking at it, then produced two knives from inside her shirt and drove them into the papery wall, pulling herself up like she was climbing a mountain. Every cut created a gash she could use as a foothold while she was moving the knives up for her next hand grip, and she moved with remarkable speed for a human woman without proper climbing gear.

Thomas followed with his own knives, making use of the holes she'd already opened to speed his own progress.

Sam snorted, then scooped me off his feet and slung me over his shoulder, beginning his own ascent at a speed that put both of them to shame. No shock there: he was designed to do this sort of thing, and they weren't. Sometimes it's good to have a natural advantage. He slowed as he pulled up level with Alice.

"Where are we heading?" he asked.

She turned toward him, looking utterly unsurprised by his sudden appearance. "Highest window. They're very fancy wasps, but they're still wasps, and they keep their prisoners as far as possible from their queens. It's instinct codified into municipal planning."

"On it," said Sam. He surged upward, ripping handholds out of the wall as he went. When he reached the topmost window, he paused, peering into the room on the other side. Only when he was confident that no one was there waiting for us did he grasp the frame and wrench the window out of the wall. "I thought someone might notice if I just pulled it out while they were looking," he said.

"Good thinking," I said agreeably. "Boost me over to the window."

"Got it." He transferred hold of the window to his tail, then swung me down and maneuvered me over to slide through the hole that he'd created, into the room on the other side. It was smaller than any of the other rooms I'd seen so far, with sides that mirrored the hex shapes of the cubbies downstairs. Apparently, the smaller the space, the more obviously it was part of a giant wasp's nest.

Fascinating. Humans evolved from early primates, but we don't live in nests of grass and mud. It seemed a little odd that the Johrlac would still live in the materials and shapes of their ancestors. Then I paused, taking a closer look while I waited for the others to catch up.

The room was hex-shaped and made of paper, yes, but there

was glass in the window—or had been, before Sam wrenched it out—and the door had something totally new to my experience of this dimension.

A lock. Metal and gleaming in the light, clearly machined. I moved closer, skating my fingers across it. It felt exactly like I would expect a metal lock to feel, and there were hinges on the door, also metallic. They had upped their security here, and that meant revealing some of the things I was reasonably sure had to be widespread throughout their culture, yet were shunted to the side for whatever logistical reason.

"Fascinating," I murmured.

"What is?" asked Thomas, sliding through the window.

I gestured toward the lock.

He crowded close, peering at it. "You're right—that *is* fascinating. If you'd asked me earlier, I would have said they didn't do metalworking on this dimension."

"No, but they do mining," said Alice, popping up behind him. "They figured out the value of their mineral deposits a long, long time ago. They trade them with neighboring dimensions, and they do all their metalworking elsewhere. Keeps their own air clean, and keeps the general population from getting too excited about the idea of using metal in their daily lives. You can only manage so much of an agrarian uprising when all you've got is bamboo."

My surprise must have shown. She shrugged.

"No hive mind is perfect. They figured out a long time ago that having one mind for the entire world made them inflexible and unable to progress: the original cuckoos happened because the locals tried too hard to cling to the idea that you could run an entire society on a single way of thinking. So they divide themselves by collectives of queens, and each collective manages a territory. They can't catch every remote farmer or woodsman. Every Johrlac on Johrlar dreams the dreams of the collective they belong to, but sometimes the ones who live in the middle of nowhere manage to wake up, even if it's not for very long. Without metal, they can't exactly challenge the collectives."

"So the queens, what, keep it all for themselves?"

"For themselves and for their guards."

Sam slid through the hole as we were speaking, then held up the window for us to see. "Should I put this back?"

"The Johrlac *do* have eyes, and they *do* see the inanimate," said Alice. "It would be best if you could, dear, yes. Please."

Sam nodded and shoved the window back into place, frowning as he asked, "If they have eyes and everything, why do they not see us?"

"Oh, they see us. We just . . . don't matter," said Alice. "We're nothing important. We can't be people, because they don't pick anything up when they look at us. Most prey species that evolve alongside telepathic predators develop natural mental shields, and the predators just look right past them. They might as well be rocks, or trees, or something else not worth bothering with."

"But a missing window would matter," said Thomas. "Someone would notice that it didn't look right, and report it to someone else, who might come to have a look. Sooner or later, they'd figure out that something was going on, and then we'd have to worry about people who were actually *looking* for something out of the ordinary. When they start paying attention to their surroundings, they can find things they wouldn't normally notice."

"So we're invisible until we're not, got it," said Sam. "That is the absolute worst superpower ever. 'You're invisible until someone realizes they might need to see you.' Why not just skip the invisibility entirely?"

"Why not spend some energy picking that lock rather than criticizing the way the brains of people from another dimension went and evolved?" asked Alice.

"Yes, ma'am." Sam turned toward the door.

Meanwhile, I began circling the room, looking for anything that might tell us what we were up against. It was a depressingly featureless space. There was no furniture: no desk to break into, no computer to poke at. Not even a filing cabinet or chair. "What do you think they do in here?" I asked.

"Best guess? They station someone to stand in here and listen to the prisoners," said Alice, with more cheer than felt entirely appropriate to the statement. "The lock helps them be sure that if anything goes wrong, they're secure in here until help can arrive. And Johrlar isn't big on written records, so it's not like they'd need to keep any sort of files in here in order to track their prisoners."

"Not sure that makes me feel better," I said, slanting a glance over at the door, where Sam was dutifully trying to pick the lock. He'd been practicing, and his natural dexterity combined with even the slightest understanding of what he was trying to do was rapidly making him one of our better locksmiths.

"Just about—there," he said, and there was a sharp clicking sound from the lock. He leaned back on his heels, looking pleased with himself.

Thomas stepped forward and turned the knob, then pushed the door inward, revealing the featureless hall beyond. Literally featureless: the walls were smooth grayish paper, with no decoration or texturing at all. Looking at them drove home just how much the downstairs atrium and map room had been intended for public use, and just how much this space, well, wasn't.

"Try to stick to the curve of the outer wall," said Alice. "Again, they're going to be doing their best to keep prisoners as far from their queens as possible."

I nodded, stepping out into the hall.

Together, the four of us moved along it, pausing when we reached the first door. It was smooth and unmarked, without any sort of window or peephole. What use would they have been? It wasn't like the guards were going to be checking on their prisoners visually.

I looked around, finally finding a low slot on the wall through which a tray could potentially be shoved. I knelt down.

"Be careful," Alice advised. "They may not know you're there, but if they see the hatch on the meal slot move, they could try to stab you through the opening."

"Stab me with what?" I asked. "You said there was no metal."

"They use bamboo cutlery. It still hurts when it stabs you."

"I'll be careful," I said, and gently eased the hatch open, taking care to keep my fingers on the very corner of the flap. It was made from polished wood, out of place against all the paper, but at least fitting with the tech level of its surroundings.

I crouched lower, peering through the slot. There was a single male Johrlac in the room, huddled in the corner next to the bed that had been provided for him, hugging his knees. He didn't look inclined to stab anyone. He also didn't look like he'd noticed me. Unlike the other Johrlac I'd seen in this dimension, he wasn't wearing a colored jumpsuit: instead, he was dressed in a loose gray-brown uniform that looked almost like pajamas. I let the hatch swing closed and looked over my shoulder at the others, shaking my head.

"Not this one," I said.

"But there was a prisoner?" asked Thomas.

"Yeah. Just a Johrlac, all by himself. He looked . . . defeated. Like he'd given up on ever getting out of here. But the room didn't look any emptier than the rest of the building."

"We don't know what their homes are like," said Alice. "Maybe he's used to lots of color and activity, and being put into a boxy little room is bad for his mental health. Maybe he's been cut off from the rest of the hive mind so he can think about what he's done. Do you want to ask him?"

"No. I want to find Arthur and Sarah."

"Then we keep moving."

The next three cells were the same story: single Johrlac, not moving or looking toward the hatch, dressed in gray-brown prison clothes. In the fourth, when I eased the hatch up, there was a Johrlac already crouching on the other side, her eyes blue and glazed with white, like she was barely holding back the urge to reach out with her telepathy.

"I see you," she said, in a dreamy tone.

I managed, barely, not to recoil.

"Kairos, yes? Little rats in the walls. I tried to tell the queens you were here, spying on us, but they told me I was overreaching my authority, said I had no right to approach them with security news, even though security is meant to be my purpose. But now here I am, locked away, and there you are, roving free."

"How can you see me?" I asked, cautiously.

"The cells cut us off from the collective, to keep us malleable," she said, surprisingly matter-of-fact. "They strip away the white noise that controls the universe. No more thoughts, no more feelings, no more ideas from the outside. Just me, alone in my head. It seemed like a fair punishment when I was on the other side of the door. Now it seems like eternity turned against me and made of teeth. I understand why the cuckoos go mad. The loneliness must swallow them alive."

"Oooooo-kay," I said. "What did you do?"

"I spoke against the will of the collective," she said. "I wanted the Kairos rounded up and removed. My queens wanted them left alone, only harvested on occasion, when we need them."

"Need them?" My voice sharpened. "Need them for what?"

She turned her face away from the hatch, looking toward the wall. "No. I'm a criminal, but I'm not a traitor. I won't tell you what you want to know if you don't know it already. I am loyal to my queens. You'll tell them? You'll tell them when they ask you what I said?"

A wave of pity crested over me, crashing down and leaving me soaked to the bone. "I'll tell them you're loyal," I said solemnly, and let the hatch swing shut. I turned to my companions. "You all heard that?" I asked.

Thomas nodded. "I did," he said.

Sam and Alice nodded in turn but didn't say anything—it wasn't necessary. I rose, and we continued down the hall.

When I opened the hatch on the fifth cell, I almost didn't realize that anything was different. Like the others, the figure in the cell was wearing loose gray pajamas, and seated in the corner with his knees pulled up to his chest. He had his forehead tucked against them, blocking his face. Still, something about the pattern of his breathing was wrong when compared to the Johrlac I'd seen before. He was holding himself too rigidly, clutching his legs too hard. His pants had pulled up slightly, revealing his feet and ankles, and I paused.

There were scratches on the sides of his feet, scabbed over and surrounded by angry red inflammation. It didn't look bad enough to be medically worrisome, but he could definitely use some antibiotics. Johrlac blood—or hemolymph—has naturally antibiotic properties. More importantly, it's clear. The inflammation meant he wasn't Johrlac.

"Arthur?" I whispered harshly.

He twitched, but didn't lift his head.

"*Arthur*," I repeated. "It's me, Annie. Come on, look at me."

He lifted his head, slowly, and gave me a mistrustful look that transformed into wide-eyed amazement as he realized I wasn't lying to him. "Annie!" he exclaimed, more loudly than I liked, and pushed himself onto all fours, crawling across the cell floor to stare at me through the hatch. "What are you doing here? How are you here?"

"I'm here to bust you out, and I'm here because our grandparents are better at dimensional travel than is honestly reasonable. Fortunately, I don't get to make the rules, so what I think is and isn't reasonable doesn't matter much." I looked over my shoulder. "Sam, get the lock. It's Arthur."

"Got that from the yelling," he said. "On it."

Arthur looked like he was about to cry. "Sam's here too?" he asked. "How many of you came?"

"Me and Sam, Grandma Alice and Grandpa Thomas. Elsie's pretty worried about you, but she was too far away to join the field trip." I smiled wanly. "She saw them take you, and I guess she didn't approve of having people teleport in and abduct her brother. She'd like you back."

Arthur pulled a face, and for a moment, I thought he was going to argue. Then he nodded. "I want to go home," he admitted, in a low voice.

That must have taken a lot out of him. Being built on the

wreckage of the person who used to own your body wasn't something I'd experienced, and so I couldn't fully understand what he might be feeling in the moment. Still, we'd managed to find him.

Sam worked at the lock, brow furrowed in concentration, until there was a click and the door swung outward. I blinked.

"All the doors we've seen here have opened out instead of in," I said. "Why?"

"Humans build our doors to open inward for security reasons," said Alice, offering me a hand so I could get off the floor. I didn't need the help, but I still appreciated the thought. It was nice to have someone worry from time to time. "It protects the hinges. Here on Johrlar, most doors are sliding. It's actually unusual to have this many hinged doors in one area. If I have to guess, I'd say the doors open outward to block off prisoner access to the hinge mechanisms."

"They're less worried about people breaking in than they are about the prisoners breaking out?" said Sam. "That seems right. Normally when you lock somebody up, you figure they'll stay that way. I wonder why they didn't go with sliding doors like a human prison, though."

"Isolation seems to be a big part of what they're going for here," said Arthur, standing and stepping barefoot into the doorway. "Sometimes at night the other prisoners scream and scream and it sounds like I'm surrounded by giant cicadas. Am I being racist or something if I say I don't like it here?"

"'Speciesist' is more accurate, darling, and no. You're allowed to dislike the people who abduct you," said Alice. "All we need to do now is find Sarah and we're all home free."

"Sarah?" he echoed, brows knitting together as he frowned. "Sarah isn't here. I would know if Sarah were here."

"I think she's gotten better at masking her presence from you," I said. "She's been to the compound in Portland a few times in the last year."

He looked hurt, shoulders hunching inward like he wanted to make himself as small as he possibly could. "She knows I want to see her. Why would she do that?"

"My dude," said Sam, who had only known Artie for a little while before he'd been deleted, and was thus more comfortable with Arthur than most of the rest of us. "You know why she'd do that. She doesn't want to see you, and she's never going to start wanting to see you."

"I can't get her out of my head," said Arthur, frustrated.

"Yeah, because she put *you* in your head, and sort of sent herself along for the ride." Sam shrugged. "Maybe we shouldn't do this here?"

"Here," said Alice, digging another anti-telepathy charm out of her bag and offering it to Arthur. "Put this on. It should make you effectively invisible to most Johrlac. It's going to be a lot easier to get you out of the building if they can't hear you thinking about escaping the whole way."

"Oh, fun," he said, taking the charm and slinging the cord over his head. Then he embraced Alice, head low and pressed against her shoulder while he gathered her close to him. "Thanks for coming to get me, Grandma."

"Of course, baby," said Alice, skating her hand over his hair. "I'd do it for any of you kids and you know it."

"Yeah, but sometimes I don't believe that 'any of us kids' applies to me," he said, letting go and stepping back. As he almost always did when in the field, he looked to me, waiting to be told what we were going to do next.

"All right," I said. "Let's keep moving."

We checked the rest of the cells along the hall. Two more of the Johrlac actually noticed the motion of the hatch and rushed over to accuse me of being a saboteur, working against their queens in some way they didn't explain but also quite clearly didn't approve of. Neither of them would tell us what they'd done to get thrown in here.

We made it all the way to the end without any sign of Sarah.

She wasn't here.

Fifteen

"A child's a child. Species is the next best thing to irrelevant."

—**Angela Baker**

The top level of a giant wasp's nest, surrounded by prison cells

We walked back toward the office we'd entered through, Alice at the front, Thomas and Arthur behind her, and me and Sam bringing up the rear.

We were about halfway there when someone shouted. We all froze, turning toward the sound, but I didn't see anything out of the ordinary, and judging by the expressions of the people around me, neither did anyone else.

"Why would they yell?" whispered Sam. "They're telepaths."

"I don't know," I replied. "But we should get out of here."

We began walking faster, and had just reached the closed office door when there was another shout, this one from in front of us. Again, we froze. This time, however, Alice started swearing softly, putting one hand on the pistol she wore low on her hip.

"Dear?" asked Thomas.

"It's a hunting tactic," said Alice, voice low. "Remember I mentioned that prey species on telepathic worlds will tend to develop shields against telepathy? They don't want to get caught and ripped apart, so they become mentally invisible."

"Yes," said Sam, warily.

"Well, if you can't hunt your prey the way that seems most natural to you, you'll find other ways of doing it. Flushing them out into the open is usually the opening salvo. They know we're in here, and they're just trying to startle us enough that we'll reveal ourselves, yell or bolt or something."

"But they can't see us," I said.

"They can, if they switch over to looking the right way. We need to consider that they might have started paying attention with other senses. Move very carefully from here, and if you see a Johrlac that isn't Sarah, don't let them touch you."

She turned and opened the office door, which was still thankfully unlocked. Of course, the room on the other side was considerably more crowded, what with the three Johrlac in blue jumpsuits inside. They all turned toward the opening door, and she had time to widen her eyes in surprise before she was hitting the ground on her stomach, leaving the rest of us to scatter. The heavy dart one of them had just thrown at her whistled by over her head, embedding itself deep in the wall on the other side.

Sam reached for the dart, lips drawing back to show his teeth. Before he could grab it, I yelped and pulled his arm away, leaving the dart where it was. He shot me a startled look.

"Just look at it!" I snapped.

He looked, face going slack as he registered the thorn-like needles arrayed around the shaft of the dart. Had he grabbed it, they would definitely have embedded themselves in his hand, leaving him injured at best, potentially poisoned at least.

I kept hold of his arm as I started backing down the hall, pulling him along with me. Thomas yanked Alice off the floor, and the two of them moved down the hall in the opposite direction. Arthur watched them go, then looked to Sam and me, and I could see the moment he made his decision. It was in his eyes, blue and familiar and strange, as they'd been since the day he woke up in St. Giles's as a stranger.

He reached up and removed his anti-telepathy charm before turning to the office, hands dropping carefully at his side. "My name is Arthur Harrington-Price," he said loudly. "I am not here of my own free will, but I *am* here, and how often does free will really come into the conversation anyway? My mother was Jane Harrington-Price, and I don't miss her or mourn her, because I don't remember her well enough to be sad that she's dead."

Alice made a choked hiccupping sound before clapping her hand over her own mouth.

"Jane was human, with a little bit of Kairos mixed in. My father is Theodore Harrington, and he's Lilu, which makes me one of the stranger hybrids you're ever likely to find. And I broke myself out of my cell all on my own. Your operational security sucks."

He grinned at the occupants of the office, showing his teeth in a way I knew Sam would take as a threat, and I knew was actually intended as one. I wanted to run over and grab him, pulling him away from his captors, but I respected his right to make this choice too much to take it away from him. He was making a last stand, using his body to buy us the time to get away. As long as they had an unknown number of semi-invisible invaders, the Johrlac would keep on coming. Give them an easy answer and a successful catch, on the other hand . . .

"Impossible," snarled one of the Johrlac in blue, stepping into the hall. He didn't look in either direction, all his attention focused firmly on Arthur. "Our cells are secure. You were helped."

"But here I am," said Arthur. "And I'm alone. How do you explain that, if I didn't break out of my cell?"

"You had help," insisted the Johrlac, but he was starting to sound unsure, like he wasn't as convinced as he wanted to be. The other two emerged from the office behind him, moving to flank Arthur.

Oh, screw last stands. There are always other options, always plans that don't involve leaving anybody behind. I pulled back my hand, calling silently on the fire that always burned in my bones, as much a part of me as my blood or marrow, innate and inseparable.

The pneuma here was sturdier and faster to respond than the still-healing pneuma of Earth. The air above my palm burst into flame, hot and lambent and very nearly searing my skin. I pulled back farther, then let fly, flinging the fireball directly at the nearest Johrlac.

They didn't register us as important because they couldn't appreciate the existence of thinking creatures without readable minds. But they knew what fire was. One of them yelled, less words than pure surprise, and then the fireball impacted the nearest guard, catching his hair and jumpsuit. They went up like oiled parchment, and it was his turn to yell, howling pain and distress. He lurched away from Arthur, careening into the nearest wall.

The nearest *paper* wall.

To say the wall burned was to understate the sheer spectacle of what happened as soon as he brushed against it. The paper went up so fast it virtually exploded, consumed by roaring flames that were immediately on their way to becoming a conflagration.

"Get Arthur," I snapped, pulling back to do it again.

Sam nodded and leapt, a streak of motion that crossed the distance between himself and my cousin so quickly that all I could do was hold my second fireball to be sure I wouldn't hit him by mistake. He returned with Arthur and I threw again, only to be answered by one of those massive metal darts.

"We'll meet up outside!" yelled Alice, and then she and Thomas were running down the hall, the guards who weren't actively on fire following after them. Sam, Arthur, and I turned to run in the opposite direction, trying to move away from the flames as quickly as we could.

We ran, and behind us, the fire consumed all.

◆ ◆ ◆

The Johrlac had abducted two members of my family, and the family creed said if they hadn't wanted collateral damage to follow on this terrible, terrible choice, they shouldn't have done it. I didn't feel bad about the fire, or the inevitable property destruction. That didn't mean the people in the cells deserved to die.

I ran until the fire was far enough behind us that it felt safe to stop, even if only for a moment, then slammed my hand into the nearest cell door, fingers spread to frame the lock. The papery substance that made the body of the door crisped and blackened, then gave way as the lock fell inward. I wrenched the door open.

The prisoner huddled in the corner looked up, eyes wide and glazed with white.

"I know you can't see me very well, but the building is on fire and you need to get the hell out of here," I snapped and moved on, running toward the next cell.

Realizing what I intended to do, Sam went bounding down the hall, beginning to punch holes in the doors and pull the lock mechanisms out that way.

"This is a lot faster than lockpicks!" he yelled back at me.

"Property destruction generally is," said Arthur, diving into the cell I'd just opened to grab the prisoner by the sleeve and steer him out into the hall. He was careful not to touch the man's skin, proving that even if he was making strange choices, he still remembered his training.

Arthur making strange choices was nothing new. He was a person built almost entirely from other people's memories, essentially "born" with someone else's experiences and emotions preloaded. Grandpa Martin was a Revenant, made of the bodies of dead men; Arthur was a new kind of Revenant, made from the memories of a dead man. And sometimes that made him glitch, in a way, reacting to stimuli and situations in unpredictable ways. He'd been depressed after his mother died, not because he was sad that she was gone, but because he *wasn't* sad. He hadn't known her well enough to mourn for her.

In the time since then, he'd seemed to get more stable, but had continued to have strange mood swings and what he described as patches of absence, places where the memories used to build him had been improperly anchored, leaving them to fall off and drop into the void. We'd thought that was a terrible thing in the beginning, a sign that he was going to fall apart entirely, but more and more I'd come to suspect that it was like a scab coming off of a scraped knee: he was settling into himself, becoming his own person and sloughing off the remains of what had been Artie. It broke my heart a little, because I loved Artie, but it wasn't Arthur's fault.

One of the first things any member of our family learned was that you should never touch a cuckoo's skin if you had any way to avoid it. When you're touching them, all the telepathic resistance in the world won't keep them out of your head; they can scythe through the protections we inherited from Great-Grandma Fran like a hot knife slices through butter, and once they're in, it can be hard to get them out.

Arthur yanked the prisoner he was trying to save out the door and let go of him, pointing toward the fire. "Look, fire," he said, maybe needlessly. "Run now, okay?"

The man ran, his eyes flashing white, and I grabbed Arthur by the wrist, jerking him along as I ran down the hall after Sam.

"What?" he asked.

"White eyes means they're contacting the collective," I said. "We have to save them, but they're telling on us as soon as we do."

"Fuck," said Arthur, with heartfelt earnestness. "Anything we can do about it?"

"Hope the fire is a big-enough distraction to let us get the hell out of here, and hope that these are the only cells." The thought that Sarah might be in another burning hall, locked in with no way out, was a terrible one. Not as terrible as it might have been, but bad enough to make me feel a little queasy.

"I think they are. From the way the guards talked when they shoved me in here, they don't get a lot of people who need to be detained like this."

"Less talk, more escape before getting barbequed," suggested Sam. He kicked through another door, revealing an empty room on the other side. It was a mirror of the room we'd arrived through, down to the wasp-wing window on the far wall. He rushed toward it, wrenching it out of its frame, then gestured frantically for the two of us to join him.

I stopped in the doorway. "Get Arthur out first," I commanded, and turned to face the fire.

It was working its way steadily along the hall toward me, not as fast as I would have expected. That made sense: Thomas's element was also fire, and if he was pulling on the flames from the other side of the fire, he could slow them down. I put my hands up, feeling for the outline of the inferno.

It was still too far away for me to feel the heat it was generating, but this was my fire; I'd created it, and it knew me. It answered my reach with a reach of its own, surging toward me. I pushed back, telling the fire I wanted it to leave us alone.

Fire is a living thing. It's not a very obedient one—fire doesn't like to be told what it's supposed to do—but it's alive, and like all living things, it can be communicated with if you only know the words you're supposed to use. I pushed and I spoke to it silently, in the language of the flame. It wasn't like Johrlac telepathy. This was something older and more primal, and it transcended language to become its own creation.

Stay, I told the fire, and *Burn but not too close to me.*

Home, said the fire. *Return?*

But alas, that was the tragedy of setting my fire free. It could never truly come home again. Even if I pulled it back into myself—and this was too much fire for me to extinguish it like that—it would remain apart from the rest of the fire, burning inside my bones and never entirely mine again, not the way it had been before. We were separated now, this fire and I, and yet it still remembered it belonged to me.

Burn, I replied. *Stay, spread, burn.*

Burn, replied the fire, and actually turned around, moving with patent disregard for the way fire normally behaved. It rolled back down the hall, consuming what it had missed the first time, burning holes in the floor and dropping to the next level, basically continuing to do what fire has always done after encountering a firebreak. I turned back to Sam and Arthur, wiping the sweat from my forehead with one hand.

They were staring at me, Sam with Arthur half-boosted to the open window, and kept staring as I trotted over to greet them.

"Well?" I asked. "Why are we just standing here? This whole place is going to be coming down!"

"It is *so hot* when you do that," breathed Sam.

"Can we go?" asked Arthur. He grabbed the sides of the window and pulled himself the rest of the way out, stepping away to make room for us.

"He's focused, I'll give him that," said Sam, and boosted me out.

This time, we didn't bother putting the window back in place. The building was on fire: it wasn't like a little hole was going to be the most noticeable thing about it.

Sam slid out the window barely a beat behind me. I grabbed his hand and took off running, heading for the large branches that overhung the building. We quickly passed Arthur, who had never been much for fieldwork. He struggled to catch up with us. I let go of Sam, freeing him to double back and sling my cousin over his shoulder like a sack of potatoes. He turned and ran back toward me, passing me as he moved to toss Arthur up into the foliage. Arthur yelped and grabbed on to the limb, dangling, as Sam grabbed me and leapt.

Behind us, the fire worked dutifully at swallowing the building whole, ripping it down one piece at a time. There had been no sign yet of my grandparents, but I believed in them; they'd be popping out somewhere on the other side any moment now. Sam lowered me to my feet, and I turned to grin at him, pausing when I saw his eyes.

His pupils were huge, so blown out that they had almost swallowed his irises, and his whole expression was glassy and drawn. I knew at once what was going on. Sighing, I hugged his arm.

"You breathed too close to Arthur, didn't you?" I asked.

Arthur, like Artie before him—same body, after all—was half-incubus, making him a walking, talking sex bomb. His pheromones were unpredictable, but more likely to cause problems when he was under stress. The Johrlac wouldn't have noticed: their non-mammalian nature made them immune to his allure. I hadn't noticed, because we were blood relations, and Lilu pheromones were supposed to expand their breeding pool. As one of the only known species to be cross-fertile with virtually everything, the population of people with at least some Lilu heritage could quickly skyrocket. Blood relatives being immune was the only way to prevent some pretty gross hook-ups.

Sam, though, was not genetically related to Arthur. He also wasn't particularly attracted to men, which kept the pheromones from hitting him like a lust-hammer. He still looked drunk or drugged at the moment, and that wasn't how we needed him to be.

"Arthur," he breathed, the word sounding like an ordeal, like I was infinitely cruel to ask him to speak.

Right. That was quite enough of that. I grabbed his collar and hauled him down toward me, then kissed him firmly. He was stiff at first, not resisting or pulling away, but not yielding either, like he thought kissing me was somehow wrong. Then, bit by bit, he melted into me, until I felt his tail snake around my waist, followed by his arms, followed by him lifting me off my feet and clutching me against him. I let go of his collar and draped my own arms around his neck, continuing to kiss him until he sighed. Only then did I pull back, looking into his eyes.

They weren't glossy anymore, and his pupils had returned almost to normal. He exhaled hard.

"You okay, buddy?" I asked.

"You kiss all your buddies like that?"

"I do. My trapeze instructor told me it was the best way to teach them not to drop me. I don't want to be smeared across the tent floor."

"A worthy perspective." He set me carefully down on my feet. "Woof, that was a bad one. Thanks for knocking me out of it."

"Anytime." I stepped back and turned to look at Arthur, grateful for the broad surface of the tree limb. It was about as wide as a twin bed, which seemed extravagant for a tree, and close enough to flat that I didn't feel like I was going to fall.

Arthur was sitting down about six feet away, back in the knee-hugging position he'd been in when I'd first found him.

"You okay over there?" I called.

"I'm sorry I doped your fiancé," he replied, miserably.

"Don't worry about it," I said. "No harm done."

He shot me a furious, almost feral look. "But there could have been. It would have been so easy."

"I know."

When Artie's pheromones had first started manifesting in earnest, we'd all been goofy teenagers, and I'll admit, there had been a certain fascination in the idea that he was just sweating pure aphrodisiac. I hadn't been very interested in dating back then, so I hadn't been jealous, exactly, but it had still seemed cool.

And then he'd sat me down and explained that he couldn't control them, which made them a constant risk to his health and safety. Not only could he force someone to do something they would never do intentionally, but he could get seriously hurt if someone decided not to take "no" for an answer. The only way to avoid that potentiality was to stay locked in his room most of the time. Arthur had quickly come to the same conclusions, and was no more social than his predecessor had been.

I walked over to Arthur, offering him my hands. "There's lots of weird vegetation around here," I said. "I'm sure something will have some stinky-ass sap you can smear on yourself to block the pheromones."

"Really?"

"Really. And you're Lilu, which means you won't be allergic to it the way I might be." Lilu get some advantages to go with the whole "basically a sex-pollen factory" problem. The breeding is a big one, from a species perspective. They're never going to die out, not with the way they reproduce. Extinction is not a worry for them.

For the individual, Lilu who have better control of their pheromones can use them to influence people without driving them into a lustful frenzy. And they're not allergic to anything. Dad thinks it's connected to their seemingly infinite cross-fertility: no good being able to reproduce with something if doing so will lead to a massive allergic reaction. They don't get itchy from mosquito bites, they don't catch poison oak . . . really, it's a big-enough bonus to make the downsides seem almost reasonable. But only almost.

Sam walked over to join us, looking faintly embarrassed. "Sorry about that, Arthur," he said, rubbing the back of his neck with one hand. "Didn't mean to get all weird on you back there."

"I appreciate the assist," said Arthur, waving it off. "And now we're in a tree. Why are we in a tree?"

"I like the tree," said Sam.

I looked back toward the building. Fire was licking at the walls, charring the papery exterior, and generally making a nuisance of itself. It didn't look like it was going to crown into the tree, however, and the patch of roof beneath our limb wasn't actively burning just yet, which meant we had a little time. "The tree is not on fire, which makes it a lot better than the alternative," I said grimly.

There was a commotion on the street below us. I popped my head over the edge of the limb to look, sliding on the rough bark before Sam wrapped his tail around my waist again to anchor me. I shot him a grateful look, then returned my attention to what was happening at street level.

There were no sirens. There were no lights. There were just swarms of Johrlac in banded bodysuits—dark blue, then golden orange, then light blue—riding what looked like giant froghopper bugs toward the burning building. One of the froghoppers was towing a cart with a large water tank on it. When they reached the building, they spread out to form a perimeter, and the riders slid down from their insects, moving to grab tubes connected to the tank. They strapped those tubes to the sides of the froghoppers, and the bugs began first to drink, then to spew cascades of foamy bubbles onto the fire.

The froth was thick and white, and it quashed the flames with a speed that simple water could never have managed. More Johrlac in the same colors but with added helmets and heavy coats charged into the building once the fire at the front had been put out, emerging a few seconds later with workers on their arms, steering them coughing and shaken to the other side of the street. No one screamed. No one shouted orders. The Johrlac not actively involved with the situation didn't even stop to stare. They just kept going about their business, ignoring the burning administrative building as completely as they had ignored the lot of us while we were infiltrating the place.

"Look," said Sam softly, and pointed. I followed the angle of his finger.

A new group of Johrlac had appeared, moving among the rescued workers. Their jumpsuits were banded black and a yellow so pale it looked white, creating a sharp contrast to the brighter yellow worn by many of the workers.

"Medical?" I guessed.

"Probably," said Sam. "Looks like they're getting everybody out."

They were. The bugs kept spitting, and the rescuers kept charging inside, although each round of rescues took a little longer as they had to go deeper to find the people they were trying to save. It wasn't until the fourth trip into the building that some of them began coming back empty-handed, and it wasn't until the sixth that I saw the first of them come out with bodies cradled in their arms, unmoving and even charred. They still carried those Johrlac over to the medical team, who took them gingerly and placed them on gurneys like the rest, only to cover them with sheets of stiff white fabric a few moments later.

"You okay?" asked Sam.

"I am," I said, still watching. I'd set the fire, no question of that, and any deaths in the burning building were on my conscience, but it wasn't like this was the first time I'd burned something down in the process of fleeing for my life, and it wasn't the first time people had died around me, or because of me. Didn't make it any easier to face the reality of what I was and what I could do. Didn't mean I'd have done things any differently, either.

"Look, over there," said Arthur. I looked up, finding him standing over and behind me, then followed the angle of his arm to where he was pointing at the corner, and at our grandparents. Alice and Thomas looked none the worse for wear, and were standing pressed up to one of the buildings that wasn't actively on fire. They were looking around, probably scanning for us, and as I watched, Alice looked up, then nudged Thomas. He turned to see what she was looking at, grinning when he spotted the three of us in the tree. Neither of them waved. Waving is rarely a good idea when you're trying to evade detection, even if you're reasonably sure no one's going to see you.

With this many minds and this much chaos on the street, we had to assume we'd be *easier* for the Johrlac to spot, not harder. They couldn't listen to everyone's thoughts at the same time, which might make them more open to the idea that some people's thoughts just couldn't be heard. And the firefighters were clearly able to perceive bodies that weren't thinking at all anymore, or they wouldn't be able to bring out the dead. Although maybe that was down to them mentally reclassifying the fallen Johrlac as something other than people, since they could perceive and interact with the inanimate.

Really, it was all too damn confusing for me to get hung up on, and made me want to go and find a Johrlac optometrist that I could grill at length about the way their vision worked. Instead, I pushed myself upright, gesturing for Sam and Arthur to follow as I started walking along the limb toward the main trunk of the tree.

"We need to get down and join them," I said. "Once we're all back together we'll be able to figure out what we're going to do next."

"Sounds like a plan," said Arthur.

"It's not to anyone who isn't a member of your family," said Sam. "Plans involve multiple steps and actual, you know, *planning*.

This is an action at the very most, a choice. A single step in the direction of a plan."

"I love you," I said.

"I know," he replied, no less exasperated.

Together, the three of us progressed along the limb, which thickened as we got closer to the trunk, making it easy for us to walk without falling. When we reached the trunk, Sam went bounding into the high foliage, quickly vanishing. Arthur blinked at this, then looked down, expression going queasy as he saw how far we had to potentially fall.

"Did your boyfriend just ditch us?"

"Probably not," I said. "Don't worry about it too hard."

Arthur frowned at me. "You're remarkably calm right now."

"Look, I'm getting to explore a new dimension, and the anti-telepathy charms we're wearing make us functionally invisible to the locals, which is nice, since I don't want to have my brain wiped today. Did they go prodding around in yours at all?"

Arthur shook his head, sitting back down on the limb.

"No," he said. "They grabbed me from the living room. I was watching TV with Elsie. She's been a lot nicer to me since we went on that road trip with Mary last year, you know? She's treating me almost like I'm really her brother, and not just some weird obligation her actual brother left behind when he went away to college. I know we were never the *best* friends, and most of the memories have fallen apart, but I remember remembering growing up together, and I know I love her. I mean, I know it, but I also *feel* it at this point. The memory of love had time to turn into actual love. It's pretty nice." His voice dropped, and he added, barely above a whisper, "I wish there'd been time for that with Mom."

"I know, buddy," I said, patting his shoulder. There wasn't anything else to say.

Dolefully, he looked up into the tree canopy. I mimicked him, more curious than distressed. A few massive beetles wandered by, taking no real notice of us, before Sam dropped from the branches overhead, clutching a massive trumpet-shaped flower in one hand.

It was a strange sort of purple-orange ombre, and it smelled like an entire Macy's perfume counter, oddly chemical while still floral. He brandished it at Arthur.

"Here," he said.

Arthur took it, dubiously. "I thought you shook off the pheromones," he complained. "Give flowers to your fiancée."

"This is *because* of the pheromones," said Sam. "It was the stinkiest flower I could find. Rub it on yourself."

"Oh," said Arthur. Then: "Oh!" as the suggestion sank in. He turned the flower so that he was looking straight down the bell, then shoved one arm all the way into it, rummaging around.

"This feels faintly obscene," I said, turning away.

"It *looks* pretty obscene," said Sam. "I mean, he's really going for it."

"Sam . . ."

"What? I found him a flower so he wouldn't put the whammy on me again by mistake. I think I get to have opinions on what it looks like when he uses it."

I snorted. "Sure, whatever."

"Got it!" said Arthur jubilantly. I turned back to him. He had pulled his hand—now covered in a viscous liquid that dripped like artificial maple syrup—out of the flower. He began rubbing it on his face and neck, then reached under his shirt and applied it liberally to his armpits. Basically anywhere that was likely to get sweaty and start to stink.

It was an ambitious undertaking, but by the time he finished, that Macy's-perfume-counter smell was overwhelming everything else, effectively shutting off our noses.

"I can get us down now," said Sam, scooping Arthur and me off our feet and under his arms. Holding us securely, he turned around, and jumped out of the tree.

Sixteen

$$\pi_2(n) \sim 2C_2\frac{n}{(\ln n)^2} \sim 2C_2\int_2^n \frac{dt}{(\ln t)^2}$$

SARAH

"Not every choice I've made in my lifetime has been a good one. Some of them were pretty objectively bad. But they were my choices, and at the end of the day, I'm nothing more than the sum of them. They're what made me."

—**Alice Healy**

Walking through a tangled, unfamiliar jungle that still manages to feel like home

Ikko's hand was warm in mine as we walked. The longer I held on to her, the more my telepathy eroded her natural defenses, and the cheery background noise of her surface thoughts became gradually more and more evident, until I was listening to her inner monologue. I knew I should let go. I knew she might not understand what prolonged physical contact with one of us would mean. But it was so nice to know the names of the plants and insects around me without needing to break the comfortable silence we had established that I just wanted to hold on.

Wait. Silence? I glanced at Ikko. She kept looking serenely ahead, not picking up on my confusion.

Of course she wasn't picking up on my confusion. She wasn't a telepath. "Ikko, how old are you?" I asked.

"Old? Oh. I'm four full rotations in age," she said happily. "Why?"

I paused, blinking. That didn't mean anything to me. Of course it didn't: how was I supposed to know how long a year was on a planet with three suns?

"It's just that you look a certain age as we measure things on the world I'm from," I said. "And it would be very strange for someone that age to be quiet as long as you have. I'm impressed no matter how old you are."

Ikko stood a little straighter, pleased with herself. It radiated off of her, almost palpable. "I'm *very* good at being quiet," she said. "Daddy says it's a problem sometimes, when I sneak up on him and he doesn't want me to sneak up on him. I think it's good to be quiet. Means you can get in almost anywhere you want to. It doesn't just work on the stinging wasps."

"How do you know that they're wasps?"

She shrugged. "Because when they try to get into your head, they buzz, and they sting you on the inside with their sharp, sharp thoughts." She glanced at me. "I know you're in my head, but you're not buzzing. More just a quiet little hum. I don't mind the hum, and I know you need to use my eyes to know what you're looking at. Wasps don't see so good. Safe or stinging, they need us to see things for them."

"And who is 'us'?"

This question seemed to confuse Ikko. She stopped walking and dropped my hand, turning to face me. "We are. The Kairos."

I blinked. "The *what*?"

"Kairos. Silly wasp, you should know what we are. You're the reason we're here." She started walking again, heading deeper into the green. After a pause to collect my thoughts, I hurried after her. She was my only guide, and some of the insects I'd identified via her mind had jaws I didn't want to get any closer to.

Ikko turned toward me as I caught up, offering her hand again. I took it without hesitation. If she was willing to let me share her mind, I wasn't going to refuse.

Knowing that she was apparently a full Kairos made the hard shell of her thoughts more understandable, and also the way I was shut out almost entirely when I stopped touching her. I could linger in the heads of my family, but they were only partially Kairos, and getting less so with every passing generation. Eventually, that protection would give way completely, and they'd be as vulnerable to people like me as any other human.

That was a distressing thought, and not one I wanted to dwell on. The family I had now was safe, and Charlotte, Olivia, and David all had the level of resistance I would have expected from them if I'd been making guesses, but what about their kids? Or their grandkids? Johrlac have a substantially longer-than-human lifespan. I've never been sure precisely how much longer, but I know Mom looks more like my older sister these days, and she was at least sixty when she adopted Aunt Evie. I could have a lot of years to watch the people I loved get slowly vulnerable.

"You're worried," said Ikko.

I blinked at her. She shrugged.

"Your hum just went all spiky. You don't need to be worried. We're not going to hurt you. We don't blame you for things you never did. That would just be silly." She pushed aside a branch with her arm, then pointed to a lower bush covered in large clusters of peach-colored berries. "Those are tasty. To us, but also to the wasps. They love them lots. You should try one."

"All right," I said, and leaned over to pick a berry as we walked by the bush, then popped it into my mouth.

It tasted like the sweetest tomato I had ever had, tart enough not to be cloying, but not so much as to detract from the pure sugary decadence of it. I stopped in my tracks, turning to stare at the bush.

Ikko shook her head. "I guess you must *really* like berries. We can come back later with a basket."

She tugged and I followed willingly, resisting the urge to run back and fill my hands with berries, to cram them into my mouth until I choked. Everything about this world, the air, the fruit—I had evolved to exist here. My body knew how to be here. But my mind . . . I couldn't imagine giving up Earth. I needed the internet. I needed to know how my shows were going to end. I needed to see Isaac grow up, and I needed to be there for Greg. Johrlar was a sweet dream. Michigan, and Oregon, and New York, those were my sweet reality.

Ikko pulled me deeper and deeper into the trees, occasionally pointing out a bug or flower she thought I'd like, but otherwise content to walk in silence. We emerged into a clear band of grass, or what looked like grass, dotted with little flowers, white with transparent petals. She kept walking, and I kept following, until I realized the flowers were turning red where we had stepped.

I pulled my hand from hers and stopped walking, indicating the flowers. "What are these?"

"Telltales," she said. "Stinging wasps can't see them once they've changed, so they don't realize they're leaving clear trails to tell us where they've walked. We plant them around everything important to us, and that way we know when someone's been poking around where we don't want them. They'll go back to white and clear in a little bit. So if you wanted to sneak in while the suns were down, you could, but since they don't know what kind of trail they're leaving . . ."

"They don't think to be careful of the flowers," I said, thoughtfully. "That's really clever, Ikko."

She preened, but said, "I didn't come up with them. Still, it *is* pretty clever, isn't it? Guess you need some clever if you want to stay alive when you've got wasps chasing after you all the time."

"Then I hope you'll have enough clever for the both of us," I said firmly.

She laughed, pulling me through the flowers to the trees on the other side.

We walked through this patch of forest—although really, I needed to be thinking of it as a jungle. We could pass through it only because someone, presumably Ikko's people, had been cutting paths through the brush; they were tangled and almost choked with underbrush at some points, but I could still see the cleared earth under the returning vines. Bugs of various sizes moved in the greenery, some the size of Earth creatures, some large enough to provide reasonable hunting for Greg.

I could bring him here. The thought was so sudden as to be almost surprising, and I considered it for a moment as I continued to follow Ikko. The air was cleaner, and he would probably be more comfortable in a place where I wouldn't need to continually hide him from everyone else. I'd even seen giant spiders in the Johrlac city: he might be able to accompany me openly.

Assuming the collective of Johrlac queens didn't have my mind wiped to keep me from challenging the shape of the group mind they'd constructed between them. I scowled and pitched the thought away. No matter how beautiful it was here, I wasn't going to be bringing Greg. I was going to find Arthur and discover a way to take us both home, so that we would never need to worry about these people again. And if some of them got hurt or broken in the process . . .

There had been no reason to make themselves my problem. This wasn't my world. I would never have come looking for them, would never have involved myself, had they not decided to force the issue. I wasn't going to feel bad if they suffered the consequences of their own actions. I wasn't.

No, really, I wasn't.

"You're thinking pretty hard, Sarah," said Ikko, pronouncing my name with precise care, like it was some sort of magical incantation that would unlock a world of sweet rewards. "It tickles."

"Sorry," I said. I hadn't even been aware that I was projecting in her direction. "I'm sorry."

"It's all right." She shrugged. "We're almost there."

"Speaking of being 'almost there,' how are you here?" I asked. "This world doesn't really seem to do 'mammals,' as a rule, and I know Kairos are mammalian."

"What's a mammal?" asked Ikko blankly.

"Uh . . ."

"Oh, *that's* a mammal." She radiated relief and mild smugness. "The mind-mind flowers had to have the word a few times before they could understand it enough to translate. Mammals are people with red blood and bones on the inside."

"I think that's fundamentally correct," I said. "There's some other stuff, and really it's all about common ancestors, which means no one who originated outside of Earth—where I grew up—is a mammal as I understand it, but sometimes you just have to say 'close enough' when you're talking about biology."

"And wasps aren't mammals?"

"No. We're a type of insect—like all of those over there." I waved a hand, indicating a group of flying bugs clustered around a large, sticky-looking flower. "Everything I've seen that evolved on Johrlar is what we'd call an insect back on Earth. Except you. Kairos are mammals, or close enough to reproduce with Earth humans. Why are you here?"

"Humans?" she echoed, dubiously. "What is humans?"

"They look like Kairos, but they can't manipulate coincidence the way you can."

"Oh." She sounded baffled by the idea of people who couldn't manipulate coincidence. "That must be awful, living without the timing. The timing is how everything works the way it's supposed to. The timing is how I found you."

I decided not to mention that I had been the one to chase her down. Let her have her victory for right now.

"But the Kairos are here because the stinging wasps wanted people to do work for them, and when they went looking for people who could be around them without getting worn away to nothing like rocks in a river, they found us. Or our ancestors, anyway. We've been here a long, long time." She sounded totally nonchalant about that, like it was completely normal for her to be telling me that her species was in this dimension to be used for involuntary labor. I hated to use the word "slavery," but when people are taken from their home dimension and taken someplace utterly alien to their biology and needs, forced to work without choice or compensation, well. The word felt pretty accurate.

"And you . . . they let you go?"

"No. They wanted us because we could stand up against their minds for a long, long time before our own minds fell apart, but they didn't think about how that would mean all the ways they usually kept people under control wouldn't work on us. As soon as they stopped trying all the time to keep us tame, we just got up and walked away. Now they look for us all the time, but we hide really well, and they don't know how to handle people they can't see. The Eldest Living says we're the same as the stinging wasps—there's things we don't know how to handle, because they're so alien to us that we can't even prepare for what we don't all the way understand. So we have to be careful, and not try to control anybody else, or we'll get done and have nowhere to run. We just trust the timing."

"Ah." The more I learned about the people I'd come from, the less I liked them. I fell quiet as we walked on, letting Ikko lead the way, little white flowers leaving a trail of vivid red behind us.

We reached a wall of dangling vines covered in more flowers, these ones yellow and shaped like trumpets. They closed as we brushed against them, furling upward and inward as they pulled away from the contact. Ikko swept them aside with great waves of her arms, and we walked through the curtain to the other side, entering what I knew at once had to be the Kairos village.

It was a surprisingly permanent-looking settlement, with clay walls and multi-storied abodes like something out of the American Southwest. And there were people everywhere, many of them wearing red in a variety of shades, like they wanted that little additional ounce of protection from their former captors. Being able to see it soothed something deep inside me. I was still me. I was still Sarah, still a cuckoo, and they hadn't managed to pull me into harmony with their hive mind, no matter how much they might be trying.

A group of people with polearms pushed away from the building where they'd been lounging and approached us as Ikko led me down the center of the avenue that ran through the settlement. She waved, unperturbed by their approach.

"I found a friendly wasp," she informed them, once they were close enough. "She was escaping their administration building, so I let her escape with me. She can work the doors."

The figure at the front of their group waved a polearm at us, casually menacing. "Why should we trust this wasp?"

"The timing brought her to me, and I've brought her to you," said Ikko, sounding smug. "I want to take her to the Eldest Living."

"The Eldest Living has been tried deeply today," said the guard. "We found other intruders wandering in the green, and brought them to speak with her. But they fled our hospitality before we could explain our true intentions, and now they wander lost to the world's dangers."

Ikko shrugged. "My intruder didn't flee anything except the administration building, and it was on fire when we walked out of sight."

"What do you say for yourself, wasp?" asked the guard, turning on me. The bident they were holding looked incredibly sharp, and I couldn't aim myself at their mind well enough to tell whether or not they would use it against me. I couldn't even pick up on their pronouns. So I decided to go with the safest option I had.

I decided to be honest. "I'm what the Johrlac call a cuckoo," I said. "I'm outside their collective, and I don't want to be *inside* it. I want to go back to the dimension I call home and never come here ever again. But there's someone I have to find before I can do that. I can see the telltales change. Ikko says that means she knows I'm not a stinging wasp, so you should know it too. I can point out everything red in this whole street if it helps you believe me. I just want to find Arthur and go home. That's all."

"The Eldest will want to speak with you," said the guard tightly.

"Then great, take me to your Eldest, and let's get this over with," I said. "I'm not trying to cause anyone problems. I just need to stay away from the queen collective. They're sort of pissed at me."

"Why?" asked the guard.

"The usual." I shrugged. "Apparently I'm a criminal because I hurt some people who were trying to hurt me, and because I went and reached the final instar while being a cuckoo, which they do *not* like one little bit. They brought me here to stand trial. And then when they tried to take my measure, I shoved a few of them out of the collective to make them understand that they needed to stop screwing with me if they didn't want to have a really lousy day, and now I'm pretty sure they want to erase my brain."

"You . . . expelled a queen from their collective?" asked the guard.

I nodded. "Yes, I did," I said. "They pulled me into a dream space so they could taunt me about being so easy for them to catch, and I smacked them for being so incredibly rude about things. I didn't ask to come here, I didn't give them permission to mess around inside my head, and I don't think they understand that I'm not going to roll over and start letting them make the rules just because they brought me here."

Ikko radiated pride. "I found a spicy nice wasp."

"She certainly seems firm in her convictions," allowed the guard. "Are you sure you want to take a cuckoo before the Eldest Living?"

"I'm sure I should," she said, firmly.

The guards exchanged a look, some of them raising their bidents, others clearly struggling to keep them lowered. Finally, the one we had been speaking to turned back to us.

"Her time is not as long as we would have it be, but still she serves the timing," they said. "If you promise you intend her no harm, you may see the Eldest. But understand that if you harm her, you will wish for the kindness of the queens."

"Do they have any?"

"No. So choose with caution."

I sighed. "I don't really tend to mean anyone any harm unless they force me to," I said. "I spent a lot of time sort of foggy because I was traveling through instars without anyone to guide me, but even then, I didn't go around hurting people if I had any choice in the matter. My parents raised me better than that."

The more I saw of Johrlar, the more I felt like there was nothing wrong with the place that couldn't be fixed by letting Angela take it over. As a cuckoo, she was telepathically limited and often bemused by the more casually telepathic members of her own species. As a mother, she was top-notch.

That seemed to sell the guards on the idea. They stepped aside, waving Ikko onward. She squeezed my hand, then started down the street, pulling me along with her.

One of them stepped in front of her as she walked, stopping her again, and leaned in close. "Mom is going to be furious when she hears that you went to the administration building after being told not to," they said. "Best hope the timing will protect you from her."

They stepped aside again, and we resumed, Ikko paling at the thought of her mother's wrath. I smiled down at her. Some things, it seemed, were truly universal.

"Sibling?" I asked.

"Brother," she said.

"I have two of those."

"Do they ever get less annoying?"

"I don't really know. Drew's a lot older than I am. He was already basically an adult by the time we met, and most of the annoying was from me to him, rather than the other way around. Isaac is still really young, and he's not annoying at all. Watching him learn how the world works is just . . . it's amazing. I love him so much."

Watching his relationship with Charlotte develop was also fascinating, although I worried sometimes about what would happen if we ever needed to separate them. I understood what it was like to be a young telepath in a world that didn't think people like you existed; the anxiety, the otherness, the fear. But Isaac had Lottie to lean on, and she anchored and evened him out in a way I could only envy.

Artie had been that for me, as much as he could be. Falling in love with him hadn't been part of the plan, and had only made everything more difficult, but I couldn't deny that sometimes I missed how soothing his mind had been, how comforting it had been to make contact with someone whose thoughts I understood from the bottom to the top.

Ikko looked up at me as I spoke, listening attentively. "Is that why you want to go home so badly?" she asked when I was done. "To get back to your brothers?"

"That's part of it," I said. "They don't have any idea where I am. None of my family does. Isaac's a wasp like me, and so is our mother, but the rest of my family . . . we're all different species, and they'll have no way of following me here."

"That must be really scary."

"It's about the most scary thing I've ever thought of, and I've seen and done some really scary stuff," I said. "I want to go home. I want my family."

"I would, too, if someone took me away from here," said Ikko. She let go of my hand, gesturing for me to keep following her. I did, feeling her thoughts muffle themselves, like she was standing on the other side of a glassy barrier. The resistance of a full Kairos made the telepathic barriers my family had seem almost negligible. No wonder these people had been able to hide for so long.

Ikko was leading me toward a tree with a trunk that resembled a massive basket, woven from dozens of smaller trunks that had interlaced as they were growing, forming a structure full of openings that stared out on the world like unblinking eyes. Something about it sent a chill along my spine, and I stood up a little straighter, too anxious to slump. Ikko kept walking, not seeming to notice my discomfort.

"Ikko," I said. "This Eldest Living you're taking me to see. Who is she?"

"Her name is her explanation," said Ikko. "She's the very very oldest of all of us in the whole world. This isn't the only place we have where we can be safe, but it's probably the biggest, and the Eldest Living was here when the timing brought us to it. She doesn't remember Caerus, but her great-great-grandmother did, and she can tell stories about the world our from happened on. She knows everything worth knowing, and she's the nicest person ever, and she'll know how you can get your people back, and how you can get home again from here. You can trust the Eldest Living. All of us do, and you can, too."

We had reached the tree. She stopped outside, gesturing toward an opening in the trunk. "Go on inside," she said. "It'll be better if you announce yourself. That way it doesn't look like somebody made you."

She turned then, scampering away, back toward the village. I watched her go, feeling suddenly uncertain.

Then I turned, and stepped into the tree.

◆ ◆ ◆

The interior of the tree was surprisingly bright, thanks to shafts of sunlight shining through the holes in the trunk. White-winged moths fluttered in the shadows between the shafts, the motion drawing my eye for a moment before I realized the center of the room was a ring of chairs made from rough-hewn wood, more humanlike than the furniture in Fetch and Carry's home, the seats unpadded: they were just plain and hard, making them unappealing to sit on, especially when contrasted with the massive heap of soft things in the middle of the ring.

Pillows and blankets and reams of unhemmed fabric formed a virtual mountain of comforting options, and atop them sat a very old person I assumed was the Eldest Living. She was wearing a knotted shift of bright red fabric, embroidered with what looked like wasp wings around the hems. It was an interesting fashion choice, to be sure, and I paused to study her before coming any closer.

She was definitely Kairos. She could have passed for human, with her wispy white hair and pale, heavily wrinkled skin, but when I tried to brush the surface of her mind to confirm that she was who I'd come to see, I struck a shell as hard as resin wrapped around an insect that had mired itself in amber. There was no getting through that without using force, and maybe not even *with* using force—it was the strongest mental shield I had ever bounced off of.

"Hello," she said, turning her face in my direction. "Are you the Sarah?"

"What?" I came closer, unable to help myself. "How do you already know my name?"

"There are people looking for you, little wasp," she said. "They came out of the space between worlds, into the green not far from here, and my hunters brought them to see me. But they were very poor guests, and they left without allowing us to help them in any meaningful way."

"Who were they?" I asked, almost frantically. There were only a few members of my family who could potentially travel between dimensions without my help, and I didn't want any of them to be in danger, especially not because of me. Again.

"The Thomas Price, and the Antimony and the Sam," said the Eldest Living. "They had a fourth, but she had been lost to the green before my hunters found them, and they worried for her safety. They said they had come to reclaim the Sarah, and the Arthur."

So they knew Arthur was here on Johrlar? That was encouraging. I wasn't trying to rescue him alone. "How long ago was this?"

"Oh, hours," she said, waving a hand almost carelessly. "The suns have moved a great distance since they left me. Would you like to sit and speak with me a time?"

"I'd rather find my family, if you don't mind."

"I do mind, I'm afraid. The timing has brought you all before me, and the timing only serves so when the need is great. The wasps search the green for their missing prisoners. They search the green for you. If you walk away, they'll be free to find you, and possibly to find us as well."

I blinked. "Are you saying I have to stay here so the Johrlac don't learn where your village is? I thought you had protections in place to stop that sort of thing from happening. Ikko said that you put up barriers and distractions and other ways to warn the community before anything could happen."

"We have many protections," said the Eldest Living. I could tell she was looking at me, but the resin shell around her mind meant that I had no idea what she was feeling, or whether she was happy to see me here. "Some of them more clear than others. What did Ikko tell you about the history of the Kairos on Johrlar?"

"She said you'd been abducted from your home dimension and brought here as slave labor," I said dutifully. "That the ones who did the abducting wanted a service class with enough telepathic resistance to stand up against the hive, and settled on the Kairos."

"We serve the timing, but the timing works sometimes in mysterious ways," she said. "The wasps came for us when there was a great famine upon the land, and the timing saw that more of us would survive if we were removed to Johrlar. So we were taken, and over time we learned enough to escape into the green places, where we could thrive. There was enough here to eat, and we spread and prospered. There are more of us here and now than there were on Caerus when we were taken. It would be better had we never been disturbed, but as we cannot change the past, we choose to glory in what we have done here that is for the better. We are happy, and we are well."

"I'm not sure what that has to do with what Ikko might have told me," I said. "I'm glad for you. It's awful not to be where you belong. But we have a lot in common, you and I. The queens who rule here banished my ancestors, and I was born in another dimension, where I had to figure out how to be happy in a place that was never intended for me."

"So you understand," she said. "When you have little, what you do have seems like everything. It's not worth the risk of losing it."

Something about her tone was making me uneasy. I took a step backward. "No, it's not. What I have right now is my freedom, and that's a lot to lose."

"But do you really have that, when you're on someone else's world and your family is being held prisoner? Or do you have the illusion of freedom egging you on, and need to let go of the idea that you have anything left to take away?"

Alarm bells were ringing in my head. "What did you do?" I asked.

To her credit, she didn't try to deflect, just looked at me and said, in a cool tone, "Only what was necessary to protect my people. They don't question how we can be so close to the city and so established without being discovered. They trust the timing, and fail to realize that sometimes even the timing needs a helping hand. I am their Eldest. I am the daughter of the man who was Eldest before me, and my own daughter has been raised knowing that one day she will take my place. She will speak for the timing. She will be the helping hand our people need to thrive. And she, like me, will speak to the collective on the behalf of the Kairos, and will offer them whatever they require to leave us alone. We do not give them our own people, ever. We do not sacrifice what we grow. But everything else is expendable."

She stood, aged legs shaky but still strong enough to hold her, and began making her way down the side of the piled-up pillows and bedding. She held her head high as she descended, chin tilted slightly upward in a way that gave her an almost-regal bearing. When she reached the bottom she held out her hand, clearly expecting me to help her with the final steps from uneven fabric to solid ground.

I moved forward again, eyeing her warily. Could she possibly not know about skin contact making it easier for me to read her mind? If these people had been avoiding the Johrlac for as long as it sounded like they had, it was actually possible that they'd forgotten that little trick of living alongside us.

I reached out and took her hand. The color in the room shifted, reds becoming brighter as my vision aligned with her own, and I felt the unpleasant sensation of my thoughts sinking into thick, sticky toffee, getting mired and dragged down in something that clung and tangled and refused to let me go. I tried to pull my hand out of hers, but my arm refused to respond to the command. It was like my tangled-up thoughts couldn't reach the nerves to tell them what to do.

"I do know about skin contact with the Johrlac," said the Eldest Living. "And I know that faces aren't a strong suit for your kind, but you should work harder at schooling yours—I could all but read your delight at the thought of crossing my defenses. The queens long ago set traps inside my mind, with my consent, to stop any others of their species from intruding where I didn't want them. Don't fight it. You're mired now, and you'll be pulled down soon enough, into the peaceful place they've made to hold you. Inside my mind, your mind will be able to dream until the time comes to carry you away. They're already coming."

She delicately extricated her hand from mine, shaking it like she'd just touched something unpleasant, then wiped it against the fabric at her hip before she turned to climb back up her fabric mountain.

My knees gave way, and I toppled gently forward into the pile of pillows, feeling little muscular twitches race along my limbs and spine. I'd never had a seizure to my knowledge, but this felt like the beginnings of one, my whole body starting to shake involuntarily as the twitches continued.

Johrlac can set traps inside a person's brain. I knew that. I'd encountered it before, when the hive had been trying to force me toward the queen instar: they'd trapped Artie's brain, turning it into a prison meant specifically for me. This didn't feel quite like that. This was more like sinking into a tarpit, too deep and thick for me to pull myself free. I felt my bladder give way, warm wetness running down my thighs and sinking into the pillows beneath me, and I couldn't even rouse myself to feel shame: if anything, I felt a grim satisfaction in knowing that I had at the very least ruined some of this deceptive liar's pillows.

It was a small delight. It was the only one I currently felt likely to receive. And so I held on to it as the toffee dragged me down, down, deeper down, back into the whiteness of the void, and then the pride slipped away, and then everything else slipped away, and I was alone with my thoughts.

Seventeen

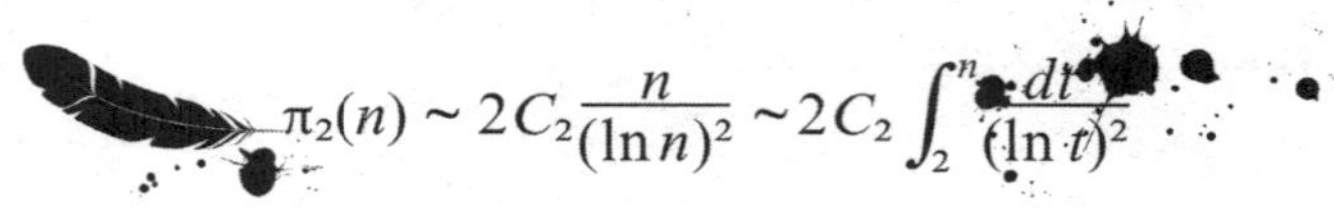

> "There was a world before you existed, and there's still going to be a world after you're gone. But it's not going to be the same. Everything is different now, forever, because you were here."
>
> —**Mary Dunlavy**

Back in the white place,
which is honestly getting sort of old

THERE IS NO TIME IN the white place, not really. Minutes can feel like hours, and hours can feel like minutes. Meaning I had no idea how long I'd actually been down there. I knew I couldn't wake up just by wanting it, although I could still rearrange the space to a certain degree: I thought about my wardrobe and I was back in my preferred oversized sweater and long skirt combination. I thought about how much I hated to be bored and a whiteboard appeared, complete with dry-erase markers and erasers to help me fix any errors.

I picked up a marker, uncapping it and inhaling the sharp, familiar fumes before setting the tip to the clean, glossy surface of the whiteboard, ready to begin writing out the first steps of the equation that would take me home. Then I paused, frowning. I couldn't write that equation. I didn't *remember* that equation. It had deleted itself as soon as I'd finished it the first time. It was gone.

But . . .

I knew it was possible to mathematically travel between dimensions, and I knew I'd been able to do it once. I knew the Johrlac had a better equation than the one I'd used, meaning it was possible to achieve this with more mathematical elegance and less brain-eating ferocity. All I needed to do was define what I needed the numbers to be able to do.

Biting my lip in concentration, I leaned forward and started to write.

What felt like an eternity later, I had fully defined all the functions I needed my new equation to perform. It had to cross dimensional boundaries, and it had to do so in a manner fast and clean enough to not kill the people it was transporting. That would be difficult, no matter how I approached it. But I thought I could see the outline of what it would have to do in order to work, and in that outline, I could also see the issues with the original equation. It wasn't just that it was hostile and inclined to attack: it was that the equation the cuckoos used was feral, broken by the number of times it had been stripped down and forced to become more efficient. Truly advanced Johrlac math was essentially alive, and like any living thing, it wanted to go on living, and it didn't want to suffer.

For generations, the cuckoos had been abusing the equation, hurting it as they chopped pieces off and tossed them aside in an effort to make the core more streamlined and easy to control. And at some point, it had stopped taking the damage lightly. It had stopped playing along with its own mutilation. It had been tame once, and now it was a threat to anyone who got too close. It was hungry.

The Johrlac were using an older form of the same equation, and a newer one at the same time, a version that had never been butchered, but had been carefully refined over the course of generations, helping it to achieve its full power and potential. I added a few more conditions to my outline, mapping out the strange and dangerous country of what I needed this equation to do.

If I was going to get my family home, I needed a version that could transport six people—because no way in hell was I going through all this only to leave myself behind—and wouldn't require me to offload more than the smallest functions onto any other processing centers. I needed the mathematical equivalent of a suitcase nuke, small and powerful and primed to blow the second I hit the button.

I could do this. It was possible. I could almost see it, and the one benefit of being banished to the white place was the total lack of distractions. I kept writing until I had filled my entire whiteboard, then summoned a second and continued onward, working toward a solution, working toward salvation. I could save us all. I could get us out of here. I could—

"Whoever taught you had some skill, we'll grant them that," said a cool female voice from behind me. "Fascinating, given how primitive they must have been. There's no possible way you could have located a real teacher in that backwater dimension you keep considering your home. If you'd been taught by someone who truly understood the ramifications of what they were doing, you would never have committed your many, many crimes."

"Collective," I said coldly, and replaced the cap on my pen. I did so with careful precision, not rushing before I turned to face the cuckoo woman I knew would be standing there. She smirked at me. I resisted the urge to roll my eyes. I hate it so much when the bad guys gloat. "I don't remember inviting you into my mind. This is the second time you've trespassed without my permission."

"We don't trespass," she said, with a sneer. "We are the collective and this territory is our own. The territory and all that it contains. You are here, therefore you are ours, and we can no more trespass against you than a body can trespass against a bone. You belong to us. The sooner you accept that, the sooner we can end this whole charade."

"I am not anyone's property," I said. "I belong to myself, if I belong to anyone. I am a queen and a collective in my own right, and you took me from my territory. I'm only contained here because you forced me to be."

"The weaker collective is absorbed," she said dismissively. "If we were able to take you, it's because you were weak. We've won. We've already won. Stop fighting us."

"I thought I was here for a trial, not a conquest."

"So allow us to try you."

"No."

She raised an eyebrow. "No?"

"No. I don't recognize your authority over me, or over my family. Let me go. Let my cousin go. We'll leave, and you'll never need to hear from us again. That's my final offer."

"You're not in a place to be making demands right now, little cuckoo. We were afraid of you at first—the cuckoo queen, the thing we've been dreading for centuries. And when you caught us by surprise, you did a little damage, true. But you're just a jumped-up version of your peers. You're not strong. You're not clever. You got lucky somehow. We know how to handle luck."

"Subvert it and use it to trap innocent people, apparently," I snapped.

"The Kairos and their precious timing do complicate things," she said. "Still, they're all but guaranteed to encounter every person we bring here who manages to evade us, and so we can use them to catch our runaways. And we're not here to fight with you. We're here to offer you a bargain you might find worth pursuing."

"What's that?" I asked warily.

"Agree to stand trial. Agree to let us measure you against your crimes, and to abide by what we find in that analysis. If you do, we promise to return your family to their home dimension, and to leave them peacefully."

"But you won't be returning me."

"Oh, no. Not unless you're somehow found innocent—which you won't be." She smiled venomously, slow as a snake in winter. "Your bones will join all the other criminals who've come before us or, if we find your mind to be of unexpected value, we'll erase your malfeasance and your wickedness, and the woman you become will join us. Either death or apotheosis."

I stared at her, briefly too stunned to speak. She kept smiling, apparently unbothered by my long silence. Finally, recovering my voice, I said, "I thought the greater punishment would take priority, but no. This was the plan all along, wasn't it? Get me here, and then make me over in your own image. Why even pretend this has something to do with the law? Why bother with the pretense of a trial if you've already made up your minds?"

"We aren't the only authority in the multiverse," she said, smile dropping. "There are busybodies out there who believe we have a responsibility to the worlds the cuckoos damage, that because we freed them upon the dimensions, we share some culpability in their crimes. Simple fools, but it serves us better to pretend as if we respect their authority than it does to defy them. Traveling to another world to pluck one of its residents away would be an act of war were we not doing it to enforce our laws. So we use the law. A cuckoo queen should have been an impossibility, and the strength you've already demonstrated . . . we can't allow it to belong to another collective. You'll be ours."

"I'll eat you from the inside out."

"No, you won't. The you who believes in threatening her sisters won't be here any longer. But the people you would kill to defend will be going safely home, unharmed, their minds intact. Isn't that worth it, to you?" She leaned closer, voice dropping conspiratorially. "We can see your guilt, like a velvet worm wrapped around your throat. We know how much you loathe what you've become. Here's the way to put paid to everything you've done, to cap it all off with a single act of penance. All you have to do is stop resisting us and this can all be over."

It was tempting. It was *so* tempting. And that was how I knew it was almost certainly the wrong thing to do: anything that sounded that appealing was probably a cover for something I was going to like a lot less. Not that it mattered how much I did or didn't like it when I was talking about the actual death of the self. My body would still be here, as a power supply for the collective, but the person in control of it wouldn't be me.

"I don't want it to be over," I said, voice quiet. "There's too much left in the world that I want and need to do. I want to see the next Pokémon game. I want to find out what happens with the X-Men. I want to see my baby brother grow up, and know that he's a cuckoo with a sense of ethics, just like our mom. I want to see my friend Mark reunite with his little sister, and I don't want to make the people who love me deal with losing me. They've already lost so much in the last few years. It's not fair to ask them to lose even more."

The collective's face contorted immediately into a scowl. "You act like you have an actual choice in the matter. We were trying to be polite."

"I'm not interested in being polite. I'm just interested in going home."

"You have committed crimes against the collective, Sarah Zellaby. You have acted against your own kind; you have killed without concern or discrimination for the innocent and the unwell. You are a criminal by any measure of the term, and for the sake of Johrlar's treaties with our surrounding realities, you must be held accountable for what you've done. It's nothing personal."

"Really? Because it feels pretty damn personal."

Between one breath and the next, the collective was gone, and I was alone with my whiteboard once again. I turned back to it, but the math had lost some of its allure; it no longer beckoned me quite as openly, no longer seemed like a fractal flower caught in the moment of unfurling. It was just numbers, pressed flat as insects under glass. I still uncapped my pen and tried to go back to work.

I had to finish this equation.

I had to find a way to get us all home.

My life—my mind—might very well depend on it.

✦ ✦ ✦

I barely noticed when the white began to fall apart around me. I was too deep in the math, focused on the task at hand, and not paying attention to my surroundings. Anyway, when the world is made of a single unrelenting, unadorned color, having spots appear in your peripheral vision will eventually become enough of a distraction to be worth noticing. I turned toward the spots. They were gray and black, dissolving the edges of the void.

"Huh," I said, replacing the cap on my pen. "Would you look at that."

The spots continued to spread, nibbling away at everything. There were already limits on my void, reducing it from an endless expanse of nothingness to a floating disk about the size of a carnival's central ring. If I closed my eyes, I could almost see the walls of the big tent surrounding me, keeping me safe from the oncoming collapse.

But they weren't really there. None of this was really there. I was deep in the recesses of my own mind, trapped in a rapidly disintegrating mental prison, and when it finished falling apart, I was going to wake up and need to deal with whatever was going to happen next. I didn't want to spend the rest of my life hiding in the depths of my own thoughts, but I also didn't want to wake up and deal with these people.

I didn't like my distant relations very much. Being the same species wasn't enough to make us family, and they needed to stop acting like they got to have a say in how I or any of the members of my actual family lived our lives. And at the same time, I knew I needed to be the face of whatever came next, lest they go looking for someone else to blame.

There weren't many cuckoos left on Earth for them to accuse. I didn't want them going anywhere near the survivors. I especially didn't want them anywhere near Mark or Isaac. If they didn't already know how to find them, they could easily pull that knowledge from the minds of my family. Thomas and Sam didn't have any natural resistance to Johrlac telepathy. They would crumble, and they wouldn't even realize they were doing it.

No. I needed to wake up. I eyed the encroaching dissolution, sighed, and closed my eyes again, folding my arms across my chest like a vampire in a horror movie, then fell backward.

I didn't hit the floor. Instead, I plunged through a substance that felt like thick foam on top of a cup of coffee, then kept sinking, down into warm, viscous fluid that surrounded and enveloped me in a softness like I had never known. I could still breathe in the sea of whatever it was, and so I just relaxed, letting it take me wherever it was going.

When the softness faded, taking the sensation of rocking in the tide with it, the transition was almost jarring. I kept my eyes closed, cataloging everything around me. I could hear the same distant buzzing that had been present since I arrived on this world, now split into only three bands of sound, like competing swarms of cicadas. I smelled flowers, floral and sticky-sweet and somehow more appealing than any flowers had ever been before. And that . . . that was all. There were no other sounds, no other scents.

I opened my eyes, finding myself looking up at a ceiling made of the gray-brown papery substance that was their dominant building material. I pushed myself into a sitting position. I was on a bench crafted from slotted-together bamboo boards, in a small white room no larger than the pantry back at home. There was a single door, more like the doors I knew back home than the sliding doors I'd seen so far: the hinges, if there were hinges, were on the outside. There would be no jailbreaks here.

I took a deep breath and pushed outward, looking for another mind. I struck resistance almost immediately, running into invisible walls that stopped my reaching thoughts cold. They hurt, in a way that was and was not pain, like the idea of pain was being weaponized against me. I withdrew my thoughts, furling them back into themselves, and rose to pace the dimensions of the room.

It was eight by eight, roughly, and the walls were approximately as tall as they were long, making it a perfect cube. Mathematical precision was exactly what I would have expected from these people, and yet somehow it managed to be almost surprising despite that predictability. I returned to the bench, sitting down, and realized for the first time that I was no longer wearing the jumpsuit that had marked me—erroneously—as a municipal assistant. Instead, I was wearing plain white pajama-type slacks and a matching top, all woven out of some sort of thin linen that barely felt like wearing anything at all. I plucked at the fabric. It was perfectly temperature-regulating. I was neither warm nor cold.

It was like the entire place had been designed to synthesize the experience of being held in stasis, or to recreate the white void without the ability to summon anything I wanted. Just to test that theory, I concentrated for a moment on how much I wanted a whiteboard, how nice it would be to get back to work. Nothing happened. The room remained exactly as it was, and I was left without even a pencil.

Charming. I took another look around, taking note of the silence, which wasn't oppressive, but was probably horrifying to someone who was accustomed to existing inside the comforting rhythm of a hive mind. I was alone inside my head. It was pleasant, in its own way. This was the sort of silence I'd been seeking since puberty, the kind that was normally only accessible in rooms that had been specially warded with anti-telepathy charms to keep my thoughts inside and the rest of the world outside. I liked it, and I continued liking it as I closed my eyes and drifted into a natural, void-free sleep.

It was oddly restful, sleeping in the silence. When I yawned and stretched, I felt refreshed in a way that I hadn't for years, which raised the question of why I had woken up in the first place. I paused, eyes still closed, to consider my surroundings.

The silence had changed.

It was still heavy as a blanket, covering and smothering everything around me. The droning cut through the silence without actually diluting it, and it hadn't changed in the least, but the silence . . . oh, the silence was profoundly different now, in a way I couldn't quite define. I tried reaching out, experimentally, and physically recoiled as my mind brushed against two others, one to either side of me. Their presence was a shock severe enough to almost make me lose my grasp on what I was trying to do.

I withdrew. The silence had changed because someone had removed or modified the dampeners that had been keeping my mind in and all the other minds out. I reached out again, more cautiously this time, and touched the two new minds I'd discovered.

They reacted, both of them, by pushing what felt like the mental equivalent of business cards at me. I picked them up, reading their pronouns—female—and positions—civic assistants—before I found their names. It wasn't much of a shock when I did, but it was something of a relief.

Fetch, I said. *Carry. Are you all right?*

There was a long pause, long enough for me to start worrying that the break in the silence had only been large enough for me to push my thoughts out, not for them to reply. Then, in a mental voice that was barely above a whisper, Fetch asked, *Sarah? Is that you?*

It's me! It's definitely me. Are you all right? What are you both doing here?

I got the distinct impression that Carry had started crying. She wasn't answering in words, only in a feeling of despair that broke over me like a wave, threatening to wash my own composure away.

Carry's here? asked Fetch, almost frantic. *They came for us while we were working, and they pulled us apart, and then the white walls came down, and when they fell away I was here, and I couldn't reach anyone outside myself. Is she all right?*

I'll ask her. I'm getting words from you and only crying from her. Is that normal?

She may not be strong enough to reach you. Fetch's thoughts turned heavy, dripping with regret. *We came from the same creche, but her first instar was delayed, and she's never been the strongest in the silence. It's part of why they kept us together when choosing our specific municipal placement. I can bolster and support her.*

And Collate?

There was a long silence in answer to that question. It wasn't the same silence as before: that had been an inability to communicate. This was an absence, marked by the soft, inaudible hum that told me her mind was still connected to my own.

Finally, in a regretful tone, she replied, *Collate was the strongest of the three of us. It fueled her desire for self-determination, and we didn't discourage her, because we didn't see the harm. We didn't believe they would revise her for her crimes. But they did. They ripped her from us, and they claimed her as their own. We—I—I hate the collective for what they did to her.*

There was a light, almost-guilty hiss to her last words, like a child admitting to hating their teacher or a loyalist whispering rumors against their dictator. She spoke like she was breaking some essential law of reality. I caught my breath.

The story here was obvious, and straightforward. Fetch and Carry hadn't known that Annalist was already compromised; they'd been arrested for helping me escape, and imprisoned behind the same anti-telepathy wards as I was. They couldn't reach each other, or anyone else. For telepaths in a telepathic society, that was a form of torture. Why I could reach them, I didn't know, but I was willing to bet it had something to do with the fact that the queens in the collective kept themselves so firmly apart from "ordinary" Johrlac: they were trying to remain distinct to reinforce their authority. But that meant the cells here—because these were cells, no matter what they looked like—weren't constructed with queens in mind. And I *was* a queen, no matter how little the collective liked it. I had just as much power as they did. Walls not built to contain me would eventually give way, whether I wanted them to or not.

Fetch and Carry were isolated in their individual cells, but that hadn't been enough to keep my sleeping mind from seeking them out and opening the channels between us. Not all the way, just enough to let us communicate. They couldn't reach each other because the anti-telepathy charms were still in place. I could reach them because those charms had never been intended to truly contain someone like me.

The fact that they could contain me at all was probably a choice. If the queens of the collective were anything like me as people, they wanted to sleep without other people in their heads from time to time. Sharing someone else's nightmare is a terrifying thing, and even when no one's having bad dreams, having waking people's mind impinging on your sleep can be awful. It's not restful, and it's not restorative. So make charms that can contain queens, at least enough to let them sleep when they want to, and you improve your world.

Honestly, I could see sleep being the entire reason they'd even bothered to figure out anti-telepathy charms on a world of telepaths. The queens couldn't maintain their control over the hive mind if they couldn't reach their people whenever they wanted them, which meant anything that blocked them out wasn't likely to be very popular.

It also explained why the Eldest Living was willing to work with them. She probably felt she had to betray anyone like me, who ran from the collective, because the queens would eventually be able to wear through the resinous shell of her thoughts if they focused long enough. The Kairos were safe, yes, but it was a safety bought with blood, and it would always be conditional, as long as the collective had any reason to look for them.

"I hate it here," I muttered, aloud. Dropping back into silence, I said, *It's not your fault. Part of self-determination is taking risks because you want to take them, and it sounds like Collate knew what she was doing. Are you hurt?*

No, she replied, sullenly. *They were rough, but they didn't physically hurt me. I saw them as they dragged Carry away, and I don't think they hurt her either. Where did you go? Why didn't you stay like we asked you to?*

Annalist put something in the salad he made for me. It knocked me unconscious, and the collective came for me. They wanted to get my measure, I think, to figure out whether I was going to be a problem. I smirked. The expression was only for myself, but I knew the feel of it would travel through my words. *I showed them I was definitely going to be a problem. I was able to shove several of the queens out of the collective before they let me go.*

That must be how they got a feel for the shape of you, said Fetch. *I am sorry. We didn't think he would . . . He came to us. He should have been willing to keep his word, and help you.*

I'm not sure he thought of what he was doing as wrong. I got to commune with the collective, after all. Maybe he thought he was helping us all.

I felt Fetch's disdain like a ripple down our tenuous connection. *That communion told them who we were. They came for us because they had been with you. They would never have known to come if not for Annalist. That was not help. That was serving us up to the queens like a prize. I just don't understand why he would do that.*

You hate the queens because they took Collate away from you. Is there any reason he would be loyal to them?

All Johrlac are loyal to our queens, even when we have reason not to be. We don't have a choice. The closer they are, the harder it becomes to be anything other than loyal. I would still die for them if they commanded me to do so, and I would be joyful at the opportunity. We are all one swarm, even if some of us are restless and ungrateful.

I didn't know how to respond to that. It was so alien to my own way of thinking, a sort of self-annihilation shaped by culture and proximity into something immutable. Very much, she was who I could have been if I'd grown up here, and I couldn't be angry at her for it. It wasn't like she'd had a choice. I forced my thoughts to calm, and tried to sound soothing as I replied, *There's nothing ungrateful about wanting to live as yourself, not an extension of someone else. You've done nothing wrong. I'm going to try to reach Carry now. Do you have anything you'd like me to tell her?*

Tell her . . . in case we're never in the same place and these selves again, tell her I loved her very much. Tell her she was probably my favorite thing about being Fetch.

You'll be able to tell her yourself, I said resolutely, and pulled my thoughts away, shifting them off to the side, where the vague impression of Carry lingered.

No matter how hard I focused on her, I couldn't get much more than the shape of her. She was more idea than individual.

Can you hear me? I asked.

No words, but a wave of affirmation from her direction.

Fetch is here too, I said. *She can't reach you, but she wanted me to tell you that she loves you very much. She's going to be here when I get all of us free. You have to hold on for her.*

Confusion, and then resignation, and sorrow. She didn't believe she was ever going to see Fetch again, and maybe she was right; she understood the situation far better than I did. But I had one advantage that she didn't.

I was a Price. And Prices don't give up on their people when they're in danger. I had to survive this in order to save my people, which now included Fetch and Carry. I opened my eyes, taking another look around the small white room. There was nothing here that I could use as a weapon, not even the bench I'd been sleeping on. It was fastened to the wall with some sort of adhesive, no bolts or screws in evidence, and even when I got off it and pulled, I couldn't get it to shift in the slightest. I had myself, and that was all.

I'd done more than enough with less. I stood at the center of the room, reaching for the math that defined the world around me. It could be used to freeze rain in the act of falling, to open tesseract passages through the fabric of reality. It could get me out of this cell.

The numbers weren't so different here on Johrlar. Math is a universal constant. I didn't dare tesseract my way much further than Fetch and Carry's house: this math wasn't complex enough to move me from one dimension into another, and I didn't know many of the places I'd been so far on Johrlar to feel confident jumping for them. Throwing myself heedlessly into the void has never been my idea of a good time.

I reached for the numbers, beginning to move them into position, and stopped as they came apart in my mental hands, dissolving into nonsense. I blinked, shaking the idea of the failed equation off my fingers, and tried again, to the same result. No matter how hard I tried, I couldn't catch the math the way I needed to. It was like it was somehow evading me.

Their shields weren't good enough to keep a queen fully contained, but they were enough to knock me back to where I'd been two instars ago. If I focused hard enough to make my head swim, I could see the math I needed, the glittering guidelines of reality . . . but that was all. No matter how hard I tried, I couldn't catch it. It refused to be contained.

I was trapped.

I dropped my hands and sat back down on the bench, resisting the urge to start punching the walls. I don't get physical very often, but when I do, I'm better at bruising my knuckles than I am at doing any real damage. If I was going to be stuck here for a while, the least I could do was not distract myself with unnecessary suffering.

My family was here, on Johrlar. They knew I was here, too. They would be coming for me soon. I knew they would.

All I had to do was be patient and they would come for me.

All I had to do was wait.

Eighteen

ANTIMONY

> "The best thing about being adopted is knowing, with absolute certainty, that I was chosen by the people who raised me. They wanted me more than anything. The worst thing is not knowing who I might have been. That version of me died so I could be born."
>
> —**Evelyn Baker**

In the jungle near the Johrlac city called Ka'krin, and really, I do not understand a damn thing about their language

When Sam jumped out of the tree, my traitorous limbic system cheered. Having a fiancé who can throw me around like a sack of potatoes—and does, on a fairly regular basis—has done some strange things to my emotional wiring. It was almost a pity my sister lived on the other side of the country these days; our mutual delight in being dropped from great heights might be the first real thing we'd ever had in common.

Arthur, on the other hand, screamed and clutched at Sam's neck, trying to hold on as tightly as he could. Sam swore, pushing his hands away, and Arthur transferred his clutching to me, getting a handful of hair and boob.

We hit the ground, Sam bending his knees to absorb the impact as much as he could, then dragging us both behind the tree. We had landed distressingly near the sidewalk, and needed to hide before any of the nearby pedestrians could figure out where that scream had come from.

What's the point of having a jungle if you're going to fully integrate it with your city? It just makes everything a liminal space, neither here nor there, and confuses everyone.

Once we were safely out of sight of the street, Sam let us both go, although he rewrapped his tail around my ankle immediately after, still holding on. I looked down at Arthur's hand, which was also still holding on.

"Ahem," I said blandly.

"What? Annie, your boyfriend just *threw us* out of a *tree*," he said.

"He didn't throw us, he jumped down and took us with him," I replied. "And if you could let go of my boob before he punches you in the throat so hard you taste cartilage, that would be cool too."

"Wha— Oh!" Arthur yanked his hand back like it had been burned, dancing backward a few feet for good measure. Shaking his hand as if to cool it, he stared at me in obvious mortification. "I'm sorry. I'm sorry! I was just trying to find something I could hold on to."

"They're pretty great, aren't they?" asked Sam, his natural urge to boast about my tits winning out over the impulse to be offended by what had just happened. With the way he could sometimes go on about them, you'd think he grew my breasts himself. Which was fine, really. It was sort of nice to have a fiancé who was so totally into my body.

I elbowed him anyway. "Sort of nice" didn't mean I wanted him discussing my breasts with my cousin. "Maybe try trusting the trained trapeze artist next time, and keep your hands to yourself," I suggested.

"I will, I promise!" said Arthur. "You're my cousin. That's gross. I would never—"

He trailed off, cheeks burning red. I could almost see him remembering that Sarah was his cousin too, even if she wasn't a blood relation. He absolutely would, under the right circumstances, with the right cousin. Which wasn't and had never been me.

"Standing around and being embarrassed at each other is fun and all, but it's not getting us home any time soon. Let's go find your grandparents," said Sam gruffly.

"Good plan," I agreed.

"I just want to get back to my basement and never go outside again," said Arthur.

"Sounds like a great idea," I said.

We started walking, circling the tree we'd been hiding behind and angling ourselves toward the back of the still-smoldering administration building. Smoke clouded the foliage around us, chokingly thick and strangely herbal thanks to all the burning brush. We were careful to avoid coming too close to the street or moving back into view; Alice might still be content to rely on the anti-telepathy charms to keep us hidden with everyone on edge from the fire, but I wasn't, especially not out in the open. There had to be kids here. Sarah was a child once, and logically, that meant all Johrlac started out as children.

Kids didn't care if they couldn't see the source of a strange noise. They cared about the strange noise, and finding its source. One of us would sneeze and we'd have a whole damn Johrlac kindergarten hanging off our arms, shouting for their adults to come and see the funny things they'd found. We needed to be cautious, even if we had a layer of protection on our side.

As if to illustrate that thought, something came crashing out of the canopy above us, slamming through the green until it hit the ground in front of us and bounced back up, revealing itself as a Johrlac in a red-and-brown jumpsuit, clutching what looked like a broom in both his hands and looking frantically around. All three of us froze, trying to emulate the trees around us.

There were charred holes in the sleeve of his jumpsuit, and the bristles of his broom were smoking. He'd clearly fled the building through an open window to get away from the fire; given the way some of the trees overhung the structure, it was impossible to guess how far he might have fallen.

Carefully, I looked him up and down. He didn't seem to be armed, and from the way he was still looking around, eyes bright and unfocused, he hadn't managed to spot us yet. Our camouflage, such as it was, was still holding. He looked up into the branches above him, then over his shoulder toward the administration building. Spinning on his heel, he started running in the direction of the sidewalk, crashing through the undergrowth between us and it.

I exhaled, sagging in relief.

"That was close," said Arthur.

The man stopped running.

We all froze again, and stayed frozen as the man slowly turned and started walking back toward us, lowering his broom so that it was held almost like a spear. He was moving slowly, scanning the greenery around him as he did, and I realized he was really *looking* at everything, each leaf and vine, with the sort of attention to detail I hadn't expected to see from anyone native to this world. For whatever reason, he'd learned to see the world around him, not just focus on the nearby minds.

Maybe it was the broom. Anyone who thought to bring their broom with them as they jumped out of a burning building would have to be good at paying attention to their surroundings. Dust doesn't have a mind, but it still needs to be swept up.

Of course, that raised the question of how much not seeing us was a choice the other Johrlac made, a more advanced version of the way Verity had never been able to see the dirty dishes clogging the sink when she didn't want to deal with them. If it was a choice, then it was presumably one they could stop making any time they wanted to.

Oh, we needed to find my grandparents. But before we did that, we needed to get away from the man who was still moving closer and closer to where we stood frozen.

Sam could move faster than the Johrlac could react. And if he moved at full speed, he'd be hitting like a freight train: he could very well kill this man without intending to, and even though the stranger represented a threat to us in the moment, he didn't deserve to die for the crime of being able to pay attention. That left me and Arthur.

Arthur's main defense was his pheromones, which didn't work against Johrlac. And mine . . .

Well, mine wasn't very far away at the moment. I reached out for the fire, feeling my way through the smoky air. We were still very close to the administration building: there was nothing that could keep me from getting to my goal. I extended the tendrils of my magic, and the fire answered me, ready to come at my command as always.

If I pulled it into the jungle, things were going to get a lot more exciting, very quickly. The man was getting closer. I didn't really think I had a choice.

Come, I commanded the fire.

The fire came so fast and so hard that it blew a hole in the back of the administration building, bursting through the papery wall like it had been fed with some sort of accelerant—which, in a way, it had been. My magic was better than gasoline where the fire was concerned, twice as flammable and infinitely more pure.

The jungle was alive and growing, wet with sap and juices. It didn't want to burn. I pushed more magic into the flames, and what the jungle wanted didn't matter anymore, because it was burning, bright as a candle and fiercely hot. Its joy was palpable, and I took a heartbeat to glory in it, letting the ecstasy of the flames burn over and through me. The man with the broom yelped and whipped around, raising his arms to shield his face as he stared, horrified, at what was rapidly becoming an inferno.

Then he ran again, faster this time, away from us . . . and away from the fire, which was coming right at us.

"You can turn it off now, right, Annie?" asked Arthur.

"It doesn't work that way, dude," said Sam. "Once she sets the fire, it's pretty much out of her control."

Not entirely. I could call it closer if I wanted to, could bring it to where I could wrap it around myself and let it warm me. Everything in this world was alien, but the fire was so familiar. The fire was here for me, and because of me, and I loved it so.

I didn't say any of that. Loving the fire was irrelevant. No matter how much I wanted it, I was still flesh and bone, and even an elementalist can be consumed if they linger too close to the flame.

"We need to get out of here," I said, looking up at Sam. "Can you carry us both?"

"Not very far, but hopefully far enough," he said, and scooped each of us under an arm, holding tight as he tensed, then leapt forward, beginning to race away from the fire, which was quickly turning that patch of jungle into an inferno. His choices of direction were limited by the wall of flame and the fact that the man from before had already taken the most effective escape route.

So he ran, leaping over obstacles and parkouring off tree trunks like he was being timed, and Arthur and I held on, me pulling my legs in as much as I could to prevent being jounced around more than was absolutely unavoidable. Leaves and small branches slapped me across the face and shoulders, but Sam was doing a decent job of dodging anything overly large.

And then there were two figures ahead of us in the brush. Sam dodged around them, still running. I leaned over, getting as close to his ear as possible, and shouted, "Those were my grandparents, Sam!"

He jumped again, using a nearby limb to redirect his momentum as he bounded back the way we'd just come. Landing a few feet in front of my bemused-looking grandparents, he set me and Arthur back on our feet.

"Sorry," he said. "I was in 'Don't burn to death or get caught' mode, and I wasn't really looking where I was going."

"I'm going to be sick," said Arthur, staggering toward a nearby bush.

I would normally have said something catty, or at least attempted to tease, but I was preoccupied with trying to get my intensely tangled hair out of my face and back behind my ears.

"You're all uninjured?" asked Thomas. Sam and I made sounds of assent, while Arthur began retching into the brush. Thomas looked past us to him, a faint look of amusement twisting his mouth upward. "I suppose vomiting isn't an injury."

"He never liked rollercoasters either, the poor lamb," said Alice, then grimaced. "I mean Artie didn't like roller coasters. It's the same body, so I'd assume things like 'does not enjoy getting recreationally rattled' would still apply."

Arthur tried to straighten and reply, only to double over again, continuing to retch. I grimaced and turned away from him, trying to keep the sounds he was making from unsettling my own stomach.

"How did you get out?" asked Sam.

"Made a hole," said Alice.

I rolled my eyes. "Is that a semi-polite euphemism for 'threw a grenade'?" I asked.

"It worked," she said serenely.

"And no one was injured," said Thomas. "How did *you* get out?"

"Asked the fire to back off long enough for us to get out a window, then made for the trees," I said. "We ran into a Johrlac down on the ground level, which is why we were moving quite so fast when we found you: he was about to send up the alarm when I called the fire to come to us."

"Which would be why the forest is in the process of catching fire," said Sam.

"Poor thing. It's not the greenery's fault that it grew so close to terrible people." Alice cast a sympathetic look at the nearest tree. "I hope it's wet enough that the fire gives up soon."

"Whether it's wet or not, there's still a forest fire kicking off behind us, and we should maybe be getting the hell out of here," I suggested. "Any thoughts on what we're going to do next?"

"A few," said Thomas. "Come along. Arthur, if you're not up for walking on your own, we can ask Samuel to carry you."

Arthur promptly straightened, wiping his mouth with the back of his hand. "I can walk," he said. "I've had enough of being carried for today."

"Excellent. This way."

Thomas began walking boldly forward, forging a new path through the tangled brush. It tried to push back a time or two, and he merely raised his hands, fingers radiating sufficient heat that leaves and boughs withered, going limp and becoming easy for him to brush aside. The rest of us followed, Alice offering an arm to keep Arthur upright and steady on the uneven ground.

The ground. For the first time since we'd broken him out of his cell, I looked down at his feet. They were bare.

"The cuckoos took your shoes," I blurted, horrified.

Arthur gave me a weary look. "Of course they did. They took everything. My shoes were part of 'everything.'"

My cheeks burned, but I kept my chin up as I looked at him, refusing to be cowed. "I'm sorry I didn't notice sooner. I was a little preoccupied with the whole 'running for my life' part of things. How are your feet?"

"Sore, but I'm being careful where I step, and Sam carrying us for the serious outdoor chase sequence was a big help. I may not have enjoyed it much, but I bet I'd have enjoyed being punctured even less." He reached up to wipe a bit of half-dried nectar from his forehead, flicking it to the side. "Also not a fan of the makeshift perfume barrier, but I understand the necessity."

"Who knew flowers had that much nectar in them?"

"Bees, I guess."

"And we'll need another flower before long," said Sam, slowing a bit so he could join the conversation. "The juice from the last one is starting to dry up, and then I'll have a problem."

"I know," said Arthur mournfully. "I guess I just stay sticky until we get the hell out of here."

"All we need to do now is find Sarah." Easier said than done. I hadn't picked up on the crackle of her static, which was normally inescapable, since we'd landed on Johrlar. It was like she didn't exist. Her range wasn't infinite, but if Arthur was here in Ka'krin, she should be too. There was no point in abducting them both just to separate them. That made the absence of her telepathic signal worrisome, and a little bit scary.

The cells back in the burning building had clearly been designed to blunt telepathy. But Sarah hadn't been there, and I didn't know if they *could* build an anti-telepathy ward strong enough to contain a queen as powerful as she was. They had good reason to know how basic wards worked: if nothing else, they would never have been able to punish the original cuckoos if not for the fact that they could be cut off from the collective. Punishing a queen was something entirely different, at least based on what I'd been able to learn about them so far. Would they even be able to do that?

Sarah hadn't been in the cells, and I was reasonably sure we'd have been able to pick up on her hum if she'd been in the building. Unless— I touched the anti-telepathy charm hanging around my own neck. Had we been blocking her out this whole time?

"No," said Arthur, apparently predicting my thoughts. "She wasn't in the building. I'm not *very* sensitive, and she's never willingly touched me, not even once, but she touched Artie all the time. I have half a dozen people's memories reminding me of that. I'm so tightly skin-attuned to her that I'd have been able to feel it if she'd been anywhere near me."

"They had blockers built into the cell walls," I said.

"Fine, then, I can say for sure that she was never on the same floor as I was." Arthur shook his head. "If she were that close, there's nothing that could have kept her out of my head."

"You say that like it's a good thing," said Sam.

"I love her," said Arthur. "I love her like I love . . . like I love air, or water, or anything else I need to stay alive. The world is hollow when she's not with me."

"I know," I said quietly, forcing my face to stay composed. Whenever Arthur described his love for Sarah, her reasons for staying away became easier to understand. She'd constructed him as a frantic last-ditch effort to save Artie, the man she had actually loved. All she'd done was collage together a pile of unrelated memories into the rough form of a person, and most of the family had remembered Artie as hopelessly in love with her from the time we were all children. One thing I knew from talking to my siblings, and to Elsie: Artie had genuinely loved Sarah, truly and completely, to the bottom of his heart. But while I'm not silly enough to say that love is a choice, it does have to be chosen, and he'd chosen it again and again, loving her despite it being a provably terrible idea.

Arthur never got to choose anything. Arthur came into existence with so many of his choices already made. Even with as mad as I still was at Sarah, I knew she hadn't intended to do that to him. She'd been acting on instinct and panic, trying to save someone who was already gone, and she'd made a mistake. That was all.

No one would say it would have been better if Arthur hadn't existed. I liked him well enough. The ways he reminded me of Artie hurt, but the ways he didn't were an endlessly unfolding delight. Still, it worried me when he talked about Sarah: his love was too deeply rooted in who he was as a person, and it consequentially verged on becoming obsession, something that might eventually harm them both.

"So we haven't managed to find Sarah yet," said Alice. "But finding Arthur means we're in the right place—dimensional crossings of this distance are expensive enough that they wouldn't have sent multiple groups over unless they had a central working."

"It didn't seem that expensive for Grandpa," I said.

"Your grandfather is working with a different set of rules," she said, delicately.

"Tell me," I said.

Thomas looked back over his shoulder at me, brow furrowed. "I don't want you getting ideas about attempting dimensional crossings on your own," he said. "I've been avoiding the topic until we'd finished more of your foundational schooling."

"I don't want to go dimension-hopping for funsies," I said. "Mary would kick my ass. She's never forgiven herself for not doing a better job of convincing Grandma it was a bad idea."

"And I'd pout for days if she said she was going to run off like that," volunteered Sam.

Thomas sighed and stopped walking, looking around until he spotted a bush covered in large, peach-colored berries. "Imagine each of these is a world," he said. He reached over and plucked a berry, holding it up for inspection. "The Johrlac travel via concentrated, somewhat destructive mathematical means. They can bend their numbers so that inserting them into another world's sphere of existence doesn't rupture anything, but rather passes cleanly through. This takes an immense amount of power and effort from the caster, as the energy consumed is either channeled through or created by the mathematician." He twisted his free hand, working a needle free of his shirt cuff, and slid it through the surface of the berry and out the other side. "The punctures they make are so small as to do functionally no damage, when the math is done correctly. When done incorrectly, we get the scenarios I've been told the cuckoos intended to play out with Sarah shortly before my return home. Worlds end."

He tossed me the berry. I turned it over in my hand, but a quick inspection didn't reveal the puncture marks. Only squeezing it slightly made beads of juice form where the needle had passed.

"Okay," I said. "Surgical and precise, got it."

"Surgical, precise, and limited by the power the cast can generate or have fed to them. Sorcerers, on the other hand, use the pneuma they've collected or carried with them to fuel the crossing." He plucked another berry, holding it up. "This causes more damage, but means they don't need anyone else to feed them power." He picked at the delicate edge of skin left around the hole where the berry had attached to its skin, finally pulling a thin strip away. Again, he tossed me the berry. This time, the damage was easy to see.

"It will heal, given time, but dimensional crossings are expensive for the worlds, rather than for the caster. We can still exhaust ourselves channeling that much power, but we do it on our own, without large groups to help us shape the spell. Indeed, sorcerers are more likely to experience complications when we try to work with others."

"Sarah brought us back on her own." But that wasn't true, was it? That had never been true. She'd done the math herself, but she'd bolstered it with the power and storage capacity of hundreds of minds, using them to do the brute force computing while she shaped the equation to her will. She wouldn't have been able to make the transition without all of us to support her. Even Artie, although we would never know for sure whether he had been aware when he touched her that he was going to be trading his life for our ticket home.

"What about Grandma?" I asked, trying to make sense of all this. "She can't bend pneuma."

"Can't even see the stuff," she said cheerfully. "I was shocked as anything when I found out I was covered in it. Could have knocked me over with a feather."

"If that serpentine bastard hadn't been holding you down and flensing you alive on a regular basis, you would have been carrying enough pneuma to make yourself the most terrifying magician the worlds have ever seen," said Thomas.

"So let's be glad that didn't happen," she said, still far cheerier than she had any right to be under the circumstances.

Thomas sighed. "Your grandmother can't manipulate pneuma, but she can be given objects, whether physical or representative, that are attuned to it and allow her to utilize what she has. The result is almost a hybrid of the human and Johrlac methods of crossing. Like the human, they use pneuma as a base, and work by expending it. Like the Johrlac, they also draw from their users."

"That's why I had horrible traumatic flashbacks every time I crossed dimensional walls using one of my tattoos, and why it could exhaust me so badly that I had to carry glucose packs to be sure I wouldn't pass out before I could get to safety." As was almost always the case when she was describing something objectively horrible, Alice's tone remained upbeat and even delighted with the subject. It wasn't the strangest defense mechanism in the family.

Thomas clearly also recognized it for what it was. He reached over and squeezed her shoulder with one hand, then looked back to me.

"Me bringing us all here was expensive in terms of pneuma consumed, and since Earth is still recovering from what the crossroads did to us, it's better if I don't try to repeat the process more than strictly necessary, which is why we're not going back until we're all together. The Johrlac coming for your cousins was expensive in terms of risk to both the mathematician and the people powering the spell, which is why we don't have to worry about them doing it on a regular basis. And your grandmother going home on her own would be expensive in terms of the toll it would take on her body, which is still recovering from the beating she took getting us all out of the bottle dimension I'd been imprisoned in."

"Got it," I said. "Thank you for taking the time to explain."

"Under the circumstances, it seemed like the best way to avoid something happening that we wouldn't be able to recover from quite as well as we could a brief delay. Now. We need to find your cousin."

"I have a suggestion," said Sam, slowly. He didn't sound happy about it. "We've all been wearing those charms Alice handed out since before we got here, and we know they make us basically invisible to most of the Johrlac. Arthur didn't have a charm, but he was in a cell designed to stop telepathic contact. Even if none of those things are enough to *stop* a queen on their own, they might be enough to turn down her volume."

"Sam . . ." I began.

He held up a hand, signaling for me to let him keep going. "I'm just saying, Annie set fire to their capital building, after they figured out Alice was here for nefarious purposes. Pretty sure this is no longer a stealth operation, if it ever really was. Maybe one of the people who's more attuned to Sarah than me or Alice should take their charm off and see if they can make contact."

Arthur opened his mouth, already reaching behind himself to remove his charm. Before he could, I grabbed mine by the strap and heated up my hand, burning through the leather cord in a matter of seconds. The charm dropped harmlessly into my other hand, and the world of Johrlar came alive around me.

The four hums I'd already been able to hear were joined by a dozen more, the jungle harmonizing with itself. One of those hums was discordant, a whimper of pain cutting through the chorus, and I knew from the tone of it that it was the forest, a single mind made up of all the interconnected root systems and mycelia under our feet. This was a telepathic world, and never had I been able to understand that better than when I let myself be open to it.

And under the louder hums surrounding me, there was a thin, almost silenced tone, one muffled and deadened by some sort of barrier, one that I still knew all the way down to my bones. Sarah had stolen my memories of her, intentionally or not, but she couldn't change the things my flesh remembered. My skin knew she was my cousin, barely short of a sister; my skin knew she was family, and beloved. I heard her with my body as much as with my mind, and I knew she was here, and I knew she was captive, and I knew she needed us. More than anything else, she needed us.

"Annie?" said Sam, anxiously. "You okay, babe?"

I shushed him, then closed my eyes and turned in a circle before I stopped and pointed in the direction the hum seemed to be coming from. "She's that way," I said. "Over there."

"One small problem, pumpkin," said Alice. "That way takes us back toward the building you set on fire."

"Maybe it's done being on fire by now," I said. "We know she wasn't there when we were inside. They must have her someplace nearby."

"That, or they moved her while we were walking," suggested Arthur. "Annie's the only person here who's better at picking up on Sarah than I am. If she says that's the way, then that's the way. I trust her."

"Thank you," I said, still pointing. "Sarah's this way. I think she's behind some kind of dampener, but it's not quite strong enough to block her out completely."

"All right," said Alice. "Lead the way."

◆ ◆ ◆

Traveling back through the jungle without the speed added by Sam's panicked flight slowed us down considerably. We'd been walking for what felt like over an hour before the air began smelling of smoke again, and shortly after that, we emerged into a clearing that had clearly burned, and recently. Ropes of foamy white clung to the newly crisped foliage around us, having been used to control and extinguish the blaze, and Arthur yelped as he tried to keep walking.

I turned to look back at him. He grimaced sheepishly.

"Ground's still hot," he explained.

"Let me get that," said Thomas. He raised and then lowered his right hand, a stern expression on his face. Arthur watched this with wide eyes, and when Thomas beckoned, he once again tried to step into the clearing. His eyes widened with surprise, and he kept on going.

"The ground's cool now," he said. "I thought you could just make fire happen, not cool things down."

"Wait until you get to experience one of your grandmother's holiday dinners," said Thomas. "As soon as she realized I could shunt the heat away from objects as well as summon it, she threw out all her trivets and declared roast roc a reasonable substitute for turkey."

"Don't exaggerate, Thomas," said Alice. "It took at least a year before I believed you wouldn't freeze my gravy doing that."

Arthur looked utterly baffled. Thomas smiled at him, visibly taking pity.

"Antimony and I are both elementalists, and the easiest manifestation of what we can do is fire, but really anything to do with moving heat around falls under our purview. Once Antimony has been fully trained, she'll be able to cool things down as quickly as she heats them up. Heat will always come more naturally."

"Huh," I said. "Does that mean that eventually James will get heat to go with his cold?"

"Yes," said Thomas. "Assuming he can focus on his studies."

"Hey!" I protested. "James focuses just fine when he needs to. It's not his fault that he's still getting used to the idea of having a family that actually likes him. He gets distracted sometimes. You would too, in his position."

"You *did*, too," said Alice, bumping her hip against his as they walked. "When I first started sleeping over, you damn near burned the house down, you were so distracted."

"A man has that reaction to finding a beautiful woman he's wanted to hold for years suddenly available and waiting in his bedroom," said Thomas, with stiff dignity. "I doubt James is having the same experience with Sally."

"No, I would think not," said Alice, almost laughing.

James and Sally—my adopted brother and their adopted daughter, respectively, which made our specific familial relations a sort of whacked-out macramé no one could follow without a flow chart—are both about as queer as it's possible to get while still adhering to a binary gender. He likes boys, she likes girls, and never the twain shall meet. She'd been his beard for a few chaperoned dances when they were in high school together, back when his father had been convinced he could bully the gay out of him.

That shit has never worked. Not from the beginning to the end of time. Bullying your queer kid isn't going to get you a straight one. If you're lucky, it'll get you what James's dad got: a living queer kid who doesn't consider you family and will never voluntarily speak to you again.

If you're unlucky, it'll get you what so many families receive. It'll get you a dead queer kid. And yeah, dead queer kids are still queer. Just ask Mary.

We had reached the center of the burnt-out place. We all paused there for a moment, going quiet and listening for any sounds from the nearby street. There weren't any. Even the bugs were quieter here, having been driven off by the smoke and flames. If the fire brigade was still out there, they were working in total silence. Not outside the realm of possibility, but that implied that they had moved on to cleanup. Throwing sheets of foam makes a sound, even if it's not as loud as people yelling or flames crackling.

I took my anti-telepathy charm and tied it around my throat again, securing the knot against the back of my neck so that it hung like a very unfashionable choker. The distant buzz of Sarah's presence immediately flickered out, and I felt a strange hollowness where it should have been. It was difficult not to pull the charm off again, just so I could know she was all right, which made no sense. I didn't like her. I certainly wasn't so worried about her that I needed a constant reminder that she was okay.

But I still missed that sound when it was gone.

I shook my head like a dog trying to shake off a flea, and turned to look at Sam. "From here, we're as quiet as we can be," I said.

"Arthur, you're with me and Thomas," said Alice. "Sam, if Annie's in danger, get the two of you out of there as quickly as you can."

"Why are we splitting up?" asked Sam. "I don't see any good reason for it."

"We're not going to be able to use the door openly," said Thomas. "That means going through in smaller groups, to avoid detection. We'll cover more ground in two groups, and this way, each of us has a fire specialist. If you have no other way out, set the building on fire again. I can keep it from reaching us long enough to evacuate, and I'll do the same thing if it gets bad where we are. The goal is to find Sarah and get outside."

"How do I tell you if we've accomplished that?" I asked.

He smiled, more mischievously than I would have thought possible. "Set the building on fire and we'll figure out that it's time to go," he said.

"Great. So fire means either 'danger' or 'success,' and the only way to find out which is to meet up behind the building again?" asked Sam.

"That's correct," said Thomas.

"Annie, I love you, and I can't wait to marry you, but your family is like, big fucking weird, you know that, right?"

"Yeah," I said, grinning at my cousin and grandparents. "I do."

He rolled his eyes and the five of us kept walking, moving toward the edge of the jungle, Sam and I pulling slightly ahead while Alice, Thomas, and Arthur angled off to the right.

Emerging from the verdant if slightly charred green into the city was jarring. The sounds that had been everywhere in the trees died almost instantly, the buzzing and squeaking of insects replaced by the sound of feet on the sidewalks and the distant grumbling of the livestock in the parking garage. I was relieved to see that the fire hadn't managed to spread that far: the stromopods and other riding animals were safe.

The fire brigade was gone, as was the triage area they had established; all the injured and deceased Johrlac had been removed. I was embarrassingly relieved by its absence. I knew at least one person had died in the fire I'd set. That didn't mean I wanted a full list of the lost. Death is always a tragedy, even when you're not on the same side, and these people hadn't necessarily done anything wrong: they'd just been in the wrong place at the wrong time, and that shouldn't be an offense worth dying over.

The administration building was singed but standing, with globs of foamy white stuff all over the front of it. Johrlac were going calmly in and out. Maybe they had a different approach to structural damage than we did back on Earth? At home, a building that had been this recently on fire would have been closed for days if not weeks, getting repaired before someone fell through a floor or something.

A group of Johrlac in red-and-brown jumpsuits like the man who'd fallen into the forest went through the door, carrying buckets and what looked like strangely shaped spatulas. Maybe they just had a more efficient means of repairing what we'd broken.

No one seemed to see us. The street was as busy as ever—busier, in some ways. There were substantially more children moving through the crowds, sticking in small groups of three to five, as silent as the adults around them. Interestingly, the children were clearly chatting with each other: their eyes were solidly white from side to side, occasionally flaring bright as a firefly's luminescence, then dying back down again. Mental silence must come later, when they were more solidly themselves and more deeply absorbed by the collective.

Alice's group turned directly toward the doors, while Sam looked at the damaged front of the building and scooped me off my feet again. "Hold on," he suggested.

I held on.

He tensed, then leapt, landing on the side of the building around what I judged to be the two-story mark. From there, he began to climb, moving toward windows and pausing to the side of them while I leaned over to see whether there was anyone on the other side. The locals might be inclined not to allow themselves to see us when they couldn't mentally "see" us, but that wouldn't stop them from noticing a window being pried out of its frame.

The first three windows, I shook my head no, and we kept on going. The scenes I'd spotted through the wasp-veined glass were surprisingly mundane, people standing around or moving things from point to point. Sure, some of them moved those things without using their hands, but whatever. Light telekinesis was one of the first lessons Thomas had taught me, and Sarah sometimes forgot whether she was using her hands or her mind when she picked something up. We were not a family that demanded things be done manually. Still, no one looked disturbed or even particularly inconvenienced by the fact that their place of work had just recently been on *fire* and at least one of their coworkers had died.

At the fourth window, I held up a finger, signaling Sam to pause, and leaned in close to scan the room for any Johrlac I might have missed. There was no one there. The room was utterly empty. I looked back to him and nodded, then pulled back against his chest as he reached up and pulled the window out of its frame.

A moment later, we were inside and he was replacing the window where it belonged. The air smelled even more strongly of char than the forest outside did, underscored with a sharp smell like acetone. I pinched my nose before I could sneeze, but the tickling remained. Sam took a breath and wrinkled his own nose, looking almost comically offended. I snorted lightly and looked around the room.

It was featureless, which seemed to be, forgive me, a feature of the stand-alone rooms in this place; only the prisoners' cells had been outfitted with anything I recognized as furniture, and there, it had been nothing more sophisticated than rough bunks to keep the prisoners from sleeping on the floor. The map room had been more properly outfitted according to my Earth sensibilities, but that had been about the function of the space: these rooms . . . I didn't know why they existed, but whatever their purpose, they didn't need flat surfaces or seating.

"I do not get these people," I said lowly, and moved toward the door, Sam close behind me.

It didn't take long to pick the lock and let ourselves out, into another long, featureless hall. Based on the angle, it was entirely internal: we'd be walking parallel to the outside wall, not moving any deeper into the structure unless we found a juncture. Shrugging, I started to my right, Sam still following. Either we'd find a turn or we'd make ourselves an exit and try again elsewhere in the structure.

With the telepathy blocker back against my skin, I couldn't pick up on Sarah if I was trying. We needed to find more cells, and try to get her out of wherever she was being held. Once we did that, we could all go home together. This could be over.

We reached the hoped-for juncture and turned, finally starting to make our way deeper. After about ten feet, the hallway widened into a sort of lounge area, like the waiting room at a hospital, only without the desks, plastic plants, or uncomfortable chairs. There were also no doors. This space didn't seem to *lead* to anything. It just existed, incongruously shoved into the middle of everything. I hesitated at the threshold.

"Annie? What's wrong?" asked Sam, voice low.

"This whole thing is . . . it doesn't feel right," I said.

He frowned, and when I stepped forward, he didn't try to stop me.

The attack came when we reached the middle of the room. The walls fell away, revealing a larger room filled with Johrlac in blue jumpsuits. They had us on numbers alone, but we fought as hard as we could before they overwhelmed us, Sam throwing punches while I threw fireballs. Several of them went down, their eyes glinting white as they fell, but the rest just kept coming.

Then a hand closed around my wrist and it was all over. The anti-telepathy charm I was wearing wasn't enough to protect me from skin contact with an actual Johrlac. I was slammed immediately out of connection with my body, and into a featureless expanse of infinite whiteness.

A woman who looked like Sarah in the way a cobra looks like a garter snake was waiting for me there, wearing an iridescent bodysuit that gleamed like an oil slick in all the possible colors of the rainbow and a few additional ones that my brain didn't know how to make sense of. She was smiling, which was almost as unnatural as the cold detachment in her icy eyes.

"You lose, little hive destroyer," she said, and her voice was and was not Sarah's, and I knew she was the collective, infinite and enormous, looking down upon me from whatever height they chose to watch over their people.

I fell into a fighting stance, raising my fists, and her smile turned cruelly amused.

"Such a mammalian response. We'll never understand how you became the dominant life form on so many, many worlds. You've lost. Let yourself lose. It's time to stop now, mammal."

Her eyes gleamed white, and the fight drained out of me.

I barely noticed my eyes closing.

I certainly didn't notice myself hitting the ground.

Nineteen

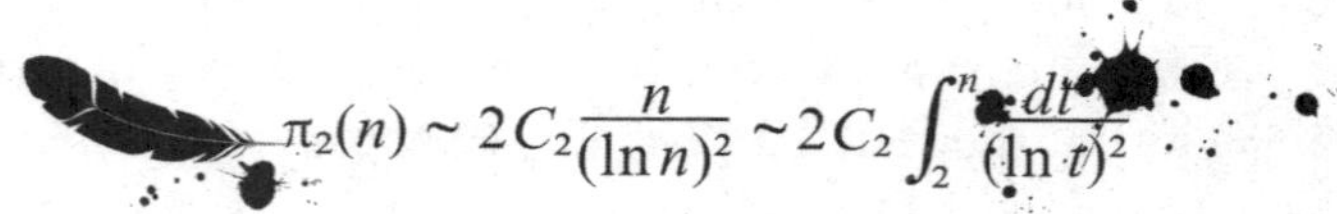

SARAH

> "Time may come where someone comes along and says they've got a claim on you from something they did without asking you first. You can be polite to them if you like, but you've got no obligation. They have no power over you."
>
> —**Frances Brown**

The Ka'krin Hall of Justice and Law

I DON'T KNOW HOW LONG I sat there before they came for me, eight guards in blue jumpsuits who grabbed me roughly and pulled me out of my cell, dragging me down the hallway to a small room where they thrust a bundle of fabric into my arms and snapped aloud, "Get dressed."

Interesting. They didn't even want to risk making mental contact with me. As soon as they'd pulled me out of the cell, the world had returned to its usual depth and focus: I could feel their minds around me, self-contained and bright, like little candle flames I could have reached out and dragged my fingers through. I kept my thoughts to myself—literally—and didn't try to communicate telepathically with any of them. Better not to feed their fears when they'd already decided I was a monster.

As for me, I was still trying to decide how monstrous I was going to become. Their collective had brought me here against my will, and now that same collective was afraid of what I could do to them. But was I willing to do it? So much hinged on Arthur's condition. If they had him and he was unharmed, I might just stand down. Let them have their trial, let them promise to send my family home, and then . . .

After that, I didn't know. I'd meant what I said before. I still had things to do. I wanted to see Isaac grow up, whether having Charlotte and Mom and me around would mean he was a better example of our species than Mom or I had been able to become. I wanted to meet Cici. I wanted to take care of Greg. But even more than all of that, I didn't want to hurt anyone else, and hurting people seemed inevitable if I continued on as I had been. I didn't belong on Earth. I was an invasive species there, and I always, always would be.

Maybe we'd all be better off if I just stopped fighting and let the collective do whatever they wanted with me. At least if they erased the Sarah-I-was and replaced me with a Sarah-they-made, they'd know they had someone who could be useful and wouldn't go around accidentally deleting people's memories or wiping their minds.

But that would be rewarding them for their terrible behavior, and I didn't want to do that either.

The bundle of fabric they had handed me was another jumpsuit, this one arctic white with bands of pale gray that I guessed would be pink if I had a pair of mammalian eyes to orient myself with. Interesting. I wondered which of their castes this aligned with; it seemed odd for them to have a whole color scheme for prisoners.

One of the guards made an impatient gesture, clearly signaling me to get on with it. I removed the loose shirt and pants they had dressed me in, leaving them discarded on the floor. I shook the jumpsuit out to remove the wrinkles, stepping into it and easing it over my hips before doing up the seam at the front, which wasn't a zipper but might as well have been. It adhered to itself when I pinched it, sealing the fabric around me. I couldn't figure out how that worked. I wasn't sure it mattered.

Turning, I walked the short distance back to the guard who'd handed me the jumpsuit in the first place. "Do I get shoes?" I asked. The jumpsuit covered the soles of my feet, but it was so thin that anything rougher than the interior floors would probably tear the fabric.

"No," the guard replied tersely. "Come with us."

They turned then, starting down the hall, while the others fanned out to surround me, leaving me with no choice but to accompany them. I didn't particularly want to run away again. This whole thing had been like one big game of cat and mouse, and I was tired of it. I wanted to see my family. I wanted to know they were okay.

I wanted this to be over with.

So I didn't resist and I didn't run, and I didn't reach out and mentally squeeze the guards around me until they collapsed and I could get away. I just walked.

The building smelled like the inside of a cheap barbeque joint, all smoke and char and the sharp, almost fruity tang of acetone. Someone had managed to light a fire here recently. I blinked, looking around as we left the hall for a large atrium—the main atrium, if the pattern of the dome above us was anything to go by. Some of the walls were blackened, and janitorial crews were already hard at work cutting away sheets of damaged material and replacing it with fresh panels, using a muddy substance to glue them in place. This really was a giant wasp's nest, with little adjustments made where necessary to adapt it to bipedal uses.

I faced front again as we crossed the atrium, feeling fleeting touches from all the minds around us. The people were intensely curious. From a few of them I caught glints of recognition, and the meaning of my jumpsuit: it was their signal for "cuckoo." As long as I wore this, I was branded as an exile, someone outside their system. I immediately liked it better for knowing that it was accurate, it actually described me, and liked it less at the same time, because it would make running away harder, if things came to that. Now anyone who looked at me would know what I was.

As if they wouldn't have known already. I tried to reconstruct the partition I'd been using with Fetch and Carry, then paused as

I realized that I was out of my cell. Experimentally, I reached for the numbers that would let me take myself away.

They were back, all of them, a beautiful Fibonacci spiral of possibilities that could take me anywhere I wanted to go if I could just define my destination to the eighth decimal place. That was easy. That part had always been easy. I could pull on the underlying threads of reality to put myself someplace else, someplace I could be, however momentarily, safe.

But if I did that, I'd be running again, and I'd just be delaying the inevitable. It was enough to know, however briefly, that the option was open to me. I *could* go. That meant I didn't need to.

We had reached a large set of sliding doors, with more guards outside, these ones standing at full attention. The eyes of the guard leading my group flashed white, and the other guards nodded before stepping to the side to let us approach.

The doors slid open. We stepped through, into a short, dark tunnel with light at the far end.

"Move, cuckoo," snapped one of the guards, and something prodded me in the center of my back, urging me to move forward, toward the light. I did so, and was almost there when someone stepped out of the shadows and snapped something around my wrist.

"Hey!" I yelped.

Too late: they were already gone. I lifted my arm, trying to see what was on my wrist. Whatever it was, it was heavy, and when I shook my arm, it slid up and down by a few inches, too tight to remove, loose enough not to cut off the circulation.

I was prodded again, and I stepped forward into the light of an arena like something out of a gladiator movie. I was standing on the ground level, and all around me were tiers and tiers of seats, almost all of them occupied. The Johrlac around me were wearing all manner of jumpsuit—everything but the cuckoo white-and-gray.

At one end of the space was a high box, cut off from the rest of the seats by privacy walls, occupied by Johrlac in iridescent black jumpsuits, their hair all styled in the exact same manner, all sitting on the same level as they stared toward me. I looked at them and swallowed, hard.

The collective. The five queens who controlled this whole territory, in front of me and in the flesh.

There were other boxes scattered around the edges of the arena, all of them closed off by heavy curtains. I looked at the object on my wrist again, and managed, barely, not to groan.

It was a heavy bracelet, some sort of polished wood wrapped around what looked like uncut opal. Opal is one of the best gems for incorporating in anti-telepathy charms; the water trapped inside the gem acts as a conductor for the magic. I couldn't feel the power embedded in the gem, but the more I looked at it, the more I thought that was what it was.

An opal of this size *could* be tailored to contain a queen. I glanced up again, at the box containing the collective. They were looking at me, eyes glowing white, and I didn't hear anything. They might as well not have been there. I was completely blocked off.

The one at the center of their formation stood, moving the short distance to the front of the box. "Bring the cuckoo," she said, her voice echoing through every corner of the arena. The acoustics were incredible, and the fact that my designation was "cuckoo," not "prisoner" or "accused," explained why: if this was where they did their show trials for exiles, they would have to conduct them at least partially aloud. They couldn't trust us in their minds.

The guards pushed me forward, and I didn't resist, allowing myself to be pushed onto the bamboo disk set at the center of the open space. As soon as we got there they stepped away, leaving me alone. The ground rumbled below my feet, the bamboo platform beginning to slide upward. I couldn't hear any sort of mechanism. I looked back to the central box. All five queens were standing now, their eyes lit up like searchlights, so bright that I couldn't look at them directly.

There was no mechanism. They were lifting me with their minds. Since I hadn't been able to do that until after my final instar, it was a good way to remind the people of their power, and why they were in charge. I could respect the showmanship of it all, even as it failed to lessen my desire to crush them for what they'd done. Not just to me: to this entire society, all the people like Fetch and Carry who were being born into a world where their choices had been taken away from them before they even existed. I glared at them, aware that they wouldn't be able to read my expression, but taking a small pleasure in how human that gesture was. I knew what I was feeling. I could still feel independent of their desires. They couldn't take that away from me without allowing me access to their minds.

The queen at the center of the collective focused on me, and when she spoke, the acoustics flung her voice effortlessly. She didn't have to yell. She didn't even have to speak loudly. "The cuckoo, designate Sarah, stands accused of destruction of her own kind, both mental and mortal; of the unwilling revision of someone who claimed her as an ally; of the invasion of another dimension without the consent or approval of the locals; and of countless small violations of the ethics by which all telepathic peoples are expected to comport themselves. How do you plead?"

I knew they weren't actually speaking English, although I wasn't sure how I could still understand them with as hard as they had locked my mental abilities down, and despite this, I still gaped at her for a moment, stunned. She raised an eyebrow, looking prepared to continue whether or not I opened my mouth, and so I straightened my spine and snapped, "Not guilty."

Eyes flashed white around the arena as the watching Johrlac did their equivalent of muttering to each other about my response. The collective allowed it to go on for several seconds before the one in the center spoke again.

"Silence," she said. "Designate Sarah, you committed the acts of which you stand accused. That is not in question. How can you plead not guilty?"

"Simple," I said. "I didn't commit any crimes. Even if I did those things, I did them in self-defense, or because I didn't know what I was doing. If anyone here has committed a crime, it was you. By exiling the cuckoos and leaving them to wander with no true understanding of their capabilities, you made situations like mine inevitable. Any blood I've shed is on your hands."

Once again, the silence was broken by eyes flashing like strobe lights, telepathic messages flying through the ether. I almost wished I could listen in on them. At the same time, I was almost grateful I couldn't. That many people shouting at once would have given me one hell of a headache.

"You do not get to make accusations against us," said another of the collective. Her voice was exactly the same as the first's, even down to the inflections. They really had given up their individuality for the sake of power—although not all willingly, considering what they'd done to Collate. "You are a cuckoo, outside our hive, outside our people. We are not held to the same laws."

"I am held to the laws of Earth," I countered. "And by the laws of Earth, I've done nothing wrong. The only people I harmed were harmed in self-defense. I refuse to acknowledge your authority over me."

"We have the proof of your crimes," said the first queen. "You cannot pretend to be innocent when the evidence is placed before you."

"I *am* proof of yours," I snapped. "I wouldn't be here if you hadn't thrown my ancestors out to wreck other worlds and become other people's problem."

They ignored me. The speaker raised a hand, and the curtain over one of the smaller boxes dropped, revealing Arthur. He was held in place by manacles around his hands, but he was still standing, and he didn't look injured.

Of course I couldn't read his face, but he didn't look like he was crying or like he had been recently. I lurched automatically in his direction, stopping myself before I could go over the edge. "Arthur!"

He turned toward me, standing a bit straighter. "Sarah?"

"Are you all right? Did they hurt you?"

He managed a small, nervous laugh. "No, and no," he said.

"Silence. The accused will not speak to the evidence," snapped the queen at the center of the collective. "This individual is a revision, and has no right to speak. This . . . person is a collage of memories and experiences not his own, collected by the accused and assembled into the shape of a man. He does not want for himself, but only as he has been instructed by the accused. He is not real, and has no right to existence."

Around the arena, eyes flashed white, and I didn't need to hear their mental mutterings to know what they were saying. The queen's tone told me everything. She was revolted by Arthur's existence, and so were they.

Arthur tried to jerk to the side, fighting against his manacles. "I'm real!" he shouted. "I exist!"

"You are improperly made, incomplete and unanchored," said the queen. She reached out and took the hands of the queens to either side of her. "We may require your testimony before this is done, so we will not delete you, but we will repair the damage that has been done."

Their eyes gleamed white, all five of them. Arthur made a choked-off sound, then slumped where he stood, not quite toppling over. I rushed to the edge of my platform, barely stopping before I could topple the seventy or so feet to the ground. With the psychic blocker on my wrist, if I fell, I'd have no way of catching myself, and I wasn't Verity. I hadn't been practicing safe falls from more than twenty feet since I was in middle school. I would die.

Watching Arthur folding slowly inward on himself like an animatronic that had been forcibly separated from its power source, it was hard not to feel like I would deserve it.

A familiar voice screamed outrage into the echoing air, and I turned to see the curtains blocking another box jerked forcibly aide, revealing a group of four figures. By their hair and clothing, I identified them as my grandparents, Antimony, and Sam. Antimony was the one screaming, her hands balled by her sides and limned with flickering white coronas. She and Thomas were wearing bracelets similar to my own. I wasn't sure how sorcery suppression would even work, but it appeared they'd been at least partially cut off from the pneuma that fueled their magic. It explained why neither of them was setting the place more enthusiastically on fire.

"Fuck you! Fuck you all!" shrieked Annie. "You have no *right*!"

"We have every right," said the queen at the center, calmly. "We are the law. You are uninvited, and your own trial is coming."

"Leave my family alone!" I yelled.

The queen switched her attention to me. The weight of it was oppressive. I didn't need to be able to receive her thoughts to feel the sheer power behind her gaze. "The choice is yours, Sarah," she said. "The choice has always been yours. You know what you need to do if you want them released unharmed. How long are you willing to be selfish? How far will you go to put your needs before theirs? All this ends when you say the word."

My heart sank as Annie turned toward me, hands still limned in white. "Sarah," she called. "Whatever they want, just give it to them. Please. Arthur can't take much more of this."

"I . . . can't," I called back. "What they want is me. They want me to join them."

For a moment, the fire burned brighter. "So join them," said Annie. "You've said before that you don't understand how to be a person anymore. You can stop. Go be a better cuckoo."

"Annie . . ." said Sam uneasily.

"We are not *cuckoos*," said the queen, disdain dropping from her voice. "We are proper Johrlac, as we have always been, as we will always be."

"You all look like big fucking wasps to me, lady," snapped Annie.

Arthur shuddered in place, still moving as jerkily as a broken animatronic, and then, with agonizing slowness, he stood up again. The process took the better part of a minute, during which we all just watched him. Annie stopped yelling at me, which I found much more reassuring than I probably should have. Maybe she could forgive me. If Arthur was all right, maybe we could be all right, too.

He straightened, putting a hand against his forehead like he was trying to hold his head in place, and groaned. That sound, like every other, was amplified by the shape of the arena, but something about it itched at the back of my brain. It was wrong, in some subtle, almost indefinable way.

Then he took his hand away and straightened fully, opening his eyes. He looked around the arena, and even I could tell he was confused. That subtle wrongness followed his every motion, making him look like a familiar stranger, like someone I should recognize but somehow didn't, just so slightly to the left of my expectations.

"Where the hell am I?" he asked. He looked around at the stands full of identical Johrlac, at the five queens in their box, and then over at the boxes containing the rest of his family. He blinked before focusing on me. "Sarah?"

I went cold, feeling suddenly as if I might collapse. I wobbled, unreasonably close to the edge of the platform, then staggered back from the edge, just staring at him.

"Sarah!" He gripped the edge of his box, pulling it like he thought he could snap the bamboo in half. "Are you all right? Where the hell are we?"

My mouth didn't want to work. I tried to reach out telepathically, and hit the barrier created by the bracelet, rebounding into the confines of my own mind. Finally, brokenly, I managed to rasp, "Artie?"

"Sarah," he replied, and looked around again, eyes finally landing on Annie. "Annie, what the hell is going on here? Who's that man with Grandma? Where are we?"

"Artie," said Annie, disbelieving. "You can't be here."

"What do you mean?"

"I mean, you're dead," she said. "Sarah killed you. You can't be here."

He actually laughed at that. "Sarah would never hurt me," he said. "I don't think she'd know where to begin. I'm not dead, Annie. I have a hell of a headache, but I know Grandpa Martin. I know what dead looks like, and I still have a pulse and everything."

"Entered into evidence, designate Arthur 'Artie' Harrington-Price, pre-revision owner of the physical form in front of us," said one of the queens, with utter, painful calm. "The cuckoo may believe herself capable, but she is untrained, and her mathematical proficiencies are based on instinct and raw power, not understanding. Her revision was performed via brute force, slamming through the designate's mental defenses and erasing the information beyond them. It was not properly removed, and was thus possible to recover."

I got the distinct feeling that while she was saying these things at least partially for my benefit—and the benefit of the rest of my family—she was also restating this for whatever portion of the crowd was meant to serve as my jury. I might not have committed the full scope of the crime I had been accused of, she was saying, but not for any lack of trying. I would have killed him if I'd been able. I just hadn't known how.

And none of that mattered, because I wanted to faint, throw up, and burst into tears, all at the same time. Artie. This wasn't Arthur, wasn't the collage I had created from the people who loved him: unless the queens were lying to us, this was Artie.

I almost wanted them to be lying to us. If they were lying, nothing had changed except for their capacity for cruelty. If they were telling the truth . . .

If they were telling the truth, this changed absolutely everything. This made it all so much harder.

"The cuckoo designate Sarah did hurt you," said one of the queens. "She performed an unauthorized revision on your mind. She destroyed you. Does that not make you condemn her?"

"What?" Artie turned to face the queens. "What the hell are you talking about? I'm not condemning Sarah."

"You were brought here to provide evidence of what she's done," said the queen, implacably. "You were removed from control of your own world, and ownership of your self was given to another."

"I . . . I feel like I've been asleep," said Artie. "I was . . . we were in Iowa, and all the cuckoos were coming together to force Sarah to end the world, and I didn't want her to do that. I like the world. I didn't want her to have to live with that. So we went to Iowa to stop her before she could do something she wouldn't be able to take back. We . . . stopped her?" He paused, then turned to look at me. "I feel like we stopped her, but everything gets fuzzy after that, and then it all goes away. And then I was dreaming. I feel like I was . . . I was dreaming for a long time. A long, long time."

"You died," said Annie. "The dreams were the person who replaced you living your life in your place."

"Artie, I'm sorry," I moaned. "I didn't understand what was happening. You touched me while I was in the middle of finishing the math to get us home, and the equation jumped into you and hollowed you out, the same way it had all the cuckoos. Then you wouldn't wake up, and when I looked into your mind there wasn't anything there to look back at me. I was so scared. I thought you were gone forever, and your body didn't know how to survive without someone inside it, so I reached into everyone around me, everyone who loved you, and I built you from all the pieces I could find. Only it wasn't you, not really. He called himself 'Arthur,' and he didn't know the parts of you that you kept secret. He couldn't work computers or log in to our chat rooms, and he . . . he loved me, but only because other people knew you loved me. He loved me because he didn't have a choice. I'm so sorry, Artie. I never meant to hurt you. I would never, ever have hurt you on purpose."

"I know." He turned back to the queens. "You called me evidence and asked me to condemn her. Well, I won't. She didn't do anything on purpose except try to repair what she hadn't meant to do in the first place. I don't know why I was stupid enough to touch her when she was in the middle of an equation. We grew up together. I know what happens if you touch a cuckoo when their eyes are lit up. I knew better. So this is on me. It's my fault."

It wasn't, but I didn't want to interrupt to tell him that. He'd touched me because he hadn't remembered growing up together, hadn't remembered how much touching me when I was that far gone could resemble grabbing hold of a live electrical wire. I'd wiped myself from his mind before we reached that point.

"I love her," he said, and his voice was firm and clear, unwavering. "I'm in love with her. I have loved her for most of my life, and if she hurt me, she didn't mean to, and I am not going to side with you against the woman I love. I have—I have no idea what's going on right now, but I know two things for sure: Sarah would never intentionally hurt me, and Sarah loves me as much as I love her. Everything else is irrelevant."

"Irrelevant?" asked the central queen, sounding very nearly amused. "She broke our laws. She stole years of your life from you. She prevented you from knowing when your own mother died—you weren't here to mourn her. Your poor sister had to do her grieving by herself, with no one who could understand her sorrow . . ."

Artie paled. "My mother? What are you talking about?"

"Sarah can tell you. She's the reason you missed it, after all."

Regret washed through me, bitter as bleach, wiping everything else away. "The Covenant came," I said. "Aunt Jane went to the carnival with Annie and Sam and Grandma Alice, and me. I was holding the Covenant operatives in stasis and it . . . it slipped. One of them got loose. He shot Aunt Jane."

"Now I know this is a dream," said Artie. "Mom would never get in a car with Grandma on purpose."

"She did, sweetheart," said Alice. "I'm so sorry, but she did."

"Grandma?" Artie's voice was quiet and confused. "But—no. No, Mom can't be dead. My mother can't be dead."

"She is," said Antimony. "I'm so sorry this is how you're finding out."

His head snapped around, attention focusing on me, and for once, I was grateful I couldn't properly understand his expression. "My mother died because your powers failed you," he said. "And I died for the same reason."

"Yes," I agreed, miserably.

"And you know what? I don't care. I mean, I care about my mother being dead—I care a *lot* about my mother being dead—but I don't care whether your powers glitched or what. I know you loved her, and I know you love me, and I know you didn't do any of this on purpose. This is all bullshit. I'm not going to be evidence against you, and I'm not going to help these people do whatever it is they're trying to do." He looked at the queens. "I don't know why you're doing this to us, but it's not going to work. Whatever your goal is, you may as well give up on it. I'm not going to turn against her for you."

"Brave little creature," said one of the queens, her eyes flashing momentarily white. "You owe us, you know that? She erased you improperly, shoved you to the bottom of your own mind where you would have withered into nothing if not for the revision anchoring you where you were. You would never have surfaced without our help. We were the rope that let you pull yourself out of the darkness. We could put you back there."

"Over my dead body," snarled Annie.

I looked over at the four of them. They were all facing the queens. Alice had moved to the front of their little cluster, with Sam standing directly behind her.

"You are not going to harm my grandson," she said—shouted, almost, her voice raised to turn the acoustics to her advantage. "Let us all go, or this is going to get ugly."

"The cuckoo has the ability to make this stop whenever she wants to," said the queen. "All she has to do is let us in and this can all be over for the rest of you."

Bringing Artie back made me want to go home even more than I already had. I'd been grieving him since I'd lost him, and while I'd come to terms with the idea of spending the rest of my life without him, that didn't mean I'd been excited about the idea. The thought that we could finally be together was very nearly intoxicating. And all I had to do was hold out until we all got to go home.

Which was never going to happen. I could tell from the way

Alice was standing that she had the beginnings of something she would truly, earnestly think of as "a plan." But because it was Alice, the plan would probably be "grenade." Thomas could usually be counted on to serve as her common sense . . . only right now he couldn't say anything without all the Johrlac hearing him, which meant he could neither help her come up with a better plan nor convince her that "grenade" was not the answer to everything.

As soon as she started blowing things up, Sam and Annie would get involved, and people would get hurt. I didn't care all that much whether the Johrlac got hurt, but I wanted my family safe. Most of all, I wanted them to make it home alive. I couldn't give Uncle Ted his wife back. I could give him his son, and maybe that would be almost as good.

I looked at the bracelet on my wrist, then held up my arm.

"Can you take this off me, please?" I asked.

The queens turned toward me, all of their eyes flaring white. "Why should we do that?" asked one of them. "Asking nicely does not end your trial."

"No. But you told me what I had to do to end it. And if you promise my family—my *entire* family, Artie included—goes home unharmed, I'm willing to agree."

"Unharmed?" asked one of them, and snapped her fingers. Her eyes flashed brighter. Annie screamed, the sound short and quickly cut off, and collapsed backward against Sam.

"Hey!" I shouted. "That is the *opposite* of 'unharmed'!"

"We're only undoing the damage *you* did," said the queen.

Annie was straightening. Like Artie, she pressed a hand against her forehead as she did. Sam kept his hands clamped on her upper arms, helping her stay upright.

She groaned and lowered her hand, looking toward me. "Sarah?" she asked, sounding bewildered. "What the hell did you *do*?"

"Oh, good, they didn't melt your brain," said Sam, and crushed her in a hug. "Don't *do* that to me!"

"They didn't melt my brain, but I feel like they put parts of it back where they belong," said Annie sharply. "Ow. It feels like my whole childhood is rearranging itself. Sarah—Sarah, I remember! I remember you! We found you on the way home from Lowryland. I was so worried for a long time that finding you meant we'd have to leave one of us in a ditch for someone else to find. And Elsie was so mad when we came home with a new cousin and she wasn't sure she'd be included!"

"Oh," I said. "They gave you back your memory."

Taking her memories of me away had been an accident, a combination of needing the space for processing and storage and a subconscious attempt to make sure she wouldn't have to mourn me when I died. I hadn't known what I was doing when I did it, but I hadn't tried to undo it, either, because she'd deserved the ability to move on and let me go. And now, just when I was going to leave her for good, she remembered me. Everything we'd been to each other, and everything we were never going to be again.

"They did," she called. "I know you, Sarah Zellaby, almost better than you know yourself, and I just want to tell you that whatever noble, self-sacrificing bullshit you're about to pull, you need to cut it the fuck out. We're not leaving here without you."

"I think you're wrong about that." I held up my arm, showing the bracelet to the queens. "Please. I'll do whatever you want. Just make sure they get home."

"We can do that," said the central queen. Her eyes gleamed white, and my family vanished. All five of them—Alice and Thomas, Annie and Sam, and Artie.

My Artie. I hadn't killed him after all.

I closed my eyes, and felt, rather than saw, the moment when the bracelet clasp let go and the whole clumsy apparatus dropped to the platform. Then the collective crashed down on me with the full might of the five queens comprising it, their minds tangling around mine and bearing it down, down, down into the abyss without end.

I didn't fight them. There were things I wanted in the world, yes, but Alice would care for Greg if I never came home, and Isaac would have Charlotte for his sister no matter what, and the life of one cuckoo was more than sufficient payment for having Artie returned to the world. A thin thread of guilt tried to penetrate my peace—what about Arthur?—but I dismissed it, focusing on the fall. The queens had said they weren't going to delete him, that they might need him later. I had to believe they'd meant it, that they hadn't thought we were important enough to lie to.

Then the fall was everything, and the abyss was all, and we descended ever deeper, and I was gone.

Twenty

$$\pi_2(n) \sim 2C_2\frac{n}{(\ln n)^2} \sim 2C_2\int_2^n \frac{dt}{(\ln t)^2}$$

"Sometimes there's nothing left to do but take a bow and leave the stage. The most powerful words in the world are all too frequently 'goodbye.'"

—Enid Healy

The abyss without name or end, eternal in its emptiness

THE COLLECTIVE CONTROLLING THE TERRITORY around Ka'krin was comprised of five queens, all survivors of the final, sometimes fatal instar that saw them to the pinnacle of our species' power. As they rasped against me like sandpaper against a rough piece of wood, I began to learn them. Two had been here for hundreds of years, solidifying their positions in the city: two were more recent members of the collective, brought in to replace queens lost in a local conflict. The fifth was Collate, who still remembered her original name, even as she viewed it with distant disdain, like it more properly belonged to someone else. She didn't need it anymore. She had been revised.

But as Artie and Annie proved, revision could be undone. I didn't know how it was accomplished, but it had to be something any member of the collective could do. That was the danger of sharing your mind so completely with others that the boundaries between you dropped away: the four older members of the collective could no more keep secrets from Collate than I could keep secrets from my own left knee.

She brushed against me, the sharks circling my small sphere of telepathically etched safety, and I unfolded a tendril of thought, dangling the bait in front of her. *Fetch and Carry grieve you,* I informed her. *They have never forgotten you. They have never forsaken you. They would gladly welcome you home if only you came back to them.*

Those are the names of menials, she shot back, before I cut the connection. *They are beneath me. They will be beneath you. Release your barriers and join us. You promised.*

I pulled back, hard, retreating into myself. My family was gone. They'd been sent home, and I truly believed that, because I had been able to find nothing in my brief brushes with the collective to imply they had lied. Still, my family had been returned to Earth because I'd agreed to become a part of their collective. If I didn't keep *my* word, what was there to stop them from going back to steal my family away again? Or all of them this time—Elsie and Alex and the children?

The thought of Charlotte and Isaac in the hands of my birth species made me feel physically ill, despite my current lack of a true physical form. I could only play this game for so long. I would need to make my next move with tactical care.

When the queen who had been Collate circled around again, I opened my shell a little wider, trying to make it seem like an accident, like I was so eager to tell her how much her former friends missed her that I had forgotten the danger I was in.

They know revision can be undone, I thought. *They just want you to come home. Remember who you are, Collate. Remember, and return to them.*

As I had hoped, she darted forward, wedging her thoughts into the gap I had opened and reaching for my mind like a starfish forcing its way into a clam. I pulled away from her, fleeing as far as my sphere would allow, and she pursued.

She began to wrap her mind around mine, and I twisted and writhed, trying to put on the appearance of a good fight, even as I started the function I had been mentally preparing, a series of numbers designed to mirror and record everything she did to me. She wrapped herself tighter. I felt the other four queens behind her, egging her on, lending their support to the fight. I went limp, letting her pull me in, and she began, as she had planned from the start, to revise me in the image they desired.

It hurt. It was like having new channels cut into my mind with a rusty scalpel, ripping and shredding and leaving devastation in its wake. I felt pieces of who I was dropping away, and I couldn't even mourn their loss: once they were gone, they were gone, like they had never existed to begin with. I was an equation in my own right, complete within myself, but I could be streamlined and made to fit.

I didn't try to resist. The function I had created while my mind was still entirely my own was ticking away, noting every snip and cut, every piece of the process, and it was small: it was tucked behind most of who I was, hidden in memory and motivation. As long as she didn't notice and stop it, there would be a guide to putting me back together buried deep inside the person I became, like a pearl inside an oyster or an encysted tapeworm tucked into muscle tissue.

It was a gross comparison, but it made me feel oddly better. I held to it as Collate—no, the queen—no, the *collective*—continued to revise, cutting away all the pieces of me that I wasn't going to need anymore. *Was this how Arthur felt when my construction began to fail?* I wondered, and then wondered who Arthur was, why I would be worried about someone I didn't know.

Deeper and deeper she cut, and the shell around us dissolved into thought and memory. The other four queens came rushing in then, the five of them gathering me close as they spun around me, remaking me in their own image. The *best* image, the only image anyone could ever truly want. Why had I been fighting this? Why had I wanted to? Fighting didn't make any sense. This was peace. This was perfection. Just me and my sisters, spinning in the void, ideal and untouchable in our flawless union.

The last of the cuckoo I had been fell free and the five of them poured into my thoughts, and we were six and we were one, a collective, powerful and poised to lead our people into the brightest of all possible futures.

And deep within my psyche, a pearl nestled, glossy-shelled and impervious, filled with the instructions for reversion. I was of the collective now. No one would ever be able to access such an unimportant token. So we left it as it was, untouched and unremarked-upon. It didn't matter anymore. In a way, I put the contents of my mind out of my mind, and focused only on the restorative unity of our collective in combination.

We were six and we were one, a single mind in many bodies, so tightly harmonized that we were the living manifestation of a single mathematical phrase, a single scintillating song. The awareness of my body returned by inches, until I knew the shape of my own skin and with it, the shape of five more skins which were now equally my own. Five sets of eyes opened and looked at a crumpled form on a floating platform, dressed in the striped grays of a cuckoo whose transgressions had been great enough to summon her home for punishment.

That would have to change. Whatever she had been before her revision, she was of us now, part of the immutable we, and we couldn't be seen in cuckoo's colors. That body would receive a new jumpsuit in the proper colors soon enough, to show caste and status to anyone whose eyes were open.

But first, we had to remember her singularity enough to move her. That was one of the hardest parts of apotheosis: first you had to move beyond what you had been, dismiss and transcend your limitations. Then you had to find a way to put them back on like a bra that didn't fit properly anymore, twisting and contorting enough to squeeze it on.

Like a—what? Lingering bits of who I had been were still sticking to my thoughts, unwanted and serving nothing of any true use. I tried to shake them off as best as I could, feeling their residue staining my perfection.

Returning to the body for the first time after unification required a comprehension of singularity that felt as difficult and transgressive as the concept of zero had been to the earliest mathematicians. They'd known it was necessary, but it had defined a thing as it wasn't, rather than something as it was, and that had been difficult.

This was difficult now. The collective detached itself from me as much as it could, leaving me almost alone, still reeling with the speed of everything that had happened, now devoid of any past before the moment they embraced me, and I was "I" again, cold, lonely "I," shivering in a world without unity or unison. I hated it. I hated it as I imagined I must have hated my former existence, to agree to the assumption into this one, and so I turned and reached for the collective, trying to rejoin the harmony. My questing thoughts hit a wall, the rest of the collective pushing me away.

Somehow the worst of it was that I actually understood why, thanks to the knowledge they had already shared with me. Many queens could ascend to the part of apotheosis, combining themselves into a collective mind. Few of them could handle the process of returning to their bodies. If one Johrlac in ten could become a queen without dying in the process, one queen in ten could become part of a collective without severing their connection to their physical body. A disembodied existence was all well and good, but it would inevitably mean my dissolution. When my body died, I would go with it, coming to pieces in the thoughts of my sisters. That could poison the entire collective. Unless I was strong enough to go back, I was doomed, and if I was doomed, they would revise me away and try again.

I had only existed, inside or outside the collective, for a few minutes, but I was alive, and like all living things, I wanted to go on existing. That thought briefly raised a concerning flag—why hadn't the me who had existed before me fought? The collective remembered her, and so I did too, and she had simply acquiesced to her own erasure. She hadn't tried to fight them. Why?

The collective had promised to release her family—a petty word for what those people had been to her. None of them had been Johrlac. They could never have come together in collective, no matter how much she wanted them to, and so she could never have known true apotheosis, never have reached her true potential—and she must have known the collective could still reach them, no matter where they were. She had given herself away to save the people she cared about, and that was almost admirable, in its misguided way. Not that it mattered why she'd been willing to lie down without a fight. Her surrender allowed me to exist, and now that I existed, I was going to continue for as long as I possibly could.

The collective brushed against the edges of my self, encouraging me, urging me onward toward the body that belonged to me. All five of them had survived this part of the apotheosis, the long, hard crawl back into flesh and bone, the freezing cold of separation. They knew the way. They showed it to me.

Bit by bit I folded myself smaller, bending the pieces of my mind into the shape they needed to fit if I was going to contain them in a shell of skin. Bit by bit I let my sisters go, until only the thinnest of tethers still connected us, and I was able to slide back into a body that no longer felt fully like my own.

It was cold there, and dark, and all but dead. The lungs were empty, pressed flat of air, and the muscular systems that were supposed to pulse autonomically, keeping the hemolymph flowing through the venous structures, had gone still. The first thing to do was to start them up again. Without a working circulatory system, this body wouldn't last for long.

It wasn't dead, only in a sort of torpor brought on by the departure of the guiding consciousness. I focused on the need for circulation and managed, barely, not to throw myself back out of it again as the pulses resumed, aching like a pulled tendon, slow and grinding and agonizing in a way I knew they hadn't been before. Chronic pain that severe would have desensitized the body's responses in a way that had nothing to do with the controlling mind.

The lungs began to expand, pulling in air without my explicitly ordering them to do so, and bit by bit, sensations other than pain returned. The body breathed, and the air fed into the systems that needed to be fed, and it was going to live. My mind would continue to possess an anchor, and I would continue to belong to the collective. I was no longer this body. None of us were the bodies which housed us. But as long as I had it, I could endure.

That was better than the alternative.

Moving slowly and using all the focus I could muster, I opened the body's eyes, and saw the world from my own perspective. It was mixed with the perspectives of every other mind in the arena, all of them combining to form a single compound image of my surroundings. It was kaleidoscopic and stunningly beautiful, and as I pushed the body to its feet, I marveled at how fortunate I was to be part of a collective, to be able to see and understand such beautiful things.

The body answered smoothly to my commands, and I turned it to face my sisters. Their eyes flared white as they reached out to tangle their minds with mine once more, and I was safe, and I was home, and I was at peace.

Twenty-One

ANTIMONY

"I wasn't planning on becoming a mother. My own mother didn't give me very good examples to follow. But once I did, there was nothing I wouldn't do to protect my children. No matter what, I was going to be a better person than my mother was."

—**Jane Harrington-Price**

Buckley Township, Michigan,
the basement of the Old Parrish Place

SWITCHING DIMENSIONS WITH SARAH AT the helm had been a traumatic experience, at least the one time I remembered it. She and Artie had both gone down before we could make the crossing, and when the spell had taken effect, it had been like all of reality was being compressed and forced through an opening the size of a garden hose. Not fun or pretty.

Doing it with Thomas taking the lead had been easier, just a ritual circle, some chanting, and then a light so bright it left afterimages on my retinas but didn't cause any actual pain. And no one I cared about had been broken or unconscious at the time, making it practically pleasant.

Making the transition under the power of the Johrlac collective made the other two methods seem like child's play. One moment we were standing in the box in the bullshit pantomime the Johrlac called a court, and the next moment we were back in my grandparents' basement, all four of us, now with the sudden addition of—

"Artie!" I squealed, throwing myself at my cousin and locking my arms around him as tightly as I could.

He made a confused noise and embraced me back. "Annie? What the hell is going on?"

"Um," I said, and paused, letting him go. I took a step backward, looking at him. He looked back, open and bemused and so utterly Artie that it threw every difference between him and Arthur into stark relief. They really weren't the same person.

The thought awoke a pang of regret. We had Artie back, but where was Arthur? Certainly not here with us.

"Everything the Johrlac said was true, just presented in the worst possible light," I said finally. "They abducted Sarah to make her stand trial for what they called her crimes, and they took Arthur—the other version of you—as evidence. We followed to try and get them both back. We got caught, and all wound up in their court." I reached up and touched my aching temple. "Before you got deleted, when we left Iowa for a whole dimension full of shitty giant bugs, Sarah wiped herself from both our minds. Just snipped our memories of her right out of our childhoods. So nothing made much sense for a while, and I really only agreed to go to Johrlar because we needed to recover Arthur. I hope he's okay."

"And Mom?" Artie looked past me to Alice, desperation in his face.

She shook her head, her own expression going grave. "I'm so sorry, sweetheart. There was nothing I could do," she said.

Artie stared at her, slow tears gathering in his eyes. "Mom," he said, softly. Then: "How's Dad? Elsie?"

"They're both fine," said Alice. "Your father's still very sad, of course, and your sister has been grieving in her own way, but she's been preoccupied with trying to keep Arthur as stable as she could, and I don't know how she is overall. Distressed by having a group of Johrlac appear in her house and snatch her brother away."

"And who's this?" Artie's gaze shifted to Thomas, turning wary.

Alice smiled, bright as the sun. "This is your grandfather, Thomas Price," she said. "I finally found him. He's finally home."

"You went jumping across dimensions until you found the love of your life, and then you brought him back to his family, even though it was dangerous," said Artie. "Got it. So when do we leave?"

"Leave?" asked Sam.

"To get Sarah back," said Artie. "I mean, we have a precedent, right?"

"It's not that simple—" began Thomas.

"Pretty sure it is," said Artie. "You got there once. You can get us there again, right? So when do we leave?"

I put a hand on his arm. "Artie, we just got you back," I said. "You can't really expect us to—"

"Save a member of our family? Do for her what she would do for any one of us? You heard her at the end there! She gave up in order to get us out! We have to go back for her!" He sounded borderline frantic. I couldn't blame him for that. I would have had the exact same reaction if it had been Sam who'd been left behind.

I would have had the exact same reaction if it had been anyone other than Sarah. My memories were still sliding back into place, and until they were finished, I presumed she would keep feeling like a person I knew but didn't have much of an emotional attachment to. I hated feeling like my world could be that easily manipulated, but what are we apart from collections of memories and experiences, all webbed together with emotional reactions? I loved Sam with all my heart. If someone started knocking out the experiences that had formed the foundation of our relationship, how long would that love be able to endure?

I didn't want to think about it, and so I focused on Artie. "They let us go this time, because Sarah said she'd stay," I said. "They're not going to let us just walk away a second time. We don't have anything to offer them in exchange for letting us have her. I'm sorry, Artie. I lo-loved Sarah, too. But we can't."

"If you're not going to help me, I'm going to find a way to do it without you," threatened Artie. He took a step backward, jaw set and hands balled into fists, clearly furious.

Honestly, I couldn't blame him. He'd been gone for years. Now he came back, impossibly, wonderfully, and his mother was dead, while the woman he loved was lost in another dimension. This was a lot, even for one of us, and it was perfectly understandable that he wouldn't be handling it well.

"You can't cross dimensions on your own, Artie," said Alice. "And I'm sorry, but we're not going to help you right now. We just got you back. I can't do that to your father."

"My father doesn't know," snapped Artie. "And if he did, he'd say I needed to go and get her back. He'd have done it for Mom. You did it for Grandpa. Why are you not willing to let me do exactly what any member of our family would be doing right now?"

"Honestly, Artie, I don't have a good answer for that, and we just met, so it's not like you have any reason to trust me anyway," said Thomas. "But I can't open a tunnel to Johrlar again so quickly after the first one. I don't have the power. We need to sit down and come up with a plan that doesn't just count on us blundering into an answer, and give me time to recover. Then we can go back for Sarah. Once we have a plan."

"We're *going* back," said Artie firmly. "This isn't a discussion and it isn't a request. I refuse to leave her behind after everything she's been through, and everything she's done trying to save us. Mom raised me better than that."

"All right, sweetheart," said Alice.

I had the distinct feeling I was overlooking something. I watched as my grandparents left for the kitchen, and mice began swarming onto the table, staring at Artie like he was some sort of impossible miracle. None of them seemed confused in the least about who he was. I guess Aeslin mice don't have the same issue telling identical people apart as humans would, because they started to cheer and praise the return of the God of Chosen Isolation.

Sam's tail snaked around my waist, and I leaned back against him as he wrapped his arms around my chest. "This has been . . . a lot," he said, watching Artie and the mice.

"Yeah, it has," I agreed. "And I can't help feeling like I'm missing something that would make this all come together. What am I forgetting?"

"We just left your cousin, possibly two of your cousins, and a whole bunch of your distant relatives in a dimension swarming with Johrlac," said Sam. "Oh, and now the only friendly cuckoo we have access to can't telepathically receive, which makes her a lot less useful when it comes to stopping hostile telepaths from breaking into our brains . . ."

He stopped talking and craned his neck around so he could eye me suspiciously.

"Annie, what are you thinking?" he asked. "Because you have that look again."

"I'm thinking that sometimes I can be really stupid for a smart person," I said. "I totally forgot about our backup cuckoo."

"Our . . . Oh!"

"Yeah." I dug my phone out of my pocket, relieved to see I still had almost 80 percent battery charge. "Mark started this mess by calling me. Now I'm going to finish it by calling him."

Finding Mark's number wasn't hard: it was the only recent unknown in my call history. I pulled it up, put the phone on speaker, and pressed the button, setting the phone down on the table as it began to ring. Artie detached himself from the still-cheering mice and wandered over to eye the phone warily.

"Who are you calling?" he asked. "It better not be my sister. She'll just try to talk me out of this."

"I wouldn't dare," I said. "I'm calling Mark."

"Mark? As in the cuckoo?"

"The cuckoo *king*," I said.

He was still eyeing me in disbelief when the phone clicked and the ringing stopped. For a moment, I thought Mark had decided to hang up on me rather than answering the phone. Then an unfamiliar female voice said, sweetly, "If you're calling about my brother's hospital bills, I will extract your larynx through the front of your throat before you have time to name a number, you fucking health insurance ghouls."

"I told you, Cici, my hospital bill's been covered," said Mark in the background, barely managing to contain his laughter.

"Never put anything past these collections assholes," said the girl—Cici, presumably. Mark's human little sister. Not so little anymore, from the sound of her.

"Yes, you're wiser than I in the way of hospitals," said Mark. "Give me back my phone."

"Why should I?"

Mark didn't answer verbally, but Cici's shrieks of laughter told me he was tickling her to get his phone back. The laughter died out and then he said, "This had better be important, I'm a little busy right now."

"Your sister sounds really happy to have you home," I said.

He paused. "Annie?"

"Yup."

"I did *not* expect to hear from you so soon."

"Because I'm supposed to be off on a suicide mission recovering my cousin?"

"Something like that."

"Well, I was. And then I got tossed out of Johrlar by the collective that's in charge of the place. Only they didn't return Sarah when they made us leave, and Artie's pretty insistent that we need to go back and get her before she can get hurt."

"Artie?" Mark sounded utterly baffled.

Artie leaned closer. "Hello, Mark. Glad to hear you're not dead, not sure why we're calling you. Just so you know."

"Mark, I know you're a king now, whatever that means. Can you bend space the way Sarah can?"

"Getting right to the point, huh?" Mark lowered his voice. "Yes, I can manage a tesseract. Why do you ask?"

"I will text you the latitude and longitude of my grandparents' house in Michigan," I said. "I need you to come here."

"What? No! Cici—"

"Just got you back, which means she'll understand if you say you need to help rescue the woman who made sure you were taken care of while you recovered," I said. "Sarah needs us, and I'm not going back to Johrlar without at least a little protection. Don't argue with me. You're only going to waste your time and mine."

"Your family still sucks," he said sullenly. "Text me the info, and I'll be right over. But only this one time, and only because you're right—Sarah took care of me while I was going through my final instar. I'll help you bring her home."

"Thank you," said Artie.

"Don't thank me too much—once she's here, she's your problem," said Mark. "I am not going to take over babysitting the most neurotic mathematician in the world."

"I'd fight you for her," said Artie.

Mark laughed and the line went dead. I grabbed my phone off the table. "Be right back," I said to Sam and Artie, before running into the kitchen to get the data I'd promised Mark.

A cuckoo king on our side could swing the balance from "impossible" to "improbable." And improbable is where I've historically done some of my best work.

✦ ✦ ✦

As expected, Thomas knew the exact latitude and longitude of the house to a full eight digits, meaning we could aim Mark either inside or outside. Which was why Sam and I were back in the field behind the house, this time joined by an anxious Artie who couldn't seem to stop himself from fidgeting.

Sam looked at him sidelong. "My guy, I'm usually the one who can't sit still. Can you try to chill? Just a little, maybe?"

"Sarah's in another dimension surrounded by people who abducted her to put her on trial, and I can't help her until I find a way to get back there, so yeah, I'm anxious as hell, and no, I'm not going to chill. Not even a little bit." Artie looked stubbornly at Sam. "I don't think you'd chill if you were in my position."

Sam winced. "Fuck, dude, it's still Iowa for you, isn't it?"

"Effectively, yeah," said Artie. He sagged in place, looking suddenly exhausted. "This is all going to hit me like a ton of bricks real soon, and when it does, it's going to put me on the floor. I don't even know how long it's been. But you're telling me I've been dead, and my mother died, and Sarah's been living with the weight of having killed me—killed us both—when she didn't kill either one of us. And for me, I just followed her through a rift in the world to save her from a ritual that would have ended everything and taken her away from me forever."

"I forgot how awful that was while it was happening," said Sam. "I got a little wrapped up in how awful everything that came next was. I'm sorry, Artie. I'd be freaking out just as hard as you are. I *did* freak out just as hard as you are, when I came back from patrol and got told that the air had become a door and Annie had gone through it without me, and no one knew where she was, so it wasn't like I could even go after her." His gaze turned briefly distant. "I would have freaked out even harder if I'd realized that it was going to be a whole year before she made it home. Time doesn't always work the same between dimensions. I don't know how long we were in Johrlar."

"Long enough for the leaves to change," I said, gesturing toward the forest. "Long enough for the woods to get cranky about how long we were gone."

I don't have the same relationship with the Galway Woods that my grandmother does, and that's a good thing, since Sam can be the jealous type. Alice has been in a three-way relationship with the woods and my grandfather for almost as long as she's been alive, and don't ask me how it works, because I don't understand it. I don't think anyone does. The woods are self-aware and questionably sapient, and knowing that has been enough to keep me from pissing them off beyond the point of making amends.

"We'll figure out the timeline when we have Sarah back," said Artie stubbornly. "We're not giving up on her."

"Wow, nerdy boy with the bad taste in women, long time no see," said Mark from behind us. I turned. He was standing in the field, looking surprisingly good for a man who'd just come out of an eight-year coma. As always, he looked enough like Sarah to have been her brother, and was wearing cargo pants and a gray cable-knit sweater. His hair looked freshly cut, and had been styled with a quantity of gel that was ambitious if not advisable. He was eyeing the three of us with one eyebrow cocked and lips pursed in faint disapproval. "And the pyro and the monkey for good measure. Hail hail, the gang's all here."

"Hi, Mark," I said, not bothering to sound too enthusiastic. "How's being awake treating you?"

"Oh, great, now that my little sister doesn't want to strangle me for getting myself hurt in the first place," he said. "She's twenty, and I'm mad about it. I missed so much. Fortunately, she missed me too, and I've looked through her memories. It's almost like I was there."

If he wanted it, his sister would gradually start to believe he'd been there all along. Cuckoos are tricky that way. It was part of why I'd had so much trouble trusting Sarah after she erased my memories of our mutual childhood. Anything that felt like affection or compassion had just seemed like an illusion after that, making it difficult for me to believe in her sincerity.

Now that I remembered who we were to each other, I felt bad about the way I'd treated her. Not bad enough to leave her behind when we might be able to get her back, but bad, like I was a smaller person than I'd ever realized.

"So she's good?" I asked.

"She is," he said, a beatific expression spreading across his face. "She never forgot about me, and she's going to law school to try and help people like me—people who aren't technically human, but still have to exist in a world where humans write the rules. She was an awesome kid, and she's an amazing woman now."

He sounded utterly besotted, and well he should. Mark was the only cuckoo we knew of who had broken his prenatal programming without outside help. Sarah had been deprogrammed by her mother. Mark had gone through a normal cuckoo puberty, waking up one morning with an innate desire to destroy anyone who got in his way. His human baby sister had managed to distract him long enough for the initial rush of homicidal urges to pass, and he'd decided to let his family live for her sake. Anyone who could convince a cuckoo that a rampage of destruction was less important than playing tea party was someone I could respect without ever meeting them.

"Okay, can we go?" asked Artie.

Mark turned to frown at him. "Hey. I didn't agree to go anywhere, and I'm not sure where you want us to go, so no. Not without more information."

"I told you Sarah was on Johrlar," I said.

"You did," Mark agreed. "But I don't know how to get to Johrlar. I've never been there. I'm an American citizen. I was born here. Telling me Sarah's in the cuckoo equivalent of the old country doesn't help me navigate."

"The collective of Johrlac queens tossed us from their dimension back into my grandparents' basement," I said. "I'm betting the traces of the math they used will still be there. You can use that to follow the trail back to where we were. That's the last place we saw Sarah."

"All right," said Mark. "You three stay here. I don't trust you not to break something while I'm gone."

"Gone?" asked Artie, sounding stunned.

"My sister just got me back. You're right that I owe Sarah—she may have triggered my instar, but she took care of me until I could recover, and she took care of my family. Cici loves her. It's hard not to love someone who visits you and brings you gifts for eight years when your brother can't. She'll want me to save Sarah. But I'm not vanishing on her for six months or whatever without telling her where I'm going. No one gets to ask that of me, ever again."

His eyes flashed white and the air next to him tore, creating an opening. He stepped through it and was gone. Artie blinked.

"That's like the rift Sarah made."

"Yeah, she does that all the time now," said Sam. "Getting her to hold still is sort of basically impossible. But I bet she'll hold still more with you home. She's missed you real, real bad, Artie."

"I know I haven't been me, technically speaking, but I've missed her too," said Artie.

Something was moving at the edge of the woods off to our left. I lit my hands, wary of the many things that could come out of the Galway. Bears and moose were possible, but unlikely; they didn't tend to survive long around here, not with all the nastier options the trees kept tucked away. Whatever it was didn't look humanoid, which meant it wasn't the neighbors, friendly or otherwise. That left way too many options for me to be comfortable.

Then the shape put several of its legs past the tree line, into the light, and I relaxed, even as Artie shrieked. Sam gave him a curious look.

"What's up?"

"That is a *spider* the size of a *bear*!" shouted Artie.

"I think of him as more the size of a draft horse," said Sam. "Look, Annie, Greg's okay."

"He must have gone into diapause to survive the winter," I said. "Plenty of good hunting for him out here in the woods, even if Cynthia hadn't been bringing him sheep."

The giant spider continued making his cautious way toward us, emerging fully into the light and keeping low to the ground.

"It's all right, Artie," I said. "This is Greg. He belongs to Sarah. He's basically her emotional support animal."

"None of us were qualified for the job," said Sam. "She needed something she could hold on to, and a giant spider from another dimension turned out to be just the thing."

"What," said Artie.

Greg was still approaching. Spiders don't have ears, as such, but they can still hear by picking up vibrations with the small hairs on their bodies. Jumping spiders are especially good at detecting human voices. He moved faster and with more ease as he recognized our voices. It's hard to say what excitement looks like in a spider, but he was walking tall and waving his pedipalps at us like an eager puppy.

"Hey, buddy," I said, as he got closer. "Sarah's not with us yet, but we're going back to get her. Yes, we are. Yes, we are. Who's a good horrifying abomination of the local laws of nature? You are. What a good boy."

He walked up to me and nudged his massive head against my leg. I scratched him gently behind the eyes, on the flat part of his head, while Artie just stared.

"I feel like I should remember something about this, but it's all hazy, like a dream," he said, in a stilted voice.

"That's because she adopted him after she scrambled our memories, and it sounds like that's the demarcation for you. Everything that happened after Iowa."

"His name's Greg?"

"To be fair, she wasn't thinking about the long term when she called him that, just about having a name for him so we'd treat him like a dog or something and not a terrifying arachnid nightmare."

"He looks like a Greg," said Artie, moving closer to the spider. That was a pretty good sign. Of multiple things, really. He was feeling enough like himself to want a closer look at Greg, and he wasn't going to try making Sarah get rid of him or anything ridiculous like that. Every little test the universe threw at him, he was passing.

He was really back.

Artie had been the first member of our generation to go down—until Dominic, the only member of our generation. We'd all grown up knowing that we were in a dangerous line of work connected to half a dozen dangerous hobbies, but it hadn't been until I saw Artie on the ground staring blankly at the sky that it had really started to sink in. We could die. We weren't immortal.

Having him back didn't change the bone-deep horror of that moment.

Artie began to scratch the top of Greg's head, emulating me, and Greg leaned against him, apparently content. Artie grinned at me, looking momentarily unburdened in his sheer delight. "I think he likes me," he said.

"What's not to like?" asked Sam.

Artie eyed him. "Do you want that in alphabetical order?"

"Boys, let's not fight," I said. "We have an ill-advised cross-dimensional rescue to attempt." Where the hell was Mark?

Greg perked up, and I turned to follow the line of his gaze. My grandparents were making their way across the field toward us.

"I tried to open a path to Johrlar," said Thomas, once they were close enough to speak without shouting. "It fizzled, hard. I think they've blocked the passage."

"Which makes a certain amount of sense, under the circumstances," I said. "We're still going. They won't have blocked the passage against their own flavor of magic."

"Blocking the universe's access to basic mathematics isn't something you can do without disastrous consequences," said Alice. "Anyway, we're willing to come with you if you want us. We've talked about it"—the glance she sent at Thomas made it clear that she'd been the one doing most of the talking—"and I can use one of my remaining crossings if we need me to."

"By which she means she'll be using *all* of her remaining crossings, as Johrlar is not a direct transit from here by her methods, and that she'll only be able to bring one person with her if she wants to bring Sarah home."

"So that's out," I said bluntly. "We all know you're not letting her go alone, and we also know Artie's not staying behind. I think it's better if the two of you stay here in case we don't come back."

The air tore and Mark stepped out, now with a backpack slung over one shoulder. He stopped dead, blinking at the scene in front of him. "Okay," he said, in a strangled tone. "Two tattooed weirdoes I can see fitting in with the rest of the family, but why is there a giant spider here? And why are we not running and screaming and maybe also dying?"

"Do you remember the giant spiders on the other side of Iowa?" I asked. "Well, Sarah brought one of them back with her when we all came home. His name is Greg, he helps with her anxiety, he's a very good boy. And the tattooed weirdoes are my grandparents."

"Does your asshole family not age?"

"We do," said Thomas. "My wife and I just stopped for a little while so we could find each other again."

"You say that like it's totally reasonable and not actually sort of insane," said Mark. "All right, assholes. Cici says you'd better bring me back in one piece and before she graduates from law school. I was gone long enough that she's sort of resigned about me going away, so you'd better never ask me to do this again. I am not spending the rest of my life with my baby sister waiting for me to disappear."

"Believe it or not, we understand the feeling," said Alice. "What's the plan?"

"If pyro here"—Mark hooked a thumb in my direction—"can really take me to the place where the Johrlac threw you people back into this dimension, I should hopefully be able to reconstruct their math. From there, I'll open a tunnel to the other end."

"And how do we know this is going to work?" asked Alice. "It took Sarah quite a while to get a hang of transit like that."

"I have some advantages she doesn't," said Mark. "I slept through the bulk of my instar. The hive woke her up and put her to work while she was still sore and off-balance. I've had time to recover. And I've already been through a dimensional crossing while I was conscious. I know what the math feels like. It's not going to be smooth and it's not going to be pretty and the more information you can give me, the better. But I should be able to do this, and I should be able to transport myself and three other people. Four is a stable number. The math will support it."

"What about Sarah?" asked Artie. "She'd make five."

"Sarah is a cuckoo queen with years of experience on me," said

Mark. "The only reason she can't tunnel between dimensions is that no one's really shown her how. Well, she was transported by the people you say took her, and now I'm going to transport us in, which means I can give her further instructions. She'll know what to do. She'll be able to get herself back."

He didn't remind us that if she couldn't move herself between dimensions, it would probably be because her captors had broken her in some irreparable way. He didn't need to, just like I didn't need telepathy to see the understanding flicker in Artie's eyes. We all knew how high the stakes were, just like we all knew there was no way he was going to let us leave her there. If we tried, he'd just do what Grandma Alice had done, and claw at the walls of the world until he found a way through them to the other side.

As a family, we knew how toxic that could be, and how hard on the people who loved you. So we were going with him now to save him from making bigger mistakes later.

"Greg, go back to the trees," I said, tapping Greg on the head and gesturing toward the woods. "Grandma, can you go play with Greg for a little while? He needs someone to pay attention to him."

"He's been lonely, the poor boy. Come on, Greggie. Let's go for a walk." She began bounding toward the tree line, waving for Greg to follow her. After a moment, he did, which really meant leaping ahead of her and then stopping to let her catch up with him. Thomas stayed where he was, smiling fondly as he watched her go.

"So I suppose that means I'm staying here," he said, once Alice and Greg had vanished into the trees. He turned to face me, expression going grave. "Be careful, Annie. I don't want to tell your parents that we lost you." Unspoken was the fact that if Artie didn't come back, his father and sister would never know that he had returned to begin with—not unless they spoke to the Michigan Aeslin mice. It would only hurt them more to know that they could have had him back again, only to lose the chance before they knew they had it.

"You won't," I said. "We'll be home before you know it."

I started for the house, Mark, Sam, and Artie following me, and every step took us closer to doing something we weren't going to be able to take back, and that was part of how I knew it was the right thing to do. The right thing is almost always hard. That's what stops some people from doing it.

The fear of being taken apart by a hive of angry telepathic wasps stops the rest.

I climbed the steps to the back door and opened it, waving the others into the kitchen. Once they were through, I let the door bang shut behind me as I followed them inside.

Twenty-Two

"While you're alive, you fight, little girl. You fight to stay that way. That's the only thing I'm ever going to ask from you. You have to fight."

—**Angela Baker**

Buckley Township, Michigan,
once more in the basement of the Old Parrish Place

Mark looked around with undisguised interest as we walked through the kitchen to the dining room, then through that to the living room to the basement door. He balked when I pulled it open, revealing the descending darkness on the other side.

"I am not going into the murder hole with you people," he said.

"If you want those coordinates, you need to," I replied. "That's where we left from, and where the Johrlac collective returned us. That's where the echoes of the equation are going to be."

"I didn't want to do this in the first place," he complained—but he started down the stairs, and the rest of us followed him.

As we walked, I tried to see this space as it would seem to a stranger. The racks of weaponry on the walls, the work tables scattered around the edges of the room, and of course, the ritual circle at the center. All in all, it could have been an unused sound stage for a horror movie. I tried to keep that in mind as I waved Mark toward the ritual circle, stepping into it first so he'd see that there was nothing to be afraid of.

"This is where we made both crossings," I said. "Give it a look."

"Right," he said dubiously. His eyes flared white, and the air around us began to ripple and tear, forming tiny rifts that opened just long enough to show me glimpses of auroras and cascading sheets of light, then sealed again. Mark frowned, shaking his head, and the glow died, taking the distortions with it. "Okay, I'll give you this much: there was definitely some sort of dimensional crossing here. One heading out, the other coming back."

"Can you retrace the crossing?" asked Artie.

"Patience," said Mark. "I just spent eight years in a coma. I'm not in a huge rush to leap to my death. Yeah, I can see which way to go. I can even put together the equation that's going to get us there. But there's a problem."

"Isn't there always a problem?" I asked.

"I'll need more processing power. And I'm not using my traveling companions. We already know from watching Sarah that it never works out the way you hope it will."

"Processing power?" asked Sam dubiously.

"Brains," said Mark. "I need brains I can offload some of the math onto, once it's finished but before it's ready to execute."

"Do they have to be human brains?" I asked.

"No. Anything with sufficient neuron density will work—Where are you going?"

"To get you some brains. Come on, Sam. We need to go visit your friend the bloodworm and all his little bloodworm buddies." I grabbed the banister, stepping onto the bottom stair. "Artie, you and Mark chill here. We'll be right back."

Then I was off and running, Sam behind me, with a task I could actually complete.

Sometimes it's good to understand what you can find in the Galway Woods.

✦ ✦ ✦

It's not true that leeches have thirty-two brains. Leeches have one large—by annelid standards—brain, and then thirty-two separate packets of ganglia that transmit instructions to the individual sections of their bodies. So no, not thirty-two brains. But thirty-two tidy little processing centers that someone could use to offload complicated math intended to change the universe.

I ran across the field, Sam close behind me, and plunged into the trees, heading for the nearest path that would take me to the swamp. "What are we looking for?" asked Sam, easily catching up with and pacing me.

I looked over at him as I ran. "Bloodworms."

"Bloodworms?"

"You remember your giant leech friend?"

Normal leeches were too small for Mark's purposes. They would burn out or fry before he could put any meaningful amount of math into them. Bloodworms, though . . . bloodworms were different. Largely because of scale. A leech two feet long has a lot more room for brain development than a leech that's only three inches long. And they kept growing as long as they were alive.

The swamp that bordered on the Galway Wood is a dangerous place, in part because it's one of the last flourishing bloodworm habitats in North America. We ran until the ground turned muddy, and then I produced a small knife from my pocket, using it to open a shallow cut on the back of my hand, which I turned over the nearest standing puddle, dripping blood into the water and stepping back to wait.

The puddle's surface began to pulse and churn, and several bloodworms reared their head, looking for their promised meal. I promptly leaned down and grabbed them, shoving them into the grocery bag I had snatched during our charge through the kitchen. This achieved, I moved on to the next puddle.

Sam produced his own knife and emulated me, bleeding before going on a bloodworm-snatching spree. The large invertebrates were slow and not very clever, and it didn't take us long to gather an even dozen, shoving them into my sack until it bulged. I held it out to Sam.

"Here," I said. "Get these to Mark. I'll meet you at the house."

"I don't want to leave you alone in the—"

"This is still the Galway Woods, Sam. I'll be fine. The woods won't let anything hurt me unless I'm stupid about where I walk. Just go, and I'll be right there."

Sam shot me a dubious look, then bounded off into the woods, heading back toward the house. I followed at a brisk but slower pace. I'm in incredibly good shape for a base human woman, absolutely. That doesn't mean I can keep up with a fūri, and we needed to do this quickly. Every minute we waited was another minute where Sarah was alone with the Johrlac—or not. The time difference might be working in our favor here.

Even so, we couldn't afford to screw around, and if we took too long, Mark might realize there was nothing we could do to make him help us and go back to his sister, who had waited more than long enough for him to come home to her. Absence makes the heart grow fonder, sure. It also makes love turn sour, and replaces regret with resentment. Cici deserved to have her brother back.

Just as much as we deserved to have Sarah back. My memories were almost done settling back into their places, and if I thought about the way I'd behaved during her trial, I felt an overwhelming shame. She was my cousin, my *Sarah*, and I'd told her to stop being a person and go be a cuckoo instead. I'd rejected her in a way that was personal and targeted enough that it should have been impossible without my memories, but those hadn't come until after I'd done it. I felt like a terrible person. I felt like a monster.

Anyone can make a mistake. But not everyone can throw their words like knives and be that sure of hitting the target. I kept my head down and moved quickly, intent on getting out of the woods before something else came to complicate a situation that was already overly complicated. In the distance, I could hear something crashing around with giddy abandon. I just hoped it was Alice and Greg, not something more hostile.

Since I'd been bleeding recently and whatever it was didn't seem to be tracking the scent, I was pretty sure it was them. I kept going until the trees thinned around me and I was emerging into the fields behind the house, the tall grasses springtime-green and gilded golden by the late afternoon sun. The sight of the house gave me my second wind. I broke into a run, clattering through the kitchen and into the dining room, where I paused to snatch one of the remaining charms from the table before heading down to the basement where Mark, Sam, and Artie were waiting in the circle.

Mark had arranged the bloodworms around the edge of the circle, lining them up so they formed an unbroken line. They weren't moving. Mark's eyes were glowing a faint, lambent white, and I was pretty sure those two things were connected. He looked over at the sound of my footsteps on the stairs.

"There you are," said Mark. "Why are you all so hard to see? I didn't hear you coming until you were on the stairs."

"Anti-telepathy charms," I said. "They help us stay out of sight when we're dealing with a telepathic population, and they probably also keep the ambient telepathic force of Johrlar from melting our brains where we stand. It's a weird travel accessory, but it works for us. Here." I lobbed the spare charm I'd grabbed at Artie, who caught it easily and held it up to eye it with valid suspicion.

"Put it on," advised Sam. "Johrlar is pretty loud if you're not wearing one."

I slanted him a sidelong look. "How do you know that?"

"I, uh, took mine off for a few seconds to see what all the fuss was about," he admitted. "We were in the middle of the jungle at the time! It seemed like a reasonable risk!"

"There are no reasonable risks when your brain could end up getting melted in the process," I said. Artie was still standing there, charm in his hand, not putting it on. "Artie? The cord goes over your neck."

"Will Sarah be able to see me if I'm wearing this?" he asked.

"I think Sarah would be able to see you through all the telepathy blockers in the universe," I said. "Seeing you was what convinced her to trade herself to the collective for our freedom. She'll see you."

He looked uncomfortable at that, but put the cord over his head, settling the charm against his chest. Mark rolled his eyes.

"This is all very sweet and sentimental and I'm touched, really, but the numbers change, you know? The longer we wait, the more the position of our respective dimensions can shift around, and the harder it is for me to get us where you want to go. I'm only doing this kind of favor for you assholes once. After this I'm going home to Cici, and we're going to get on with our lives, far, far away from you."

"And we appreciate that," I said. "Bloodworms good enough to work?"

"They're like little auxiliary processing units," said Mark. "It's like they have brains the whole length of their bodies, and no real sense of self to feel bad about deleting. I can just overload their buffers, let them crash, and then do it again. They're perfect."

"Glad we could help." I stepped into the circle.

Sam smiled at me. Artie looked over and gave me a nervous nod. He'd picked up a handgun from the armory, and what looked like a collapsible baton: I was just glad he wasn't going into this unarmed. When dealing with mammals, he could usually hide behind his pheromones. Well, that wasn't going to work here.

Mark looked around at the three of us, eyes still glinting. "You're ready? Because there's not going to be a second bus out of here. We go now or we don't go at all."

"We're getting her back," said Artie firmly. "That has never been up for discussion."

"Guess that means yes," said Mark. His eyes flared, going from a light glow to a halogen burn, and the bloodworms around the edge of the circle began to twitch and undulate, forming a startlingly rhythmic pattern. He didn't say anything. I was used to that from Sarah, whose math was so frequently a purely mental process.

The math began wrapping around me like an almost-physical cocoon, pinning my arms to my side and making it feel like I was wearing a snug corset, not enough to make it hard to breathe, but enough that I felt each breath individually, my lungs working harder to expand. The white of Mark's eyes grew and grew until it washed away everything else, and then it, too, shifted, becoming blackness around me, and blue ahead of me, flashing to red behind. We were racing into the Doppler shift.

And still Mark's eyes blazed white, and still the colors flickered around us, and then, with a sensation like an airplane dropping toward the ground, it all burst around us. My ears actually popped as the pressure released, and I dropped to my knees, suddenly breathing normally. Raising my head, I saw that Artie and Sam were on hands and knees as well, while Mark was bent forward, his own hands braced against his thighs to keep him upright. The bloodworms were gone. They hadn't made the crossing with us.

The basement was also gone, replaced by the lush green and brilliant floral brightness of the jungle near the Kairos village. I groaned and staggered upright.

"We need to move," I said.

"Why?" asked Artie, sounding mulish. "I need to breathe."

"Because we're near a bunch of local assholes that I don't want to deal with right now," I snapped.

"Too late," said an amiable voice from behind me, as the tine of a bident was brought to rest against the back of my neck. "The timing told us you'd be here. All we ever had to do was wait."

Shit.

Twenty-Three

"Love is a form of obsession, absolutely. And some of us never learned how to let go. Didn't much pay attention during the lessons on sharing, either."

—Alice Healy

Back on Johrlar,
being taken before the Eldest Living of the Kairos

THE GUARDS MARCHED THE FOUR of us at bident-point back through the jungle to their village, and through the village to the home of the Eldest Living. They didn't seem surprised or concerned about the fact that we had a Johrlac with us now; if anything, they were delighted to have someone else to point their spears at.

By the time we reached the tree and were waved impatiently inside, I was ready for a fight. I balled my hands into fists, pale flames surrounding them. Everything I'd seen when we were here before was flammable. Tree, fabric, little old lady who I really probably shouldn't set on fire—all flammable. All expendable if they insisted on standing between us and rescuing Sarah.

But when the guards urged us into the tree, the Eldest Living wasn't atop her mountain of cloth. Instead, we seemed to be alone. I seized the opportunity to straighten and cross over to Artie, who was looking a little green around the edges.

"You all right, buddy?" I asked.

"This is *terrifying*," he said. "Who are these people? What do they want with us?"

I paused. Oh, right. Artie hadn't been with us when we'd encountered the Kairos before, and neither had Arthur. There was no way he could remember any of this. "A long time ago, the Johrlac swiped a bunch of Kairos from their home dimension because they wanted a telepathically resistant service class," I said hurriedly. "They just didn't think through the implications of a telepathically resistant service class that happened to be close friends with coincidence and causality, and the Kairos somewhat inevitably got away from their captors and started their own settlements in the deep jungle."

"Where we've been hounded and hunted ever since," said the voice of the Eldest Living, as she stepped out of the shadows around the edge of the space. "The collective cannot let go of the idea that because our ancestors were not from this dimension, we owe them in some way for our existence. As if the timing would not have seen the ones it wanted born, regardless of the world our parents lived in. Hello, travelers. Some of you are new to me."

"Your guards were watching for us," I snapped. "What is your game?"

"Freedom," she said. "We want to be left alone. We've been bargaining with the current collective for a long time, and it's no longer serving us well. We require a new collective. So we ask and wait for the timing to provide us with the tools we need. You, and the rogue queen, are those tools."

"The rogue—Sarah?" Artie focused on the Eldest Living, suddenly intense and anxious. "Are you talking about Sarah?"

"The collective took her, and agreed to leave us in peace for a season," said the Eldest Living, blissfully unaware of how much that statement made Artie want to beat her over the head with the nearest chair. His hands flexed, and I knew he was considering doing precisely that. It would have complicated getting out of here, but after everything this lady had been associated with doing to us, I'd be fine seeing her go down.

The Eldest Living sighed as she looked around at our faces. "It was necessary to spare my people. I apologize, but you would do the same if our positions were reversed."

"How can you be so sure we're the tools your timing wants you to use to break the current collective?"

"I've spoken to the majority of you, and you don't become the Eldest Living without learning a thing or two about people," she said. "Look. We all want something simple. We want to be left alone, here, on Johrlar, and not forced to return to a dimension we don't remember in order to preserve our peace. You want your queen back. She's been absorbed into the collective by now, and we can help you recover her. They never see us coming."

Mark smirked. "No, I guess they wouldn't," he said. "I can't catch hold of your mind at all. It's like trying to see through mud when I try."

"From the way you move your head, I can tell you grew up around people who see with their eyes rather than their minds. For those who neglect the physical aspects of their senses, as the Johrlac of this world tend to do, we might as well be invisible," said the Eldest Living. "They don't see us unless we move, and even then, they lose sight of us quickly."

Mark frowned. "That's terrible operational security. If they know you're there for people who rely on vision, they should be training up guards who know how to look for you."

"That assumes a flexibility of thought that the Johrlac lose when a single collective remains in power for too long," said the Eldest Living. "We're not asking you to help us harm anyone beyond the collective, which has done harm beyond measure. All we're asking you to do is help us change an unfair system, so that we may have a moment's peace before the new system rises to replace it."

Sam and I exchanged a look. I didn't like this. I didn't like the idea of coming from another dimension to overthrow someone else's government. We'd have to leave immediately afterward, which was the definition of making a mess and leaving it for someone else to deal with. But then again, they started it when they stole Sarah and Arthur. Having Artie back was wonderful in ways I hadn't been able to take the time to really grapple with yet, but it had been so long since we'd lost him, and Arthur had become his own person. Losing him stung.

Whatever we did to these people, they deserved it.

I turned to the Eldest Living. "What's your plan?" I asked.

Slowly, she smiled.

✦ ✦ ✦

Kairos planning, which was largely based on lucky breaks and best-case scenarios, was remarkably similar to family planning, if based on even more tenuous chains of coincidence, which made sense: their connection to the timing was direct and reliable, unlike our own, which became more diluted and unpredictable with every passing generation.

Less than an hour after our arrival, we were walking along the monorail structure in the company of a massive group of Kairos guards, easily forty of them, all packed in close around the enormous velvet worm that Mark was seated atop, riding it dutifully toward the city. Artie rode behind him, more out of necessity than desire: Arthur had never been interested in fieldwork, and so while he'd maintained basic physical fitness, he hadn't kept their shared body in the sort of shape that would allow Artie to make this walk without straining something he was probably going to need later.

As we approached the series of ramps that would take us down into the city, Johrlac guards appeared, flanking the exits. Each of the travelers would approach, the guards' eyes would flash white, and then the travelers would begin their descent. As the only one of us the guards would be able to really "see," Mark was our representative. This was also our test of how well he could navigate in Johrlac society.

It was our turn. Mark urged the worm forward, and when he was in position, he met eyes with the guard. The man's eyes flashed white. Mark's did the same, brighter and harder to look directly into. The man blinked, repeatedly, and dropped his spear before staggering back against the rail, putting a hand against his forehead. Then he waved us on, and we began our descent, about half of us looking back in anticipation of the pursuit that had to be coming.

It didn't come.

"Dude, what the hell?" asked Sam. "You were supposed to be all 'These are not the droids you're looking for,' not 'Let me melt your brain for you.' And why did they just let us go?"

"I didn't mean to," said Mark sourly. "He asked what my business in the city was. You were right—he didn't see any of you people. So I told him I was taking my weird giant worm for a walk, and then he wanted to know my name. Only he didn't like my name, and he tried to push deeper into my mind. So I shoved him out. I guess I wasn't supposed to be able to do that, since he didn't even try to stop me. I didn't mean to hit him so hard."

"As long as they don't chase after us, we're fine," I said. "I think we'll be fine if they *do* chase after us, but it'll be the sort of fine that comes with a lot more bloodshed, and I'd rather skip it if we can."

Mark eyed me skeptically.

"What?"

"Just not sure I believe one of you assholes trying to *avoid* the bloodshed." We were winding down the ramp, the velvet worm's footing sure and stable, thanks to its many, many feet. There were more guards at the bottom. Mark locked eyes with them and they stepped aside, gesturing us forward.

I eyed him. He shrugged.

"Queens lead their society, and kings are supposed to be impossible," he said. "So they hit my mind, feel enough power to make me a queen, pick up on the fact that I'm a dude, and don't know how to deal with the contradiction, so they just sort of back down. I get the feeling they don't spend a lot of time thinking for themselves. It's not an encouraged skill around here."

"You think pretty highly of your own species," said Sam.

"Eh. If you get to visit the land of the shapeshifting monkey people and they're all total losers, are you really going to be their biggest fan? Or are you going to be all 'Gosh I'm glad I don't live here'?" Mark shrugged again. "These people are my species, but they're not my friends, or my family. We don't have anything in common but some shitty ancestral memories—which I don't even have anymore, by the way. Sarah ripped them out of me like a really nasty weed."

I winced at the imagery. I knew what it was like to have my memories removed, and I had resented it for a long time. Mark didn't sound resentful. He sounded bitter, but almost grateful at the same time, like she had done him an immense favor that he didn't really have the words to properly describe.

The streets were as busy as they'd been on our previous visit. Other than the char damage to the administrative building, most of which had already been repaired, there was nothing to show that we'd been here at all. People walked in every direction, some accompanied by large insects, some pushing strollers. There were more children than there'd been before, and several of them stopped to point at our Kairos guards, eyes flashing.

"Uh, guys?" I said.

An adult moved toward one of the groups of pointing children, following their fingers to look directly at us.

"Guys," I repeated, with more urgency.

"What?" asked Mark.

I pointed at the children who were pointing at us, beginning to amass a small crowd of adults who stared and muttered, their eyes flashing on and off like fireflies.

One of the Kairos guards swore. "Their children can see us better than they can, because they haven't outgrown believing the evidence of their eyes," he said. "If the children can show the adults where we are, we can be found."

"Meaning . . . ?"

"Run."

The guards took off with the ease and speed of a trained unit, running away from the velvet worm and heading down the street toward the hulking, lightly charred shape of the central building. Sam leapt onto the back of the velvet worm, sweeping Mark and Artie—our least physically fit members—under his arms, and ran after the guards. I brought up the rear, hands lighting up. If these people decided to chase us, they were going to find out the hard way that no one wants to be the main character at a barbecue.

The administration building was swarming with Johrlac, but we ran right by it, heading for the stone structure on the other side. One of the Kairos dropped back to pace me.

"We know a way in through the rear," he said. "The queens stay here when not acting in a public capacity. They recognize that stone is a better protection."

"Against what?"

"Everything," he said. "Their own people—they live in fear of another collective rising in their shadow, as they once rose in the last collective's shadow. Only one queen in a hive, after all. They've solved that by finding a way to combine many queens into one, but that doesn't change the instinctive response to a challenger."

The children had been left far behind us, and the adults they'd clued into our presence were equally far back, but that didn't mean there wouldn't be some sort of an alarm. We kept running, and when we reached the stone building, the guards circled around behind it, to a stretch of wall made from the papery material that comprised so much of the city. I blinked at it, then looked at the guard I had been running beside.

"They prefer the comfort of their nests," he said. "The paper is breathable and lets the air circulate more freely. It keeps things from getting too stuffy. They view it as almost sacred, in a way, and while they will cut it to make doors when none are present, they only do so when they can make immediate repairs."

More of the guards were fanning out to begin slicing through the wall, removing it in a single massive piece.

"We can put this back when we're done with it, and because it's unthinkable that someone would mess with the paper in such a way, none of the Johrlac will go looking for the seams," explained my guard.

I looked at him, askance. "For a telepathic society, they sure do ignore a lot of warning signs."

"They decided a long time ago what they were and were not willing to see, and they shut out everything else," said the guard. "It's the danger of reaching what you consider perfection. Anything that challenges it must be set aside."

"Did your timing tell you that?"

"No," he said patiently. "My common sense did. Now come. We're close to the chamber of the collective."

We poured through the hole where the paper had been, guards surrounding my little group, Mark walking at the very center, like he wanted to keep his presence a surprise for as long as possible. With the anti-telepathy charm around my neck, I couldn't tell whether Sarah's static was present, and I was almost afraid to check.

Artie wasn't. He reached up and took his own charm off, stuffing it into his pocket as he closed his eyes and kept walking. After a few seconds, he sagged and looked over at me. "I can't feel her," he said.

"Maybe they're suppressing her somehow?" I suggested.

"I don't think so," he said. "I think—from what they were saying while they were in my head—I think there's a good chance she isn't anymore."

"Not here?"

"Not anywhere." He looked at me bleakly. "I think they maybe did to Sarah what Sarah did to me, only they did it on purpose."

"Sounds great," said Mark. Artie, Sam, and I all shot him horrified looks. He shrugged. "What? We know that sort of thing can be undone. If she's alive and just not in her own head right now, we put her back where she belongs and everything is fine. We go home, you assholes leave me alone, we're all happy."

"You have a very pragmatic way of looking at the world," said Sam.

Mark shrugged. "I took a nap and woke up with phenomenal cosmic powers, having missed my sister's entire time in high school. I'd trade the powers for the time if that were an option. Knowing that I can't makes everything else seem a lot less urgent. All I want to do now is get through whatever's next and move the fuck on."

"It must be nice to be that sure of what you want," said Artie dolefully. He didn't put his charm back on.

"Aren't you?" asked Mark. "I thought we were here because you wanted your very own telepathic wasp to take home and call 'baby.'"

"No," said Artie. "I only want the *right* one."

"And you're stressed out because she may be taking a little break from existing? Dude, you have got to chill."

"That's normally my line," said Sam.

We were working our way deeper and deeper into the stone building as they talked. The walls here were largely made of stone, sturdier than they were in the only other Johrlac building I had seen. Harder to burn, too. I made note of the material as we walked, keeping my hands lit. The white flame was a recent development, something I'd been working hard to stabilize. It was hotter than my normal fire by a significant measure, and harder to see if you didn't know what you were looking for. It didn't take any more attention or focus than regular red flames did, so why not go with the more destructive option?

The Johrlac disdain for furniture continued in this building. The halls were empty, no shelves, no seating, and it wasn't until we had worked our way well into the building that I even started to see doorways off the hall we were walking along. Straight lines and no frills, that seemed to be the Johrlac way.

If anything could have reinforced the idea that Sarah wasn't like these people, it was the minimalism of their world. Her room—both her rooms, Oregon and Ohio—had always been a textured maze of trinkets and posters, a snapshot of her life as she preferred to live in it. She would never have chosen this sort of austere precision. I could see where a mathematician might look at the perfection of the architecture and believe that it needed to be showcased. To people who lived and breathed numeric perfection, this was probably the high of beautiful décor.

We turned a corner, and found ourselves confronted with a long wall made of paper. I could see shadows moving on the other side, backlit by whatever they were using to light their space. All conversation had died.

I looked to the guard who'd been pacing me, and mouthed, *Is this it?*

He looked baffled. The mind-mind flowers could clarify language, but not the shape a word left on the lips. I leaned in closer, whispering, "Is that the collective?"

"Ah. No," he whispered back.

I nodded understanding, and we kept moving deeper.

✦ ✦ ✦

The longer we walked, the more apparent it became that the building was constructed in a series of concentric circles, each one slightly smaller than the last. There were chambers in the rings, marked by paper walls and occasional voices, but on the whole, each ring was empty until it merged with the next along the line. We moved deeper and deeper, and the rings began to show signs of actual use.

We were maybe five rings in when we stepped into what I could only describe as a nursery. The walls were lined with hex-shaped cubbies, each one occupied by an infant or small child—I'd estimate up to two or three years old, as humans measured growth. They sucked on bud-shaped bottles or scooped pollen out of flowers with tiny hands, eating and staring blankly into the distance. None of them cried or babbled or anything I would have expected from babies.

That didn't match what I knew about cuckoo children. Isaac had cried from the beginning, cried for food, for warmth, for contact. He'd reached and wanted just as much as any human infant.

There were adult Johrlac on the nursery ring. They wore black-

and-white jumpsuits and walked in silence with glowing white eyes, presumably in constant communion with the children in their care. A few of them glanced in our direction as we walked through, and I had the distinct feeling they could see us, but none of them said anything or seemed alarmed in any way, so we just kept going, passing out of the realm of those strange and silent children, seeking our goal.

Two rings later, we encountered our first signs of resistance. A line of Johrlac guards blocked the way, holding bamboo canes like quarterstaffs, clearly prepared for a fight. Their eyes were blue: whatever orders they were following, they weren't telepathic ones. All of them focused, immediately, on Mark and Artie, the only members of our group not currently wearing anti-telepathy charms.

"Shit," I muttered, and moved to stand between Artie and the guards.

They attacked in silence, moving in a ragged line that didn't make sense until I looked at their faces and realized that in order to see us, they had shut down their telepathy and focused on the physical world as much as possible. Like humans blindfolding themselves to fight invisible monsters, they were blocking everything that might interfere with believing their eyes. They couldn't communicate or coordinate the way they normally would, and that put them at a disadvantage.

The first two swung for Artie. I grabbed their canes, wincing at the impact against my palms, and lit them on fire. It spread quickly, consuming the wood and licking at their hands, which caused them to yelp and drop their weapons. I pulled a knife out of my shirt and threw it at the closer of them, sending him to the floor as it embedded itself in his throat. The second looked at his empty hands, then lunged for Artie, only to be met with a baton across the wrists.

I shot Artie an impressed look. He pulled the baton back, getting it into a defensive position. "Don't worry about me," he said. "Knock 'em down."

Sam was cheerfully bowling Johrlac guards at one another, bouncing from place to place almost too fast for me to follow. The Kairos guards were meeting canes with bidents, and were clearly more accustomed to actual combat: when they were hit, they went down silently, whereas the Johrlac guards yelped and shouted and groaned, broadcasting their injuries more openly than I would have expected from trained security.

Mark . . . wasn't visibly doing anything. He was standing perfectly still, guards throwing themselves at him and never quite making contact. His eyes were glowing steadily white, and his hair had started to move, ruffling like he was in the path of a stiff breeze. More guards flung themselves at him, only to hit the ground behind or beside him, unable to make contact.

"This is boring," said Mark. "Can't you do any better?"

One guard, either smarter or braver than the rest, stopped at the very edge of what I would have considered the combat zone, pulling what looked like a dart gun and aiming it at Mark. He blew on the end of the gun, sending a fletched dart straight at Mark.

It never reached him. Halfway there, it stopped like it had struck an invisible wall, then flipped in the air and shot back toward the guard who had launched it in the first place. It slammed into the side of his neck and his eyes rolled up in his head before he went down in a heap, twitching and foaming at the mouth. Gradually, the twitches stopped. He didn't get back up.

"Huh," said Mark. "Guess I can do that now. Anyone else want to go?"

He looked around at the guards who were still standing, expression speculative. They shied back, and one turned to run. Sam was immediately there, standing between him and freedom. His hands came down on the top of the guard's head, fingers laced tightly together to form a solid ball, and the guard crumpled. Like so many of the others, he didn't get back up.

It was a strangely PG battle scene: Johrlac bleed clear, and so the floor just looked slick and slippery, not covered in gore. A few of our Kairos guards were bleeding, but none badly; we'd come through the encounter with nothing much worse than bruises. I turned to check on the man I'd been talking to as we walked, and found him watching our rear with a deeply concerned expression on his face.

"They know we're here," he said. "The queens only lay ambushes when they believe the hive has been compromised. We're walking into a trap."

"Why not overwhelm us? Why risk us getting close?"

"Most of their fighters can't see us even as well as these last ones could," he explained. "It takes them time to muster a defense, whereas their hive is prepared for assaults. We must go carefully from here, but we must still go. We won't get another chance this clean."

"Sarah may not have another chance at all," said Artie grimly.

"So we keep going," I concluded, and looked down the hall. There didn't seem to be any more guards there, but I had no way of being certain.

None of our fighters were down.

We kept going.

✦ ✦ ✦

We encountered more resistance another two rings in. This group was larger and better armed, with amentums and metal-tipped darts as well as the bamboo staffs. Like the first group, they fought fiercely and focused on Mark and Artie, but went down in the face of a force they couldn't properly see or organize themselves against. I found myself relieved to be fighting in a building made of stone, which wasn't nearly as flammable as the paper that they used for everything else.

We kept going. The two rings after that were empty, and warmer than any of the others had been, the air growing hot and humid, like we were moving into the outskirts of a greenhouse. I looked askance at the Kairos guards, but they just kept moving, apparently unbothered by the changing climate.

Then we moved into the center of the hive.

This wasn't a ring: it was a circular room, roughly as large as a swimming pool. Like a swimming pool, it was recessed compared to the floors around it, dropping about six feet from the threshold. There was no padding on the other side. If we hadn't been moving slowly and carefully, someone could have been seriously hurt.

The minimalist theme was continued here; there were no unnecessary furnishings, only six beds like raised garden planters, high sides with a recessed center, each one containing a female Johrlac in a black bodysuit gleaming with rainbows, like the surface of a polluted lake, their eyes closed and their hair fanned out over their pillows. Their hands were folded on their chests, and five of them weren't moving.

The one who *was* moving was in the process of sitting up as we crowded in the doorway. She turned toward us, eyes as blue as glacial ice, and shook her head in obvious disappointment.

"I suppose this was inevitable," she said, and flicked her fingers, eyes flashing briefly white.

Oh, shit.

Twenty-Four

"Bring her home."

—**Mary Dunlavy**

In the queen's hive on Johrlar, about to face the collective

THE KAIROS GUARD WHO HAD been at the front of our group flew backward, impacting the wall behind us with a sickening crunch. We all turned to stare, then looked back at the Johrlac, who was standing now, stepping delicately out of her planter.

"We've been expecting you," she said.

Sam looked at me and nodded. I nodded back.

"Then you know we'll keep coming," said one of the Kairos.

"Yes, we do," she said. "We also know you'll lose."

Sam's tail wrapped hard around my waist, and he jerked me off my feet as he leapt, spinning me around in front of him so he could get an arm under my behind and toss me gently into the air. He caught me before he hit the ground in the center air, then went bounding back to the others, grabbing Artie, who yelped.

The drop presented a genuine issue for our guards, since the Johrlac queen wasn't exactly going to wait for them to climb down. She began telekinetically grabbing them as they moved forward, flinging two more into walls before she shifted a third—fourth, really, but math is not my strong suit—forward and he stopped, hanging in midair. I looked back at the doorway. Mark's eyes were gleaming lambent white. They were playing tug-of-war.

Normally I would object to using a living person for that sort of game, but it was keeping her focused on one guard, and distracting her from the rest. Sam was able to get five of them down before she let go. Mark was still pulling, and that guard hit the wall like the others, slingshot backward by the sudden loss of an opposing force. There was a horrifying crunch and Mark grimaced, the light in his eyes literally going out.

"This is not going to end well for you, abomination," said the queen. "We have the power of six, and you have the power of but one. Give up and allow yourself to be destroyed. Kings are not to rise."

Those of us on the ground level fanned out around her, moving carefully. She still didn't seem to see us if she wasn't trying: Mark had the full force of her attention.

Or seemed to, anyway. She turned abruptly, looking at Artie. "You should not be here, little restoration," she said. "We put back what the cuckoo had broken. You're free now. Go home and leave our affairs to us."

"Not without Sarah," snapped Artie. "Where is she?"

"It was a fair and balanced exchange," said the queen. "We returned you and we retained her. She belongs to us now."

"Where. Is. She?"

"If you can't find her on your own, your claim is not so great as you'd imply," said the queen calmly. "Very well, little restoration. If you can find her, and if she wants it, we'll let her go. But if you can't, the math is in our favor, and you will leave us."

"Artie," I called, low and tight. "If you can't do this, we have to find another way. We only get one shot."

"I know," said Artie. He began walking around the sleeping queens, looking down at them. He paused a few times to get a closer look, bending down and studying their faces closely.

At the third queen, he bent further, reaching down to delicately smooth a lock of hair away her face. "This is her," he said. He looked up, focusing on the queen who had been fighting us. "She got this scar over her eyebrow when we were twelve. We were playing in the woods and she lost her grip on the rope we were using to get up into the treehouse. She hit her head on a rock when she fell, and I thought she was dead. This is Sarah."

"Are you sure?" asked the queen, almost mockingly.

He nodded. "I'm positive," he said.

"Very well, then." Her eyes flashed momentarily white, and the other queen's eyes opened.

They were icy, impossibly blue, and if he was wrong, I couldn't have said so: she looked like my cousin. She looked like Sarah. Slowly, she sat up, watching Artie the whole time. He pressed a hand against his temple, relief washing over his face in an unstoppable tide.

"There's the static," he said. "It's faint, but it's there. Sarah? We came back for you."

"I don't know you," she replied, voice uninflected and almost mechanical. "We know you—we repaired what the cuckoo had done, the damage she had allowed to fester, but *I* don't know you. Why am I outside the we?"

"This restoration claims to have come to take you home," said the first queen. "He has agreed to leave us if you refuse."

Something about this was too easy. She had already known Sarah would refuse, or she would never have allowed Artie to try.

"I didn't agree to that," I said hurriedly. "I want to know what you did with Arthur."

"The overlay? He has been set aside. Do you want him as well?"

"Yes," I said.

The queen appeared startled. "Why?" she asked.

"He's family," I replied.

Sarah—if it *was* Sarah—was still looking blankly at Artie, who was staring at her like his heart was dissolving in his chest.

Sam was abruptly beside me. "Whoa," he said.

"Indeed, whoa," I agreed.

"Can only one of your cousins actually exist at a time? Because that's pretty fucked-up."

The Kairos guards were fanning out, moving as carefully as they could as they positioned themselves behind the still-sleeping queens. The one who was awake was still looking at me, bewildered. "And you'll leave?" she asked. "If we return him, you'll leave? You won't force us to keep repeating this over and over again?"

"We want them both," I said.

"It's her choice," she said. Her eyes flashed white. "The guards will bring the overlay."

"Sarah," said Artie. "Come on. You need to stop this, and come home. I'm okay. I miss you. We finally figured things out. Now's the time when we get to try. Don't you want to try?"

"Try what?" she asked. "I don't know you. I don't know any of you. Please. Let me return to the we. I am not meant to be singular. I am not meant to be I."

Artie closed his eyes, slumping.

Mark stepped off the ledge and walked calmly on the air toward us, getting a little lower with every step he took, like he was descending an invisible stairway. "This is all fun and everything, but I don't like it," he said. "The princess isn't supposed to be a blank slate and a bunch of etiquette books. She's supposed to be deeply annoying, with passionately held opinions about the X-Men and a lot of feelings about, well, everything. Mostly the guy she's currently failing to recognize. It's weird having her sound like an empty channel. It needs to stop."

There was a commotion at the doorway on the other side of the room, and several Johrlac guards appeared, hauling an unfamiliar Kairos along with them. He was tall and blond, and struggling against their grasp in a way that was almost familiar.

The queen waved her hand and he was lifted into the air, floating gently down to land in front of us.

"There," she said.

I frowned at the stranger, who looked anxiously back at me. "Arthur?" I asked.

"Oh thank God," he said, and flung himself at me, impacting hard enough that Sam winced in sympathy. "I have no idea what's going on or what I'm doing in this body—when I asked the people who were moving me to a new cell, they said it had been empty, I didn't steal it, but it's not mine and I don't know what's happening and I want to go home and wait." He paused, pulling away from me. "Why am I over there? Why does Sarah look so weird?"

"Uh, complicated answer," I said. "That's Artie. The Johrlac collective put him back where he belonged. And Sarah looks so weird because she's been absorbed into their collective. We're going to get her back."

"Yeah, we are," said Mark. "Right now."

His eyes flashed white and he collapsed, folding gracefully to the floor. A moment later, Sarah fell backward in her bed and didn't move, even when Artie grabbed her arms and shook her.

Silence fell.

Twenty-Five

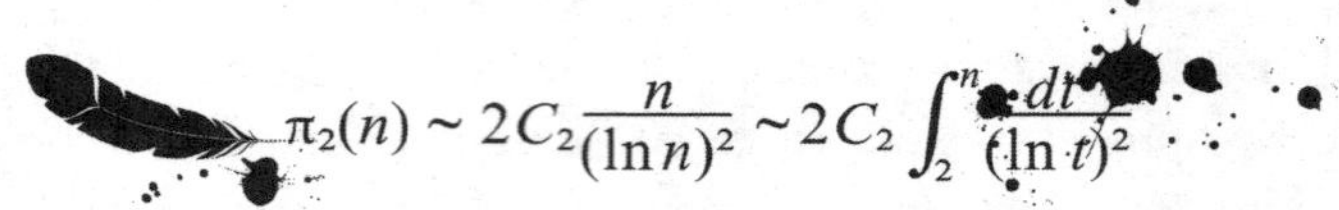

SARAH

"It all adds up, in the end."

—**Evelyn Baker**

Inside my head, which is currently singular, and that's not fun

I DIDN'T UNDERSTAND WHY I WAS awake and singular, or who the stranger calling me by an unfamiliar name was, or why I was supposed to know him. Then there was a pressure against my mind, hard and almost stabbing, sending me toppling backward into the depths of my own thoughts.

I pressed back against the intrusion, trying to shove it out, and a male voice said, *Now Sarah, is that any way to greet an old friend? Look at it this way, princess: you messed with my head. Now I get to mess with yours.*

I turned in the emptiness of my mind, trying to see where the voice was coming from. *I don't know you. I never "messed" with your head. Go away and let me rejoin the collective.*

I don't think so, princess, said the voice, and it was amused now, almost entertained. *I don't think you want that, either, because you left instructions for getting you loose.*

What do you mean?

I mean this. A pearl appeared in front of me, floating in midair, nacreous and white and about the size of my head in the waking world. *You made it for me, didn't you? Because you knew your med-*

dling cousins would drag me into this, one way or another, and you knew I'd have the strength to break it.

I didn't know what that thing was, but sudden terror filled me. If he broke it, terrible things would happen. I threw up the idea of my hands. *No, wait!*

Why should I?

I don't want to go back. I know I wasn't always part of the collective, but now that I am, I'm happy. This is peace. I'm not alone. I'm not struggling for anything. Please, give it back and go. Just let me be.

You make a fair point, princess. But I have a counterpoint you might be interested in hearing.

What's that?

Breaking this thing will probably hurt you, a lot. I've worked too hard to be a good person to relish causing you pain, but you cost me eight years with my sister, and if pain is an inescapable consequence, well. I'm not going to feel too bad about that. The pearl split down the center, and prismatic white light began cascading out, eradicating everything it touched. *Oops.*

I didn't respond to that. I was too busy screaming.

Twenty-Six

ANTIMONY

"I do my best work in the encores."

—**Frances Brown**

In the queens' hive on Johrlar

Artie was still shaking Sarah when she opened her eyes and started to scream. The whiteness overwhelmed her irises and sclera rapidly, getting brighter by the second. She sat up, clutching her head. Artie didn't let go of her. Instead, he pulled her close, holding her against his chest. He wasn't touching her skin, but it was still a risky thing to do.

Then the other four bodies of the collective started screaming. The one who'd been already awake and conducting the scene clutched the sides of her head, doubling over, but managed not to join the cacophony.

"What's happening?" I yelled, trying to be heard above everything else.

"I'm helping," Mark yelled back, the glow in his eyes dying back down to normal levels of frosted white. He shot a sidelong look at the shrieking queens. "Maybe a little more than I intended to!"

"Mark!" I yelled.

He shrugged. "You said you wanted her back!"

One of the queens stopped screaming and started to sob. The Kairos guards moved toward her, helping her out of her bed, and she latched on to one of them, wrapping herself around him and babbling, "Collate, civic assistant, service. Allow me to perform my function, please. Please, I just want to perform my function. Let me do what I was made for. Let me go home."

Another of the queens stopped screaming. She looked frantically around. "You're not my sisters," she said. "Where are my sisters?"

The queen who'd been clutching her head straightened. "We *are* your sisters!" she said, loudly. "We *are*! Give up this nonsense!"

"Imposter," snarled the other queen. Her eyes flashed, and the first queen flew across the room to hit the wall.

"I think their collective is collapsing," said Sam.

Sarah stopped screaming and clutching her head, wrapping her arms around Artie instead, burying her face against his chest. I couldn't see whether she was crying. But I could feel the moment when her static resumed, as loud as ever, audible even through the muting effect of my anti-telepathy charm. I didn't take it off. Hearing a queen through the charm was like feeling lava through heat shielding; the fact that it wasn't knocking me over meant I was still getting enough of the benefit to be worth it.

A third queen stopped screaming and sat up, looking around the room with wide, clear eyes. One of the Kairos guards moved to her side.

"Engineer?" he asked.

She looked up at him and nodded. He extended a hand to help her up.

"My Eldest Living would like to speak with you about the establishment of a new treaty, and a new collective."

She took his hand, allowing herself to be pulled to her feet. She looked around at the rest of us, frowning when she reached Collate and Sarah. "Yes," she said faintly. "A new collective would be . . . kinder. I will speak with your Eldest."

The last remaining queen in her bed stopped screaming, but didn't open her eyes. She didn't breathe, either. The queen who had taken the guard's hand looked at her and sighed.

"Singularity is a burden," she said. "Death can be a gift."

Sarah took her face away from Artie's chest and leaned back, looking up at him with wide eyes, dark eyelashes clumped together by tears. "Artie?" she whispered, and it was such a fragile question that I feared any answer but the truth might break her.

"Yes," he said, and leaned down, and kissed her.

For him, it had been less than a day since their first kiss. For her, it had been eight years since their last one. She clung to him as tightly as she could, and for once she didn't shy away from skin contact with another person. Watching her wrap herself around him really drove home how much she normally held back with the rest of us, how tightly she kept herself inside her self-imposed boundaries.

Engineer turned to look at Mark. "You are . . . something new," she said. "I was unaware a male could survive the adult instar."

"I wouldn't have if Sarah hadn't insisted on getting me proper medical care," he said, gesturing toward my entwined cousins. "I owed her this. Now we're taking her home."

"One of the two originals of this collective is dead. The second may soon join her." Her eyes flicked to the queen who had been flung into the wall. "Another is unstable, and should never have been assumed into this collective. She survived the deaths of her sisters. She should not have. I will not have her. Only two of us will remain, if you take your Sarah. Two is not a collective."

"I have . . ." Collate coughed. "I have two others I lived with before my apotheosis. I am sure they would welcome my return."

Sarah finally stopped kissing Artie and turned toward Collate. "Fetch and Carry," she said, her voice thin but carrying. "They're in custody at the administration building, for helping me."

Collate frowned. "That will need correction." She looked to Engineer. "If we offer, and they accept, I would lead them through apotheosis. I would bring them home to me."

"Four is a sufficient base for a collective," agreed Engineer. She looked to the Kairos. "We will negotiate with your Eldest Living."

"And me?" asked Sarah. "Am I free to go? Are we . . . are we all free to go?"

"There is no cause to keep you any longer," she said. "Your crimes, such as they are, are forgiven. Leave us, and do not return."

"So that's it?" asked Mark. "We can just leave?"

Engineer looked at him. "Would you prefer something more complicated?"

"Well, no, but I—"

"You are a unique and impossible thing, a cuckoo king. Be grateful we do not choose to keep you for greater examination. The mathematics which make you must be incredible."

Mark visibly backed down, even taking a step away.

Arthur, who was no longer clinging to me but had yet to let go of my arm, matched Mark's movement with his own, moving toward the queen they called Engineer. "What about me?" he asked.

"What about you?" she replied.

"Am I—do I get to exist? Is this body stolen? Are we going to have to do all this over again when its original owner comes looking for it?"

"Ah," she said, understanding. "The Kairos boy who was born to that body drowned in the sea. He sank so far that he was washed away, and we found the empty vessel in the tide. It was taken then, and kept against future needs. Why? Do you not like it? We have others."

"It's all right," said one of the Kairos guards. "The timing would not have taken him if he were not meant to go, and an empty house prefers an occupant. We will not demand your skin's return."

"Way to make this sound even creepier," muttered Arthur.

"Thank you," I said hurriedly. "Thank you for giving back my cousins. All three of them." Uncle Ted was definitely going to be surprised when we got home and he found out he had two sons now, but that was a problem for later.

"I'm not even the right species," said Arthur.

"Complain later, look grateful and leave now," I advised, catching his arm. Sarah was still holding on to Artie—I wasn't sure she'd ever really let him go again. Sam had dropped down from whatever chaos he was causing and was now planted firmly behind Mark, ready to whisk him out of danger if needed.

"You can go now," said Engineer.

She looked at us all, and her eyes flashed white, and the whiteness was all there was, and we were no longer there.

We were somewhere else.

Twenty-Seven

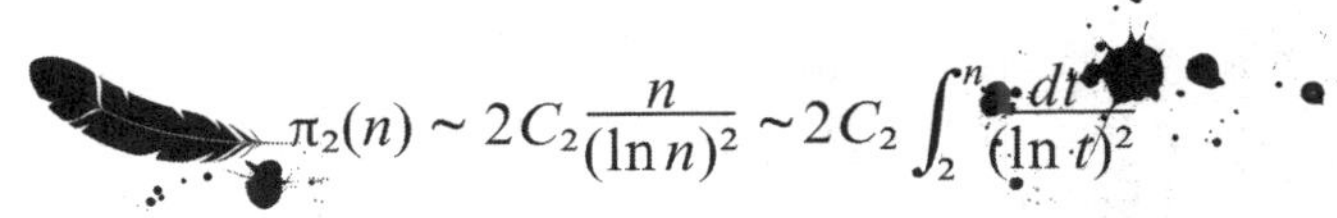

SARAH

"Welcome home, darling."

—**Enid Healy**

Buckley Township, Michigan,
the basement of the Old Parrish Place

ENGINEER'S EYES FLASHED WHITE, AND we were flung across dimensions. She was holding most of the math in her thoughts, but halfway there she handed it over to me, one last farewell from someone who had been my sister, if only for a little while. I twisted the strand of mathematics in my thoughts, filling in the final coordinates, and we were abruptly standing in my grandparents' basement in the house in Michigan. The distant hum of their minds clicked on before the afterimages could fade, accompanied by the complicated web of Aeslin thoughts, hundreds of mice reviewing the same religious texts, as they tended to do whenever not actively engaged in celebration.

"Tell them we're here before someone shows up with a shotgun," said Antimony tightly.

"All right," I said, and reached out. *We're home.*

Sarah? My grandmother's mental voice was tinged with delight. *Oh, Greg is going to be so happy to see you!*

The door at the top of the stairs banged open, my grandparents rushing down to join us, their thoughts full of fireworks and delight. Thomas was dwelling on all the things he could add to the family records, while Alice was just looking forward to calling our parents and telling them we were all safe. She paused when she realized we had an extra body with us, giving Arthur a hard look.

He ducked his head, watching her shyly. "Hi, Grandma," he said, voice making it clear that he didn't expect to be recognized.

Her wariness melted at once. "Arthur, sweetheart," she said, and opened her arms for him.

He threw himself into her embrace, while I leaned back against Artie and felt—for the first time in years—like the world made sense again. He put a hand on my shoulder, fingers brushing the skin of my neck, and I could feel him completely, comforting and complete and exactly as he was meant to be.

Mark shook his head, backing away from our impromptu family reunion. "I need to get back to Cici," he said. "Don't call me."

He vanished, bending the world around him in a cascade of equations that might as well have been written on the air, they were so crystalline and obvious. I could follow him, if I wanted to; I could step forward and be with him in his family home, leaving him with nowhere to run. I could do it.

But I didn't want to.

Everything I wanted was right here, and I was exactly where the numbers wanted me to be.

"This is gonna get real awkward, isn't it?" asked Artie.

I leaned back and kissed him on the cheek.

"Yes," I said. "Isn't it amazing?"

Because, after everything, it really was.

Turn the page for a brand-new InCryptid novella
by Seanan McGuire

WE SING IT ANYWAY

We Sing It Anyway

"Take care of your brother, Elsinore. He's little, he doesn't understand. I'll take care of you, and you take care of him."

—**Jane Harrington-Price**

An ordinary family home in Portland, Oregon
Trying to remember why I bothered coming downstairs in the first place

I STOOD IN THE MIDDLE OF the dark living room, trying to remember why I was there, and trying with equal fervor not to think about how disappointed my mother would have been if she could see the place. She'd never been the best housekeeper the world had ever known, but she and Dad had always been good about splitting the chores, and Artie and I had been encouraged to pitch in since we were old enough not to make the messes worse. Our house had always been cluttered but clean, someplace we wouldn't be ashamed to show to company.

That was over now. It had started to slip when Mom died. Dad stopped cleaning then, and so did I. What was the point in dusting or running the vacuum cleaner when my mother would still be dead anyway? I couldn't dust my way out of her death, or dry so many dishes that she'd come back and tell me I'd done a good job. She was gone.

Turning around, I stomped back up the stairs and left the destroyed living room to the shadows. My mother wasn't here, and she was never going to be here again, and I couldn't stand one more minute in the space that had been hers above all others. Maybe later, when I could remember why I'd been there to begin with. Her absence was like acid in the air, turning it toxic and impossible to breathe.

What makes matters worse is that we *know* ghosts exist. You can't be a member of this family and not know ghosts exist, because we were pretty much all raised by one. Mary Dunlavy has been our family babysitter since my grandmother was a baby, and she's been dead the whole time. You don't get toilet trained by a dead woman without coming to accept the persistence of life after death.

Only my mother didn't persist. When she died, she went straight on to whatever comes next, not lingering around for the rest of us to cling on to. She died, and she disappeared, and she was gone, forever. It wasn't fair. It was never going to *be* fair. How was I supposed to give a damn about mopping the kitchen floor in the wake of her leaving me?

But when Mom died, my brother kept cleaning as best as he knew how. Arthur wasn't the most skilled, but he tried, and he cared, and because of those two things, we hadn't descended fully into squalor. Oh, the place had been a total wreck, but it had been the sort of wreck that didn't necessarily slip over the line into becoming a biohazard. Yes, the dishes had overflowed the sink, but they hadn't been covered in mold, and the trash had been occasionally taken out. Anyone who'd looked at the place would have been able to tell that we were coping. Not well, but coping.

All that changed six months ago, when a bunch of rejects from a new production of *Starlight Express* appeared in our living room, grabbed my brother, and vanished. Not cool. Oh, and all the rejects had been cuckoos, meaning they had the face of the woman who'd accidentally killed my original brother and built a replacement out of the memories the rest of us had lying around at the tops of our minds.

Yeah, our shit is both unique and overly complicated. What about it? Beyond the fact that my overall family life is why I can't keep a girlfriend to save my life. Most of the women available in the greater

Portland area are either straight, human, or both, and the human ones always think I'm lying to them when I have to cancel another dinner or trip to the movies. The nonhuman girls, well.

For a lot of the nonhuman girls close enough to human to actually be *in* my available dating pool, their species is in a state of critical decline, which means all hands on deck for the reproduction trenches. I'm not particularly into the idea of being a mom, not even of the step variety, and they don't get to opt out of preserving their species' genetic health. So we just politely agree not to do the whole "doomed hookup" routine, and they settle down with people who can help them co-parent.

"Hey, are you endangered enough to be required to reproduce for preservationist reasons?" is not the most romantic question ever asked during the early stages of a relationship, but that doesn't mean it isn't important. The girl I'd most recently been flirting with, Amelia, was a Hockomock Swamp Beastie, a species of humanoid so rare that they're only found in one wetland region of Massachusetts. We'd only gotten as far as heavy petting before the subject of species-saving reproduction came up, and well, I might be invited to the wedding, but I wasn't going to be a bride.

And this isn't entirely relevant to what happened six months ago, so: getting back on track. A bunch of sci-fi cuckoos kidnapped my brother, and I called my cousin Annie immediately. Why her? Well, Annie had been there when my original brother died and my *other* cousin, Sarah, had constructed his replacement. She understood the score better than most people. Also, she's a sorcerer, and that means all this magic bullshit is a little more her wheelhouse than it is my own. If anyone would be able to figure out what to do next, I figured it was going to be Annie.

So I'd told her what had happened, and she'd put me on speakerphone with my sort of creepy maternal grandparents, and then they'd said they were going to handle things and hung up. Leaving me with nothing to do but sit at home with my traumatized father and wait.

Mom was the love of Dad's life. That's how you want it to be with your parents, right? You want them to be some grandiose love story that you can aspire to and be vaguely embarrassed by at the same time. Only when your parents are a love story, they're fragile. It's like having a beautiful, breakable vase and living in earthquake country. There's a risk.

They'd been stronger than some people, and they'd survived losing their only son, survived having him replaced by a relative stranger, survived the return of Mom's parents and the chaos it dragged along in its wake. But one bullet and their love story ended, and everything broke down. When I'd gone upstairs to tell my father that Arthur was gone, he'd barely looked away from his computer, only replied, in a dull, dead voice that he supposed it had always only been a matter of time.

So I'd lost my mother, lost my brother—twice—and now lost my father, effectively. I'd gone back downstairs, sat down on one of the few clear spots on the couch, put my head in my hands, and cried.

And that was six months ago, and I didn't think anyone had washed a dish since then. The smell in most of the house was an unpleasant mixture of body odor and trash, making it feel like I was walking through a dumpster. I barely noticed anymore. My entire world was falling apart. Losing Artie had been hard. Losing Mom had been cataclysmic. Losing Arthur after everything else . . .

Well, it had been unthinkable. He wasn't the brother I'd had in the beginning, but he was the brother I had left, and the brother I had learned, one awkward moment at a time, to love. Without him, it was just me and Dad alone in the dark, and I was becoming increasingly afraid that we were never going to make it out again.

I stalked down the hall, ignoring the trash and laundry on the floor, and let myself back into my bedroom, which was in many ways as bad as the rest of the house. There was less actual garbage, but the laundry had piled up until it was taller than the bed, and three-quarters of the mugs and tumblers from the kitchen covered my dresser, bedside table, and vanity. I'd have to rinse some of them out soon, or I'd have to resort to drinking straight out of the bottles.

I threw myself down on my bed—one of the few clean flat surfaces left in the house, although that status was in question, with as often as I was eating my meals there—and rolled onto my back, staring up at the ceiling. I'd only been like that for a few minutes before I heard Mary make a small noise of startled disapproval off to one side.

"Elsinore Norelle Harrington-Price, I *know* I raised you better than this," she said, in the sort of clipped, horrified tone that basically guaranteed the mice were going to turn her impending lecture into a catechism. The thought of being yelled at by rodents for the rest of my life was too much added on top of everything else. I grabbed my spare pillow and pulled it down over my face. Maybe if I pressed hard enough, I could suffocate myself before she really got rolling.

No such luck. Only a moment later, she was grabbing the pillow out of my hands and throwing it across the room, into the mess against the wall. I groaned. "Now I need a new pillowcase," I complained, rolling over to glare at the ghost in my room.

The ghost in question glared right back, folding her arms across her chest to emphasize just how annoyed she was. "You already needed a new pillowcase," she said. "And new sheets. And from the way it's crunching underfoot, maybe a new rug. What is going on here? Did you just give up?"

"Yes," I said curtly. "That's exactly what we did. Glad you noticed. Thanks for this little reminder that I'm trash and deserve to sink into the bog I've been curating beneath my bed."

Mary sighed, expression softening. "Oh, sweetheart. I suppose you're right: that wasn't very generous of me, was it? I know you've been going through a hard time."

"You haven't been here." It was impossible for me to keep the resentment out of my voice, and so after a momentary struggle, I gave up on trying. Why should I make an effort? No one else had. "How do you know?"

"I can see the house, and the mice swarmed me as soon as I popped in," said Mary. "They had a lot to say about the current state of things."

"Traitors," I muttered.

"They're worried about you. And honestly, so am I."

"So where have you been?" The question was pointless, and I knew it: Mary had been with the children. That was where Mary always was. They came first for her, and always would. She didn't have a choice in the matter, not really. She was a caretaker ghost, attached to the family specifically to serve as a babysitter. Part of how she maintained her haunting was by following its rules, and that meant that when there were kids around, she would always prioritize them above anyone else.

Which had been fine for years, when our parents had finished having children and my generation had been too young to start. But now, between Verity and Alex and one quasi-adoption, we had four kids under ten in the family, and Mary was almost always busy. Which reminded me . . .

I sat up and blinked at her, then said, "You're here," almost accusingly.

Mary, her white hair like a beacon in the dimness of the room, nodded. "I am," she agreed.

"I didn't call for you."

"No, you didn't," she said.

"But you're here. Why are you here?"

"The ten-thousand-dollar question." Mary looked around the room with unfeigned disdain. "I'm here because the anima mundi has given me the afternoon off to help you deal with what's about to happen."

"Why? What's about to happen?" I asked, voice tight with sudden wariness. The anima mundi was Mary's actual employer, the cosmic force that kept her anchored to our reality rather than moving on into the afterlife. They were the living spirit of the Earth, older than time and beyond most simple human concepts, like "gender." When the literal soul of the planet where you live says they're nonbinary, you don't argue with them.

They kept a pretty tight leash on Mary most of the time, because sustaining a haunting as involved as she was—one that could interact with the physical world at will, and pass for one of the living under almost all circumstances—was pretty energy-intensive, and it turns out the spirit of the world isn't that invested in my weird family having easy access to babysitting. Unreasonable, right? But the anima mundi did like all the other services Mary could provide, at least half of which were sarcasm-based, and so they kept her around, just limited.

If she was here when no one had called for her, that meant something big enough for the anima mundi to gauge it worth the cost was going on. I closed my eyes, still sitting up on the bed.

"Who died?" I asked.

"What?"

"You're here, and you say it's important enough that the anima mundi has given you the afternoon off, and that means someone died. No one's pregnant right now, and I'd know if anyone was getting married. So. Who died?"

"Oh, sweetheart, no. No, think in the other direction."

I cracked open an eye, looking at her suspiciously. "The other direction?"

"Yes." Mary nodded encouragingly. "The direction that says I'm going to go get Evie in a minute, because there's no way the two of us are getting this house livable on our own. I'm guessing Ted is still incapacitated?"

"Yeah," I said, voice gone flat. "I haven't seen him in a week. He never really comes out of his room anymore."

"I know he's not dead—I'd feel it if he were—but he's not my responsibility the way you are," said Mary. "I raised you better than this. Get out of bed."

"No."

"Elsinore . . ."

"*No*. My mother's dead, my brother's gone, I don't see any reason why I *should* get out of this bed." I glared at her. "Give me one good reason."

"Six months ago, your cousin told you that she was going to bring your brother home," said Mary. "She did it."

I froze.

Not quite literally: I'm not a cryomancer like James, I can't turn my own body into ice just because something startles me. But effectively. It felt like someone had wrapped spectral fingers around my heart and lungs and was now squeezing, steadily cutting off both air and circulation.

"Elsie? You have to breathe, sweetheart. Breathe now."

I inhaled, automatically following instructions, and continued to stare at Mary, silently pleading for her to explain.

She sat down on the edge of the bed, wrinkling her nose at the state of my sheets, and said, "All right, short version. The people you saw take Arthur were from Johrlar."

"I assumed it was something like that, when they didn't come back," I said. My voice sounded strange, like I was hearing it from somewhere outside of my body. "Aunt Evie said I shouldn't worry."

Which had just made me worry more than ever. Why do people *do* that, say you shouldn't worry when there's everything in the world to worry about? Some of the smartest people I know have fallen into that particular trap.

At least my Uncle Kevin hadn't told me not to worry. He'd just sighed, looking pained, and muttered something about wishing his children would *tell* him before they chased his parents off into alternate dimensions on wild quests that might or might not end in tears.

We have a fun family, is what I'm saying.

"Worrying wouldn't have done any good," Mary said. "They were very far away, and there's nothing any of us could have done to help them. Even I can't travel that far. The anima mundi's power stops at the Earth's pneuma. Once they moved beyond it, they were on their own."

"But you're saying they found Arthur?"

"Well . . ." She hesitated, expression turning complicated. "Yes and no. It's not as straightforward as all that."

"It better be," I said. "They went to another dimension and came back with a different version of my brother once. I got used to the idea of Arthur after losing Artie. I don't have another adjustment in me."

"I . . ." She sighed, shoulders slumping. "I am not doing this right. Hold on, I'll get someone who can help."

Then she was gone, leaving me looking at the empty air.

Minutes ticked by without her returning. Cautiously, I slid off the bed and began gathering laundry from the floor, tossing it into the empty hamper. It wasn't going to be big enough, but if Mary was planning to come back and resume making me feel bad about my life choices, I wanted to be able to at least pretend to have started making a dent in the room.

I am a grown woman, have been for years, but she was my babysitter. I'd still be responding to her as an authority figure when I was in my nineties, assuming I managed to live that long. In our family, living past middle age seems to be a fifty-fifty prospect at the absolute best.

Once I had a stretch of flooring clear, I could finally see why it had been crunching every time I walked: a thin layer of crinkly wrappers had been laid out over the rug, covering it in a shining patchwork of candy bar, granola, and various fast-food wrappers. It was too precise to have happened accidentally. I stared at it for a moment, trying to make sense of the array. Then, in a level tone, I called, "I need a priest."

That would seem like an odd thing to announce in most bedrooms, unless you were in the market for an exorcism. In my house, it was as normal as asking for a bedtime story. There was a moment of quiet, followed by a rustling sound from the base of the wall, and a mouse burst into view, running across the remaining laundry to scale the leg of the bed and sit, looking at me attentively.

Its fur was a light tan color where it hadn't been streaked

with half a dozen conflicting shades of hair dye. Normal mice are color-blind. I've never had the nerve to ask a member of my clergy whether the same is true for Aeslin mice. If they're not color-blind, they know exactly what they look like, and asking might hurt their feelings.

The mouse continued to watch me, whiskers trembling with anticipation. I took a deep breath. "Hello, priest," I said. "Do you know why there's a layer of wrappers covering my rug?"

"Yes," squeaked the mouse. I waited for it to continue. It didn't.

That was odd. Aeslin mice aren't known for their brevity. "And?" I prompted.

"Lo, did not the Patient Priestess say 'This Is the Time for Mourning, and It Is Inappropriate to Expect Me to Vacuum Right Now'? And she did lay tarps across the floors and plastic over the furnishings, to keep them safe and clean until the Time for Mourning had passed, and the world could be brought to lemon-scented brightness once again."

I blinked. "You covered the floor in trash so I wouldn't have to vacuum?" I asked.

"Yes, Priestess," squeaked the mouse. It glanced toward the now-overflowing laundry basket, ears going briefly flat against its head. "Are you . . . may we Hope the Time for Mourning is coming unto an End?"

For the first time since a bunch of cuckoos snatched my brother and sent half my family on a wild-goose chase trying to find him, I felt a pang of guilt. We'd been neglecting the mice something awful, Dad and me. Oh, they had enough to eat, because we were still eating: DoorDash and pizza delivery are miracles of the modern age. But when was the last time they'd had cheese that wasn't scraped off a Hawaiian special, or cake that hadn't come in a Hostess wrapper? My family had a covenant with the mice, and we weren't keeping up our end of the bargain.

"I don't know," I said, honestly. "But Mary's going to be back soon, and she's upset enough about the state of the house that I figured I should at least try to show her that I still know how to make an effort. I'm sorry."

"Oh, no, Priestess, please! It is I who should be Sorry, if I have made you feel in any way as if you have Failed us. The roof is Sound, there are no Predators, and if the Feasts have been Few in this Time of Grief, that is only as it Should Be. I have No Right to make you Regret."

"Hey," I said, trying to break the cycle of self-castigation before it could go much further. "Don't beat yourself up for having needs. I've been neglecting my duty to the colony. That's a fact, not a feeling. And even if it were a feeling, my feelings get to be valid too. I'm sorry I haven't been doing my part. I know you're all grieving too."

"Not me, so much," squeaked the mouse. "I Belong to Your Clergy, and we have not Lost our Tie to the Divine. The Clergies of the Silent Priestess, the God of Chosen Isolation, and the God of Bright Things in Broken Places are far more Filled with Sorrows."

"Wait. Did you change Artie's title?"

"No, Priestess. We merely Named his Successor According to our Custom. Were we Wrong to do so?"

My knees felt suddenly weak, and I dropped to them on the trash-strewn floor, gripping the side of the bed with both hands. My eyes stung with tears. Blinking them back, hard, I said, "No. No, you weren't wrong."

That might seem like a bit of an overreaction to a casual comment by a hyper-religious rodent, but allow me to offer a counterpoint: when your brother gets erased from his own mind and replaced with a shallow simulacrum of himself, you can tell me I'm out of line for getting a little emotional about the way the people in his life mourn. For me, it was days in bed, not washing my hair, and letting the laundry pile up until it blocked the windows. For the mice, it was renaming his clergy to better suit the man who'd taken his place.

Oh, they were both my brother, Artie and Arthur. It had taken me a long time to see that, denial standing between me and accepting Arthur as anything other than an unwanted replacement. But it wasn't his fault. He hadn't asked to be made any more than the rest of us had asked to be born, and more importantly, he was the only brother I had left. Hating him for not being Artie wasn't going to bring Artie back.

It had helped that they were different enough that I could find things to hang my acceptance on. Arthur liked coffee. Arthur voluntarily joined me to watch bad medical dramas in the living room, and Arthur liked Batman comics more than he liked the X-Men. Arthur preferred to live life without a legion of little plastic people staring at him, and had boxed up all Artie's action figures, tucking them away in the garage. We'd been starting to discuss hosting a yard sale in the spring when he disappeared, maybe turn all those old collectables into a new transmission for his car.

Not that he knew how to drive. Artie knew how to drive, but Arthur needed lessons before he'd be able to combine mental programming and muscle memory in a way that wasn't going to get somebody killed. I'd almost been looking forward to helping him out with that.

I stared at the mouse, who looked patiently back. Aeslin mice are endlessly patient when they're dealing with their gods. We're divine beings in their eyes, and any attention we choose to pay them is a gift. But that doesn't mean we should take them for granted, the way I'd been doing.

"I'm so sorry I've been too busy feeling bad for myself to be there for you," I said to the mouse, pushing myself back to my feet. Dramatics aside, I owed it the reassurance. "I'll make sure the colony gets a whole cake tonight, I promise. And Mary will be back soon. She's going to tell me what's really going on."

"And may we Listen In?" asked the mouse, whiskers quivering with excitement.

I hesitated. Mary had said both that Annie succeeded in finding my brother and that it wasn't as simple as just bringing Arthur home. He'd been in the custody of Johrlac, which was even worse than the custody of cuckoos. If they'd deleted him again, I wasn't sure I could handle starting over with a third iteration of the same-but-not brother.

And I definitely wasn't sure I'd be able to hold myself together long enough to explain things to the mice.

"Sure," I said. "Just keep quiet, and help me get all this junk off the floor, okay?"

The mouse cheered, and scurried to begin scooping up bits of wrapper.

✦ ✦ ✦

There was something nice about tackling a seemingly never-ending mess. If the room had been only a little messy, I would have needed to make decisions, to put things on shelves and organize them. As it was, all I had to do was pile laundry in and then around the hamper, and make stacks out of everything else I came across. I stacked dishes on the bed. My sheets needed to be changed anyway. What more damage could a couple of dirty plates do?

As I worked, the mouse who had answered my call for a priest ran back and forth across the floor, grabbing the tiny bits of foil and colorful trash until they were rolled into balls and ready for the wastebasket. It was surprisingly quick and efficient, especially with me removing the laundry that had been covering the mess.

We were still working when Mary cleared her throat behind me. "We're back," she said. "You've made a lot of progress."

"Not really," I said, turning. "I'd need about three days to get it clean enough to vacuum in here."

"No, but it's a start," she said.

She was dressed in more old-fashioned clothing than she'd been before, a white shirt with a starched collar and a knee-length red skirt held up by suspenders. The woman next to her looked even more like she'd just escaped from the 1950s, in blue jeans cuffed at mid-calf, a white shirt, and short, slicked-back brown hair bleached blonde by sunlight and lemon juice. Not that either of them could really be called "women," since they were no more than sixteen: the age they'd both been when they died.

Rose smiled at me, the lopsided come-on grin she'd been wearing since I was a little kid and really thought I could grow up to marry a dead girl. "Hey, Els-bells, long time no see," she said.

"Not my fault you don't hitchhike in Portland very often," I said.

"I don't hitchhike anywhere anymore if I can help it," she said.

I snapped my fingers. "Oh, right," I said, trying to cover the fact that I'd honestly forgotten her change in status.

Rose Marshall used to be a hitchhiking ghost, a type of spirit that was bound to walk the earth looking for someone who could drive her home. She could appear solid and alive only under very specific circumstances, while wearing clothing borrowed from the living.

She was my family's second honorary dead aunt, and since she was the one who had never been responsible for bedtime or telling me to brush my teeth, she got to be the "fun dead aunt," which was an unnecessary distinction in most households. She spread her arms and I threw myself into them, hugging her close.

As always, she smelled of rosemary and gasoline, and she was as solid as any living human. Mary smiled at the pair of us, then turned to my overflowing laundry hamper, wrinkling her nose.

"I'm taking this to the compound," she said. "You'll have to pick it up when it's all clean and folded, but if I leave it here, you're never going to finish cleaning this room."

She grabbed the hamper and was gone, taking it with her. Rose gave me another squeeze, then let me go, pushing me out to arm's length. "Elsie, please don't take this the wrong way, but when was the last time you took a shower? I'm dead, but you *smell* dead."

"I don't know," I said, resisting the urge to sniff myself. I'd long since stopped noticing the way I, or my surroundings, smelled. "Sometime in the last month, I think."

"You don't sound all that sure about that."

"I'm not. But I have to say something."

"Fuck, kiddo, I had no idea things were this bad. I would have swung by sooner if I'd known."

"You would?" I asked. "I didn't know you had that much freedom of movement these days."

Her expression darkened, storm clouds rolling in. "If I tell them one of my nieces needs me, I get the freedom of movement," she said.

I didn't argue.

Like I said, Rose used to be a hitchhiking ghost. Ghosts don't normally change what kind of haunting they are; they get assigned a type of dead person to be when they die, and that's how they stay until they move on to the great beyond. Rose, though . . . well, my Aunt Rose never met an authority figure she wouldn't thumb her nose at, and she'd managed to attract the attention of not one, not two, but three of the greater spirits that control the afterlife. The ghosts call them gods.

The mice call *us* gods. I'm not sure I believe in gods. I sort of think that anyone who goes looking for the divine will just find something bigger than themselves, and assign godhood to that discovery. But gods or no, the spirits who'd noticed Rose had the power to make themselves her problem, and they'd done exactly that, rewriting the limitations of her haunting until she fit the purpose they had planned for her.

She was a Fury now, a spirit of vengeance, in direct service to those three greater powers. One of them was the anima mundi, which tied her even closer to Mary than she'd been before the change. They were haunting the same house, Mary and Rose, and they were never going to be free of one another. Not really.

Although I guess that's what family means.

"Anyway," said Rose. She let go of my arms, picking her way through the mess remaining on the floor to perch on the absolute edge of the bed, eyeing my sheets with distaste. "Mary brought me because she couldn't figure out how to explain the situation. She's never been a psychopomp. She knows when members of her family are alive or dead, but she's not really equipped to escort you into the afterlife. Makes her weirdly less comfortable with the idea of death than I'd expect, from a ghost. But then, she's always been a weirdo."

"What does this have to do with my brother?" I asked.

"You have to understand, what happened to Artie . . . it wasn't exactly death," she said. "He was erased, not killed, and that isn't the same thing."

"Okay, and?"

"And when the Johrlac snatched Arthur, they took him to a place where things could be recovered after they'd been erased." Rose looked at me earnestly. "Elsie, they brought him *home*."

"What?" Numbness spread through my entire body like wine soaking into a white tablecloth, filling every inch of me. Artie was gone. I'd already mourned him. There'd been nothing for us to bury, but he was *gone*, and we had Arthur now. If Artie was somehow back, then Arthur . . . "No. I can't mourn another brother."

"Honey, you don't have to. They brought them both home. Arthur looks a little different now, and he's not the same species anymore—the body they had on hand to transplant him into was pure Kairos—but he's here. Artie and Arthur are *both* here."

"Because that's not going to be confusing or anything," I said, still numb. My knees felt like they were about to buckle. I sat down on the bed, next to Rose, our knees almost brushing. "You're not fucking with me right now? My brother's coming home?"

"He is," she said gravely. "Soon."

"How soon?"

"Tonight," said Mary, reappearing with my empty laundry hamper in her hands. "Sarah just wanted me to tell you before she showed up and scared you half to death."

"Sarah." Try as I might—and I *was* trying, I truly was; she was bringing my brother back to me, with a bonus, and I should really be able to forgive her if she was willing to go that far for his sake—I couldn't keep the disdain out of my tone. Mary heard it, I knew she did. Her expression cooled, skin around her eyes tightening with displeasure. Still, my feelings were valid, and I looked away from both ghosts as I continued: "She's coming here?"

"She's bringing your brothers," said Mary. "We don't have another way of getting them here that quickly, and Arthur doesn't currently have any sort of ID. He doesn't even legally exist."

"I guess not, if he's in somebody else's body." A thought occurred to me, sharp and stabbing and unkind. I looked back to Mary. "Is this another situation like the last one, where he's going to come to pieces and then someday they're going to get the original owner back again?"

"Not according to Antimony," said Mary. "The leadership of the Johrlac apparently keep bodies whose original owners have passed on some form of life support for situations like this one, so that they can both restore people who've been unmade and preserve the new people who replaced them. It's something to do with their legal system. Can't get testimony from somebody you've deleted."

"Wait—legal system?"

"Yes," said Mary, patiently. "The Johrlac initially snatched Arthur because they wanted him to testify against Sarah in their courts."

"What were they trying to charge her with?"

"Being a cuckoo queen. That's apparently illegal in their culture."

I just stared at her for a moment. Becoming a queen hadn't been Sarah's choice—no matter how mad at her I was, I couldn't ignore the fact that she'd been victimized by her biology as much as Artie and I had sometimes been abused by our own. She'd become a queen because other cuckoos had gone out of their way to hurt her, and trying to make that out to be something she needed to be punished for wasn't just cruel, it was utterly ridiculous.

I took a deep breath. "I'm not going to say they can't do that, since they obviously did, but are you seriously telling me that I've spent the last six months waiting to hear that my brother was dead because some extradimensional assholes decided to get overambitious with their law enforcement?"

"Pretty much," said Rose. "Now, if your room's this bad, the rest of the house has to be something out of a nightmare. You want to go down and tackle the living room before your cousin and your brothers get here?"

The plural was still jarring, and probably always would be. I shook off my momentary surprise and nodded. "That sounds like a good idea, if the two of you are willing to help."

"That's why we're here," said Mary. "Let's go."

✦ ✦ ✦

The living room was in some ways worse than my bedroom, and in other ways, better. There was more clutter—unbroken boxes, bags of recycling, stacks of mail that had been ignored until it began to cascade onto the floor—but there weren't nearly as many dishes, and there was basically no food waste.

One nice thing about living with the Aeslin mice: they're incredibly effective disposal services. Any food that had been left out had been cleared away long before it could mold, and any bugs that had been attracted to the mess had been hunted for the additional protein they could provide. The mice weren't picky about their diet, and even enjoyed the opportunity to hunt. Normal mice, rats, and various reptiles were all nice additions to their tables. A few cockroaches or houseflies were no big deal for them.

They weren't as reliable about dealing with wrappers, which was part of why my bedroom floor was such a disaster. The living room had no such issues. Mary and Rose gathered up armloads of towels, vanishing into the ether before coming back to help me sort mail or break down boxes. I felt a little awkward about sending all the laundry to Michigan for Grandma to deal with, but only a little awkward. She'd been gone for six months, along with everyone else, and if she was willing to do the washing, I was equally willing to let her.

About halfway through the first pass on the room, Mary took my hamper and came back with clean, folded clothes, carrying them up to my room. She paused on the stairs, giving me a frank look.

"I told them we're almost ready," she said. "You've got about an hour. You may want to go and grab a shower before it's too late."

"Even if you don't want to, I think you *have* to," said Rose. "Again, you smell like a literal corpse, and that's not going to make your brother feel good about coming home to you."

"He's really coming home?" I asked. "This isn't all some nasty joke to convince me that I need to clean the house?"

"He's really coming home," she said. "Come on. I'll stand outside the bathroom if you need me to."

"I'm not a child."

"You're sort of acting like one, and I'd understand if you didn't want to be alone right now."

Mary continued up the stairs with my laundry, and I watched her go before sighing and turning back to Rose.

"Okay," I said. "I think I'd like that."

"Good girl."

The bathroom was as nasty as the rest of the house, but the tub was damningly dusty and dry. I shut the door—Rose staying outside as promised, although I knew she could drop the illusion of flesh and walk through the wood on a moment's notice if she felt the need—and stripped, dropping my clothes onto the old, stiff towels on the floor. I was definitely going to be shouting for a clean towel when I got out.

The pipes grumbled when I turned the water on, air escaping like a rattle of bones. I stepped into the tub, pressing the button to activate the shower, and stood under the water, letting it cascade down over me, washing some of my confusion away.

Unfortunately, what came in after it was grief, and fury. Grief, because my brother was coming home—both my brothers, apparently, which was an impossible gift that I would never have expected or asked for, not in a million years—and fury, because my mother had died not knowing that Artie would ever come home. She'd grieved him, and she wasn't going to get this reunion. She deserved this, and she wasn't here.

That realization was like ripping a scab off the infected wound that was her absence. I slumped against the shower wall, water streaming over me, and sobbed until I felt like I'd been wrung dry.

"Elsie?"

Mary's voice came from directly behind me. I turned, and there she was, standing in the shower. The water was falling straight through her, leaving her as dry as ever, but when she reached out to put her hand on my shoulder, her fingers were solid. I sniffled.

"That's a neat trick," I said. "How are you managing it?"

"I have no idea, and if I think about it too hard, I'm going to get drenched," she said. "It's ghost stuff. Are you okay?"

"I haven't been okay for a long time," I said, closing my eyes and leaning against the shower wall. The water cascading over my back was a soothing, steady pressure. "I'm trying to be okay now. For Artie." And for Arthur, and for my dad, who was going to have to find out sooner or later that all this was happening. I knew I should go and tell him, but I couldn't face the thought of opening his office door and finding him staring off into space, unblinking, barely present in any sense of the word. I wasn't sure he'd even have been eating if not for the mice harassing him to stay alive. It's hard to say no to an entire colony of wildly shrieking rodents.

Believe me, I've tried.

"He'll be here soon, sweetheart."

"I know." I opened my eyes, straightening. "If you want to hop on out, I'll finish getting myself presentable. Give me ten minutes, okay?"

Mary looked at me anxiously, then nodded. "All right, Elsie. Rose and I are right outside if you need us."

"I'll need a clean towel."

She smiled, face softening. "I'll get you a nice warm one from the dryer."

She didn't say whose dryer it was going to be from, only vanished, leaving me alone in the shower. I wiped the water from my face, the spell of my sorrow blessedly broken by her interruption, and quickly finished the process of scrubbing off weeks of sweat and grime. I had almost forgotten how wonderful it felt to be clean. I shampooed my hair three times before I called it good enough and turned off the water.

When I pulled the shower curtain aside, the towel I'd asked for was waiting for me on the counter, fresh and clean and as warm as had been promised. I wrapped it around myself, grabbing the second towel that had helpfully accompanied it to dry my hair. There wasn't time to use the hairdryer: Mary might be able to tell them to wait until I was ready, but I had already taken long enough in the shower, and I didn't want to wait any longer.

Once I was dry, I realized I had another problem: my clothing was so filthy that it was stiff, and the thought of putting it back on was revolting. I clutched the towel a little more tightly around myself as I eased the bathroom door open and crept out into the hall, heading for the stairs.

I was almost there when Rose appeared in front of me. "I've dealt with depression before, plenty," she said. "You look more grief-stricken than some of the weeping ladies I've known, and they're ghosts whose entire existence is about grieving. Are you okay?"

"Nope," I said, almost cheerfully. "Not even remotely. But I'm doing my best, and that's really all I can do right now. So will you let me get dressed?"

"We should have been haunting you a long time ago," said Rose, stepping to the side. "Mary's gone to get you something clean to wear. Hope you're comfortable with her fashion sense, because you know you're about to be covered from collarbone to ankles."

"Yeah, but it'll all be my stuff, which means I like it." I barely remembered what it was like to have clean clothes on. I flashed Rose a smile as I climbed the stairs, trying to look as reassuring as I could.

From her expression, she wasn't buying it, but she folded her arms and let me go, not popping back up ahead of me. Sometimes hanging out with ghosts can be a little exhausting that way.

Mary had already been to my room, leaving jeans, a sweater, and the necessary undergarments neatly folded on my unmade bed. They, like the towel before them, were still warm from the dryer. I dressed quickly, not taking as much time as I wanted to savor the feeling of clean clothing against my skin, and grabbed a brush from my dresser, raking it through my hair before turning back to the door.

Time to face the music.

I walked slowly back down the stairs, following the sound of voices, and found Mary and Rose in the living room, along with roughly half of a Costco sheet cake. Mary was crouched down, clearly deep in negotiations with the small group of Aeslin mice in priestly regalia who had gathered there. One of them spotted me and squeaked in excitement, causing the rest to turn and exclaim jubilantly, "HAIL!"

"Yes, yes, I know, Elsie taking a shower is very impressive, but I need you to stay focused," said Mary, snapping her fingers. "You can have this whole cake if you'll just promise to give us a little space during the upcoming reunion. Go into the walls and don't come out until someone asks for you."

"But Priestess—" objected a mouse.

Mary fixed it with a stern eye. "I can quote the scripture as well as you can. Or do I need to remind you that did not the Patient Priestess say, 'There is a time for everything, and right now it's time to sit quietly and let people have some space'?"

"You do a good job with the scripture, but you can't pronounce the capital letters the way they do," I said, stepping fully into the living room. "But Mary's right, guys: I need to do this without an audience. I know you'll be watching, but can you do your watching from out of sight, please? For me?"

It had been long enough since I asked the mice to do anything but leave me alone that they seemed inclined to listen. They conferred briefly among themselves, then turned to me and bowed, the one at the head of their little group squeaking, "It Shall be Done!"

"Thank you," I said solemnly, and watched as they scattered for the walls. True to her word, Mary carried the cake over to the cleanest corner of the room and set it down where it could be swarmed without creating too much of a distraction. She set it down, then walked back to me.

"Are you ready?" she asked.

"As I'll ever be," I said.

Mary disappeared, and Rose and I were alone.

She bumped her shoulder against mine. "Chin up," she said. "You're gonna see your brother. I'd give anything to see my brothers again."

I glanced at her in surprise. "You have brothers?"

"Past tense. I died, they didn't, we lost touch. Then *they* died, and I was elsewhere doing my ghost gig, and now they're off in the great beyond where all good people go, and I'm never going to see them again." She shrugged broadly. "You're getting an incredible gift. Appreciate it."

"I will. I am. I do." I took a deep breath. "I guess this is a sort of a weird situation, huh?"

"Yeah. So it's okay that you don't know exactly how to feel. Nobody expects to deal with a sudden sibling resurrection. Or if they do, they're probably not the sort of person you really want to be spending time with. Resurrectionists aren't very good company. Their creations can be, but that's a matter of rebelling against toxic family traditions, not raising the dead."

"Fair enough," I agreed. With the mice hidden in the walls and Mary gone, my empty hands felt suddenly awkward, like they were supposed to be holding or cupping something, like anyone who saw me would think I was somehow unfinished. I let them rest against my sides, then immediately crossed my arms, trying to seem more at ease with my surroundings.

Rose eyed me sympathetically. "It's gonna be okay, Els. Just breathe."

"How am I supposed to do that?"

"Most living things manage the breathing part just fine as long as they don't think about it too hard."

"How am I supposed to stop thinking about it when you won't stop talking about it?"

She shrugged broadly. "That's for you to figure out, not for me to tell you."

I eyed her, huffed, and started picking up dishes from the various flat surfaces around us, stacking them up for easier transport to the kitchen. The whole house needed a focused, dedicated scrubbing-down, but that was no reason to sit idle. Now that I could see how bad it had all gotten, I couldn't *stop* seeing it.

There was no warning before the pressure in the room changed, sharp as an impending storm. I straightened and turned, and there was my cousin Sarah, wearing a weird black bodysuit that gleamed like oil on the surface of a puddle in the dim living-room light. She was holding the arm of a dark-haired man in jeans and a plain blue sweatshirt, his weight balanced uncomfortably on the balls of his feet, like he expected to need to run at any moment.

The emotions pouring off of her were concern and joy, in almost equal measure. She was worried, although I couldn't have said about what—him, my reaction, the state of the house. And she was radiant with delight, a satisfaction that was almost too big for her body to contain.

His emotions were a similar mixture. Relief, and adoration, and a spiky, uncomfortable grief. The specific mixture was new, but the shapes of those emotions were as familiar as my own. I knew.

Even if Rose and Mary hadn't already warned me, I would have known. I had grown up alongside those emotions, and had been feeling them secondhand for most of my life. Lilu—even part Lilu—are empaths, not true telepaths like Sarah. We get and can influence other people's emotions. Some of us have more trouble than others when it comes to shutting them out. I've always been better at it than Artie, who got more of the reception and less of the control. But I knew the mind that was brushing against mine.

I hadn't fully believed until that moment. I'd been told, but it was so impossible that I hadn't fully been able to accept what I was hearing. Suddenly, my empty hands felt like the least important things in the world. I stepped forward, lifting my arms, ready to embrace him.

"Artie," I breathed, tears springing to my eyes.

"Hey," he said, and stepped away from Sarah, who let him go without complaint.

We met in the middle of the room, wrapping our arms tightly around one another, and I held on to him like I was never going to let go. I never wanted to. His body had been with me almost since the moment he'd been born, but he, himself, had been gone for years. Having him back was painful and glorious at once, like lancing an infected wound and letting the rot finally drain out.

The pressure shifted again, and Sarah's emotions vanished from the swirling stew around us. Artie gave me another squeeze.

"She's gone to get Arthur," he said, voice low. "He's going to need some reassurance when he gets here. He's pretty freaked out."

"And you're not?"

"Oh, hell, Elsie, I just found out that I've been dead for like eight years, but someone else has been using my body that whole time, and now the someone else has a body of his own and he's not going anywhere," said Artie. "I am well and truly freaked out, on a scale I didn't know was possible. Oh, and Mom's dead. Mom's really dead? They're not messing with me?"

"No." I let him go, stepping slowly back. "I'm sorry, but they're not. She died two years ago. It was . . . it was the worst day of my life. Even worse than losing you. At least when we lost you, we found Arthur, and he was so confused and messed-up at first, focusing on him kept me from spiraling. But Mom . . . Mom was supposed to live forever. I'm still kind of pissed at her because she didn't."

He looked at me, utterly stricken, and I remembered abruptly that for him, Mom's death was new information. It might as well have just happened.

Cheeks flushing red, I looked down at the floor. "I'm sorry. I know this is all really new to you. I didn't mean to—"

"It's okay, El. I know you're not trying to hurt me. And I know

I've been gone for a while." He rubbed the back of his neck with one hand, looking around the living room. "Dad really needs to get a cleaning service in here. Where *is* Dad?"

"Upstairs in his office. He . . . hasn't been doing very well lately. Losing you was terrible, losing Mom was the end of the world, and then we lost Arthur, and he couldn't—neither of us could figure out how we were supposed to go on when it was just the two of us. We don't *work* when it's just the two of us."

The pressure in the room shifted again as Sarah appeared to my right, this time holding the arm of a tall stranger with ash-blond hair and a perplexed expression. The emotions radiating off of him were mostly centered around fear, in all its various flavors. He was afraid of *me*, which was strange enough to make me pause and look closer. No: he was afraid I wouldn't know him. And with that fear, I knew exactly who he had to be.

"Hi, Arthur," I said, forcing my voice to stay level. "Loving the new look."

He made a choked sound as Sarah pulled away from him. "You know me?"

"I do."

"I can't . . . I can't feel what you're feeling. I'm the wrong species for that."

"I know, buddy. Aunt Rose told me. It's going to be an adjustment—not as much of an adjustment as getting used to the idea that I have two brothers now, and who said you could outnumber me? I want to speak to the manager—but we'll manage it."

Arthur repeated that strange choked sound, and all but fell into my arms, clinging to me like he hadn't been sure he'd ever have the opportunity again. I hugged him back. He was a stranger and he wasn't, at the same time. And he was still my brother. Artie was back, but Arthur had been there when he wasn't, built from my family's love for the one we'd lost, and he was as much my brother as Artie had ever been.

Sarah had crossed to Artie while I was caught up with Arthur; her arm was looped once more through his, her head resting against his shoulder. Her contentment was as strong as his grief, and seemed to be taking the edge off of his feelings. I gave Arthur another squeeze, then stepped back, letting my hands slide to rest against his elbows.

"We're going to need to find something else to call one of you," I said. "Artie and Arthur, it's too damn confusing."

"It'll be easier if I change," said Arthur. I must have looked surprised by his easy agreement, because he shrugged and explained, "I'm going to need Artie and Uncle Al to help me get set up with a new identity, and they're more likely to help me out if I'm not being a jerk about things. Artie has his—our—original fingerprints. And blood type. And everything else. Also, it's going to be easier on Dad this way."

"He's going to be so glad to see you both," I said firmly.

Arthur smiled, a little. "I hope so. I know I'll be glad to see him. I just hope he believes it's me."

"It's you," I said. "Emotionally, you're still the person you've always been. I can see it, and he will too."

"Really?"

"Really."

I looked toward Sarah and Artie, both of whom looked anxiously back. Shaking my head, I waved my hands vaguely in their general direction. "So are you two doing this?"

"Are you still mad at me?" asked Sarah.

"Not what I asked, but sure, let's do this. I've been mad at you for years. It's not going to stop that easily," I said. "But I'm not *as* mad at you, if that's what you're really asking me. I know you didn't hurt Artie on purpose, and now you've finally managed to bring him home. You even pulled off the best-case scenario: I get to keep Arthur, too. You didn't give me time to get used to a whole new brother and then decide I didn't get to keep him after all. Now I get to share the bathroom with them both." I made a face. "Okay, maybe I *am* still that mad at you."

Sarah laughed, uncertain but beginning to relax, and squeezed Artie's arm a little tighter. I caught the jet of jealous anger off of

Arthur and looked back to him, seeing the unhappy glint in his unfamiliar eyes.

Two brothers, both with the same foundations, even if they were very different people in the real world. Two brothers, both in love with the same woman, both believing themselves to have been in love with her since childhood. And now Artie was winning. Barely back and he'd already reclaimed the girl he'd been trying to win for most of his life.

Oh, this was going to get awkward fast.

"We're going to need to figure a whole bunch of things out, really quickly," I said. "Artie, I'm assuming you want to go back to your basement—and Arthur, you *can't* go back to the basement."

"Why not?" asked Arthur, uncomfortably. "I already said I'd give up my name. Why does he get our bedroom, too?"

"Because you're not the same species anymore," I said. "You're not Lilu. He's been living in there since we were kids. His pheromones have permeated everything. I have the same issue with my room, upstairs. I don't think Dad will mind us converting Mom's office into a bedroom for you. Better for the space to be used, and the mice will be thrilled."

A rustle from the edge of the room reminded me that the mice were listening, and that their ability to give us space wasn't going to last forever. Clearing my throat, I said, in a clear, carrying voice, "It's very nice that I have two brothers, and it's even nicer that they're not being swarmed and overwhelmed when they're already tired and off-balance. Truly respectful mice would give them until morning to feel better."

"Am I still going to have mice?" asked Arthur.

"They divided your clergy from Artie's a long time ago," I said. "I wouldn't be surprised if they'd been finalizing the division since Rose said you were both coming home. You still have mice."

"You don't escape divinity that easily," said Sarah.

Arthur looked longingly over at her, emotions turning rose-tinted around the edges. Sarah's emotional landscape didn't so much as flicker. She wasn't paying any attention to him.

I couldn't be mad at her for that—she'd been avoiding Arthur since she'd slapped him together, uncomfortable with his unwavering devotion and with her own part in making it an immutable aspect of his personality. She hadn't done any of it on purpose, and when she'd realized he couldn't *stop* loving her, she'd made the responsible choice by staying away. I knew that was true, every bit of it. And it didn't dull my anger at feeling how utterly she didn't care about my now-youngest brother.

Artie loved her, and she loved Artie. That part was simple, even straightforward. That part hadn't changed in as long as I could remember. But Arthur loved her too, and I knew without asking what they'd been through that she hadn't been the one who chose to bring Arthur home. If it had been up to her, I had no doubt he wouldn't have been here now. She had never been trying to save him. Not ever, not once.

But she'd done it all the same. She cared about him as a member of her family, and sometimes that was more than enough.

"Hey," I said, pulling Arthur's attention back to me. "You ready for me to go and get Dad? He took it . . . pretty hard when you disappeared. When you were abducted, really. I did too, but he was inconsolable. He's going to be so happy to see you both."

"I'd like to see him too," said Artie. "It hasn't felt that long for me, but I'm still trying to deal with the idea that Mom can actually be gone, and I want to know that he's all right."

"He's not," I said bluntly. "Neither of us is. I think I'm in shock right now, and I'll probably have a total nervous collapse sometime after we all go to bed. But I took a shower today, and Mary's going to help get the house back into a semi-livable condition, and once it's not actually a biohazard, I'll call Aunt Evelyn to come over and help with whatever's left. We've all been falling apart since the cuckoos—"

"Johrlac," interjected Sarah.

"—assholes," I amended, "popped in and took off with my baby brother. I'm sorry I didn't have a predetermined coping mechanism for interdimensional abduction followed by the disappearance of a chunk of my extended family as they go on a semi-planned and utterly unsupported rescue mission. I spent six months thinking all of you were dead, and I'm honestly still trying to wrap my head around the fact that you're not. Dad hasn't heard any of this. He's going to be floored."

"I've heard enough," said my father, voice low and exhausted.

I turned around, suddenly certain of what I was going to see, and there he was, standing on the stairs and gripping the bannister like he thought it was about to slip through his fingers and vanish. Like me, he didn't look like he'd showered in quite some time. Unlike me, he had the additional visual signal of a short, unkempt beard, which crawled up his cheeks and down his neck until his face was an unweeded garden. He'd done nothing to groom or even it out, and tufts of various lengths jutted from his chin and jawline, dark brown speckled generously with gray.

He was wearing a stained shirt and plaid shorts, and looking at the group of us with dull, disinterested eyes.

"Hi, Dad," I said.

"Elsinore," he acknowledged, still eyeing the others. "And Sarah. Are the two of you getting along again?"

"Trying to," I said.

"Yes, Mr. Harrington," said Sarah.

"Good. I don't like you kids fighting. Makes things too tense around here." His voice remained level, almost disinterested.

His emotions were another matter. Hope was spiking off of him, hot and fierce and practically scorching. It mirrored the hope surging off of both my brothers—tender and confident from Artie, anxious and insecure from Arthur. They were standing in two very different places. Artie was still thinking of Dad as he'd been before he'd started grieving for everyone he'd ever loved, one by one. First his son, then his wife, and then his son again. Artie had his own face and his own abilities and very little reason to fear he wouldn't be accepted.

Arthur, on the other hand, couldn't pick up on Dad's emotions anymore. He looked like a stranger, his body's responses to stress were a stranger's instincts, and he knew how deeply our father had surrendered to his sorrow even before the Johrlac had come.

Dad finally looked directly at the two of them, eyes flicking back and forth between the pair, then finished descending the stairs. He walked straight for Arthur, sweeping him into a tight embrace. "We missed you, son," he said.

Arthur made a choked-off sobbing sound and clung to him.

Artie's hope flared, becoming confusion, and then, slowly, understanding. He shifted a little closer to Sarah, resting his chin against the side of her head.

Dad lifted his head and turned to look over his shoulder at Sarah and Artie. "You really my boy?" he asked.

"I am," said Artie.

"We both are," said Arthur.

"You've been different people long enough that I guess that isn't all that strange," said Dad. "How'd you come back?"

The question was vague enough that it could have applied to either one of them, and they knew it. They exchanged a glance.

"Sarah didn't actually delete me, just shoved me so deep into my own psyche that I couldn't come back, and wasn't aware of the passage of time," said Artie.

"And when the Johrlac brought him back to the surface in order to establish their right to punish her, they removed me from his brain and put me into a spare body they had sitting around for just that sort of situation," said Arthur.

"And do we get to keep you both?"

"Yes," said both of them, and "Yes," said Sarah.

Dad smiled.

"Good enough for me," he said. Letting go of Arthur, he crossed back to Artie and hugged him, firmly, before planting a kiss on Sarah's forehead. "I always knew you'd find a way to fix things," he said fondly. "My favorite mathematician."

"Thank you, sir," said Sarah. Artie gave her a one-armed squeeze.

Arthur looked doleful, and I took a step back, squeezing his shoulder with my right hand.

"Dad?" I said. He looked around at me. "Can we set Arthur up in Mom's office? He can't share the basement with Artie. He's not Lilu anymore."

Dad's eyes momentarily widened. "That's going to be an interesting challenge for all of us," he said. "But yes, we can clear out and repurpose your mom's office. She'd have been happy to do it. Anything for her children."

"Would she still have seen me as one of her children?"

Arthur sounded as miserable as he felt. Dad turned back to him.

"Yes, of course," he said firmly. "Arthur, you have two dead aunts who haven't seen that as any sort of reason to back off and stop meddling, and a whole colony of intelligent rodents that already see you as a god. A new body isn't nearly strange enough to have made your mother do anything but tell you that you need to get a haircut if you're not ready to commit to growing it out. She'd honestly be a lot angrier about my beard than she would be about your appearance; if anything, she'd gloat because you're blond now. 'See, even when he has to give up my genes, they win out.'" He said the last in an eerily perfect imitation of my mother's tone and timbre, enough to make me grateful that I hadn't been holding anything. I would definitely have dropped it.

"Really?" asked Arthur.

"Promise, champ," said Dad.

"I need a new name," said Arthur.

"How about our middle name, James?" asked Artie.

"Won't work. Annie adopted a new brother, and his name's James," said Arthur.

"A new brother? How does that work?"

"Everybody's getting bonus brothers these days," I said. "They're the hot accessory of the season."

"I don't think you really want to start arguing against new brothers," said Sarah, voice gentle. She still wasn't moving away from Artie, and I realized abruptly what was different about her.

Her emotions weren't shrouded behind a veil of choking grief and self-recrimination, the way they'd been since she first woke up after her trip to Iowa. I hadn't done anything to lessen that grief and guilt, to be completely clear: if anything, I'd worked hard to encourage it, taking every opportunity to remind her that she was to blame for the loss of my brother, for the fact that my mother cried every night. But now that guilt was gone, replaced by weary satisfaction and something that felt very much like joy.

She was remembering how to be happy, and I realized that I wasn't angry about it. She deserved to be at peace. After everything we'd been through, maybe we all did.

"How about Orin?" asked Artie abruptly.

I blinked at him. "How'd you get there?"

"It's Arthur Curry's Atlantean name," he said. "He's—"

"Aquaman," said Arthur. "I could get behind that. Not my favorite hero, but he's a good one, and there are some similarities. And it's still a human-sounding name, which is better than I'd get if I asked the mice."

Artie made a face. "Friends don't let friends accept new legal names from religious rodents."

"I guess not," said Arthur, and smiled at him, hesitant and hopeful. Artie grinned back.

"Do we have any clean sheets?" asked Dad.

"You do now," said Mary, appearing behind him on the stairs with a laundry basket in her arms. "And you've got me for the evening. I'll help get Jane's office into shape for demihuman habitation."

"Thank you, Mary," said Dad.

She smiled at him, expression going sweet and oddly maternal. "It's the least I can do. We'll get everything sorted."

"And I'll go shave," he said, rubbing his chin with one hand. "I feel like I could use it."

"You really could," she affirmed. "Go on. We've got this."

✦ ✦ ✦

She might have been exaggerating in the moment, but as it turned out, we really *did* got this, as long as "this" was getting both my brothers situated in their respective rooms. Artie's dismay when he saw that most of his possessions had been stripped from the basement was a towering shock, and calmed only when Orin admitted that he'd just boxed everything up and stored it in the garage.

"It wasn't mine, and I didn't want to look at it anymore, but getting rid of it felt wrong," he said, downtrodden.

Artie shook off his surprise and said, "I guess I can understand that. I would probably have done something similar. And this way my things won't be all dusty." He grabbed hold of Sarah's hand and pulled her with him back down into the basement.

I watched them go, deciding not to comment on the fact that my older younger brother was locking himself in his room with a girl. They were both adults, and after everything they'd been through, it wasn't my place to tease. Especially not when Orin so clearly needed me to distract him.

"Come on," I said. "Let's go see what we have to work with."

Mom's office was on the second floor, and had been closed off since her death. In a way, that was a good thing: it meant we'd be dealing with dust and mustiness, not with the incredible mess Dad and I had been able to make of the rest of the house in her absence. I opened the door and stopped, blinking.

Mom's file boxes, which had historically taken up more than half of the floor, were gone. So was her desk, a massive IKEA monstrosity that had always loomed over her like a hardwood-and-steel gargoyle. Instead, Rose and Mary were in the center of the room, assembling a bedframe.

Well, Mary was assembling a bedframe. Rose had managed to find a beer somewhere, and was cheerfully critiquing Mary's assembly efforts. Both of them paused and turned to look at us as we stood in the doorframe.

"Hey!" said Rose, waving her bottle cheerfully. "Want a beer?"

"I didn't touch the dollhouses," said Mary. "Thought you might like the company."

There was a shelf of dollhouses above the space where the desk had been, carefully arranged and surrounded by tiny fences and astroturf "lawns." A few of them even had elaborate gardens, filled with ribbon roses and doll-sized sprays of plastic flowers. It was beautiful and pastoral and a little strange, and Orin's relief was radiant as he looked at the shelf and smiled. "Yeah, I do," he said. "Thank you."

"Don't worry about it, sweetheart," said Mary. "Rose is going to help me go and fetch your mattress once we have this all put together, and then you'll need to tell me what kind of bedding you want. We're not robbing a department store. Your grandmother has a whole attic full of sheets and blankets, and having the Aeslin mice living up there means that ordinary mice haven't chewed holes in them. It'll be sparse in here, but we'll have you kitted out before dinner."

"Speaking of dinner," said Rose.

Mary shot her a hard look. "You're dead, you don't need dinner."

"I'm dead, but I'm hungry. Some of us didn't get the eternal-satiation package. And I was just going to offer to pick up burgers for everybody, if that works. Bronson's is still open for another three hours, and they're used to me."

"How have you been going to the same diner for eighty years?" I asked.

Rose shrugged broadly. "It's in Buckley."

That didn't actually explain anything. When she didn't offer anything else, I looked to Mary, pleading silently for more details. She smiled as she shook her head.

"The people who stay in Buckley live alongside the Galway Wood, and they learn early that if they saw something, no, they didn't. A teenager who never gets any older but also doesn't lure the high school boys out into the swamp to swallow their souls is nothing compared to some of the things that live out in those trees," said Mary.

"Glad Mom moved to Oregon, then," I said.

"Anyway, burgers?" asked Rose.

"Sounds good," said Arthur—Orin.

"But not until we finish putting the bed together," said Mary.

Rose rolled her eyes. "You are *no* fun."

"I'm the babysitter," said Mary. "If I'm fun, I'm doing it wrong."

"Can we help?" I asked.

Mary nodded and beckoned us closer.

Working together, the four of us got the bedframe assembled, and then Mary and Rose vanished, reappearing a few minutes later with a box spring precariously balanced between them. Orin and I moved to help them maneuver it onto the frame. They vanished again, this time reappearing with an actual mattress.

Once that was in place, Mary stepped back, dusting her hands together before resting them on her hips. "I'll go get the bedding after you have a chance to sit down and eat. Orin, you think about what you want, or you're going to wind up with whatever I think suits you, and that might upset us both."

"Okay, Mary," said Orin.

She moved toward him, dropping her hands before reaching out to take his. "You know how I can feel every member of the family, all the time?" she asked. "How I always know when you need me?"

He nodded. She smiled.

"Well, I feel you, Orin Harrington-Price. As yourself, independent and unique. I feel Artie down in his basement, and I feel you up here, because you both exist, and you're both part of this family. Don't question that."

"I'll do my best," he said.

"Good," she said.

"Now tell me what you want for dinner," said Rose. "Bronson's awaits."

✦ ✦ ✦

After taking our orders, Rose popped off to get orders from Dad, Artie, and Sarah, then vanished across the country to Michigan to actually pick up our dinner. Orin and I followed Mary back downstairs to the living room, where we resumed picking up the trash and clutter from the floor.

We'd been at it for a little while when Dad wandered down the stairs, freshly showered and shaven, wearing a clean shirt for the first time in months. He stopped to watch us for a few moments, then sighed, rubbing at his face with one hand. "It's a good thing your mother isn't here," he said. "She'd kill me for letting it get this bad."

"You didn't trash the place on your own, Dad," I said. "I think I get at least a little credit."

"Ah, but she wouldn't kill me for making the mess, she'd kill me for neglecting the mess, and I don't think we can pretend that I don't have any responsibility for keeping the house semi-livable."

"Grief is a beast," said Mary. "Sometimes when it howls, all we can do is try to get out of the way before we're swallowed whole. Jane would understand. I know she would."

Dad looked at her, then looked firmly away, eyes shining with unshed tears. He didn't argue. I think he understood that it wouldn't do any good.

One thing about having a dead woman for a babysitter: she knows everything about you, because she was there while you were figuring it out. She changed my grandmother's diapers. If she said Mom would have been able to understand why we'd let the house go to shit around us, she meant it, and there was no one who would know better than she did.

Then Rose reappeared with her arms full of takeout bags and drink holders, and the living room devolved into laughter, more laughter than the house had heard in years. Artie and Sarah came up from the basement, and we all pretended not to notice how rumpled her hair was.

"Unpacking, hey?" asked Rose, passing over their orders.

Well. Most of us pretended.

Artie's cheeks flared red, and a sharp spike of jealousy stabbed out from Orin. I threw a French fry at him, breaking the emotion, and he shot me a startled look. I shrugged and smiled. If I needed to help him shake off his natural instinct to obsess over Sarah, well, I would do exactly that. No baby brother of mine was going to be that hung up on a woman he'd never be able to have. Not if I had anything to say about it.

The living room was still a disaster, but it was a disaster with available chairs now, and as Mary distributed napkins and cans of cold soda, it was hard to think of anyplace I would rather have been. I wound up seated on the floor in front of the couch, Dad's knees against my back and a burger resting on my crossed ankles. Artie and Sarah packed themselves onto the loveseat, and Orin sat on the other end of the couch, the toes of his left foot digging companionably into my calf.

Rose sat in Mom's recliner with her burger, and I didn't tell her to get up or move. She had as much of a right to be there as anyone. Mary didn't eat, but she did perch on the arm of the loveseat, smoothing Sarah's ruffled hair with her fingers, and for a moment, everything felt like it was the way it was supposed to be. My mother was still gone, and that was never going to stop hurting. But my brother had come home—both my brothers—and I didn't have to choose between them. We got to stay together.

We got to be a family. And we got to figure out what that was going to mean.

Together.

Really, when the mice came swarming out of the walls to get their own share of the meal, it was almost a relief to have something so incredibly normal happening around us. I threw them my fries and leaned back into Dad's legs, laughing. The sound filled the room, mixed with the cheers and exultations of the mice, and we were home. We were all of us, finally home.

Price Family Field Guide to the Cryptids of North America

UPDATED AND EXPANDED EDITION

Aeslin mice (Apodemus sapiens). Sapient, rodent-like cryptids which present as near-identical to non-cryptid field mice. Aeslin mice crave religion, and will attach themselves to "divine figures" selected virtually at random when a new colony is created. They possess perfect recall; each colony maintains a detailed oral history going back to its inception. Origins unknown.

Basilisk (Procompsognathus basilisk). Venomous, feathered saurians approximately the size of a large chicken. This would be bad enough, but thanks to a quirk of evolution, the gaze of a basilisk causes petrification, turning living flesh to stone. Basilisks are not native to North America, but were imported as game animals. By idiots.

Bogeyman (Vestiarium sapiens). The thing in your closet is probably a very pleasant individual who simply has issues with direct sunlight. Probably. Bogeymen are close relatives of the human race; they just happen to be almost purely nocturnal, with excellent night vision, and a fondness for enclosed spaces. They rarely grab the ankles of small children, unless it's funny.

Chupacabra (Chupacabra sapiens). True to folklore, chupacabra are blood-suckers, with stomachs that do not handle solids well. They are also therianthrope shapeshifters, capable of transforming themselves into human form, which explains why they have never been captured. When cornered, most chupacabra will assume their bipedal shape in self-defense. A surprising number of chupacabra are involved in ballroom dance.

Clurichaun (Clurichaun sapiens). Supposedly, clurichaun are fairies, related to leprechauns, and prone to all the nasty stereotypes you can think of for the Irish. As we've never seen any indication that "fairy" is anything aside from another way to classify cryptids, and clurichaun are very real, we're not sure how much credence to place on their theory. Clurichaun are virtually immune to all forms of poison, including the mild recreational ones, leading to them developing a reputation for being great drinkers.

Dragon (Draconem sapiens). Dragons are essentially winged, fire-breathing dinosaurs the size of Greyhound buses. At least, the males are. The females are attractive humanoids who can blend seamlessly into a crowd of supermodels, and outnumber the males twenty to one. Females are capable of parthenogenic reproduction and can sustain their population for centuries without outside help. All dragons, male and female, require gold to live, and collect it constantly.

Ghoul (Herophilus sapiens). The ghoul is an obligate carnivore, incapable of digesting any but the simplest vegetable solids, and prefers humans because of their wide selection of dietary nutrients. Most ghouls are carrion eaters. Ghouls can be easily identified by their teeth, which will be shed and replaced repeatedly over the course of a lifetime.

Hidebehind (Aphanes apokryphos). We don't really know much about the hidebehinds: no one's ever seen them. They're excellent illusionists, and we think they're bipeds, which means they're probably mammals. Probably.

Hockomock Swamp Beasties (Hockomock Gigantopithecus sesquac). We are currently consulting with the doctors associated with the only known colony of Hockomock Swamp Beasties to better classify them; for the moment, it seems most likely that they're relatives of the Sasquatch, North America's most widespread known non-human primate. Hockomock Swamp Beasties possess skin closer to that of a manatee or hippo, allowing them to remain submerged for long periods without wrinkling or risk of infection. They are otherwise well aligned to other known hominids.

Huldra (Hulder sapiens). While the Huldrafolk are technically divided into three distinct subspecies, the most is known about *Hulder sapiens skogsfrun*, the Huldra of the trees. These hollow-backed hematophages can pass for human when they have to, but prefer to avoid humanity, living in secluded villages throughout Scandinavia. Individual Huldra can live for hundreds of years when left to their own devices. They aren't innately friendly, but aren't hostile unless threatened.

Jackalope (Parcervus antelope). Essentially large jackrabbits with antelope antlers, the jackalope is a staple of the American West, and stuffed examples can be found in junk shops and kitschy restaurants all across the country. Most of the taxidermy is fake. Some, however, is not. The jackalope was once extremely common, and has been shot, stuffed, and harried to near-extinction. They're relatively harmless, and they taste great.

Johrlac (Johrlac psychidolos). Colloquially known as "cuckoos," the Johrlac are telepathic ambush predators. They appear human but are internally very different, being cold-blooded and possessing a decentralized circulatory system. This quirk of biology means they can be shot repeatedly in the chest without being killed. Extremely dangerous. All Johrlac are interested in mathematics, sometimes to the point of obsession. Origins unknown; possibly insect in nature.

Laidly worm (Draconem laidly). Very little is known about these close relatives of the dragons. They present similar but presumably not identical sexual dimorphism; no currently living males have been located.

Lamia (Python lamia). Semi-hominid cryptids with the upper bodies of humans and the lower bodies of snakes. Lamia are members of order Synapsedia, the mammal-like reptiles, and are considered responsible for many of the "great snake" sightings of legend. The sightings not attributed to actual great snakes, that is.

Lesser gorgon (Gorgos euryale). One of three known subspecies of gorgon, the lesser gorgon's gaze causes short-term paralysis followed by death in anything under five pounds. The bite of the snakes atop their heads will cause paralysis followed by death in anything smaller than an elephant if not treated with the appropriate antivenin. Lesser gorgons tend to be very polite, especially to people who like snakes.

Lilu (Lilu sapiens). Due to the striking dissimilarity of their abilities, male and female Lilu are often treated as two individual species: incubi and succubi. Incubi are empathic; succubi are persuasive telepaths. Both exude strong pheromones inspiring feelings of attraction and lust in the opposite sex. This can be a problem for incubi like our cousin Artie, who mostly wants to be left alone, or succubi like our cousin Elsie, who gets very tired of men hitting on her while she's trying to flirt with their girlfriends.

Madhura (Homo madhurata). Humanoid cryptids with an affinity for sugar in all forms. Vegetarian. Their presence slows the decay of organic matter, and is usually viewed as lucky by everyone except the local dentist. Madhura are very family-oriented, and are rarely found living on their own. Originally from the Indian subcontinent.

Manananggal (Tanggal geminus). If the manananggal is proof of anything, it is that Nature abhors a logical classification system. We're reasonably sure the manananggal are mammals; everything else is anyone's guess. They're hermaphroditic and capable of splitting their upper and lower bodies, although they are a single entity, and killing the lower half kills the upper half as well. They prefer fetal tissue, or the flesh of newborn infants. They are also venomous, as we have recently discovered. Do not engage if you can help it.

Oread (Nymphae silica). Humanoid cryptids with the approximate skin density of granite. Their actual biological composition is unknown, as no one has ever been able to successfully dissect one. Oreads are extremely strong, and can be dangerous when angered. They seem to have evolved independently across the globe; their common name is from the Greek.

Sasquatch (Gigantopithecus sesquac). These massive native denizens of North America have learned to embrace depilatories and mail-order shoe catalogs. A surprising number make their living as Bigfoot hunters (Bigfeet and Sasquatches are close relatives, and enjoy tormenting each other). They are predominantly vegetarian, and enjoy Canadian television.

Tanuki (Nyctereutes sapiens). Therianthrope shapeshifters from Japan, the tanuki are critically endangered due to the efforts of the Covenant. Despite this, they remain friendly, helpful people, with a naturally gregarious nature which makes it virtually impossible for them to avoid human settlements. Tanuki possess three primary forms—human, raccoon dog, and big-ass scary monster. Pray you never see the third form of the tanuki.

Ukupani (Ukupani sapiens). Aquatic therianthropes native to the warm waters of the Pacific Islands, the Ukupani were believed for centuries to be an all-male species, until Thomas Price sat down with several local fishermen and determined that the abnormally large great white sharks that were often found near Ukupani males were, in actuality, Ukupani females. Female Ukupani can't shapeshift, but can eat people. Happily. They are as intelligent as their shapeshifting mates, because smart sharks is exactly what the ocean needed.

Wadjet (Naja wadjet). Once worshipped as gods, the male wadjet resembles an enormous cobra, capable of reaching seventeen feet in length when fully mature, while the female wadjet resembles an attractive human female. Wadjet pair-bond young, and must spend extended amounts of time together before puberty in order to become immune to one another's venom and be able to successfully mate as adults.

Waheela (Waheela sapiens). Therianthrope shapeshifters from the upper portion of North America, the waheela are a solitary race, usually claiming large swaths of territory and defending it to the death from others of their species. Waheela mating season is best described with the term "bloodbath." Waheela transform into something that looks like a dire bear on steroids. They're usually not hostile, but it's best not to push it.

Yong (Draconem alta aqua). The so-called "Korean dragon" shares many qualities with their European relatives. The species demonstrates extreme sexual dimorphism; the males are great serpents, some easily exceeding eighty feet in length, with no wings, but possessing powerful forelimbs with which to catch and keep their prey. The females, meanwhile, appear to be attractive human women of Korean descent, capable of blending easily into a human population. Unlike European dragons, their health is dependent on quartz rather than gold, making it somewhat easier for them to form and maintain their Nests (called "clutches").

Playlist

"Ordinary Town"	Dave Carter and Tracy Grammar
"Whataya Want from Me"	Adam Lambert
"What If Tomorrow Comes"	*Black Friday*
"In All My Dreams I Drown"	American Murder Song
"This Town Is Wrong"	The Nields
"Sanctuary"	Utada Hikaru
"All the Green Places"	Talis Kimberley
"Back to the Garden"	Delta Rae
"Protocoligorically Correct"	*The Slipper and the Rose*
"The Fine Print"	The Stupendium
"Alice"	Peggy
"Map of the Human Heart"	The Guggenheim Grotto
"The Web I Spin For You"	*Nightmare Time*
"This Is Why We Fight"	The Decemberists
"Try"	*The Lightning Thief*
"Feast or Famine"	*Black Friday*
"The Broken Bride"	Ludo
"Ever After"	*Cinderella's Castle*
"Crash the Party"	OK Go
"Run Away With Me"	*Nightmare Time*
"Snow White Queen"	Evanescence
"River of Stars"	Little Big Town
"She Moved Through the Fair"	Annwn
"Ash to Ash"	*Cinderella's Castle*
"Why Do You Let Me Stay Here?"	She & Him
"I Will Not Forget That I Have Forgotten"	Eluvium
"Next Time"	*Nightmare Time*

Acknowledgments

I love Sarah. She's probably one of my favorites to write (although a keen look at these acknowledgments will show that I say that about all of them—whoever I'm currently writing is pretty much always going to be my favorite), and her approach to problem-solving is refreshingly logical when compared to the rest of her family. Still, it was a surprise when I got to go back to her, especially since giving her a third outing was going to require heading for a place I'd never been sure we'd get to go: Johrlar, original home of the cuckoos.

Since the topic of extradimensional cryptids has come up a few times now, let me clarify something. As a rule of thumb, you can assume that any cryptid based on actual folklore or mythology originated on Earth. The things I invented, however, are fair game to come from basically anywhere. In the case of the cuckoos, that means Johrlar, and building their homeworld's ecosystems was unreasonably enjoyable for me.

I am still in Seattle, still happy with my house and my community, still playing a truly ridiculous amount of *Magic the Gathering*. As I write this, we're still in the middle of a global pandemic, and that makes me even more inclined to feather my nest and work on loving where I live. I hope you're still all okay with the decision not to include COVID-19 in the InCryptid setting. There was just no logical way to make it work, and unlike the real world, fictional realities *do* need to hang together narratively. Even ones as ridiculous as this.

It's early 2025 for me, to give you a fixed point to navigate from, and while I remain cautious about the ongoing global pandemic (and the burgeoning new ones), I've been traveling when necessary. A trip to the United Kingdom for Worldcon, and then another not that long after, to see the West End production of *The Lightning Thief*. A lot of theater, really, and a lot of swamp time and writing. I'm still keeping my fancy mantises, and have continued to add new species, now including jeweled flowers and African lined. They make me really happy.

And now, as always, time for gratitude. My first and biggest thanks go to my agent, Diana Fox, who remains my staunchest advocate, and is still utterly willing to go charging into battle for my sake, keeping things moving smoothly and ensuring this series is treated with respect and gravity. She takes my calls at all hours of the day, whether or not she wants to, and is just a total professional. I appreciate her more than words can say.

Thanks to Chris Mangum, who maintains the code for my website, and to Tara O'Shea, who manages the graphics. Alec Fowler manages website updates and makes sure the site has some small resemblance to the modern world, and I am so very grateful. Terri Ash is no longer the "new" personal assistant, but is still at the party—if you email through the website I just mentioned, she's the one who'll send your mail on to me, after handling what doesn't need to reach me. She's essential, and I am very glad she's here.

Thanks to the team at Tor Publishing for their part in this transition, and to our new team, including Oliver Dougherty, my new editor, who has done a remarkable job of stepping into an ongoing series without getting bowled over.

Cat update (I know you all live for these): Thomas is going to be seventeen this year. His arthritis is really bothering him these days, and he mostly sleeps and yells at people to turn the water on. Megara is unchanging and unchangeable. As a cat who doesn't really waste time on thinking about anything beyond breakfast, she's relatively unflappable. Elsie is my perfect owl, and she makes sure I eat, sleep, and do all the other things that are required for survival. Tinkerbell is a snotty little diva who knows exactly how pretty she is, and Verity would like to speak to the manager. Of life. (If that all seems familiar, it's because it is. The cats are stable, which is wonderful.) Kelpie is still growing. She's recently taken to standing up on her hind legs and walking around like a person, and it's very disturbing. Muffles is her best friend, and the two of them wrestle up one side of the house and down the other, slamming into walls and each other with giddy abandon.

And now, gratitude in earnest. Thank you to everyone who reads, reviews, and helps me keep this series going; thanks to Kate, for wandering London and for picking up the phone when I call her in a panic; to Phil, who knows what he did; to Shawn, for being the best brother a girl could possibly want; to Chris Mangum, for being here even when it's inconvenient; to Wing Mui and Natalie, for keeping me socializing outside my head; to Manda Cherry, for a heated car seat and a wonderful friendship; to Crystal Fraiser, for regular company and grilled cheese; and to my dearest Amy McNally, for everything. Thanks to the members of all four of my current ongoing D&D games. And to you: thank you, so much, for reading.

Any errors in this book are my own. The errors that aren't here are the ones that all these people helped me fix. I appreciate it so much.

Let's have an adventure!

About the Author

Beckett Gladney

Seanan McGuire is the author of the Hugo, Nebula, Alex, and Locus Award–winning Wayward Children series, the October Daye series, the InCryptid series, and other works. She also writes darker fiction as Mira Grant. McGuire lives in Seattle with her cats, a vast collection of creepy dolls, horror movies, and sufficient books to qualify her as a fire hazard. She won the 2010 John W. Campbell Award for Best New Writer, and in 2013 became the first person to appear five times on the same Hugo ballot. In 2022 she managed the same feat again!